SUPER TURBO

VS. WONDER PIG

WRITTEN BY **EDGAR POWERS**
ILLUSTRATED BY **SALVATORE COSTANZA**
AT GLASS HOUSE GRAPHICS

LITTLE SIMON
NEW YORK   LONDON   TORONTO   SYDNEY   NEW DELHI

LITTLE SIMON
AN IMPRINT OF SIMON & SCHUSTER CHILDREN'S PUBLISHING DIVISION 1230 AVENUE OF THE AMERICAS, NEW YORK, NEW YORK 10020 FIRST LITTLE SIMON EDITION NOVEMBER 2021 * COPYRIGHT © 2021 BY SIMON & SCHUSTER, INC. ALL RIGHTS RESERVED, INCLUDING THE RIGHT OF REPRODUCTION IN WHOLE OR IN PART IN ANY FORM. LITTLE SIMON IS A REGISTERED TRADEMARK OF SIMON & SCHUSTER, INC., AND ASSOCIATED COLOPHON IS A TRADEMARK OF SIMON & SCHUSTER, INC. FOR INFORMATION ABOUT SPECIAL DISCOUNTS FOR BULK PURCHASES, PLEASE CONTACT SIMON & SCHUSTER SPECIAL SALES AT 1-866-506-1949 OR BUSINESS@SIMONANDSCHUSTER.COM. THE SIMON & SCHUSTER SPEAKERS BUREAU CAN BRING AUTHORS TO YOUR LIVE EVENT. FOR MORE INFORMATION OR TO BOOK AN EVENT CONTACT THE SIMON & SCHUSTER SPEAKERS BUREAU AT 1-866-248-3049 OR VISIT OUR WEBSITE AT WWW.SIMONSPEAKERS.COM. DESIGNED BY NICHOLAS SCIACCA * ART SERVICES BY GLASS HOUSE GRAPHICS * ART AND COLOR BY SALVATORE COSTANZA * LETTERING BY GIOVANNI SPATARO/GRAFIMATED CARTOON * SUPERVISION BY SALVATORE DI MARCO/GRAFIMATED CARTOON * MANUFACTURED IN CHINA 0821 SCP * 2 4 6 8 10 9 7 5 3 1 * LIBRARY OF CONGRESS CATALOGING-IN-PUBLICATION DATA NAMES: POWERS, EDGAR J., AUTHOR. | GLASS HOUSE GRAPHICS, ILLUSTRATOR. TITLE: SUPER TURBO VS. WONDER PIG / BY EDGAR J. POWERS ; ILLUSTRATED BY GLASS HOUSE GRAPHICS. DESCRIPTION: FIRST LITTLE SIMON EDITION. | NEW YORK : LITTLE SIMON, 2021. | SERIES: SUPER TURBO, THE GRAPHIC NOVEL ; 6 | AUDIENCE: AGES 5-9 | AUDIENCE: GRADES K-4 | SUMMARY: "SUPER TURBO AND HIS PALS IN THE SUPERPET SUPERHERO LEAGUE ARE USED TO FACING DOWN THE EVIL AT SUNNYVIEW ELEMENTARY TOGETHER, AS A TEAM. BUT WHEN WONDER PIG STARTS ACTING STRANGELY ON THE SAME DAY THAT TURBO'S CAPE GOES MISSING, TURBO IS SUSPICIOUS"—PROVIDED BY PUBLISHER. IDENTIFIERS: LCCN 2020049162 (PRINT) | LCCN 2020049163 (EBOOK) | ISBN 9781534485402 (PAPERBACK) | ISBN 9781534485419 (HARDCOVER) | ISBN 9781534485426 (EBOOK) SUBJECTS: LCSH: GRAPHIC NOVELS. | CYAC: GRAPHIC NOVELS. | SUPERHEROES—FICTION. | HAMSTERS—FICTION. | PETS—FICTION. | ELEMENTARY SCHOOLS—FICTION. | SCHOOLS—FICTION. CLASSIFICATION: LCC PZ7.7.P7 SW 2021 (PRINT) | LCC PZ7.7.P7 (EBOOK) | DDC 741.5/973—DC23 LC RECORD AVAILABLE AT HTTPS://LCCN.LOC.GOV/2020049162 LC EBOOK RECORD AVAILABLE AT HTTPS://LCCN.LOC.GOV/2020049163

CONTENTS

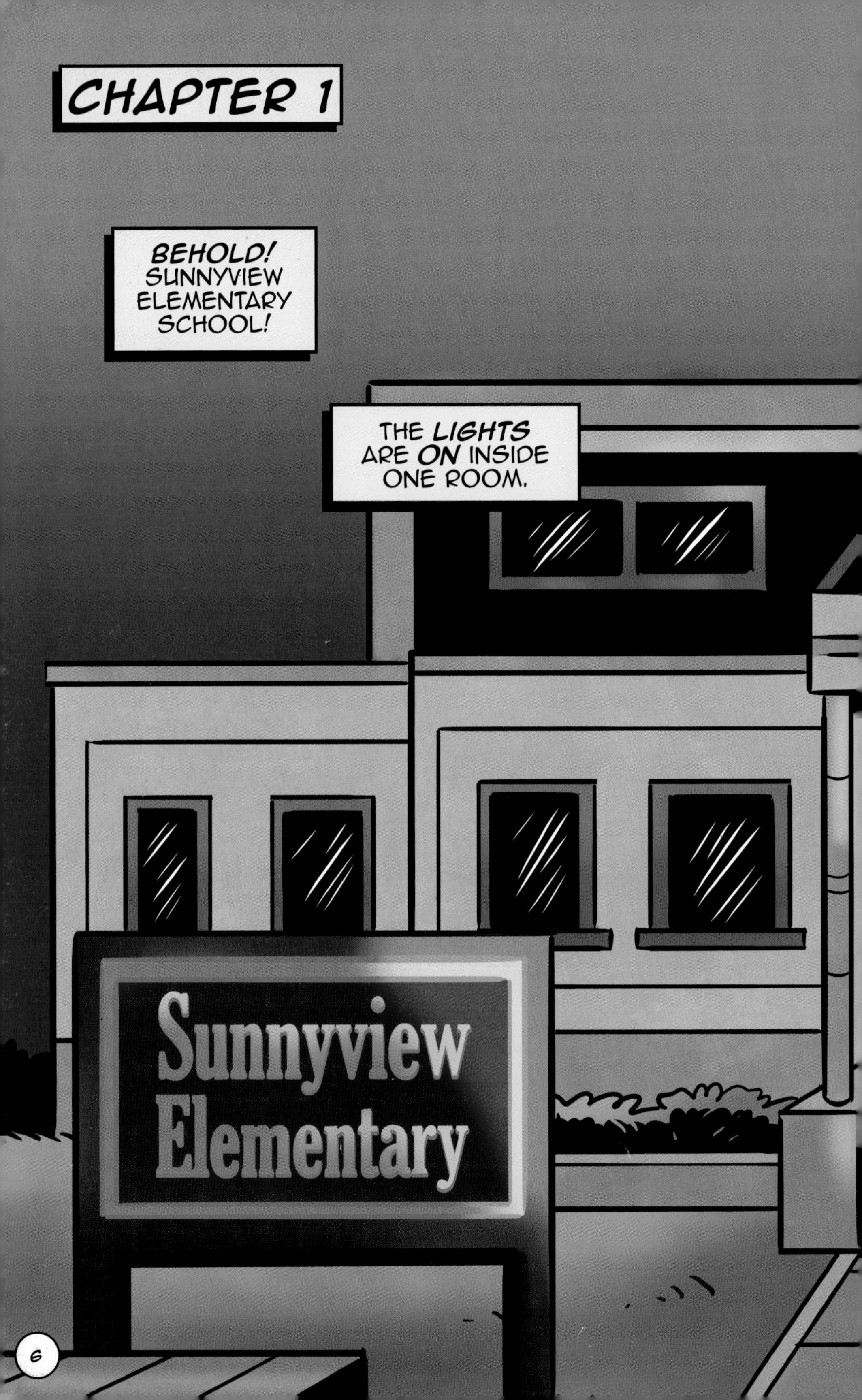
CHAPTER 1
BEHOLD! SUNNYVIEW ELEMENTARY SCHOOL!
THE LIGHTS ARE ON INSIDE ONE ROOM.
Sunnyview Elementary

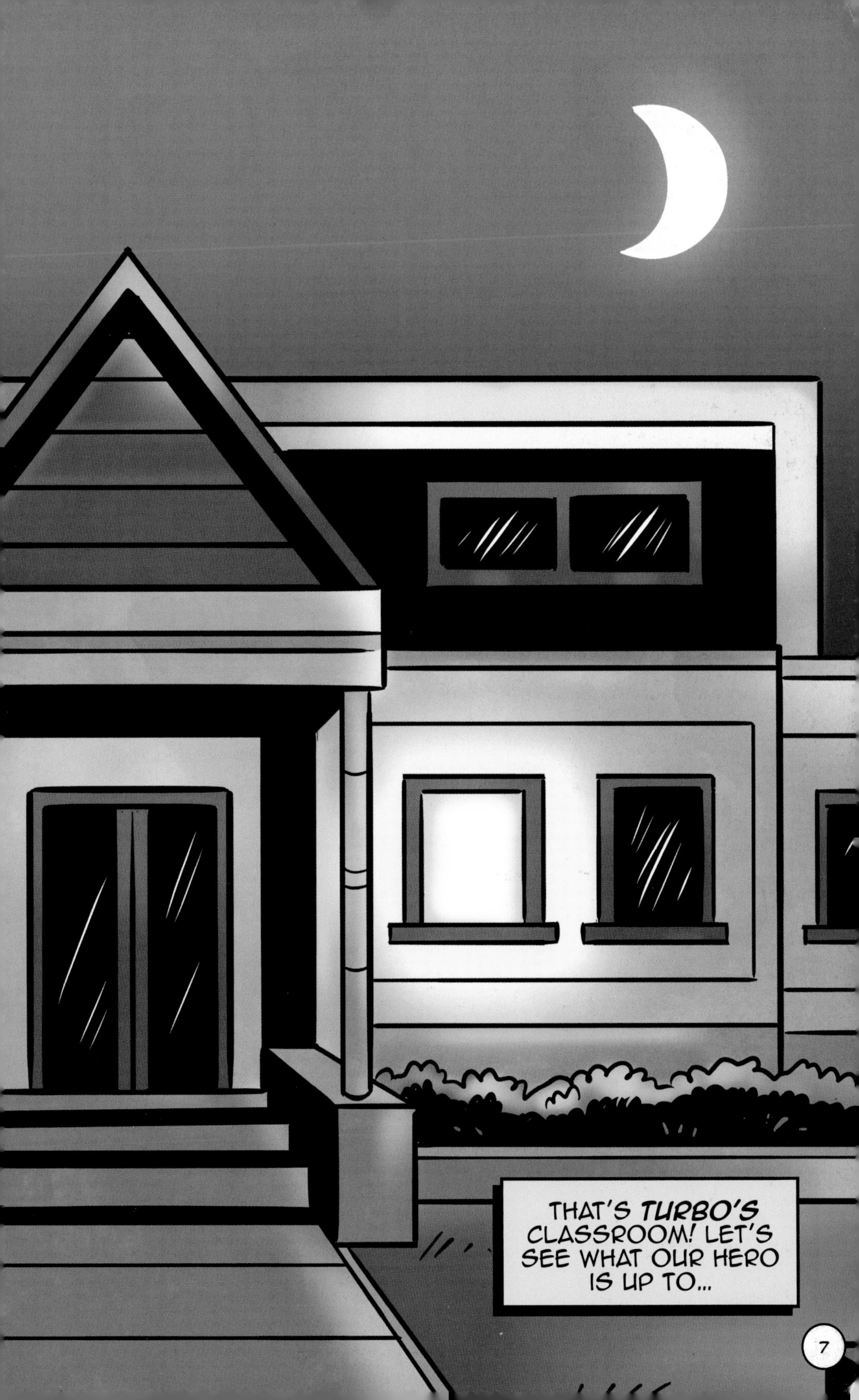
THAT'S *TURBO'S* CLASSROOM! LET'S SEE WHAT OUR HERO IS UP TO...

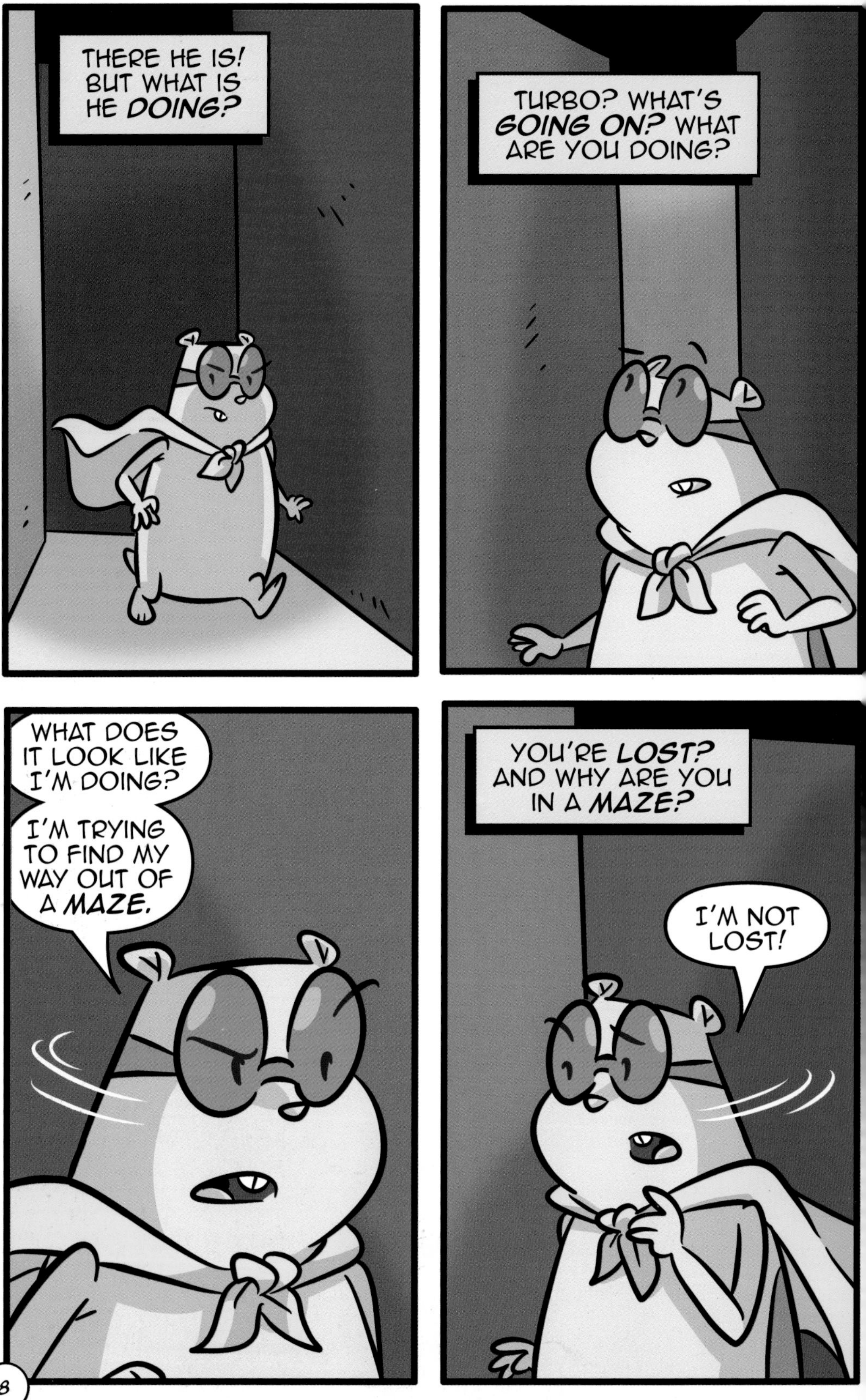
THERE HE IS! BUT WHAT IS HE *DOING?*
TURBO? WHAT'S *GOING ON?* WHAT ARE YOU DOING?
WHAT DOES IT LOOK LIKE I'M DOING?
I'M TRYING TO FIND MY WAY OUT OF A *MAZE.*
YOU'RE *LOST?* AND WHY ARE YOU IN A *MAZE?*
I'M NOT LOST!

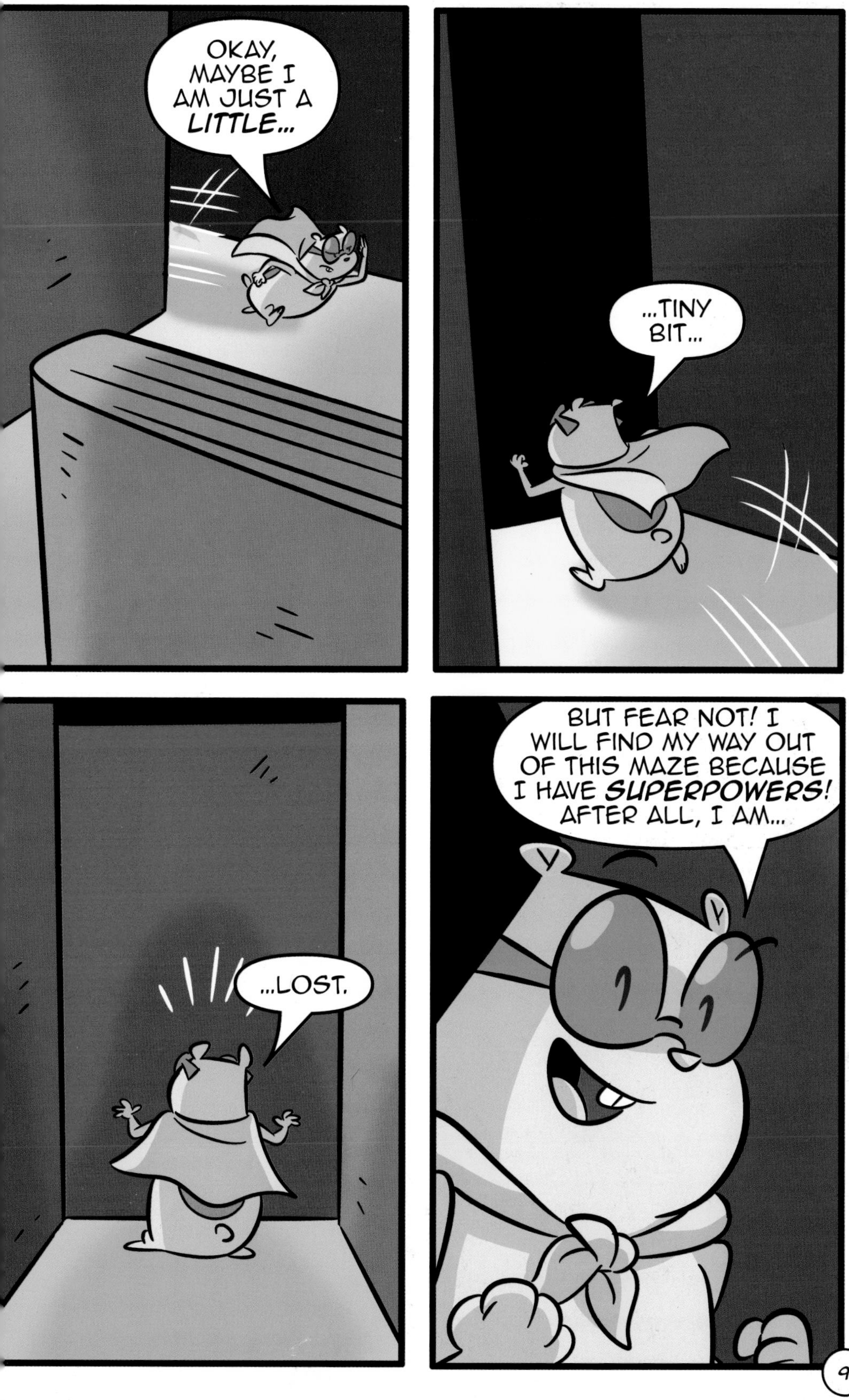
OKAY, MAYBE I AM JUST A LITTLE...
...TINY BIT...
...LOST.
BUT FEAR NOT! I WILL FIND MY WAY OUT OF THIS MAZE BECAUSE I HAVE SUPERPOWERS! AFTER ALL, I AM...

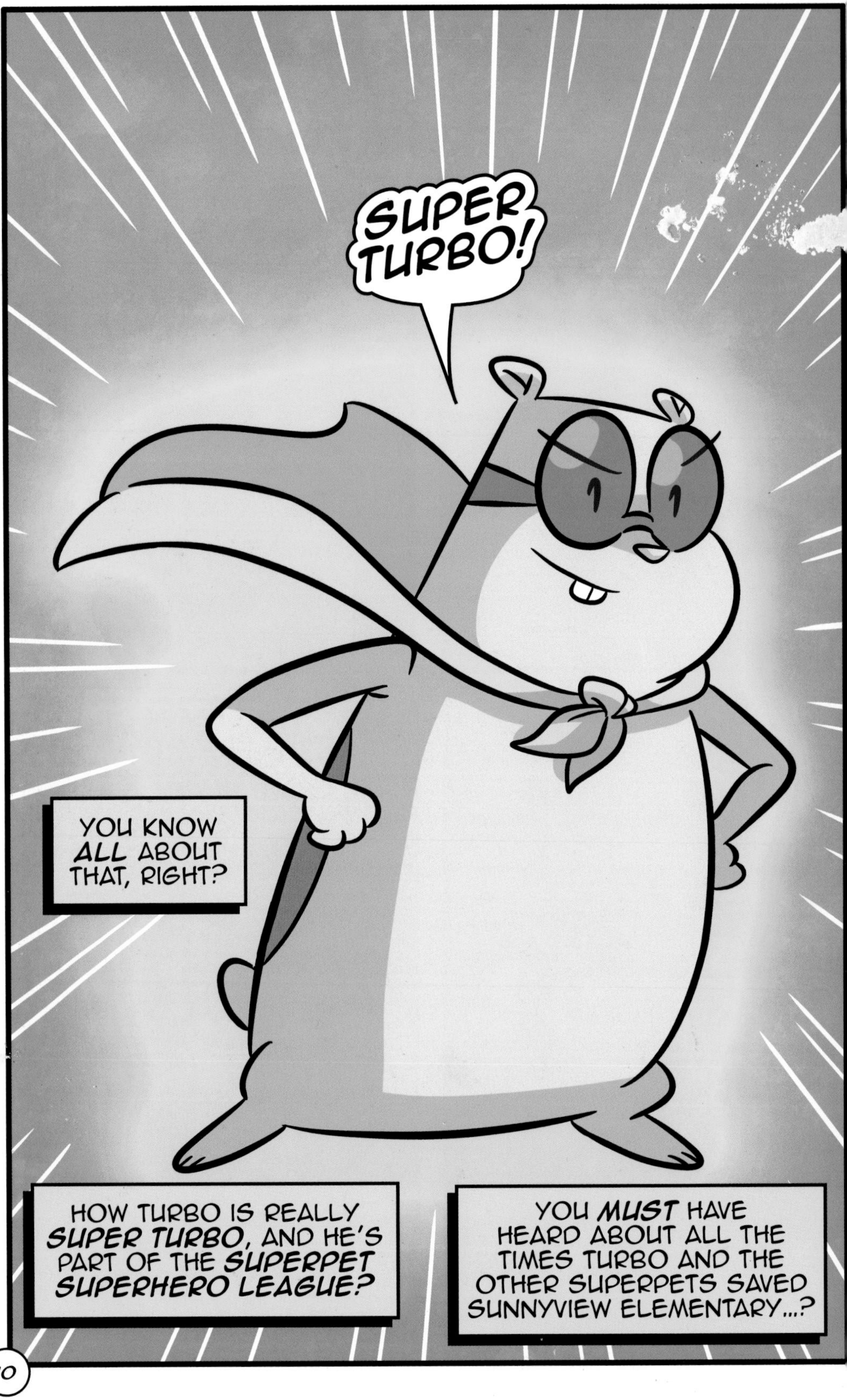
SUPER TURBO!
YOU KNOW *ALL* ABOUT THAT, RIGHT?
HOW TURBO IS REALLY *SUPER TURBO*, AND HE'S PART OF THE *SUPERPET SUPERHERO LEAGUE*?
YOU *MUST* HAVE HEARD ABOUT ALL THE TIMES TURBO AND THE OTHER SUPERPETS SAVED SUNNYVIEW ELEMENTARY...?

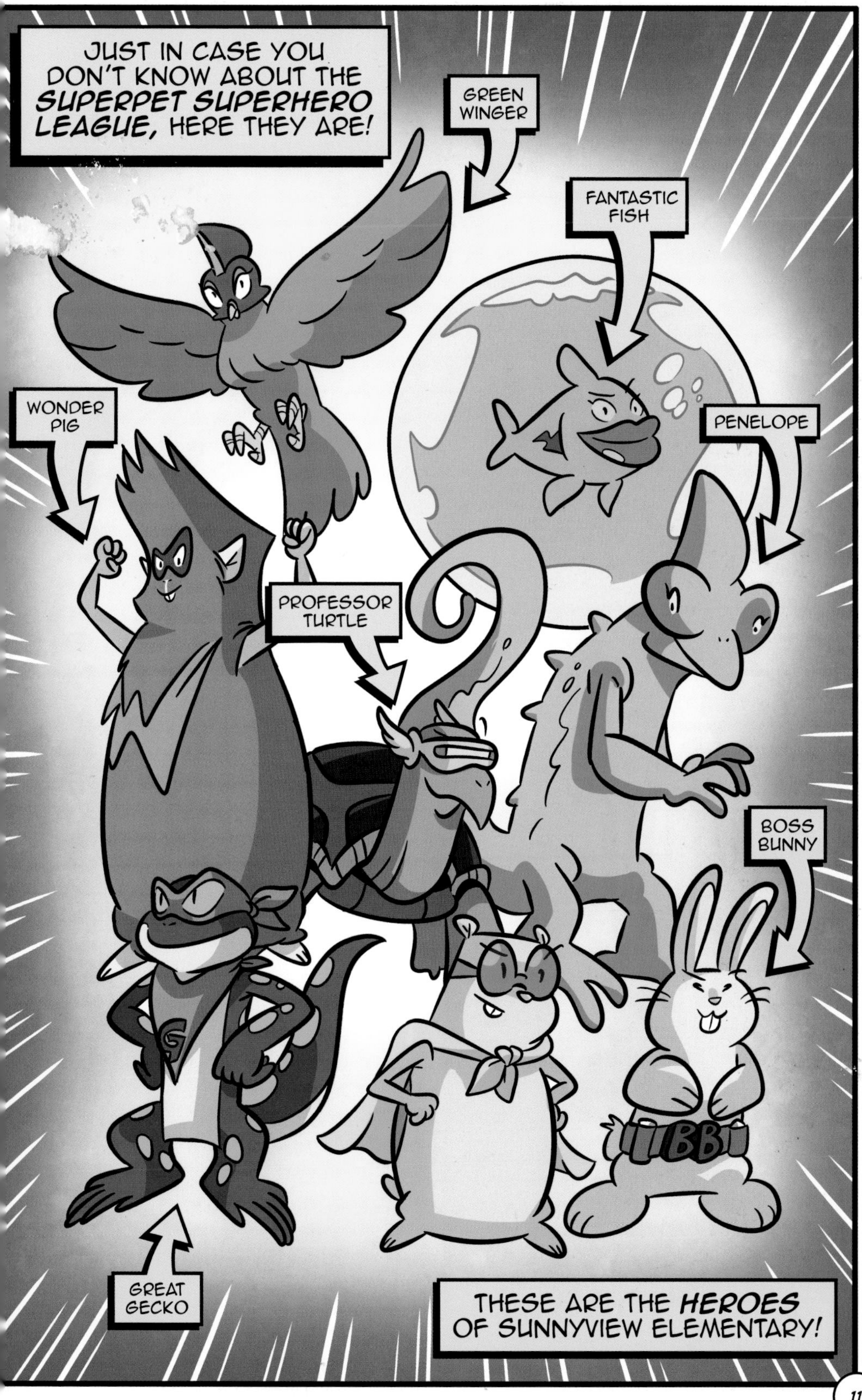
JUST IN CASE YOU DON'T KNOW ABOUT THE *SUPERPET SUPERHERO LEAGUE,* HERE THEY ARE!
GREEN WINGER
FANTASTIC FISH
WONDER PIG
PENELOPE
PROFESSOR TURTLE
BOSS BUNNY
BB
G
GREAT GECKO
THESE ARE THE *HEROES* OF SUNNYVIEW ELEMENTARY!

WITH THAT OUT OF THE WAY, WE RETURN TO SUPER TURBO, WHO IS ONLY A *LITTLE, TINY BIT* LOST IN A MAZE.

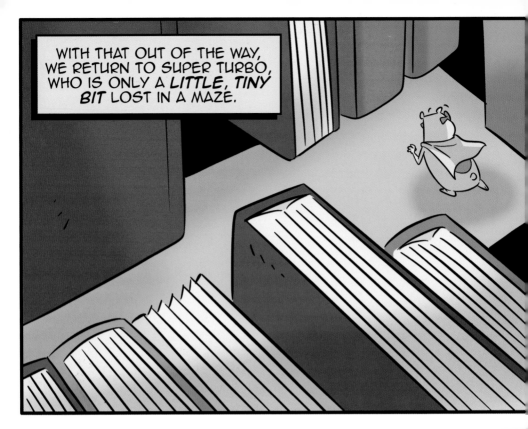

TURBO TURNED *LEFT.*

TURBO TURNED *RIGHT.*

THIS LAST TURN SHOULD DO IT...

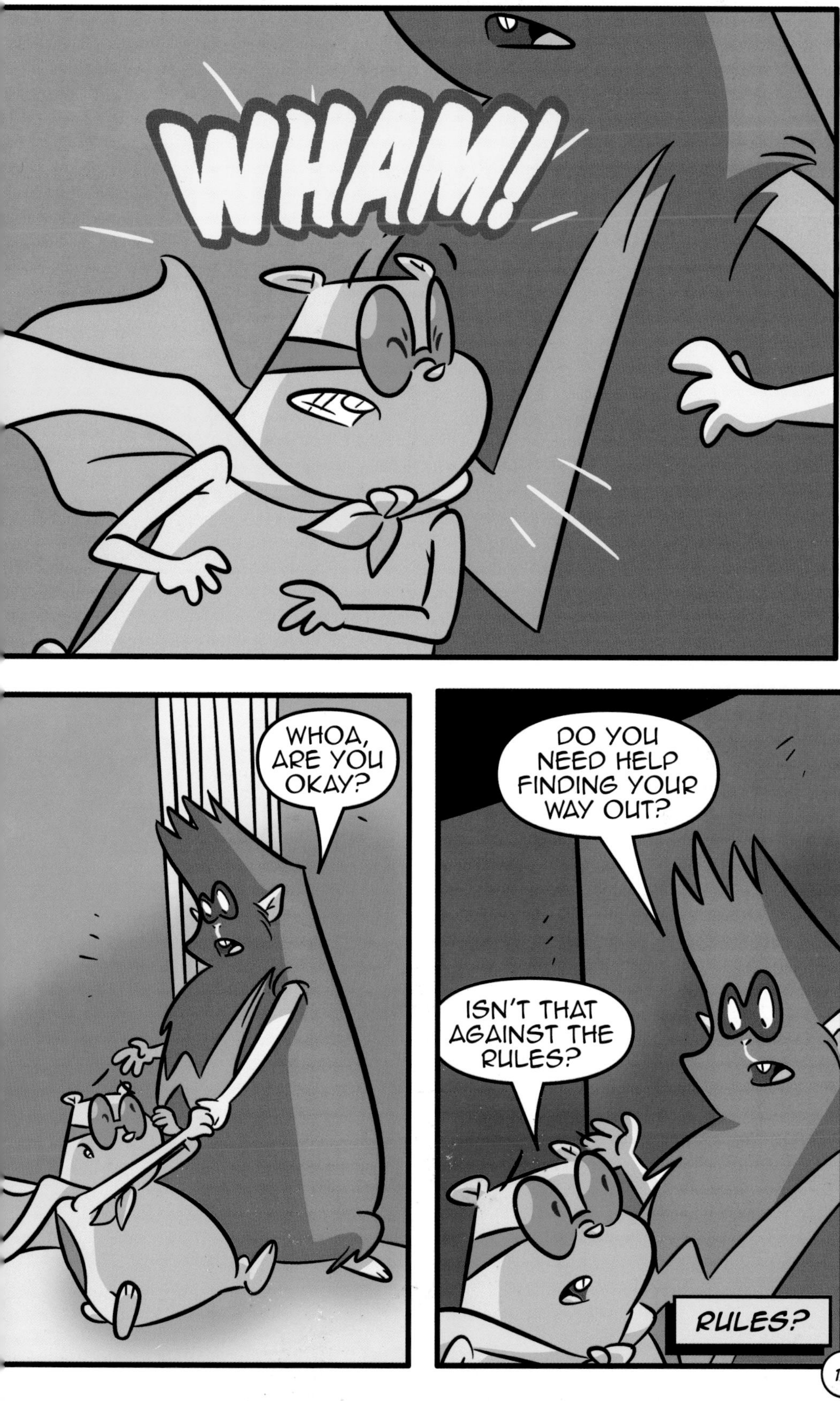
WHAM!
WHOA, ARE YOU OKAY?
DO YOU NEED HELP FINDING YOUR WAY OUT?
ISN'T THAT AGAINST THE RULES?
RULES?

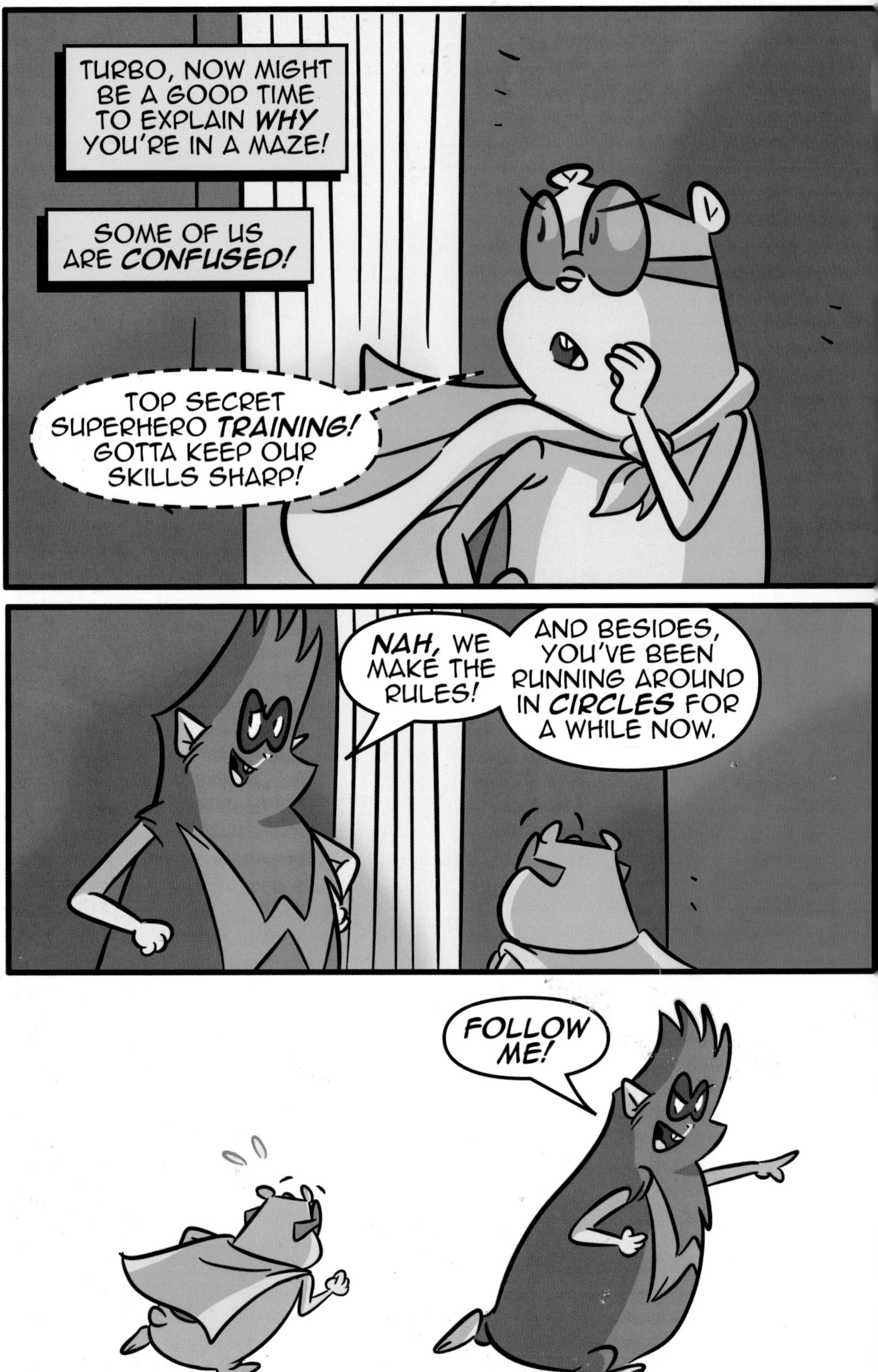
TURBO, NOW MIGHT BE A GOOD TIME TO EXPLAIN WHY YOU'RE IN A MAZE!
SOME OF US ARE CONFUSED!
TOP SECRET SUPERHERO TRAINING! GOTTA KEEP OUR SKILLS SHARP!
NAH, WE MAKE THE RULES!
AND BESIDES, YOU'VE BEEN RUNNING AROUND IN CIRCLES FOR A WHILE NOW.
FOLLOW ME!

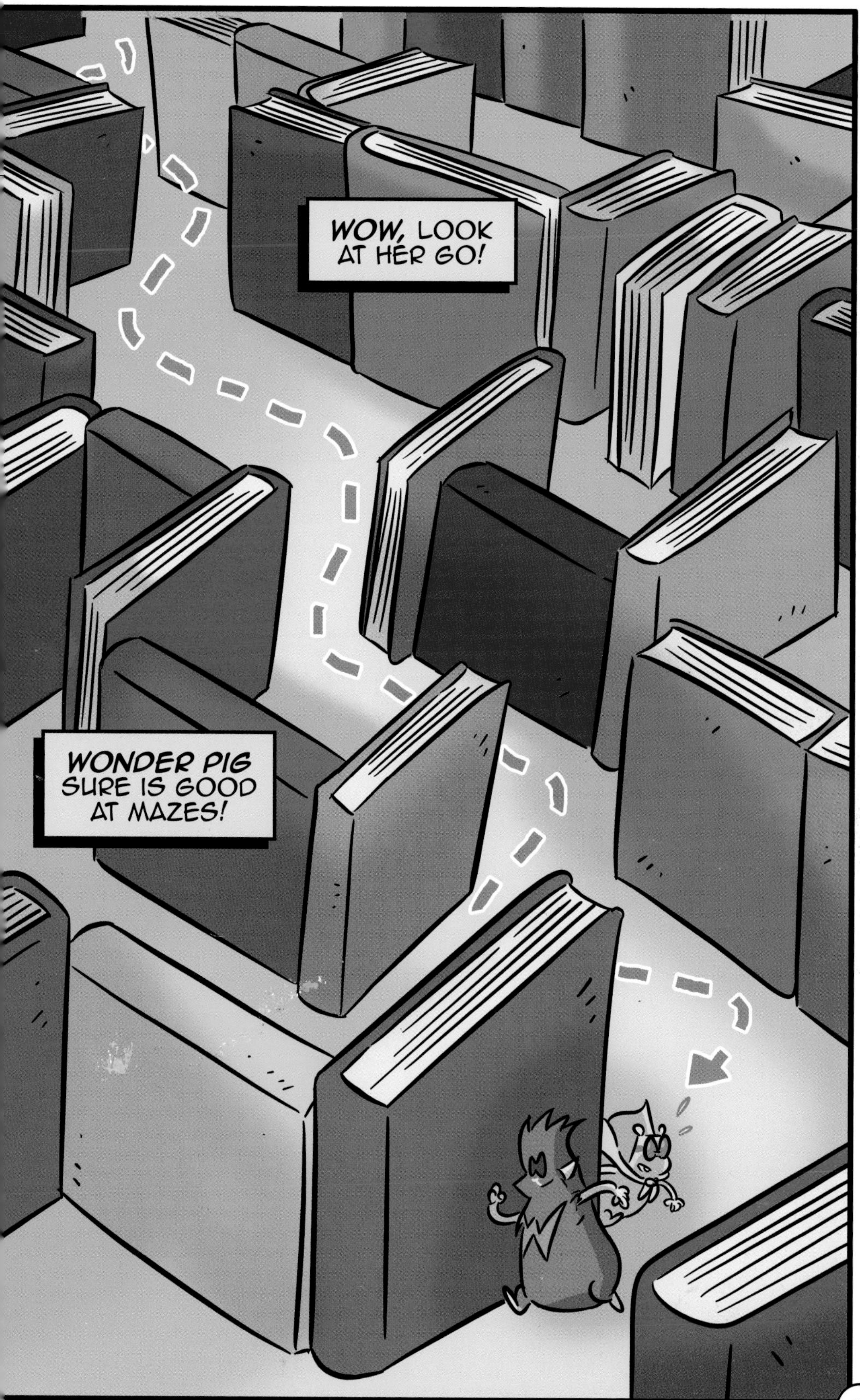
WOW, LOOK AT HER GO!
WONDER PIG SURE IS GOOD AT MAZES!

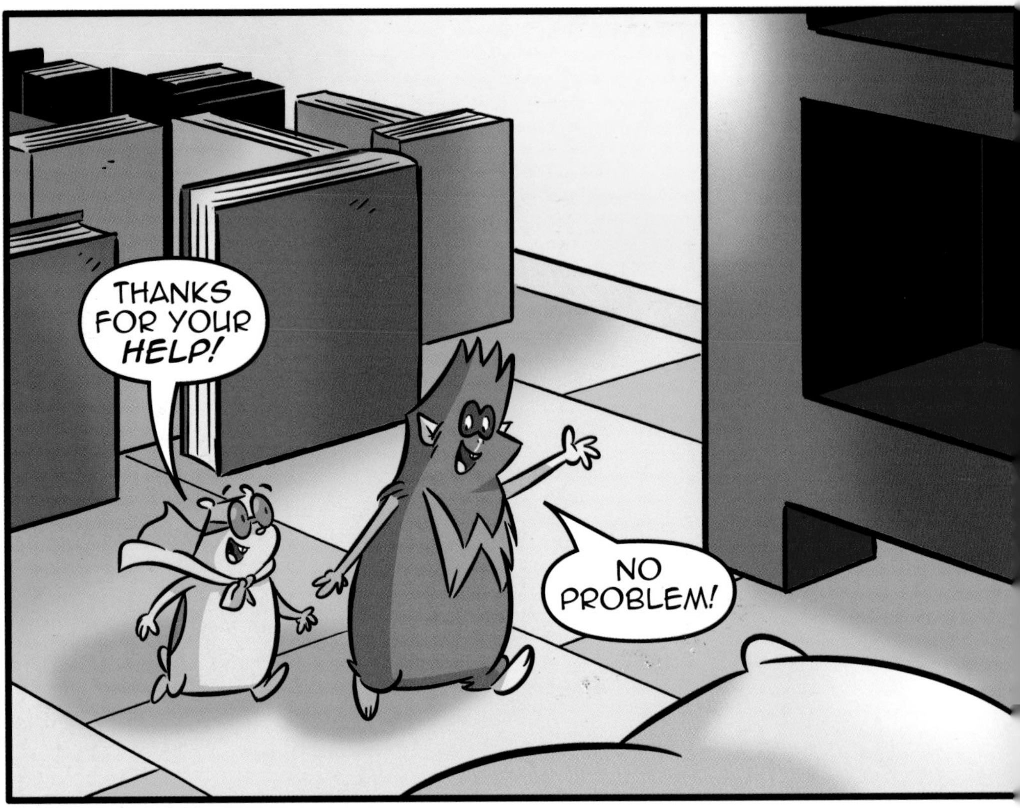
THANKS FOR YOUR HELP!
NO PROBLEM!

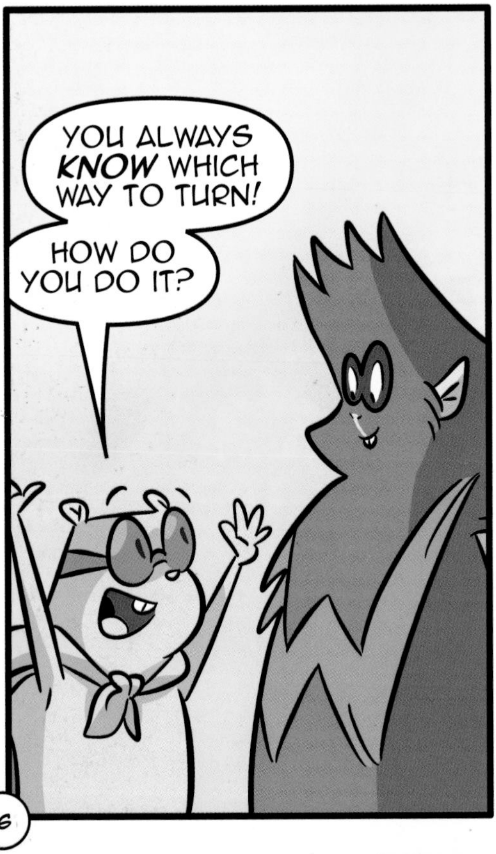
YOU ALWAYS KNOW WHICH WAY TO TURN!
HOW DO YOU DO IT?

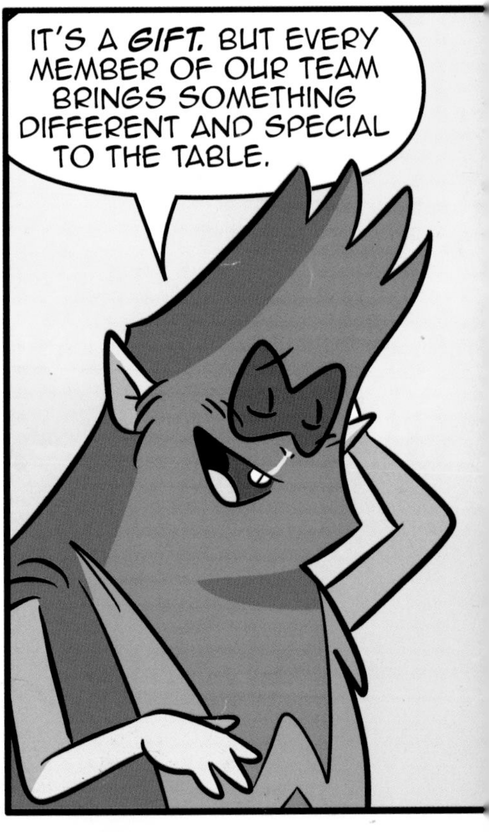
IT'S A GIFT. BUT EVERY MEMBER OF OUR TEAM BRINGS SOMETHING DIFFERENT AND SPECIAL TO THE TABLE.

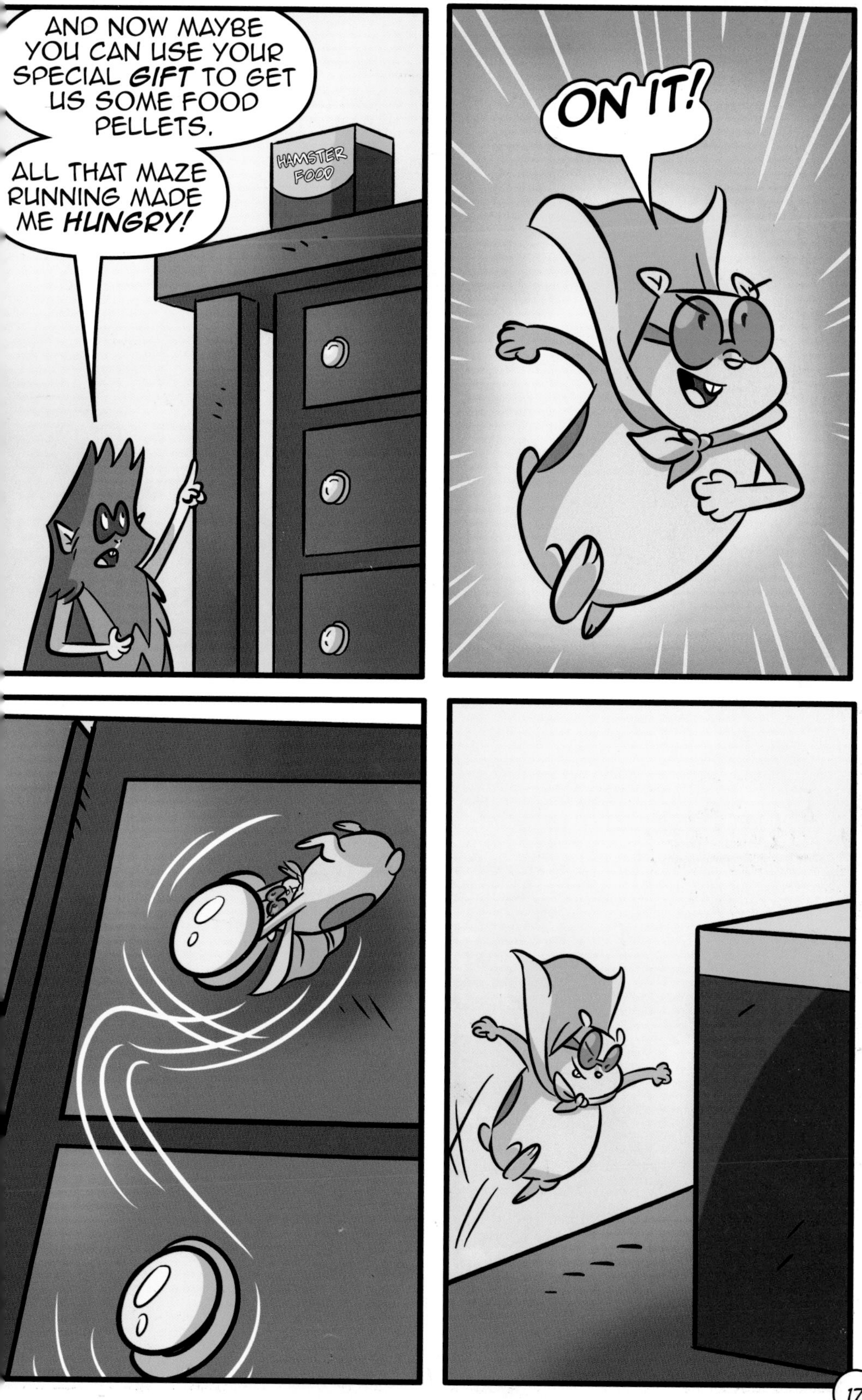
AND NOW MAYBE YOU CAN USE YOUR SPECIAL *GIFT* TO GET US SOME FOOD PELLETS.
ALL THAT MAZE RUNNING MADE ME *HUNGRY!*
HAMSTER FOOD
ON IT!

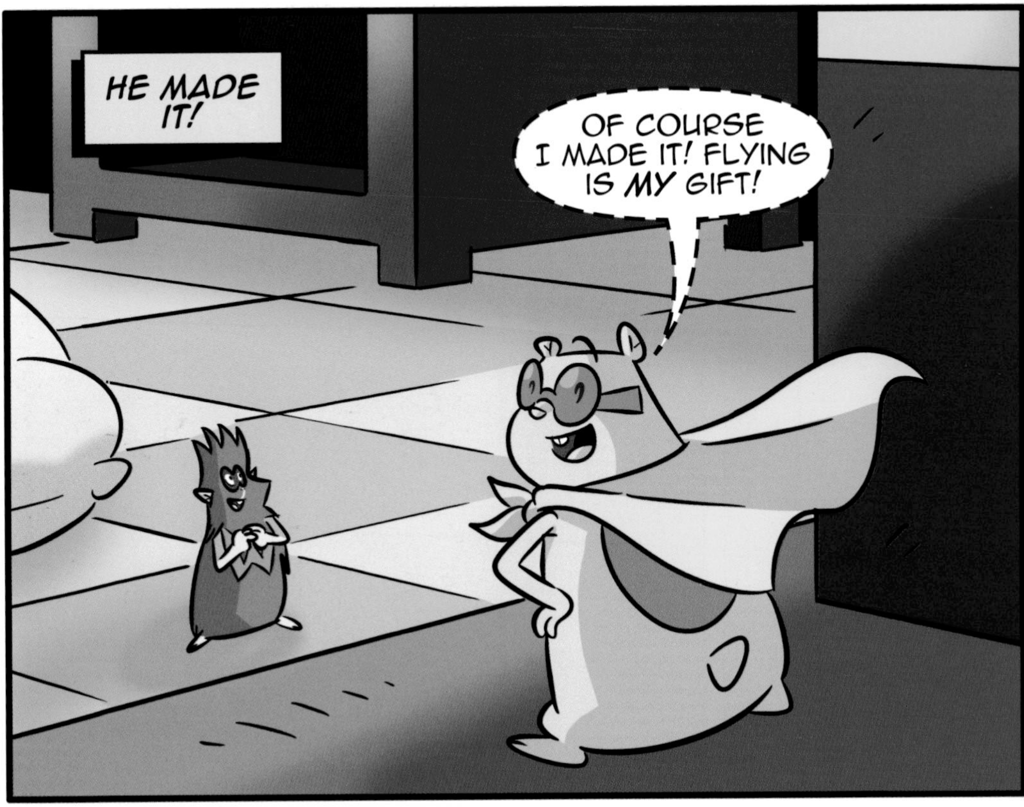
HE MADE IT!
OF COURSE I MADE IT! FLYING IS MY GIFT!

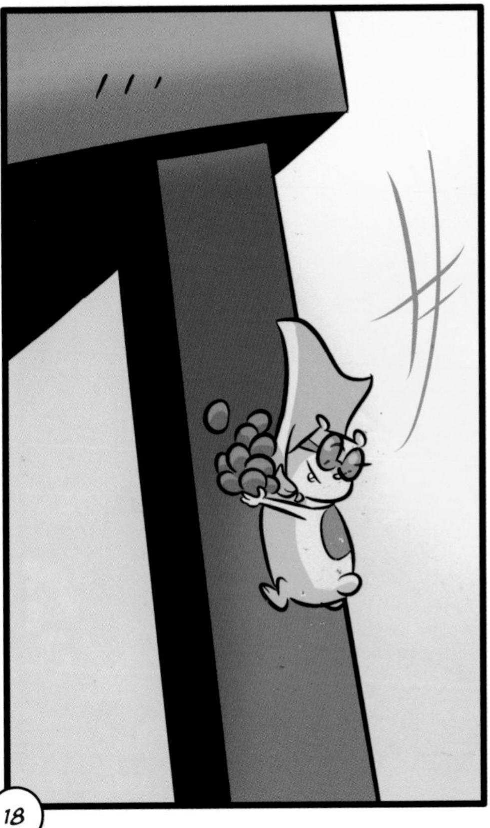

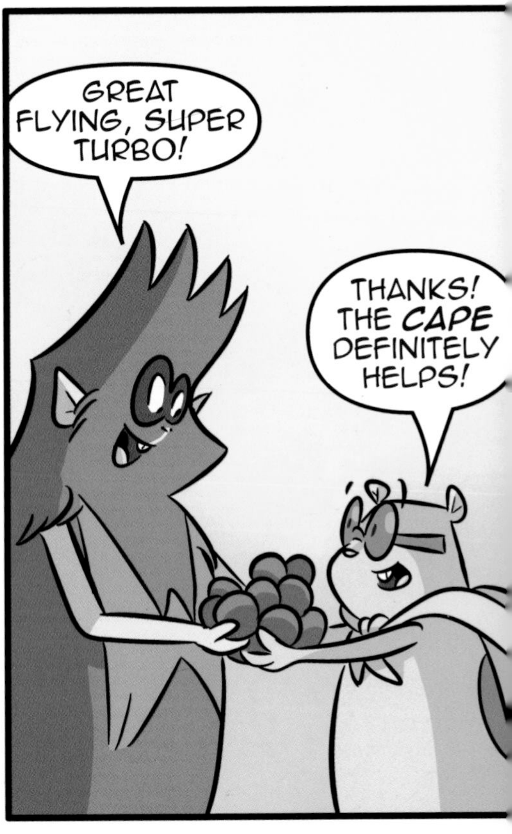
GREAT FLYING, SUPER TURBO!
THANKS! THE CAPE DEFINITELY HELPS!

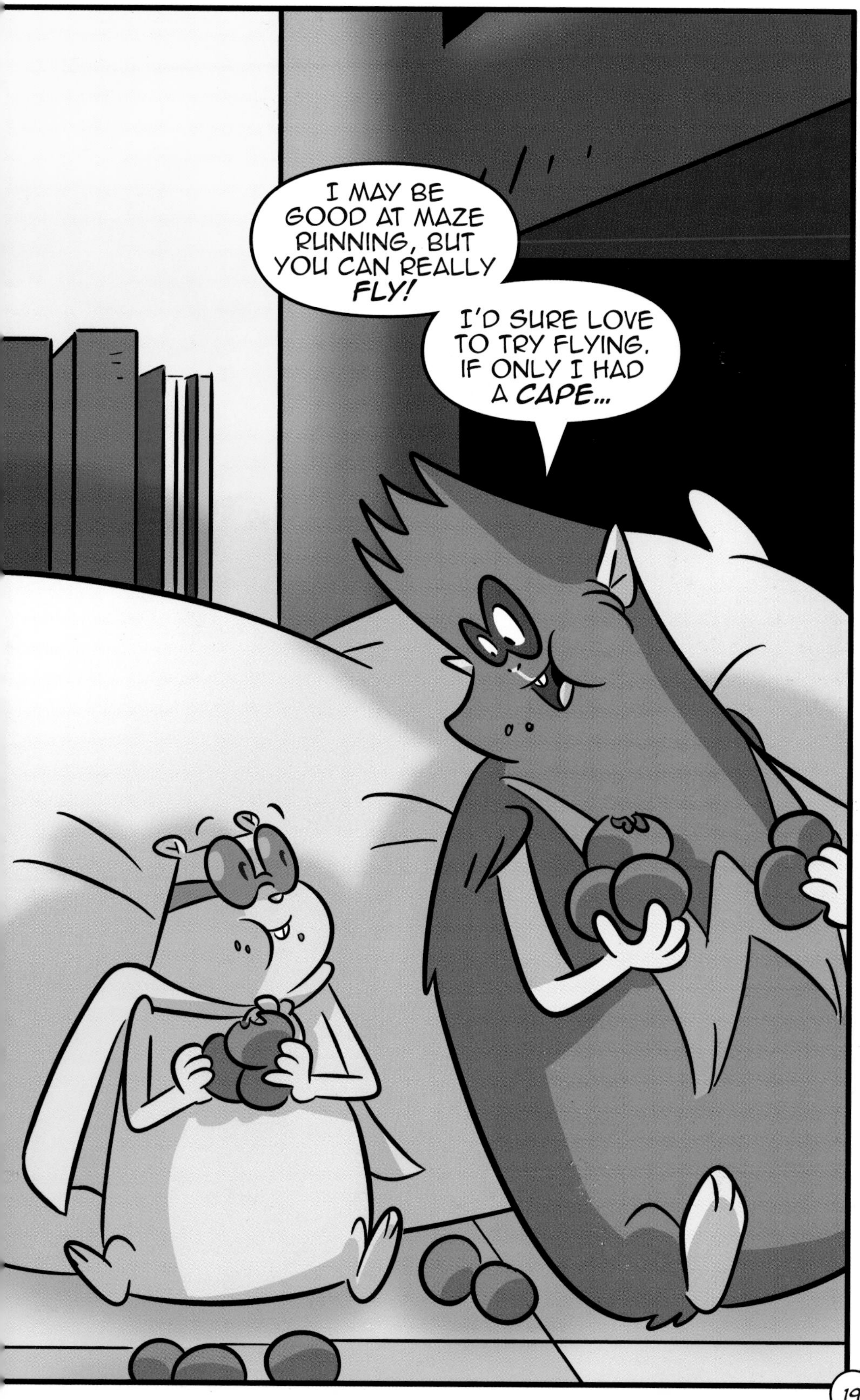
I MAY BE GOOD AT MAZE RUNNING, BUT YOU CAN REALLY *FLY!*
I'D SURE LOVE TO TRY FLYING. IF ONLY I HAD A *CAPE*...

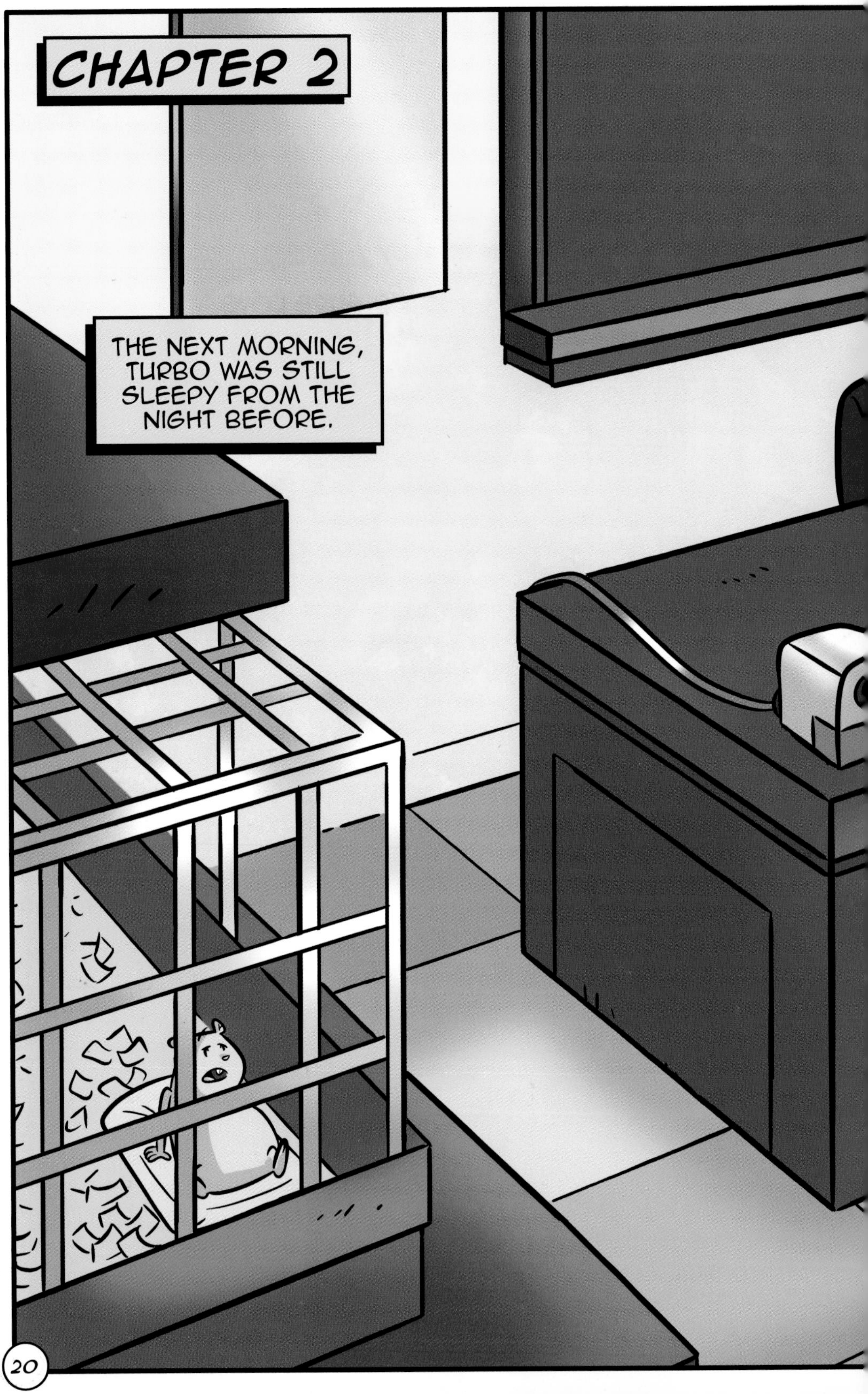
CHAPTER 2
THE NEXT MORNING, TURBO WAS STILL SLEEPY FROM THE NIGHT BEFORE.

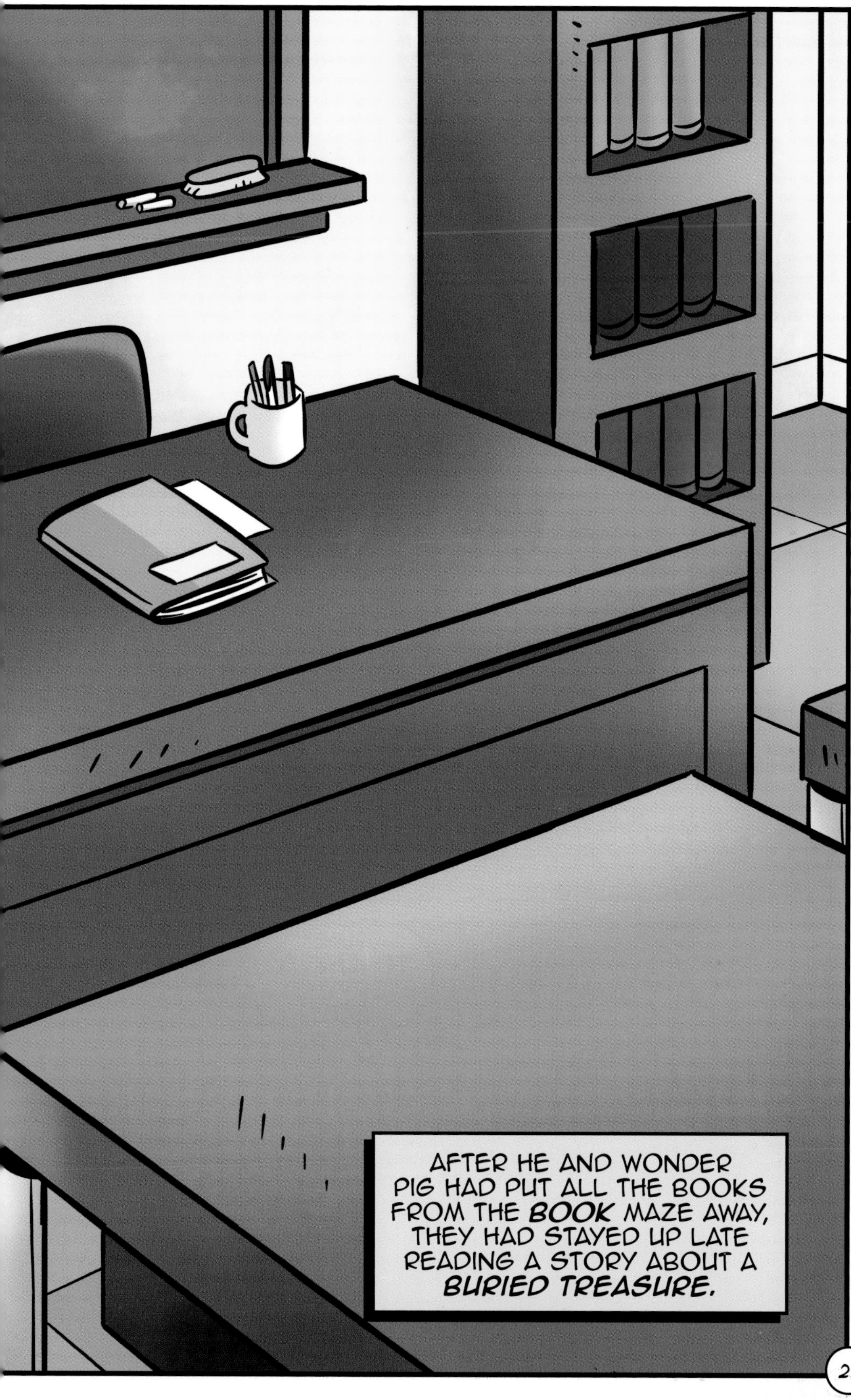
AFTER HE AND WONDER PIG HAD PUT ALL THE BOOKS FROM THE *BOOK* MAZE AWAY, THEY HAD STAYED UP LATE READING A STORY ABOUT A *BURIED TREASURE.*

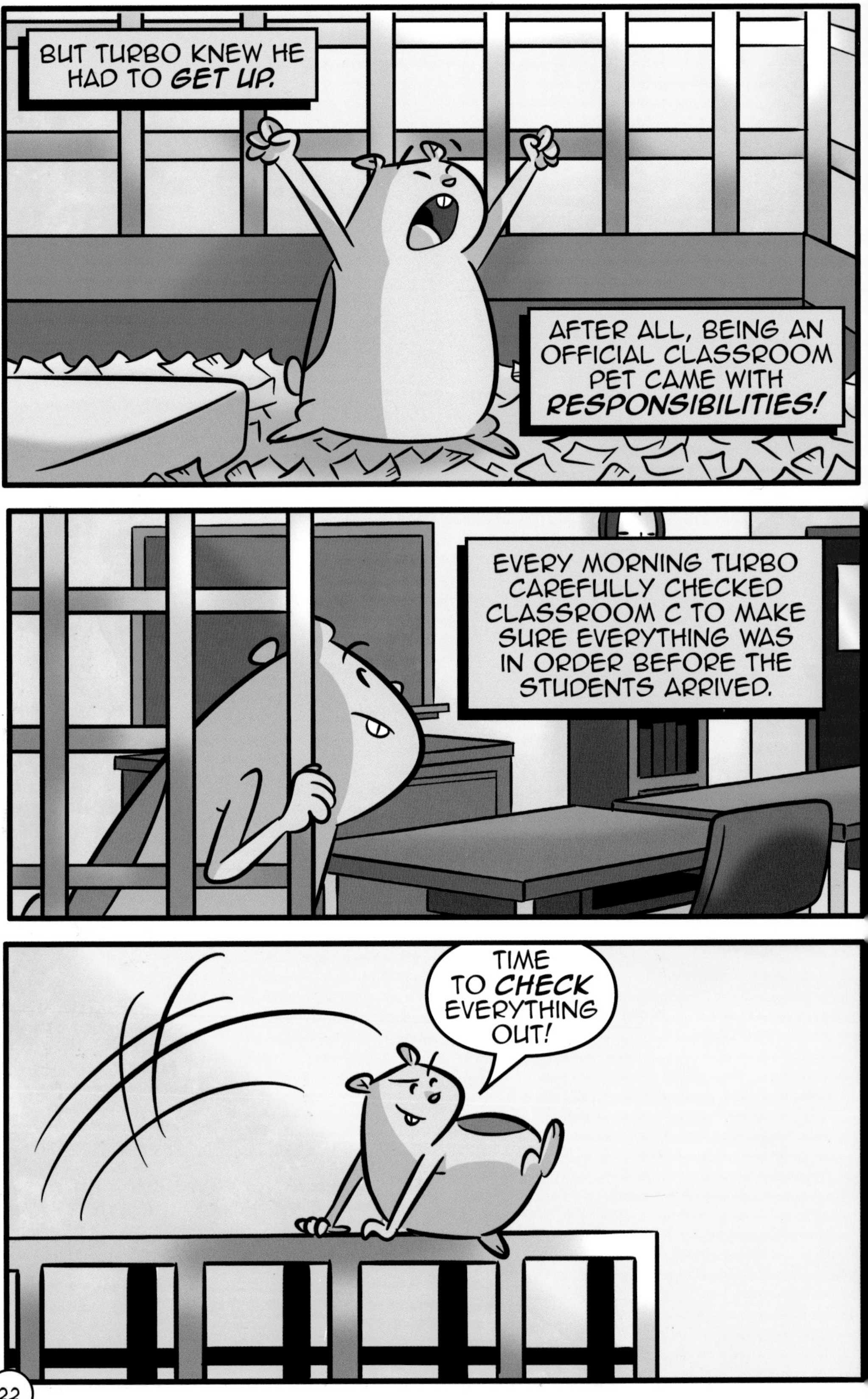
BUT TURBO KNEW HE HAD TO *GET UP.*
AFTER ALL, BEING AN OFFICIAL CLASSROOM PET CAME WITH *RESPONSIBILITIES!*
EVERY MORNING TURBO CAREFULLY CHECKED CLASSROOM C TO MAKE SURE EVERYTHING WAS IN ORDER BEFORE THE STUDENTS ARRIVED.
TIME TO *CHECK* EVERYTHING OUT!

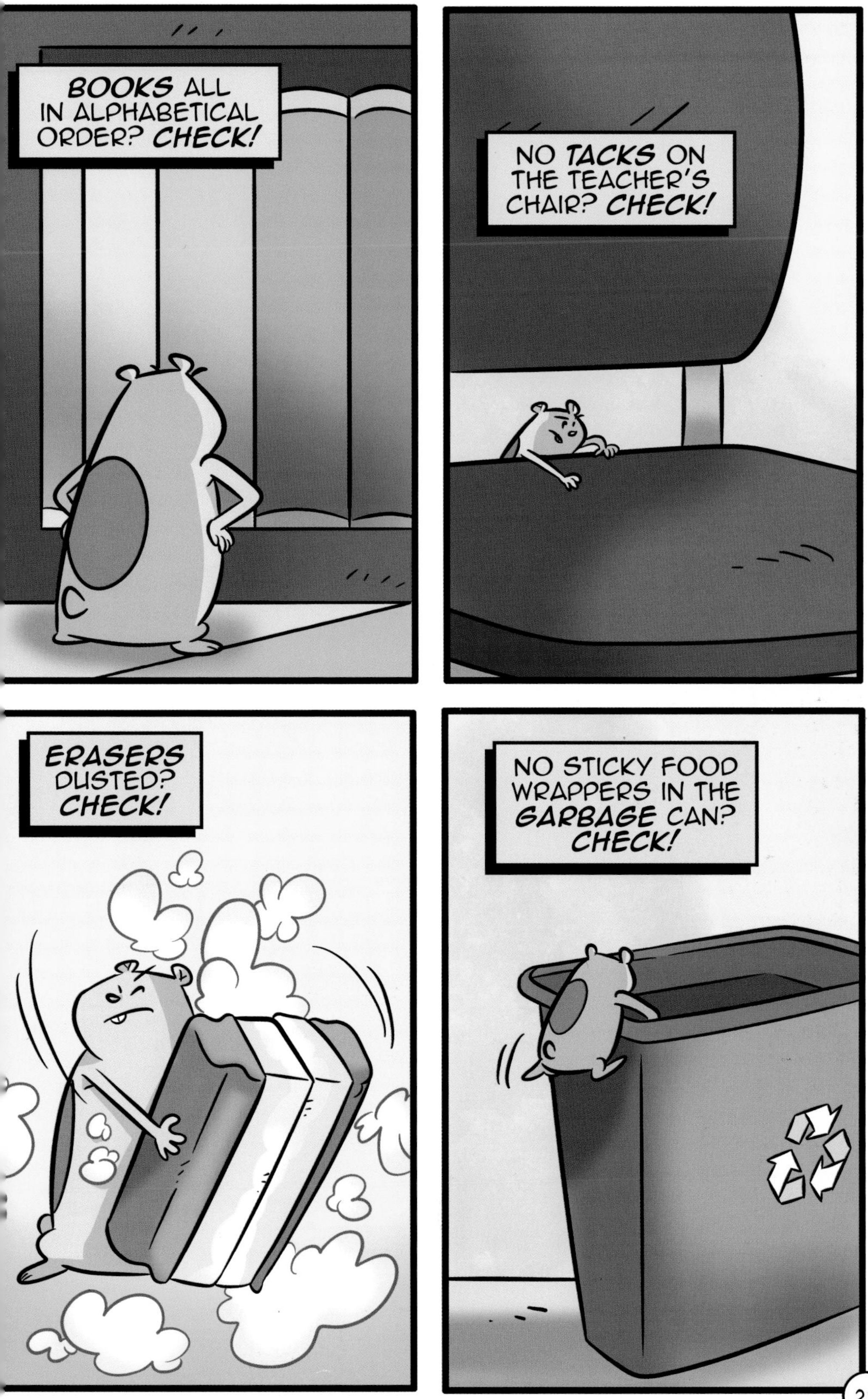
BOOKS ALL IN ALPHABETICAL ORDER? CHECK!
NO TACKS ON THE TEACHER'S CHAIR? CHECK!
ERASERS DUSTED? CHECK!
NO STICKY FOOD WRAPPERS IN THE GARBAGE CAN? CHECK!

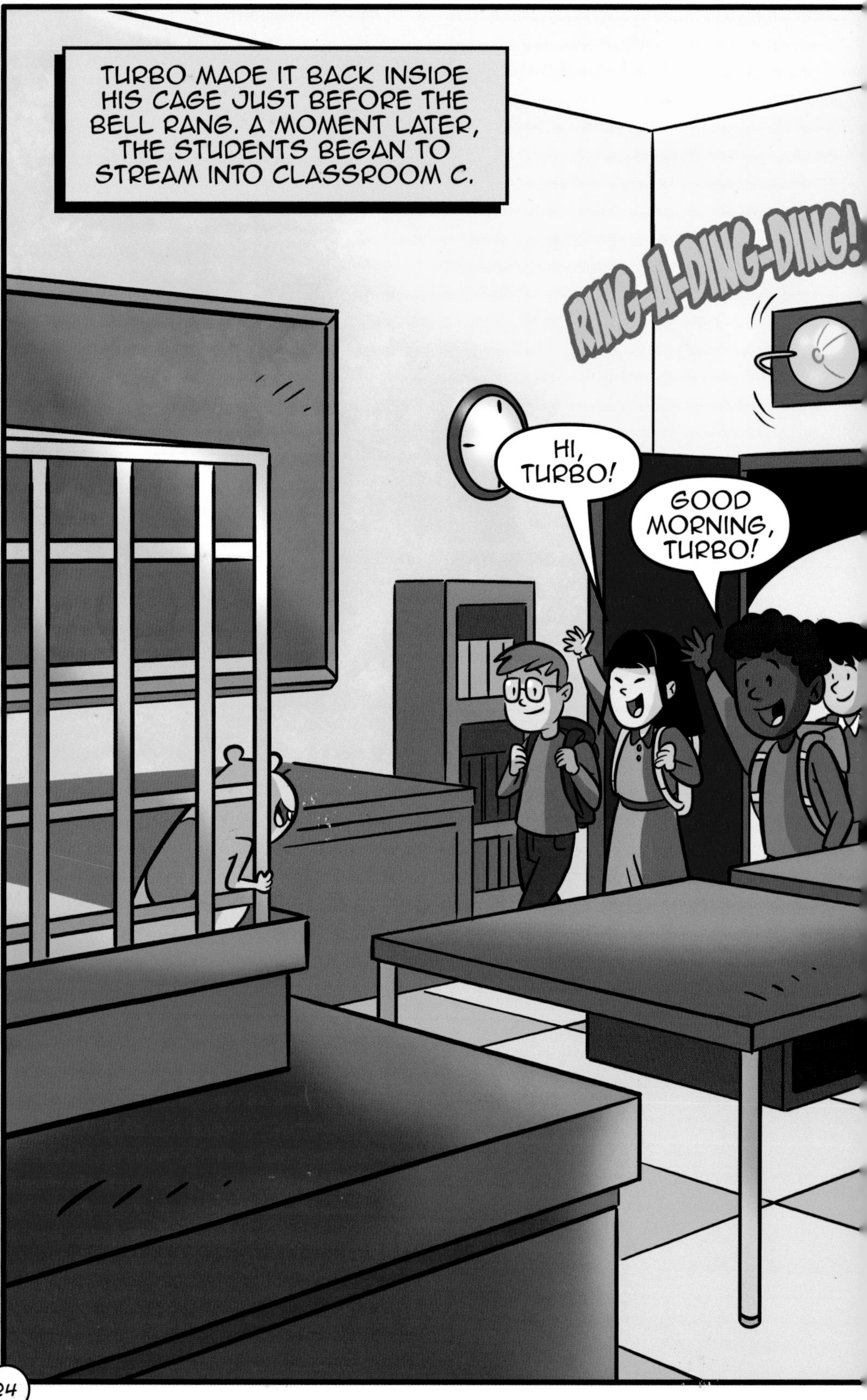
TURBO MADE IT BACK INSIDE HIS CAGE JUST BEFORE THE BELL RANG. A MOMENT LATER, THE STUDENTS BEGAN TO STREAM INTO CLASSROOM C.
RING-A-DING-DING!
HI, TURBO!
GOOD MORNING, TURBO!

IN ORDER TO KEEP HIS **SECRET** SUPERHERO **IDENTITY** A SECRET, TURBO SPENT THE DAY DOING ORDINARY HAMSTER THINGS.

LIKE EXERCISING...

...EATING FOOD PELLETS...

...DRINKING WATER...

...AND, OF COURSE, ENJOYING ALL THE ATTENTION HE GOT FROM THE STUDENTS!

YOU'RE THE BEST CLASSROOM PET IN THE WORLD, TURBO!

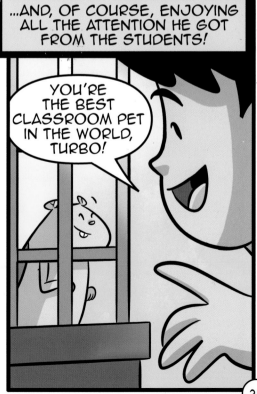

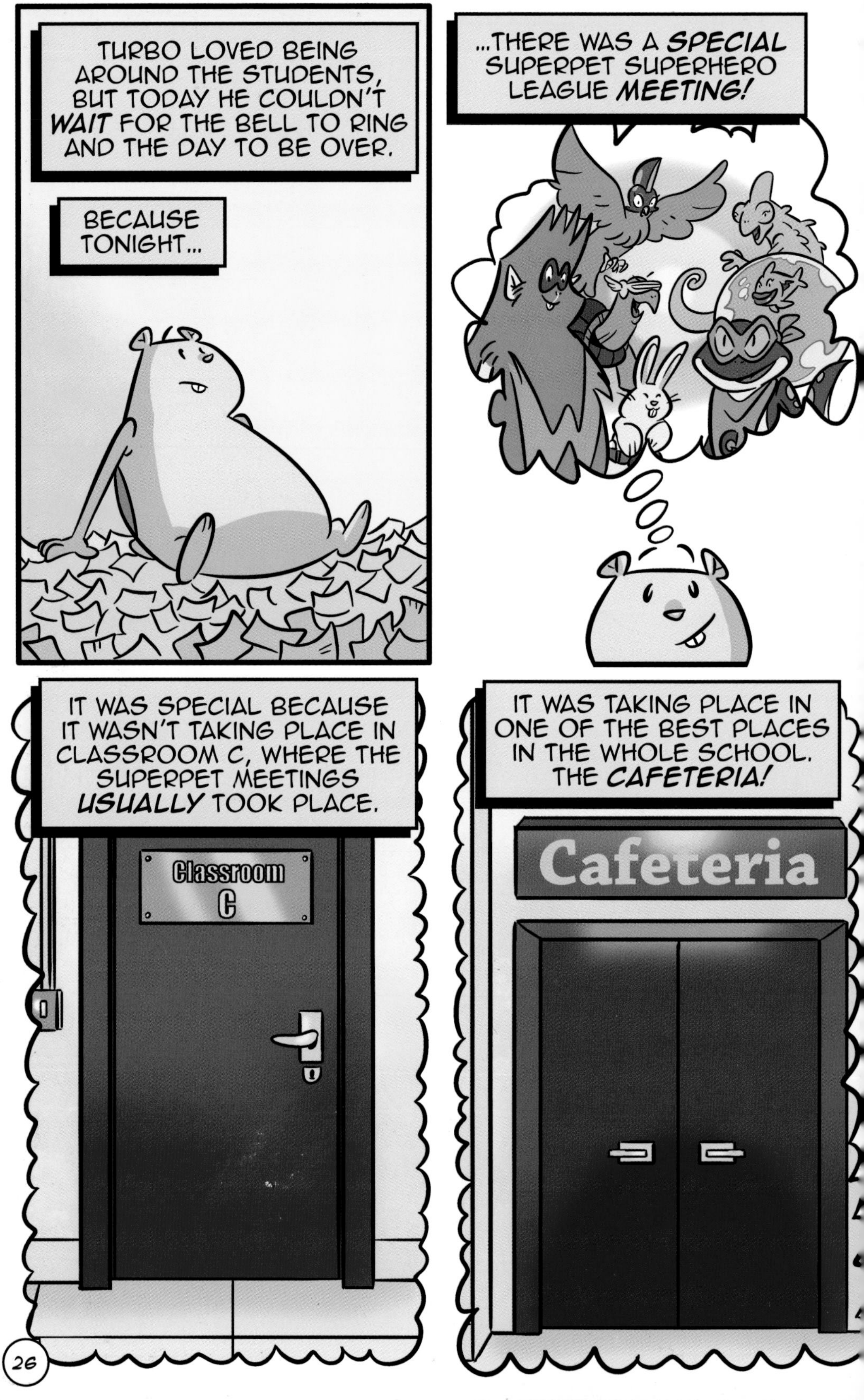
TURBO LOVED BEING AROUND THE STUDENTS, BUT TODAY HE COULDN'T *WAIT* FOR THE BELL TO RING AND THE DAY TO BE OVER.
BECAUSE TONIGHT...
...THERE WAS A *SPECIAL* SUPERPET SUPERHERO LEAGUE *MEETING!*
IT WAS SPECIAL BECAUSE IT WASN'T TAKING PLACE IN CLASSROOM C, WHERE THE SUPERPET MEETINGS *USUALLY* TOOK PLACE.
Classroom C
IT WAS TAKING PLACE IN ONE OF THE BEST PLACES IN THE WHOLE SCHOOL. THE *CAFETERIA!*
Cafeteria

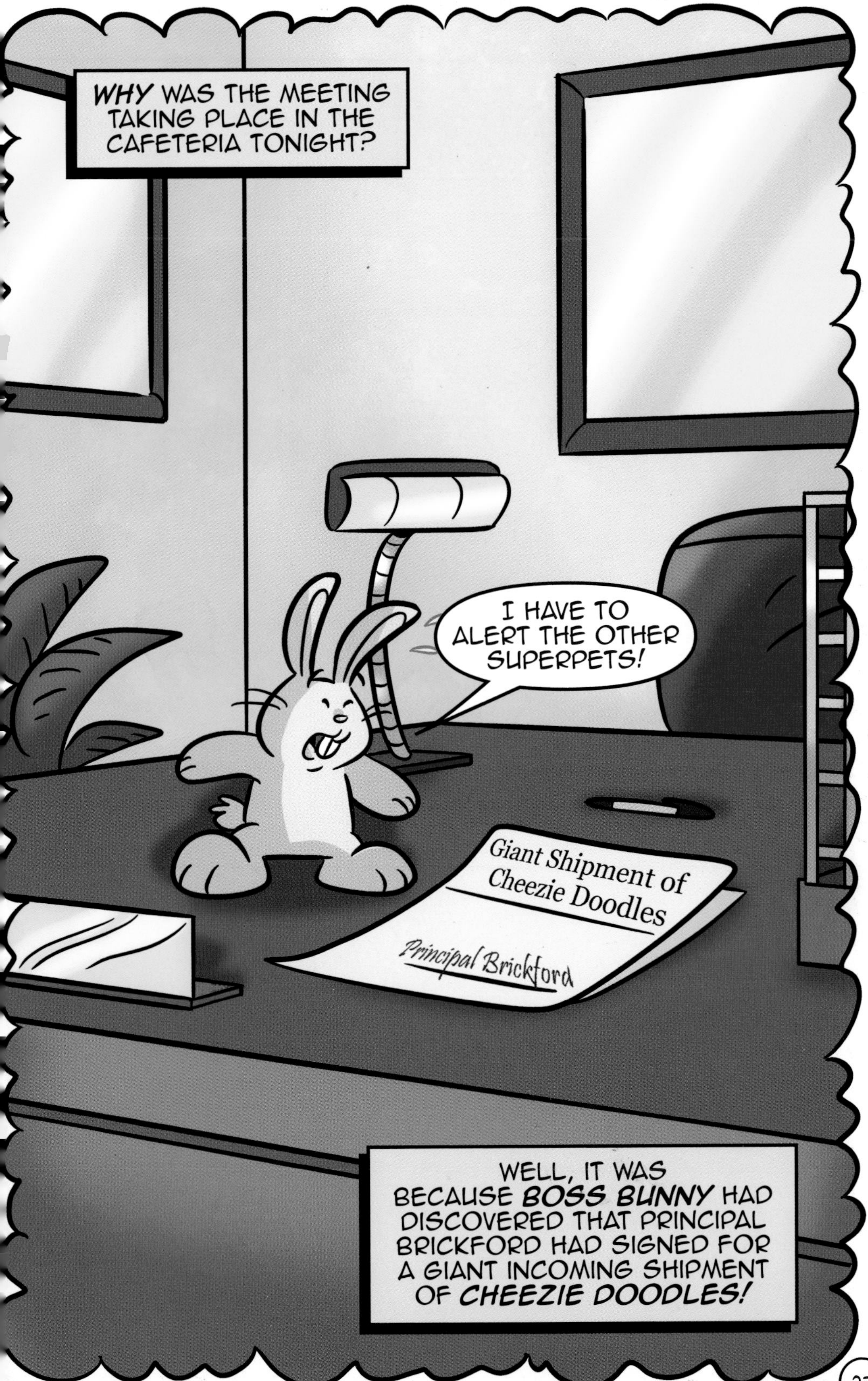
WHY WAS THE MEETING TAKING PLACE IN THE CAFETERIA TONIGHT?
I HAVE TO ALERT THE OTHER SUPERPETS!
Giant Shipment of Cheezie Doodles
Principal Brickford
WELL, IT WAS BECAUSE BOSS BUNNY HAD DISCOVERED THAT PRINCIPAL BRICKFORD HAD SIGNED FOR A GIANT INCOMING SHIPMENT OF CHEEZIE DOODLES!

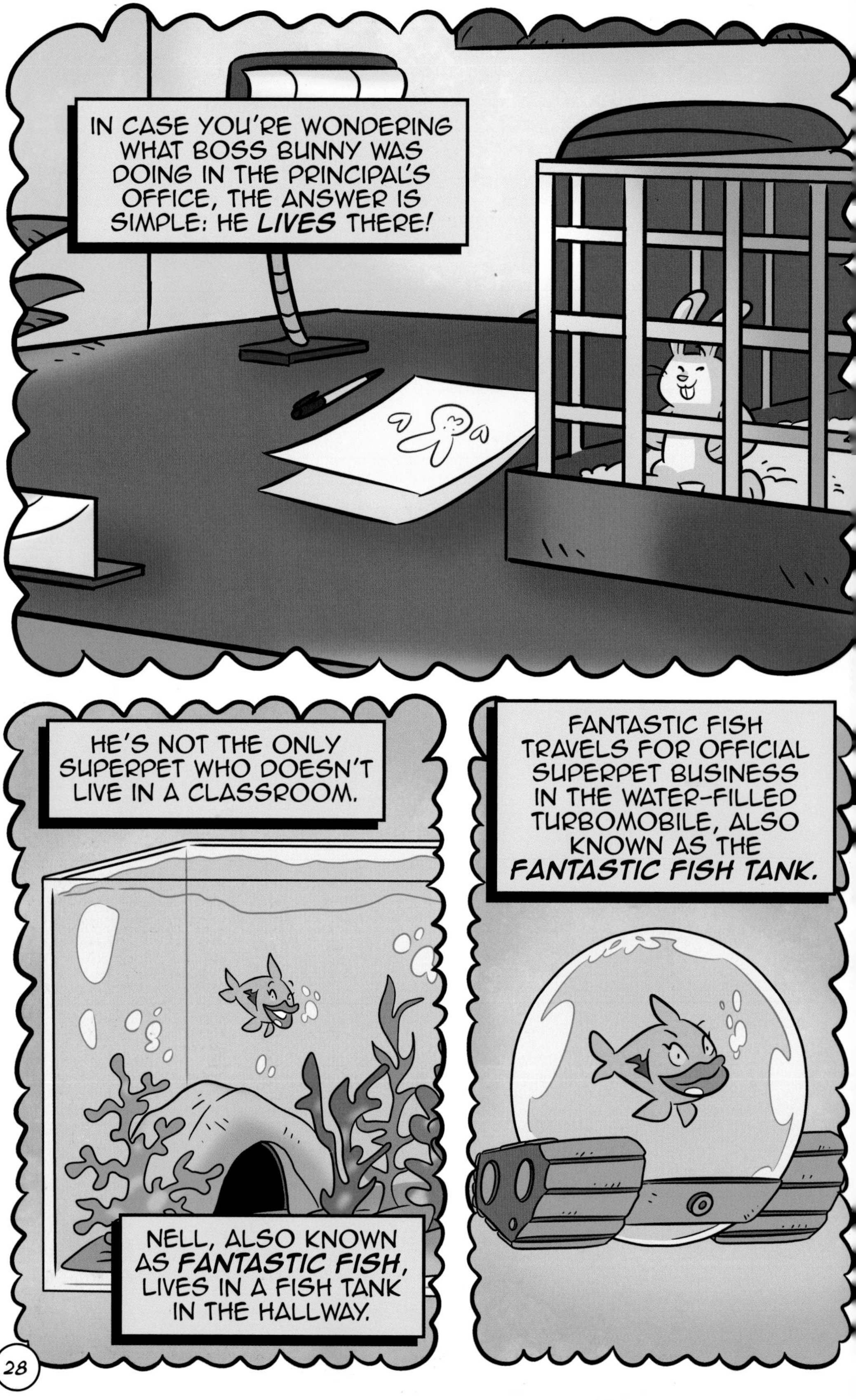
IN CASE YOU'RE WONDERING WHAT BOSS BUNNY WAS DOING IN THE PRINCIPAL'S OFFICE, THE ANSWER IS SIMPLE: HE *LIVES* THERE!
HE'S NOT THE ONLY SUPERPET WHO DOESN'T LIVE IN A CLASSROOM.
NELL, ALSO KNOWN AS *FANTASTIC FISH*, LIVES IN A FISH TANK IN THE HALLWAY.
FANTASTIC FISH TRAVELS FOR OFFICIAL SUPERPET BUSINESS IN THE WATER-FILLED TURBOMOBILE, ALSO KNOWN AS THE *FANTASTIC FISH TANK.*

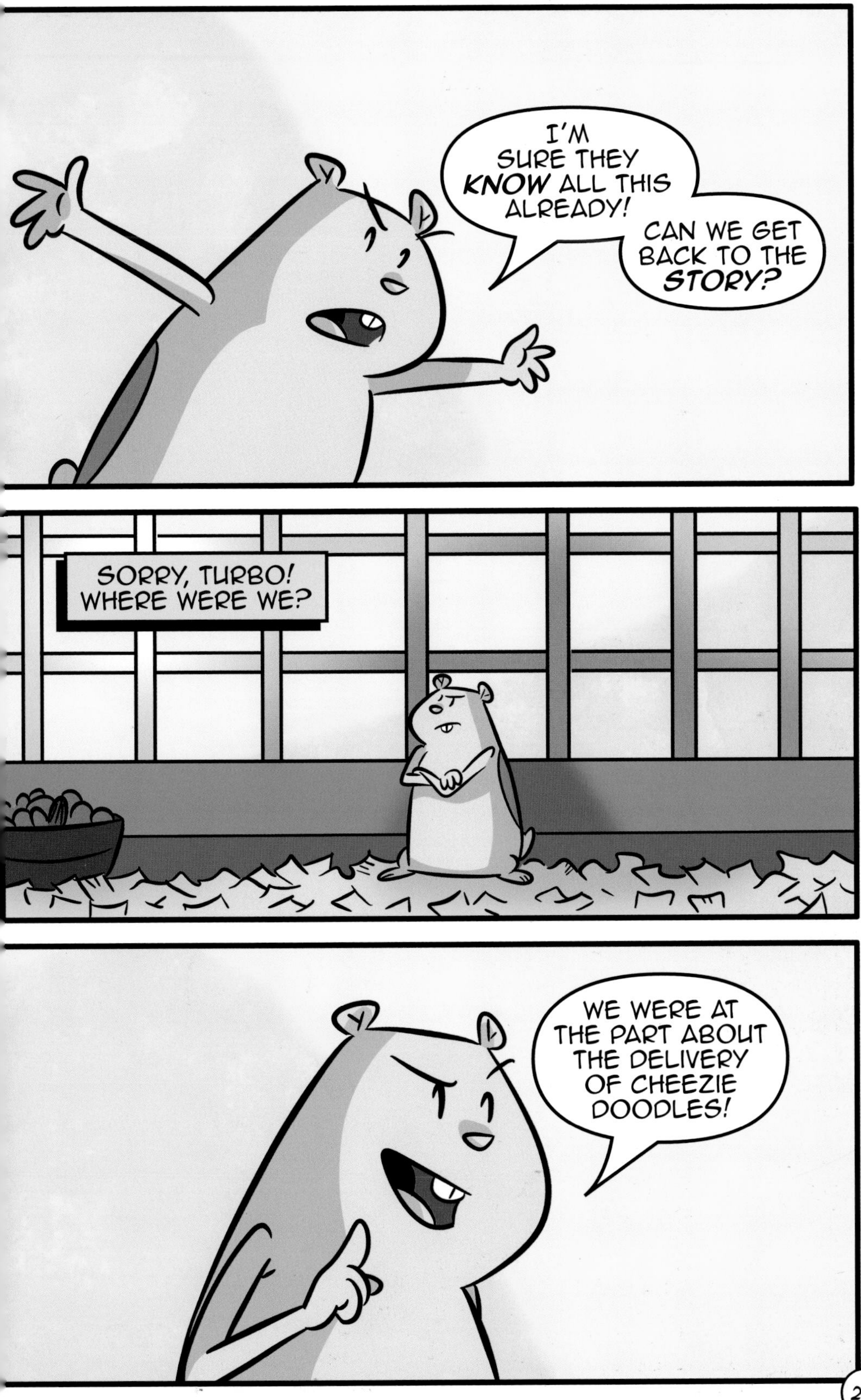
I'M SURE THEY KNOW ALL THIS ALREADY!
CAN WE GET BACK TO THE STORY?
SORRY, TURBO! WHERE WERE WE?
WE WERE AT THE PART ABOUT THE DELIVERY OF CHEEZIE DOODLES!

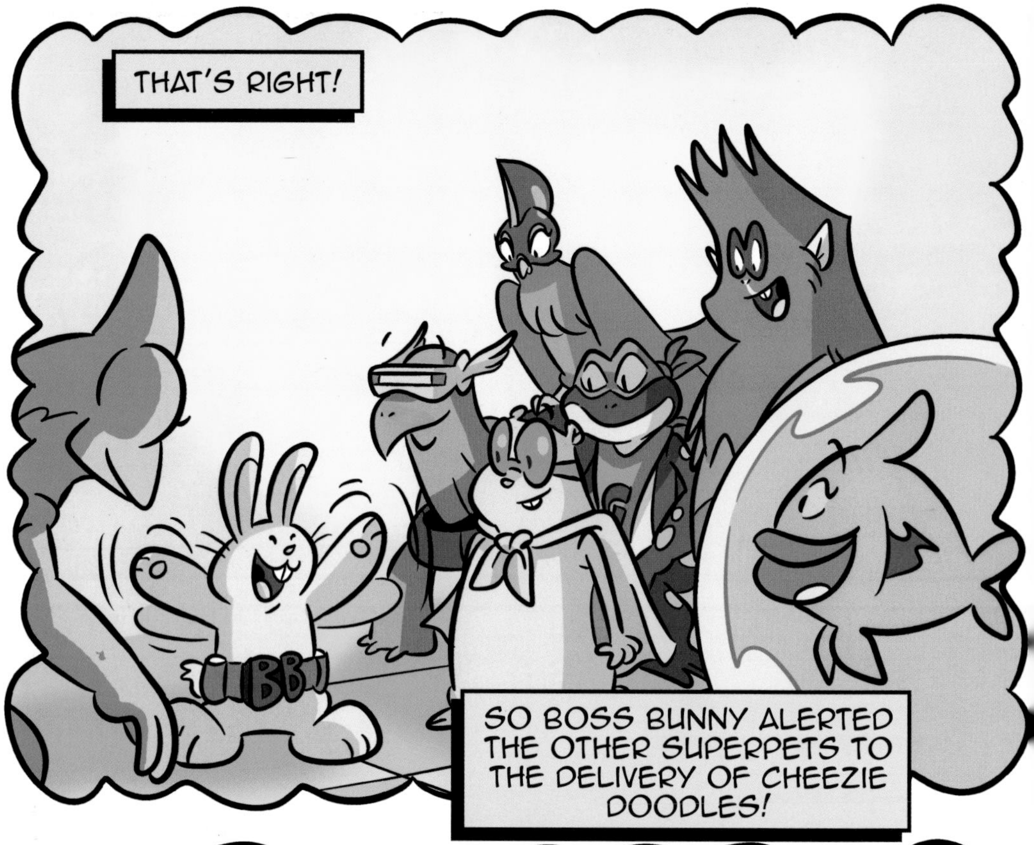
THAT'S RIGHT!
SO BOSS BUNNY ALERTED THE OTHER SUPERPETS TO THE DELIVERY OF CHEEZIE DOODLES!

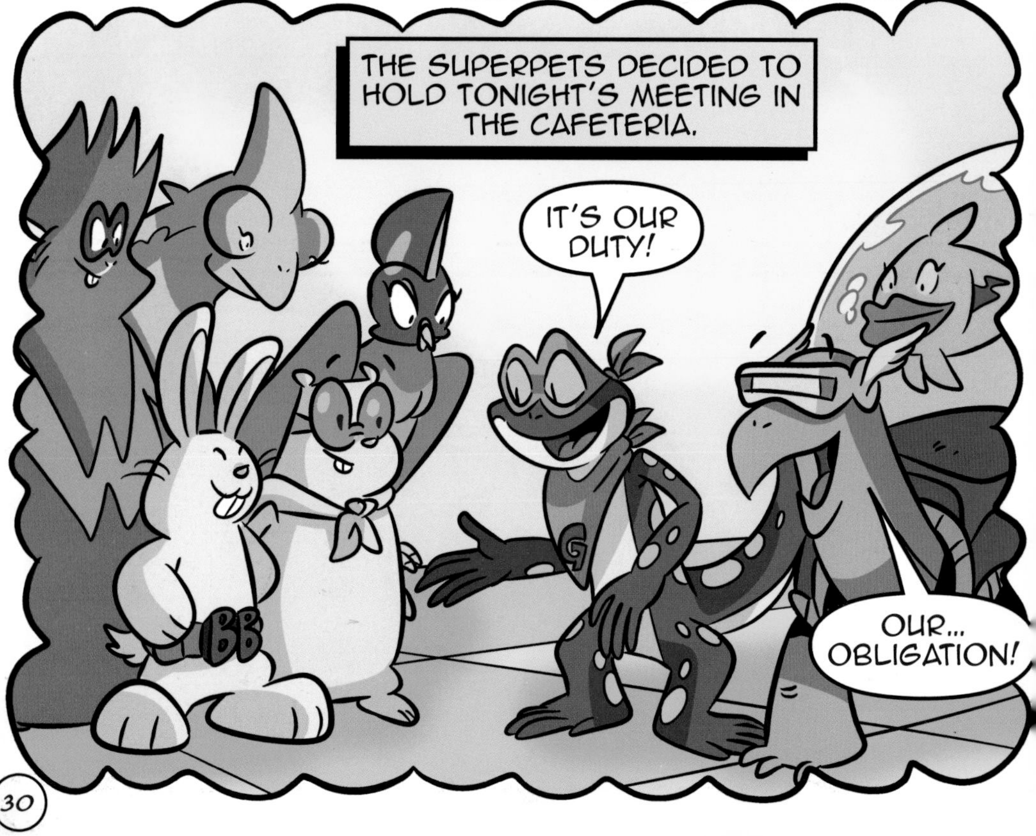
THE SUPERPETS DECIDED TO HOLD TONIGHT'S MEETING IN THE CAFETERIA.
IT'S OUR DUTY!
OUR... OBLIGATION!

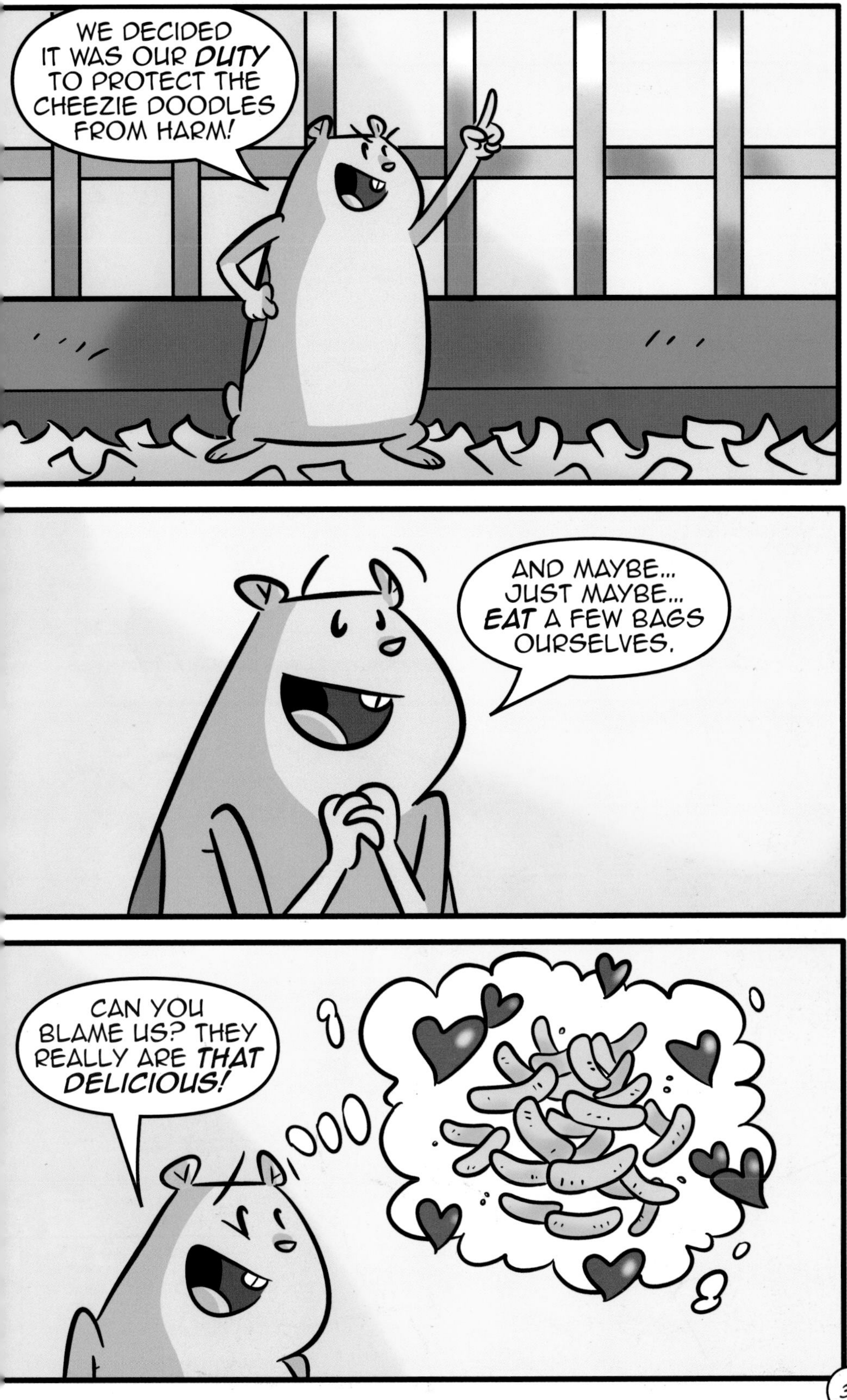
WE DECIDED IT WAS OUR DUTY TO PROTECT THE CHEEZIE DOODLES FROM HARM!
AND MAYBE... JUST MAYBE... EAT A FEW BAGS OURSELVES.
CAN YOU BLAME US? THEY REALLY ARE THAT DELICIOUS!

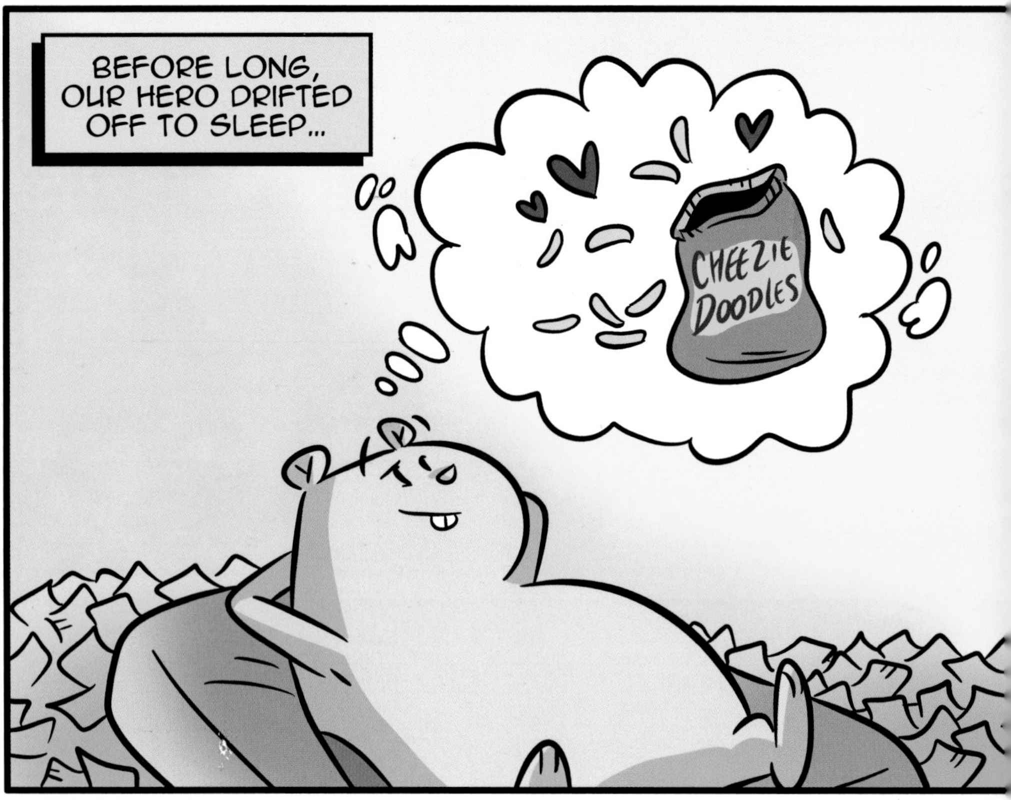
BEFORE LONG, OUR HERO DRIFTED OFF TO SLEEP...
CHEEZIE DOODLES

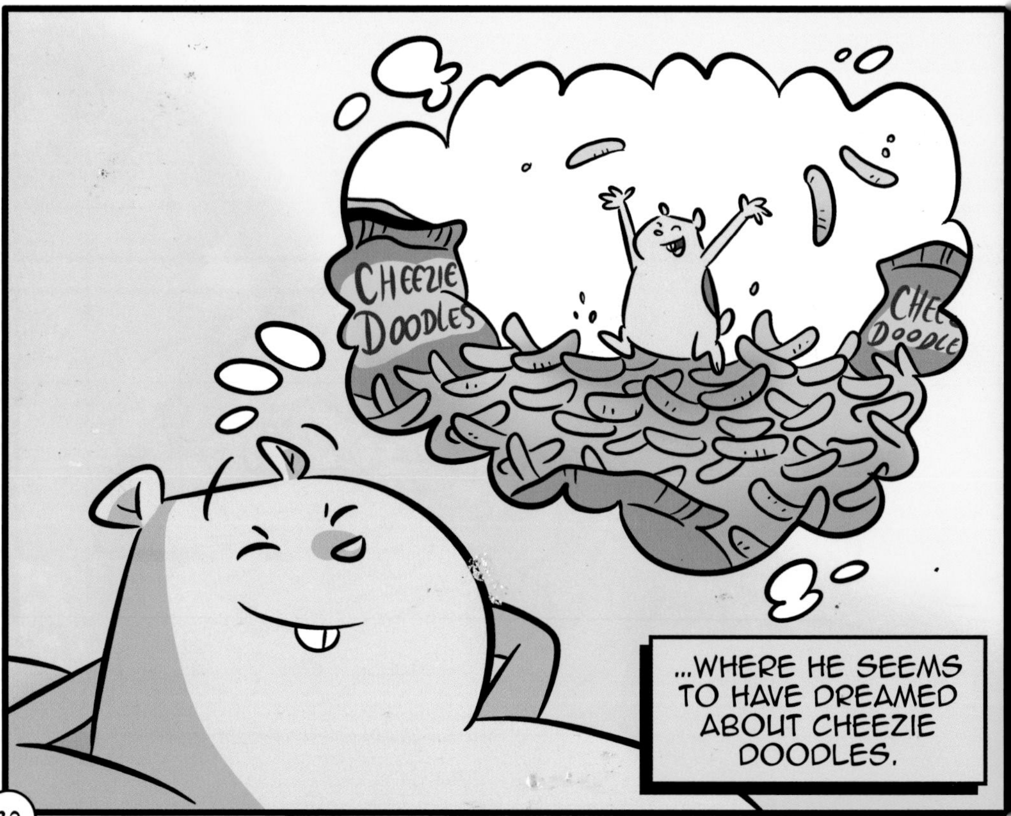
CHEEZIE DOODLES
...WHERE HE SEEMS TO HAVE DREAMED ABOUT CHEEZIE DOODLES.

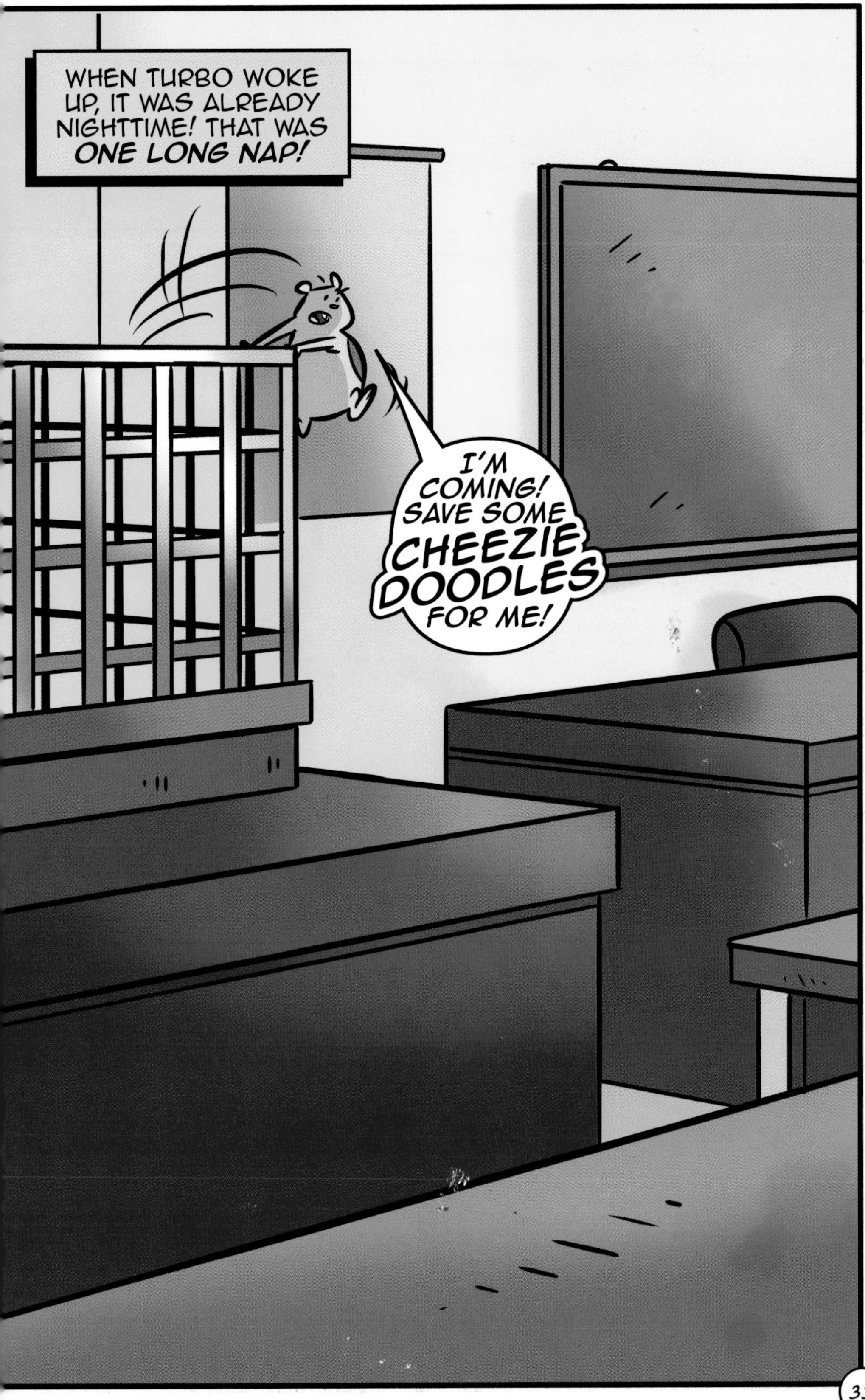
WHEN TURBO WOKE UP, IT WAS ALREADY NIGHTTIME! THAT WAS ONE LONG NAP!
I'M COMING! SAVE SOME CHEEZIE DOODLES FOR ME!

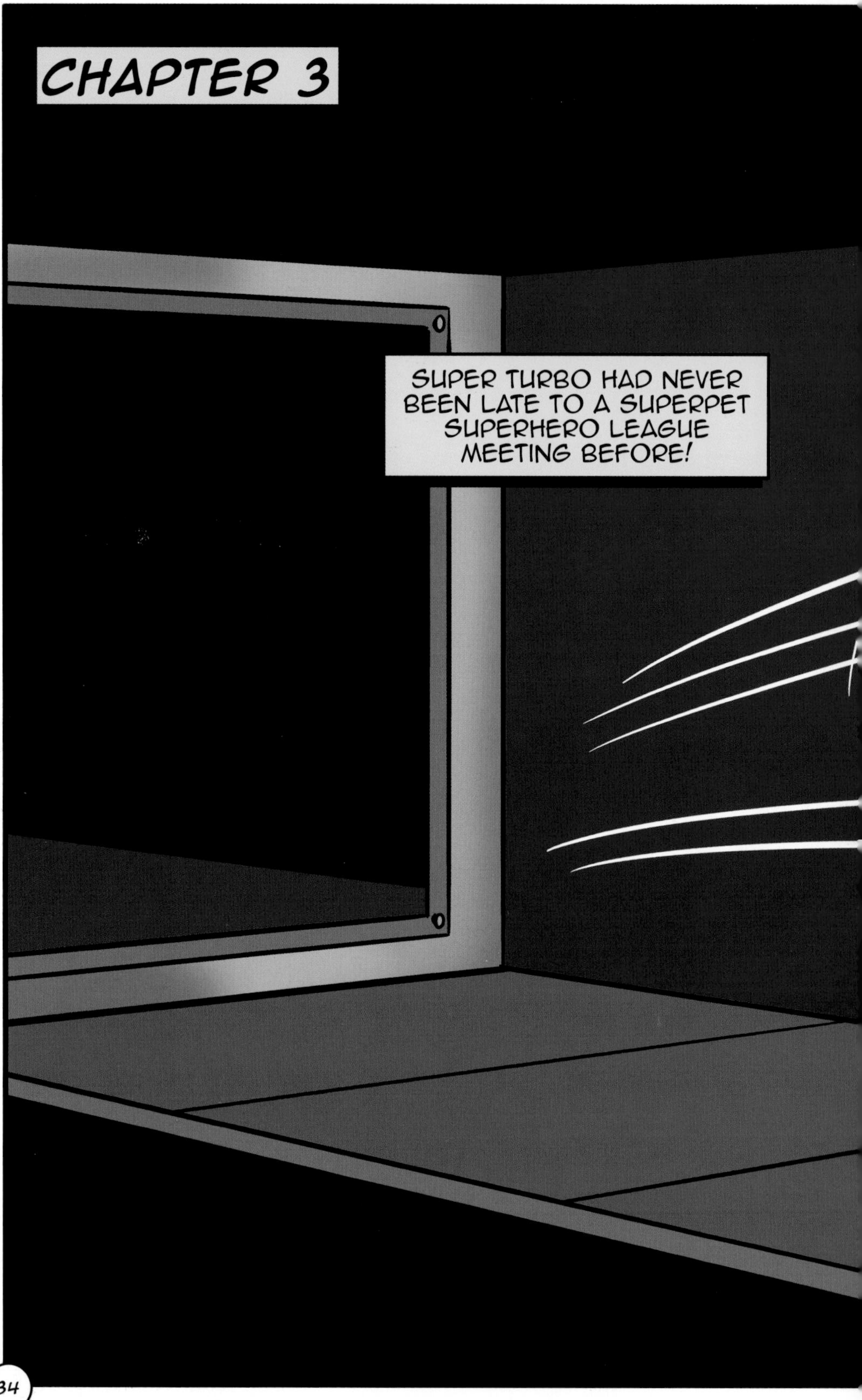
CHAPTER 3
SUPER TURBO HAD NEVER BEEN LATE TO A SUPERPET SUPERHERO LEAGUE MEETING BEFORE!

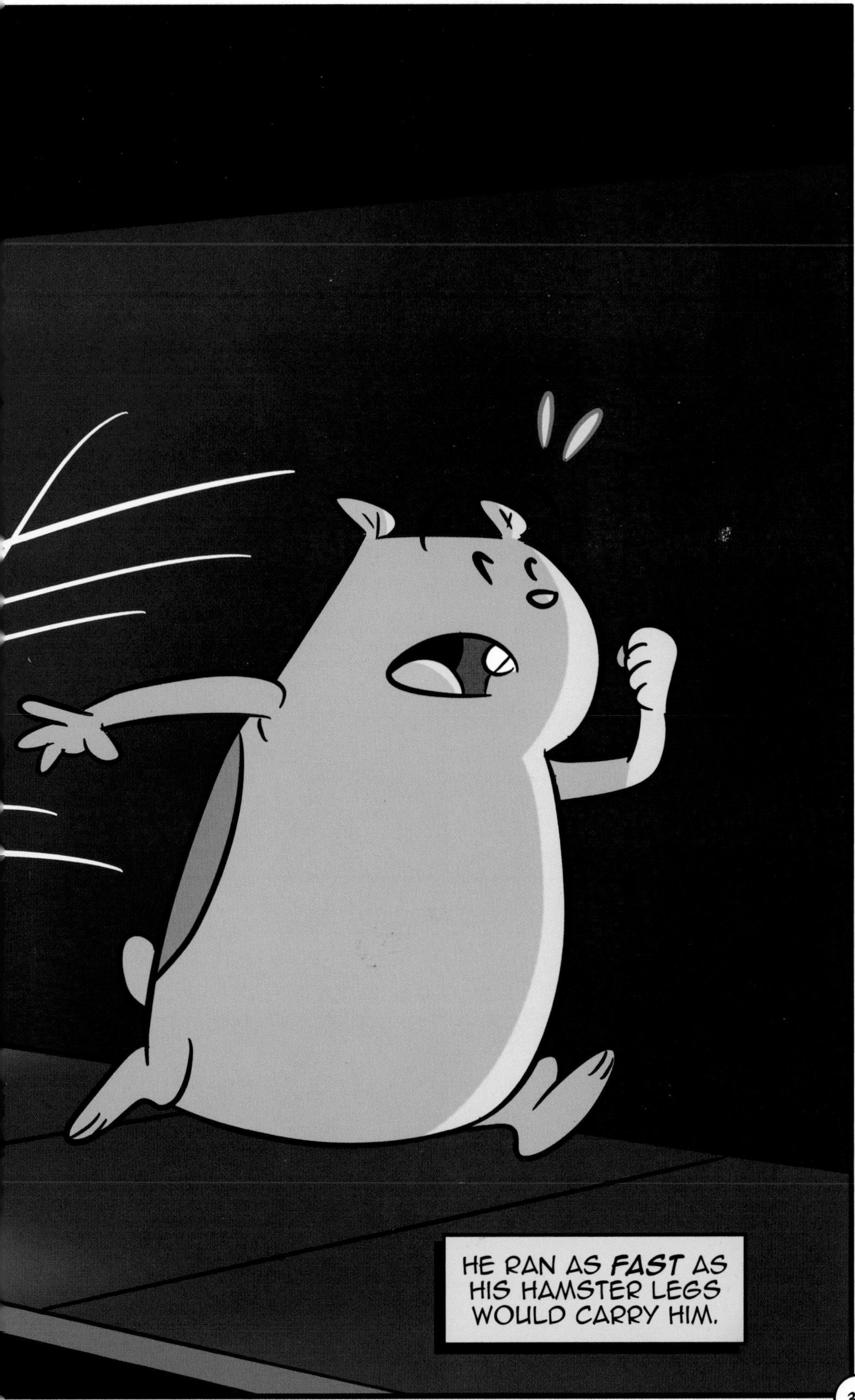
HE RAN AS FAST AS HIS HAMSTER LEGS WOULD CARRY HIM.

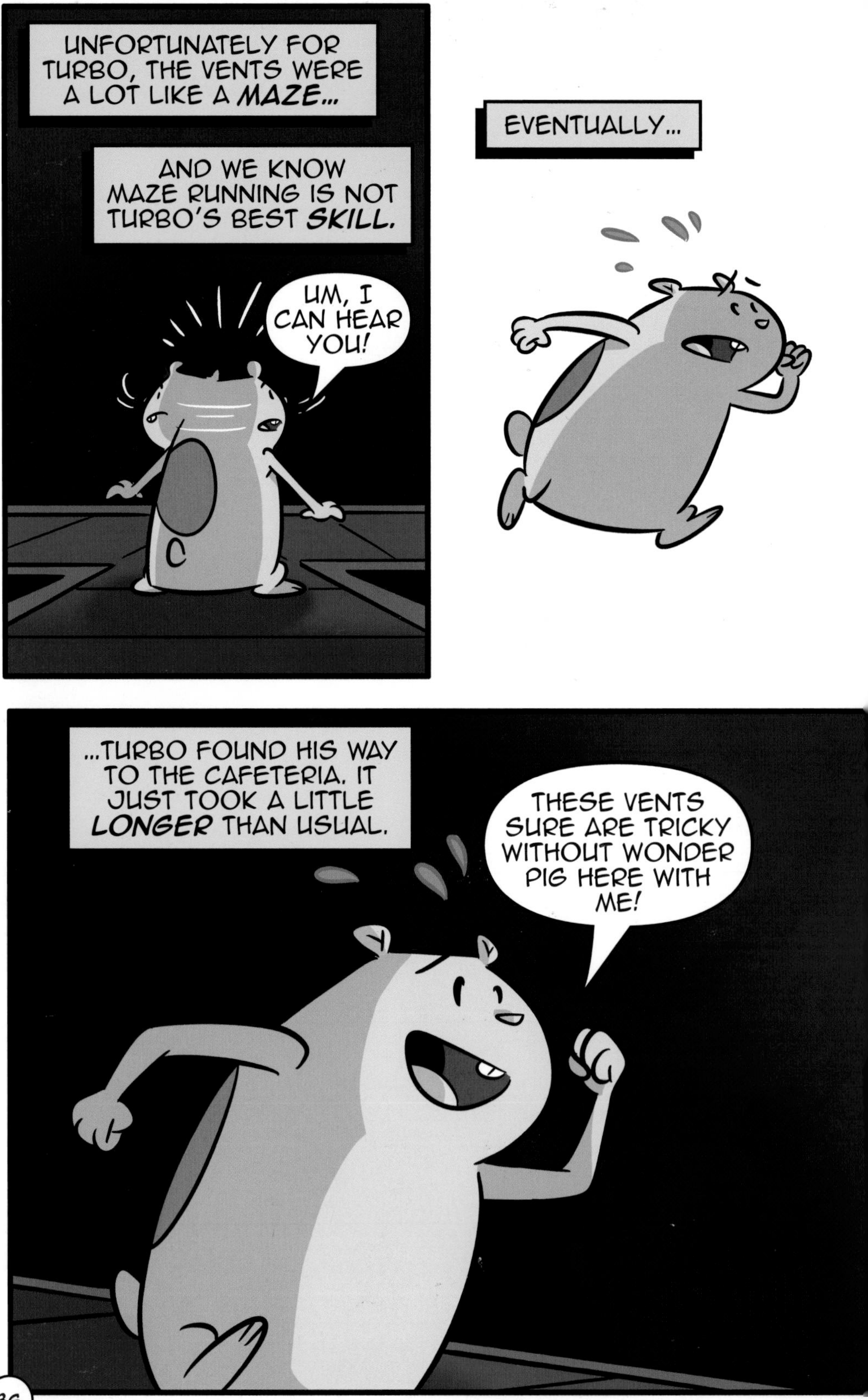
UNFORTUNATELY FOR TURBO, THE VENTS WERE A LOT LIKE A MAZE...
AND WE KNOW MAZE RUNNING IS NOT TURBO'S BEST SKILL.
UM, I CAN HEAR YOU!
EVENTUALLY...
...TURBO FOUND HIS WAY TO THE CAFETERIA. IT JUST TOOK A LITTLE LONGER THAN USUAL.
THESE VENTS SURE ARE TRICKY WITHOUT WONDER PIG HERE WITH ME!

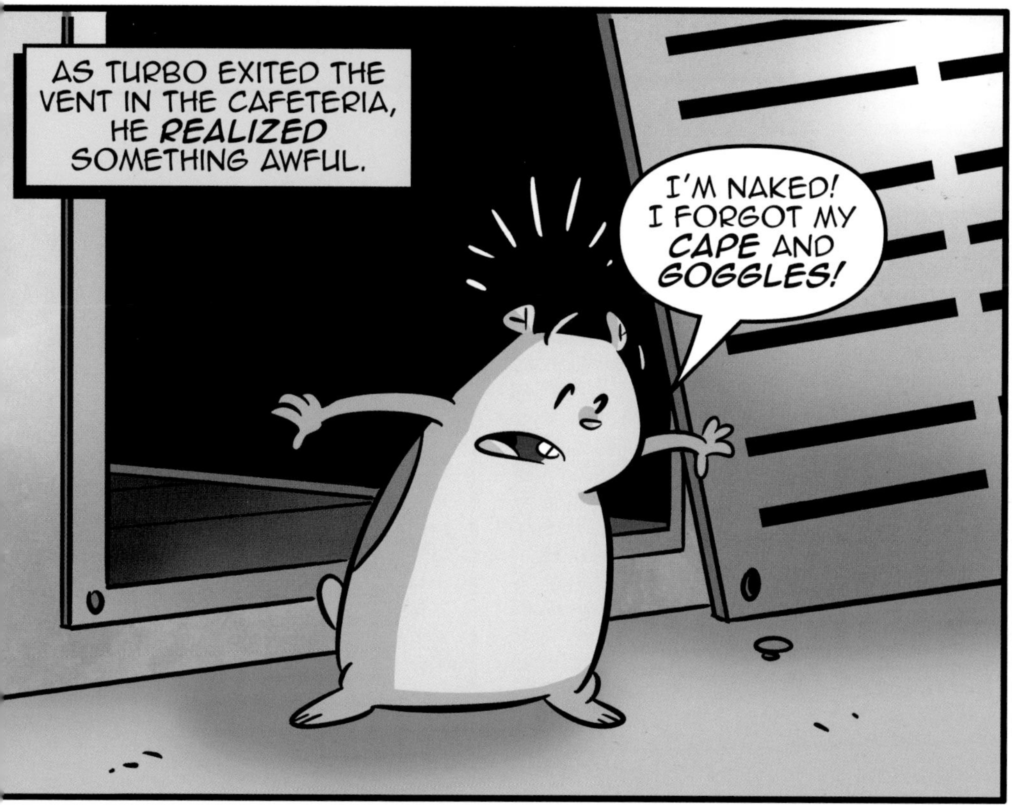
AS TURBO EXITED THE VENT IN THE CAFETERIA, HE REALIZED SOMETHING AWFUL.
I'M NAKED! I FORGOT MY CAPE AND GOGGLES!

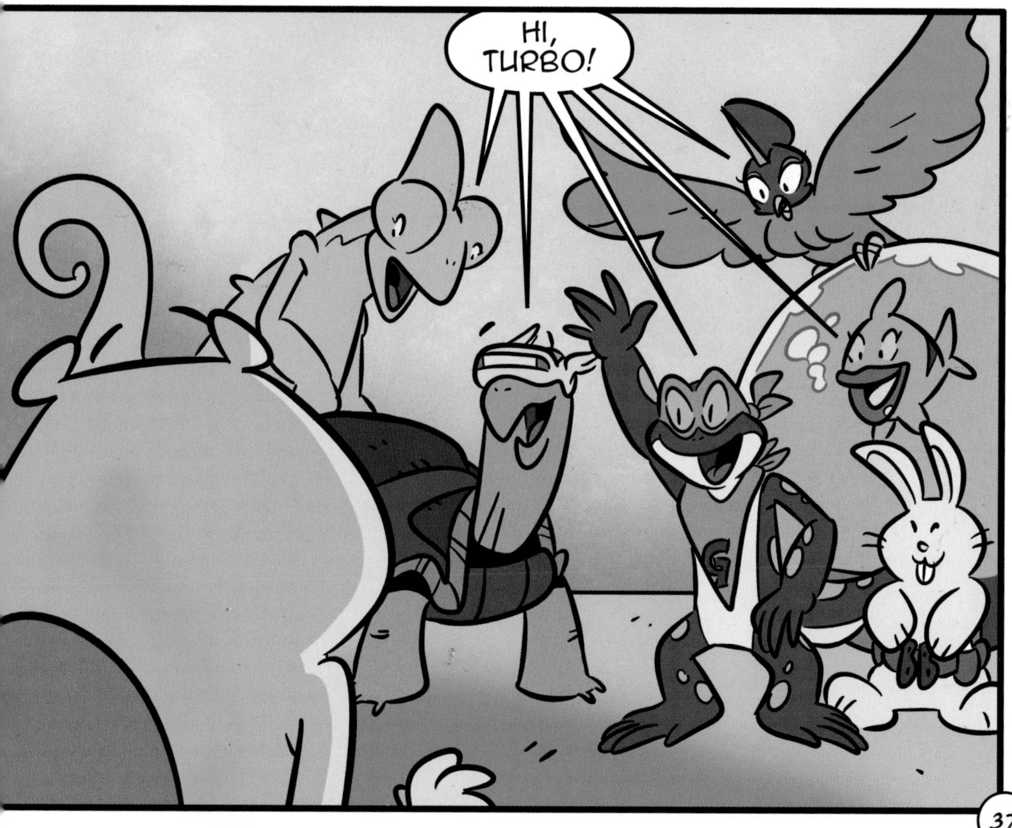
HI, TURBO!

ABOUT... TIME...YOU...GOT HERE.

PROFESSOR TURTLE SPEAKS REALLY SLOWLY BECAUSE...WELL, BECAUSE HE'S A *TURTLE!*

YOU'RE JUST IN TIME FOR *SNACK* TIME!

CHEEZIE DOODLES

CHEEZIE DOODLES

THAT'S IT, FANTASTIC FISH! ONE BIG PILE OF DELICIOUSNESS!

CHEEZIE DOODLES

SNIFFING OUT *TROUBLE*, BOSS BUNNY?

NO TROUBLE! JUST THE *SMELL* OF CHEESY GOODNESS!

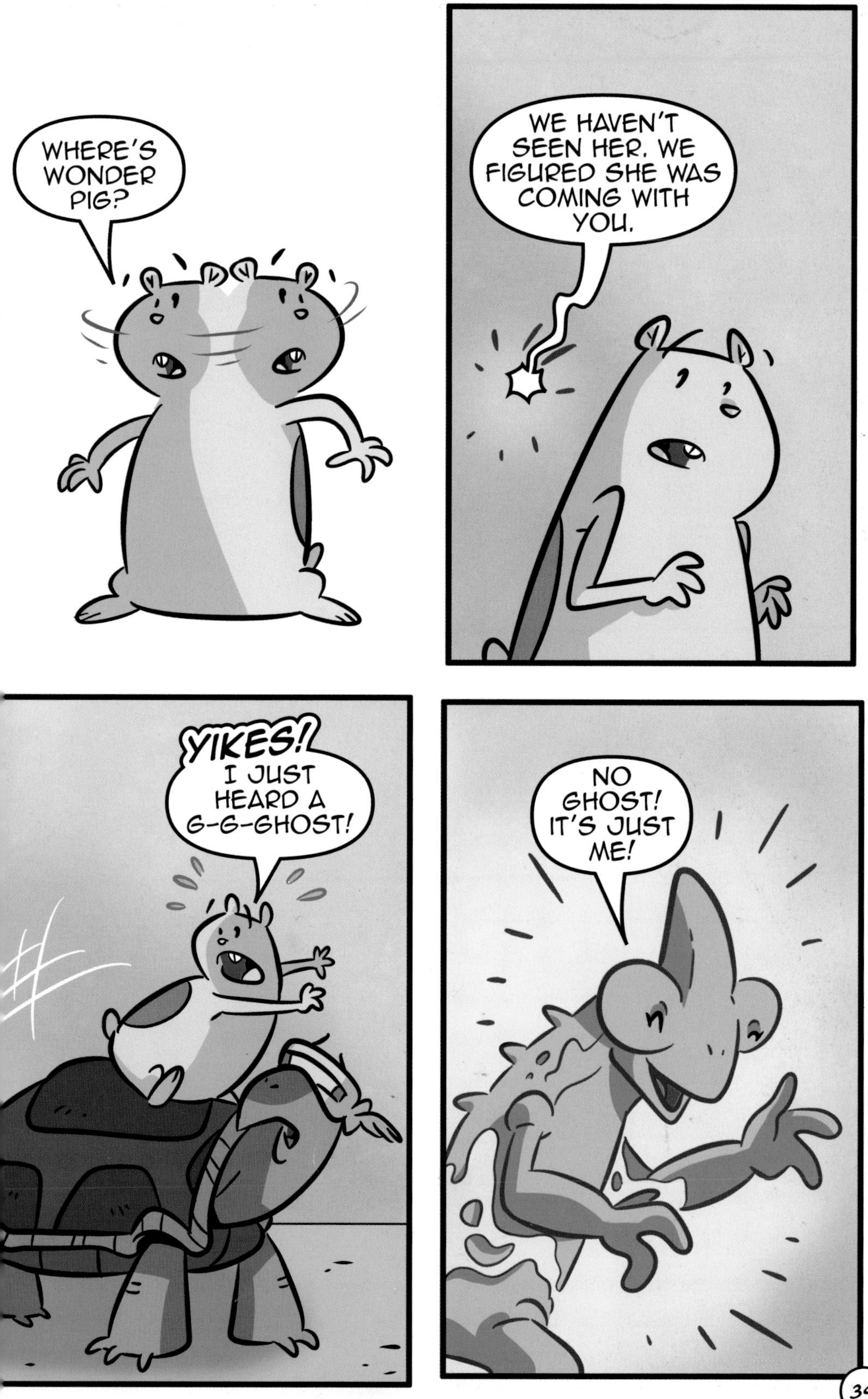
WHERE'S WONDER PIG?
WE HAVEN'T SEEN HER. WE FIGURED SHE WAS COMING WITH YOU.
YIKES! I JUST HEARD A G-G-GHOST!
NO GHOST! IT'S JUST ME!

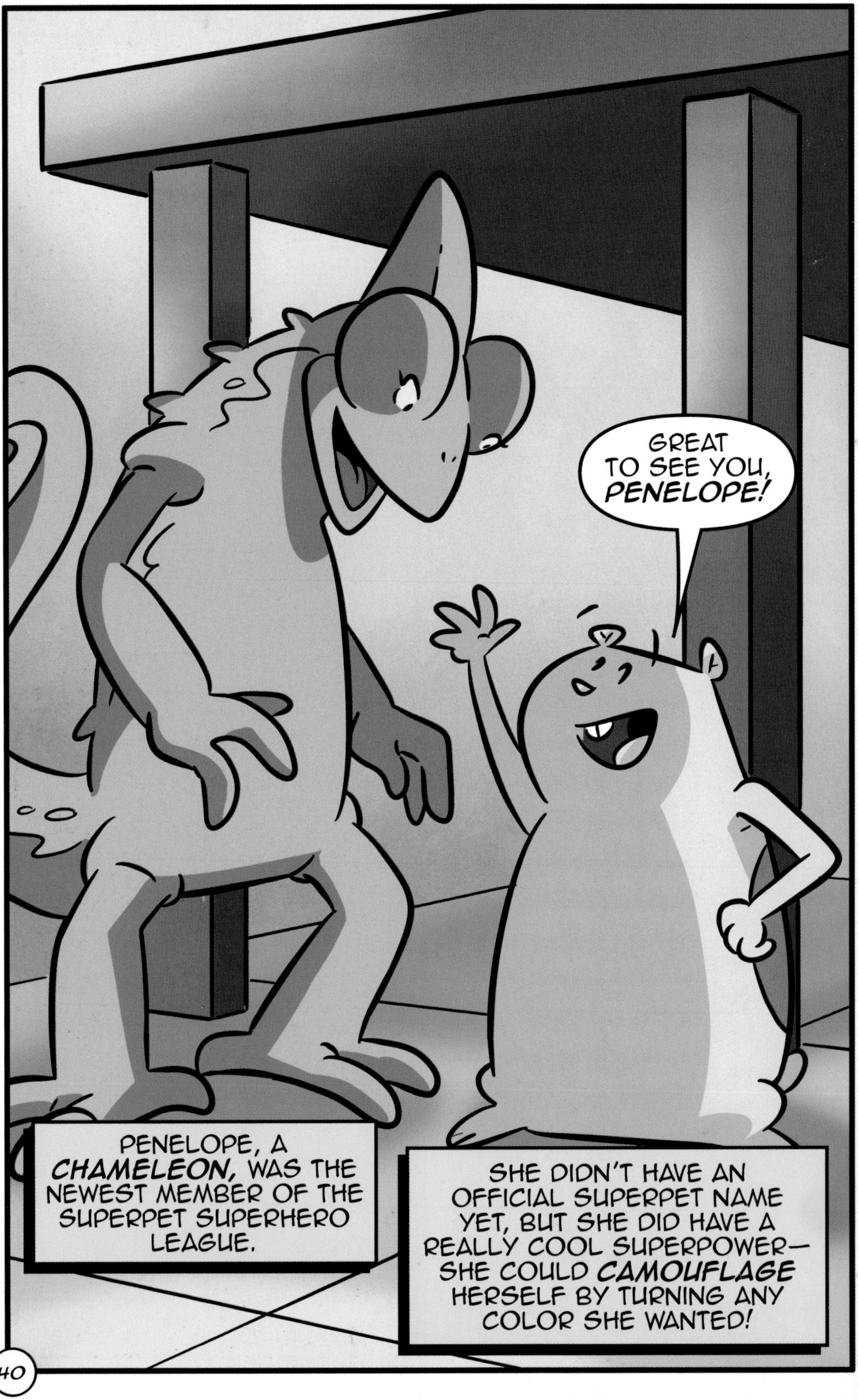
GREAT TO SEE YOU, PENELOPE!
PENELOPE, A CHAMELEON, WAS THE NEWEST MEMBER OF THE SUPERPET SUPERHERO LEAGUE.
SHE DIDN'T HAVE AN OFFICIAL SUPERPET NAME YET, BUT SHE DID HAVE A REALLY COOL SUPERPOWER—SHE COULD CAMOUFLAGE HERSELF BY TURNING ANY COLOR SHE WANTED!

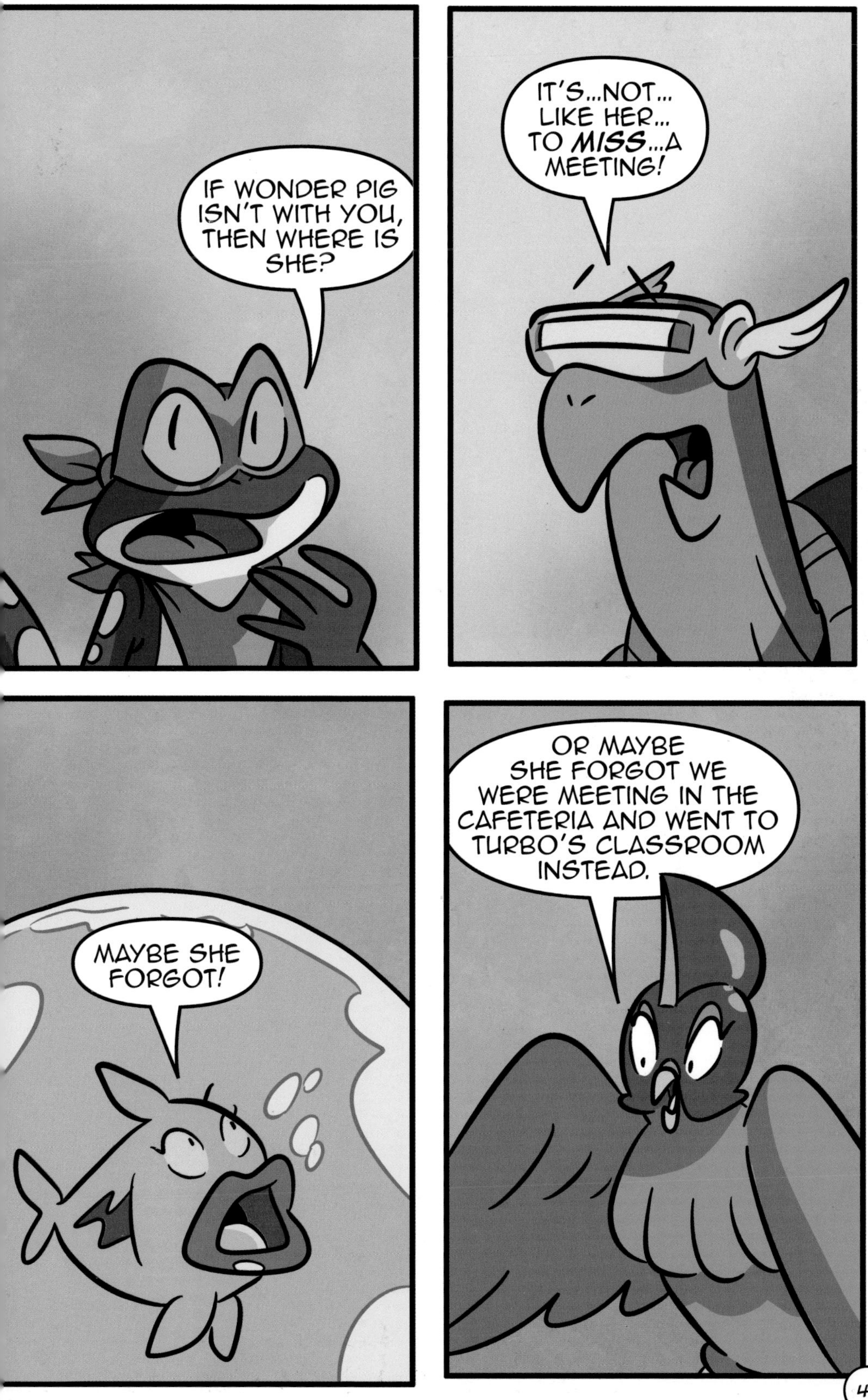
IF WONDER PIG ISN'T WITH YOU, THEN WHERE IS SHE?
IT'S...NOT... LIKE HER... TO *MISS*...A MEETING!
MAYBE SHE FORGOT!
OR MAYBE SHE FORGOT WE WERE MEETING IN THE CAFETERIA AND WENT TO TURBO'S CLASSROOM INSTEAD.

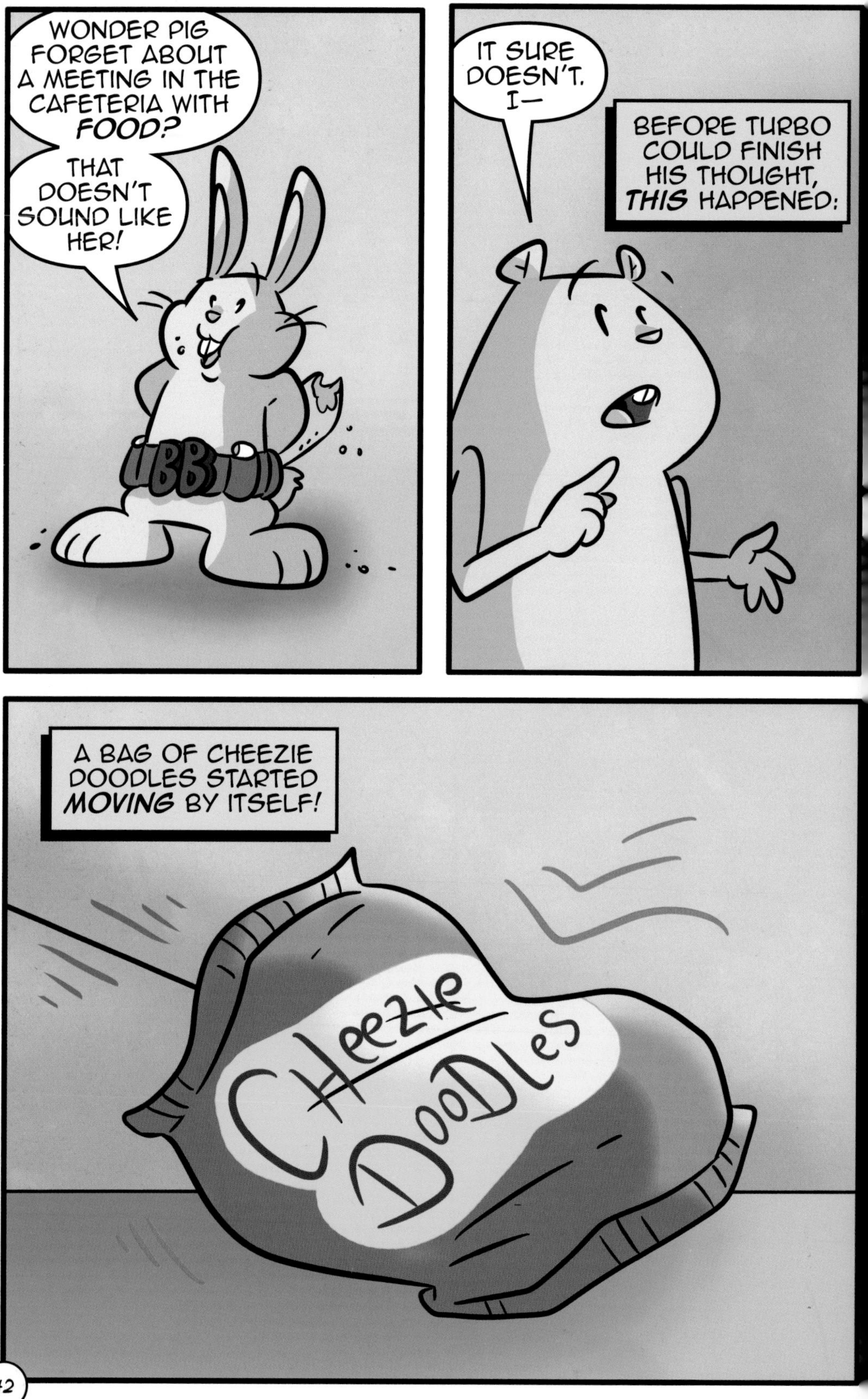

WONDER PIG FORGET ABOUT A MEETING IN THE CAFETERIA WITH FOOD?
THAT DOESN'T SOUND LIKE HER!
IT SURE DOESN'T. I—
BEFORE TURBO COULD FINISH HIS THOUGHT, THIS HAPPENED:
A BAG OF CHEEZIE DOODLES STARTED MOVING BY ITSELF!
Cheezie Doodles

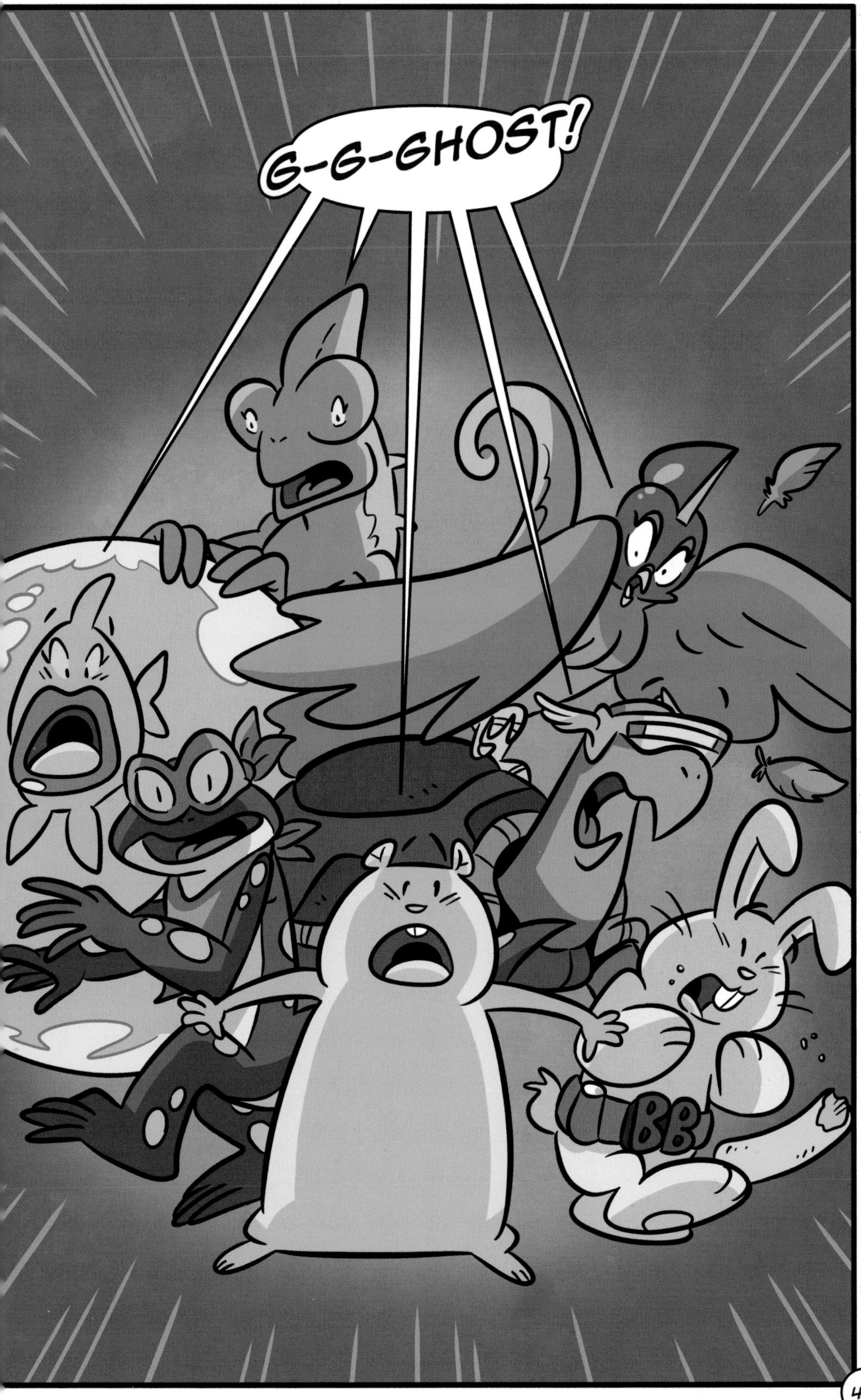
G-G-GHOST!
BB

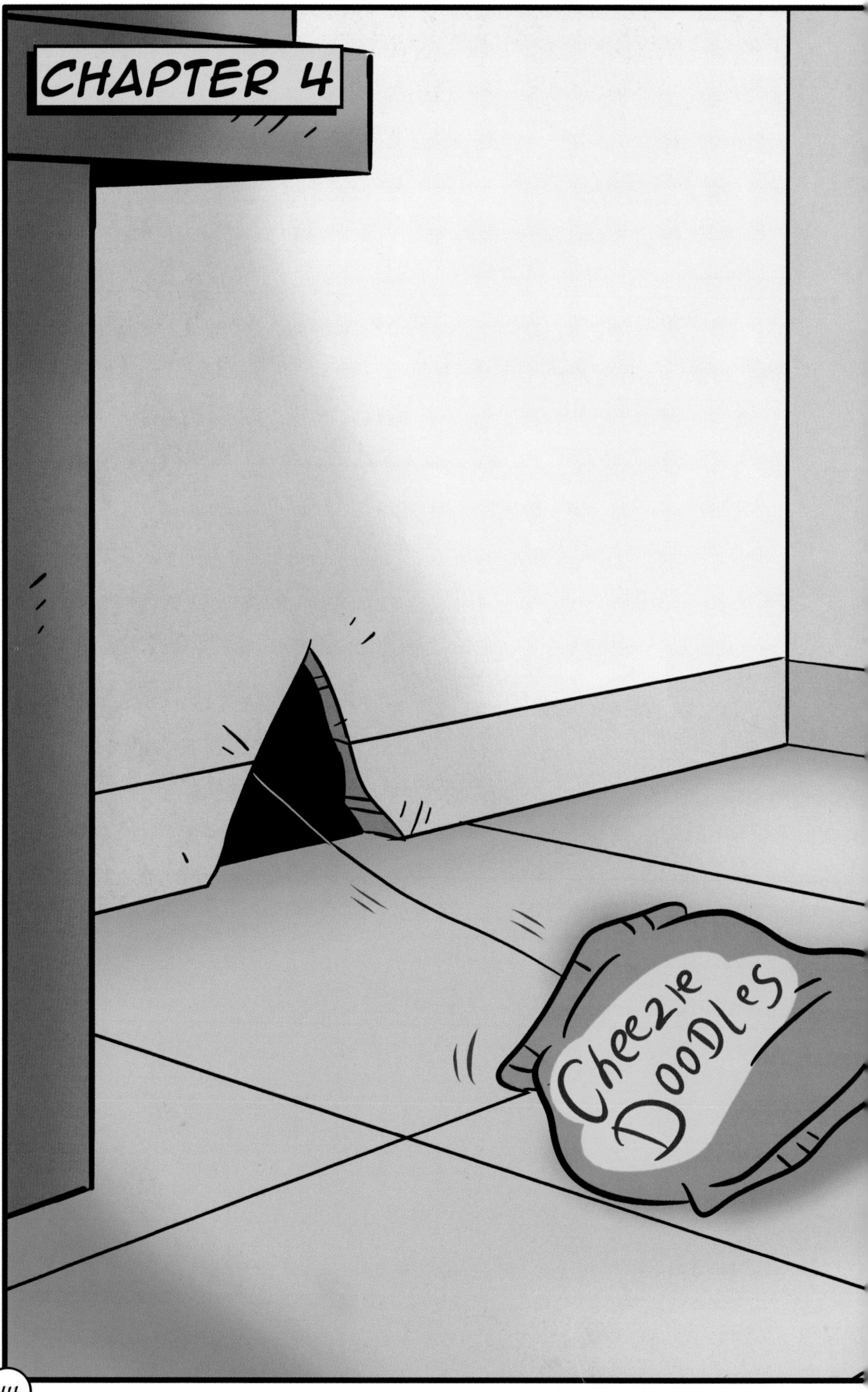
CHAPTER 4
Cheezie Doodles

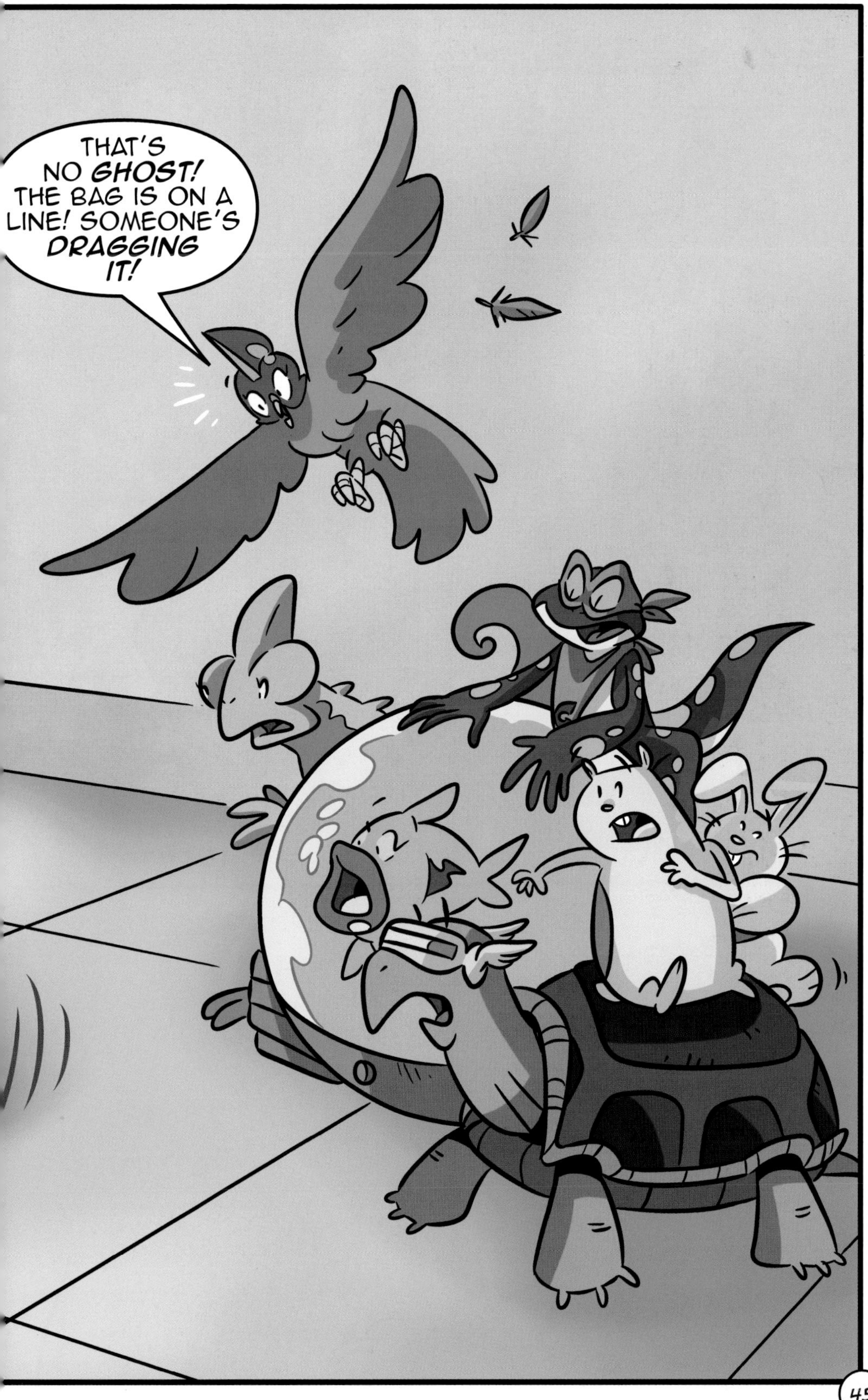
THAT'S NO *GHOST!* THE BAG IS ON A LINE! SOMEONE'S *DRAGGING* IT!

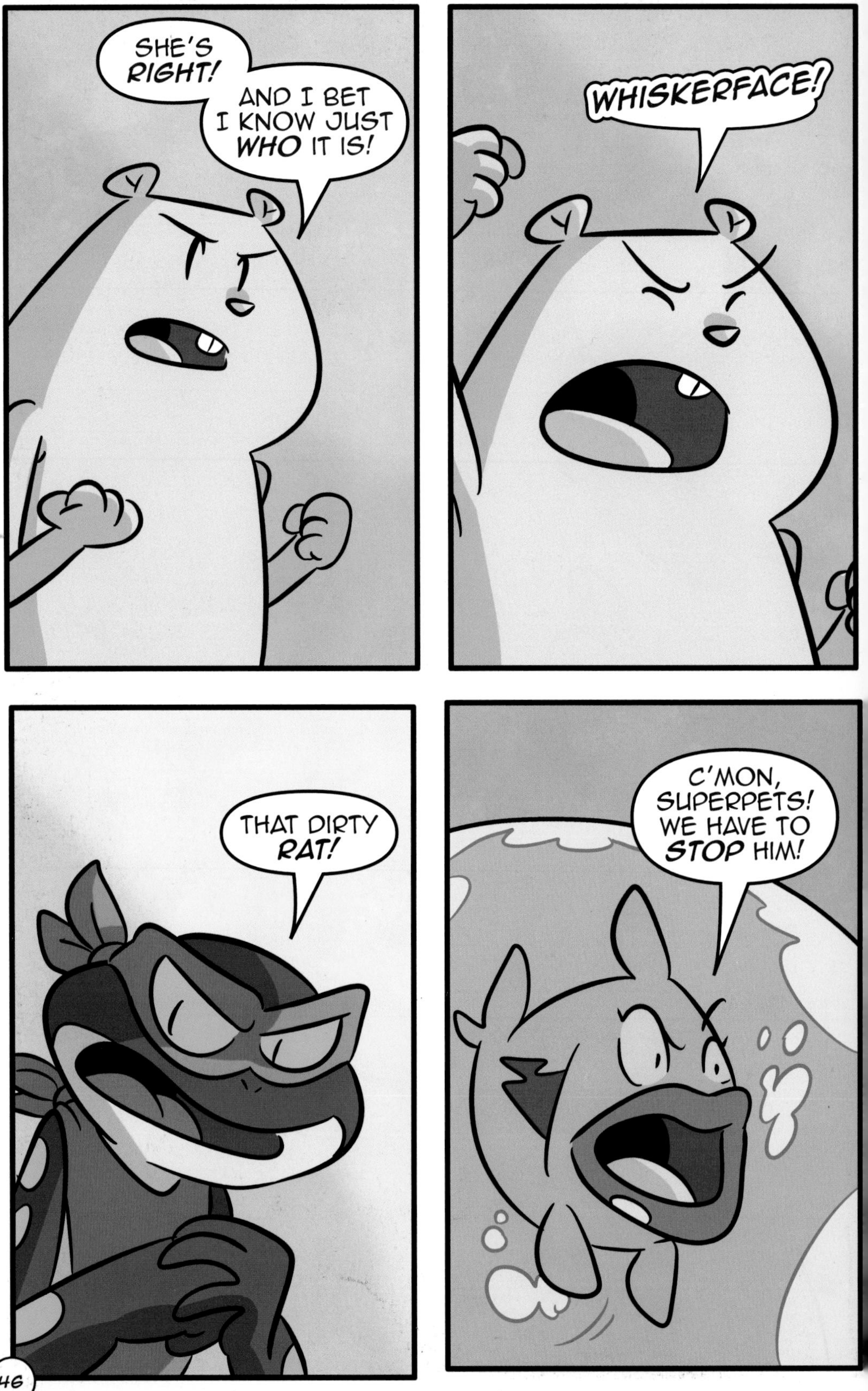
SHE'S RIGHT!
AND I BET I KNOW JUST WHO IT IS!
WHISKERFACE!
THAT DIRTY RAT!
C'MON, SUPERPETS! WE HAVE TO STOP HIM!

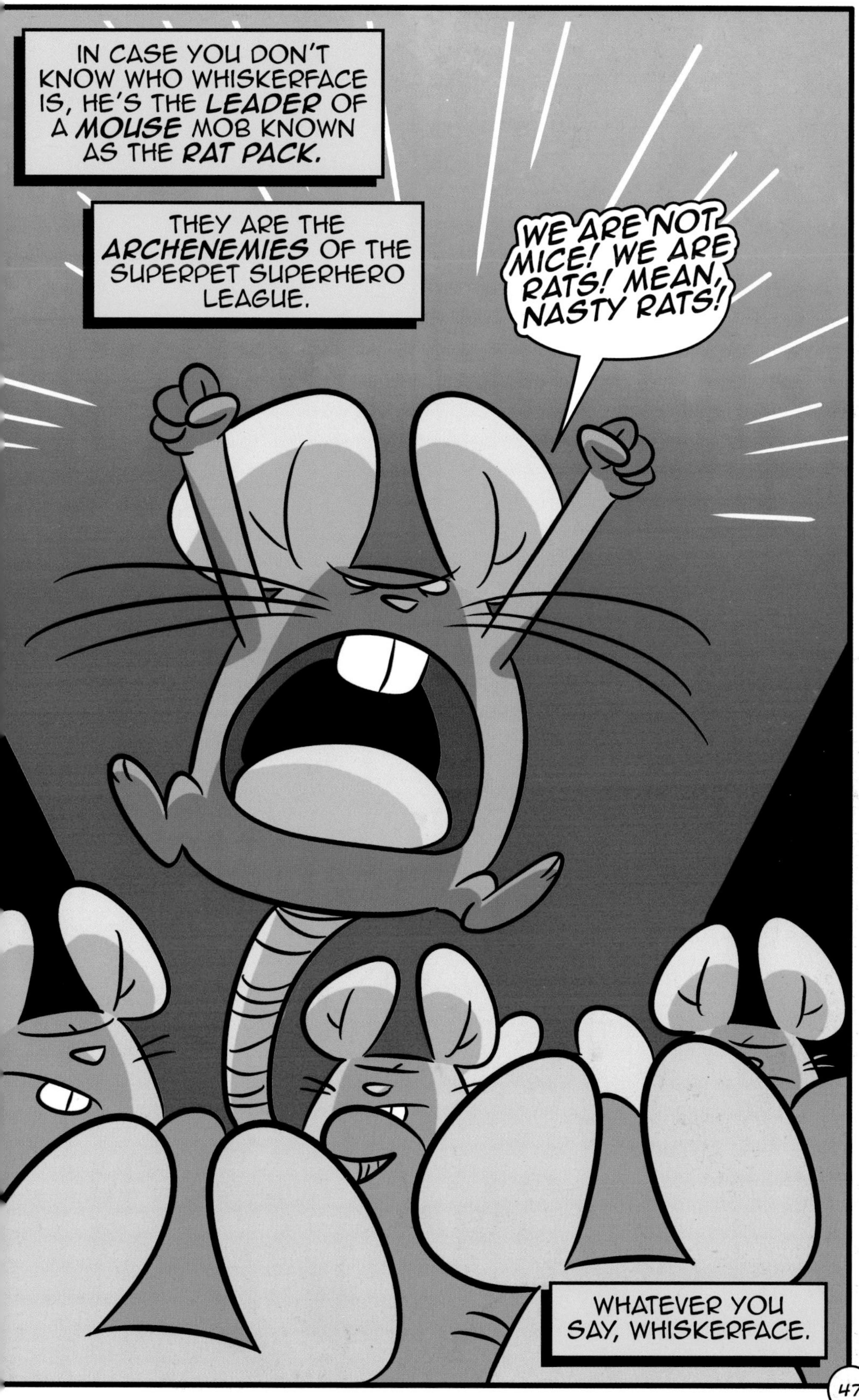

IN CASE YOU DON'T KNOW WHO WHISKERFACE IS, HE'S THE LEADER OF A MOUSE MOB KNOWN AS THE RAT PACK.
THEY ARE THE ARCHENEMIES OF THE SUPERPET SUPERHERO LEAGUE.
WE ARE NOT MICE! WE ARE RATS! MEAN, NASTY RATS!
WHATEVER YOU SAY, WHISKERFACE.

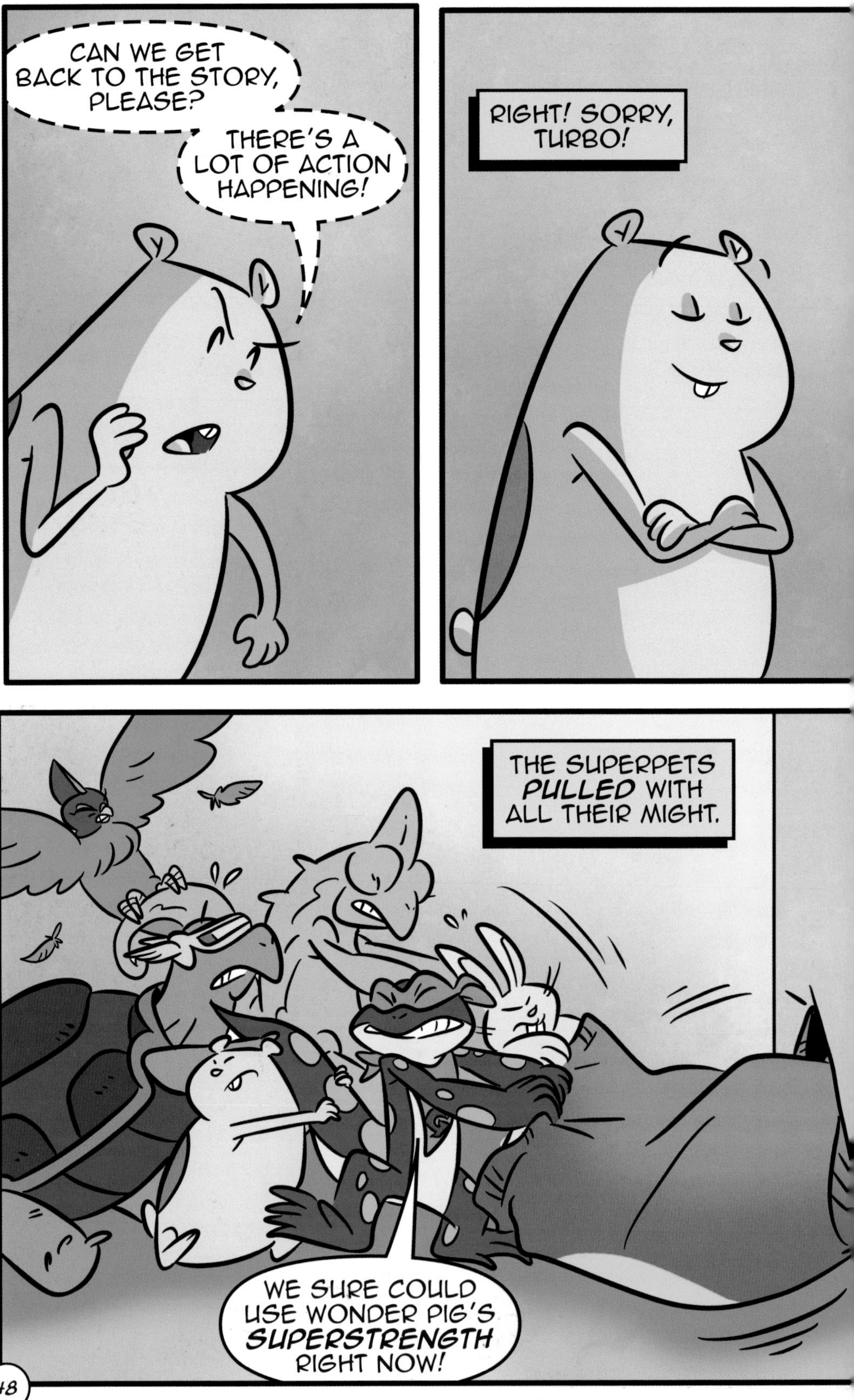
CAN WE GET BACK TO THE STORY, PLEASE?
THERE'S A LOT OF ACTION HAPPENING!
RIGHT! SORRY, TURBO!
THE SUPERPETS *PULLED* WITH ALL THEIR MIGHT.
WE SURE COULD USE WONDER PIG'S ***SUPERSTRENGTH*** RIGHT NOW!

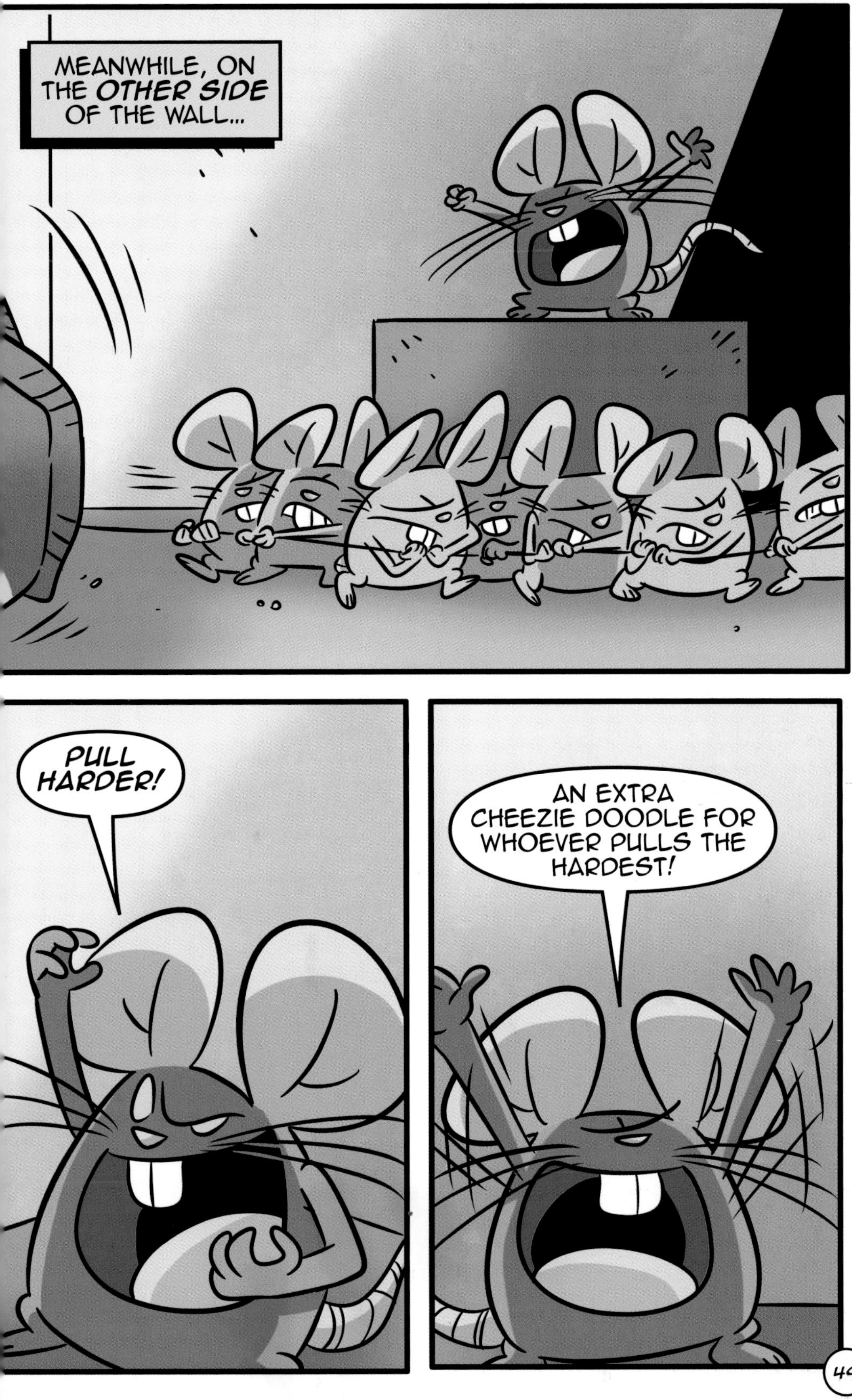
MEANWHILE, ON THE OTHER SIDE OF THE WALL...
PULL HARDER!
AN EXTRA CHEEZIE DOODLE FOR WHOEVER PULLS THE HARDEST!

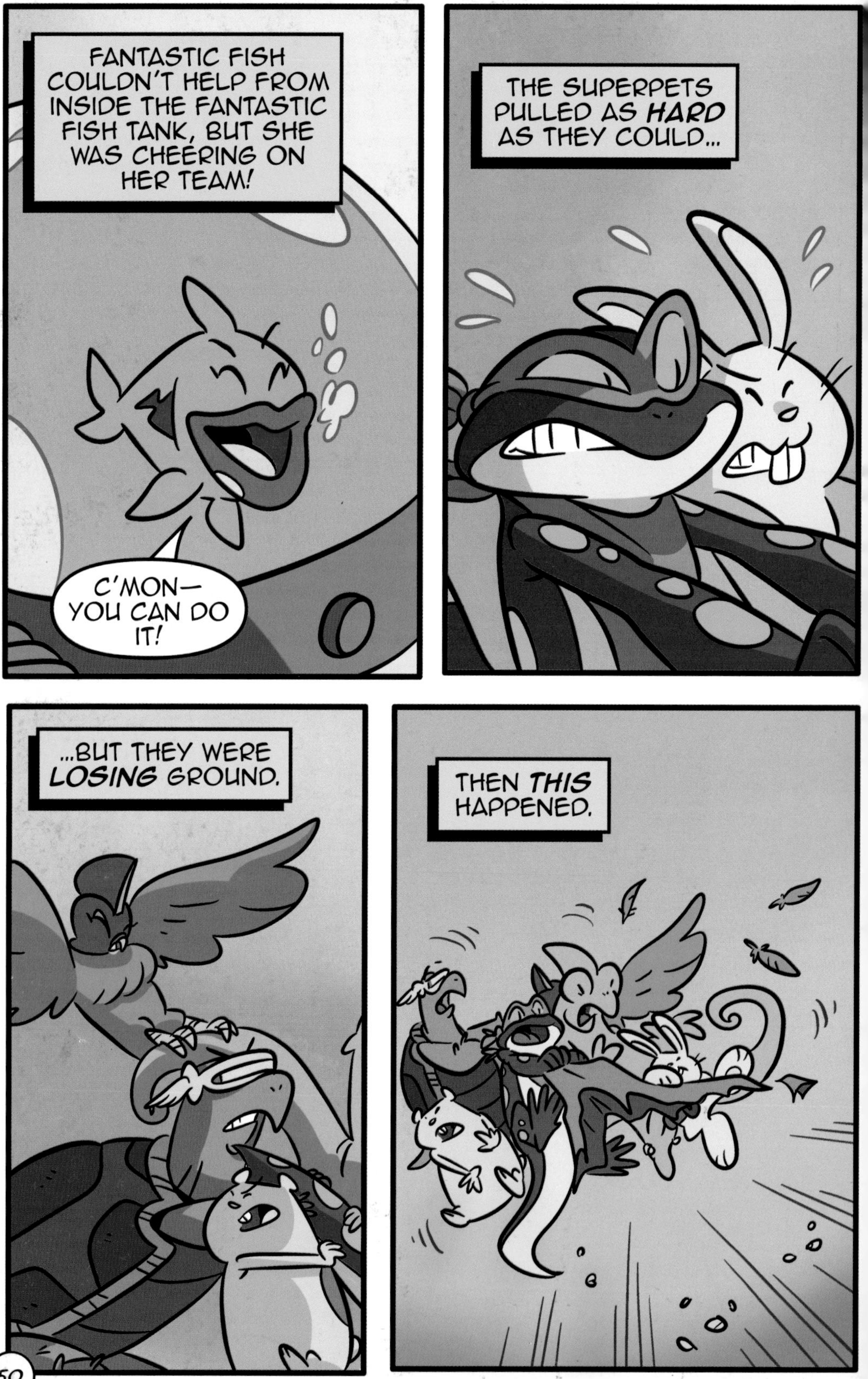
FANTASTIC FISH COULDN'T HELP FROM INSIDE THE FANTASTIC FISH TANK, BUT SHE WAS CHEERING ON HER TEAM!
C'MON— YOU CAN DO IT!
THE SUPERPETS PULLED AS HARD AS THEY COULD...
...BUT THEY WERE LOSING GROUND.
THEN THIS HAPPENED.

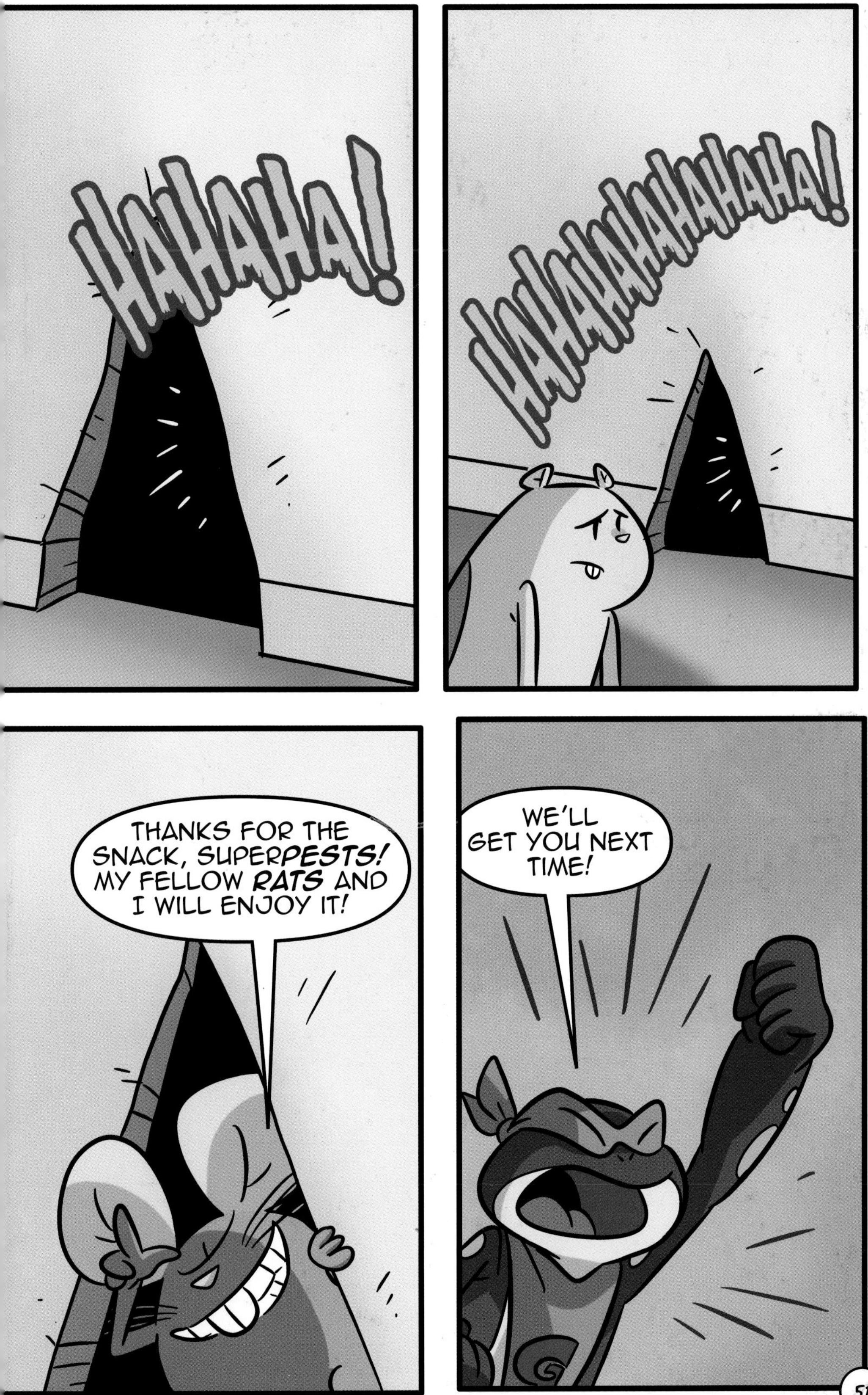
HAHAHA!
HAHAHAHAHAHAHAHA!
THANKS FOR THE SNACK, SUPERPESTS! MY FELLOW RATS AND I WILL ENJOY IT!
WE'LL GET YOU NEXT TIME!

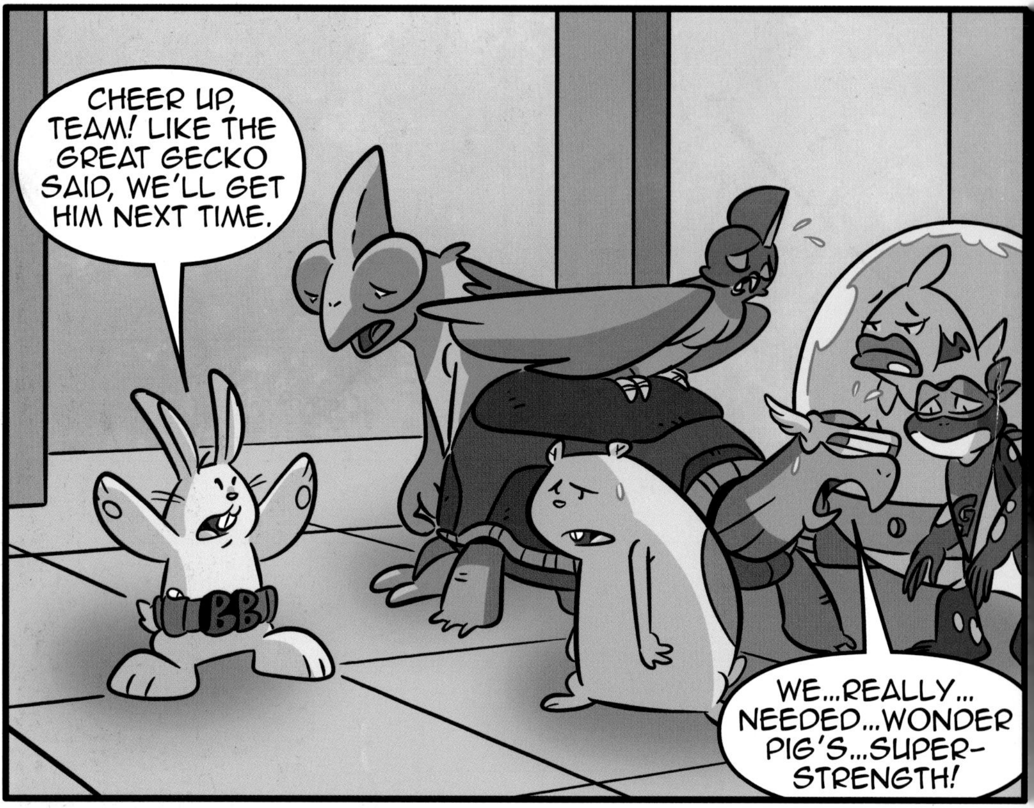
CHEER UP, TEAM! LIKE THE GREAT GECKO SAID, WE'LL GET HIM NEXT TIME.
WE...REALLY... NEEDED...WONDER PIG'S...SUPER-STRENGTH!

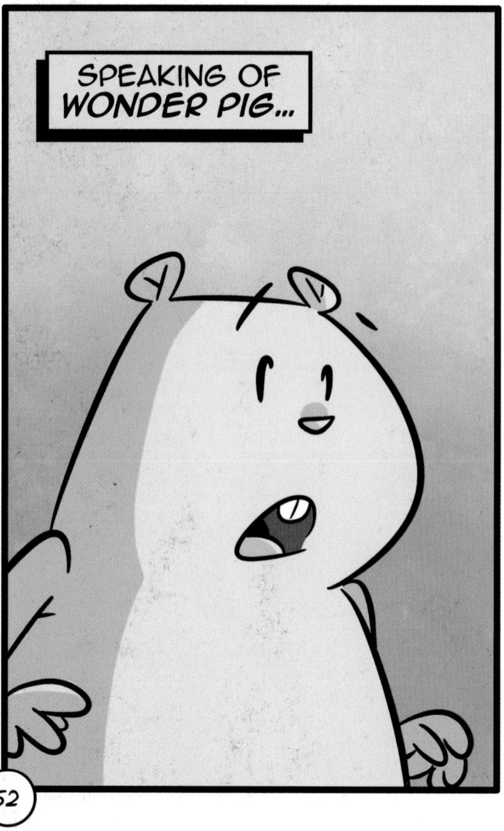
SPEAKING OF *WONDER PIG*...

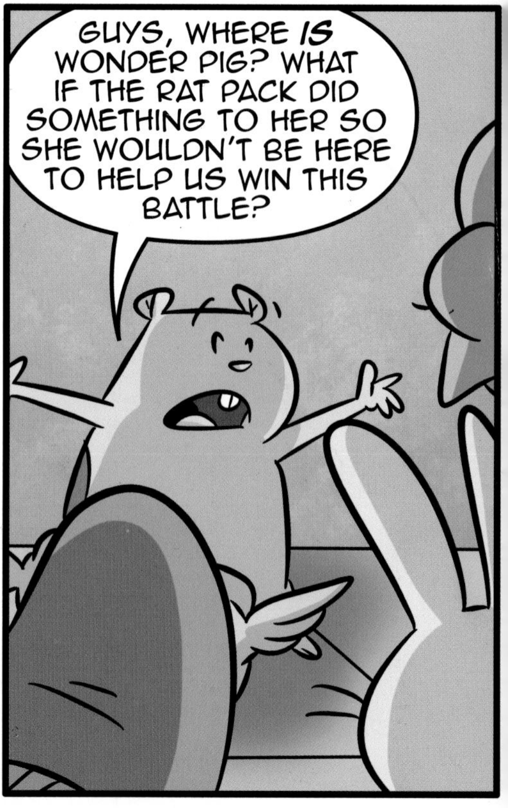
GUYS, WHERE *IS* WONDER PIG? WHAT IF THE RAT PACK DID SOMETHING TO HER SO SHE WOULDN'T BE HERE TO HELP US WIN THIS BATTLE?

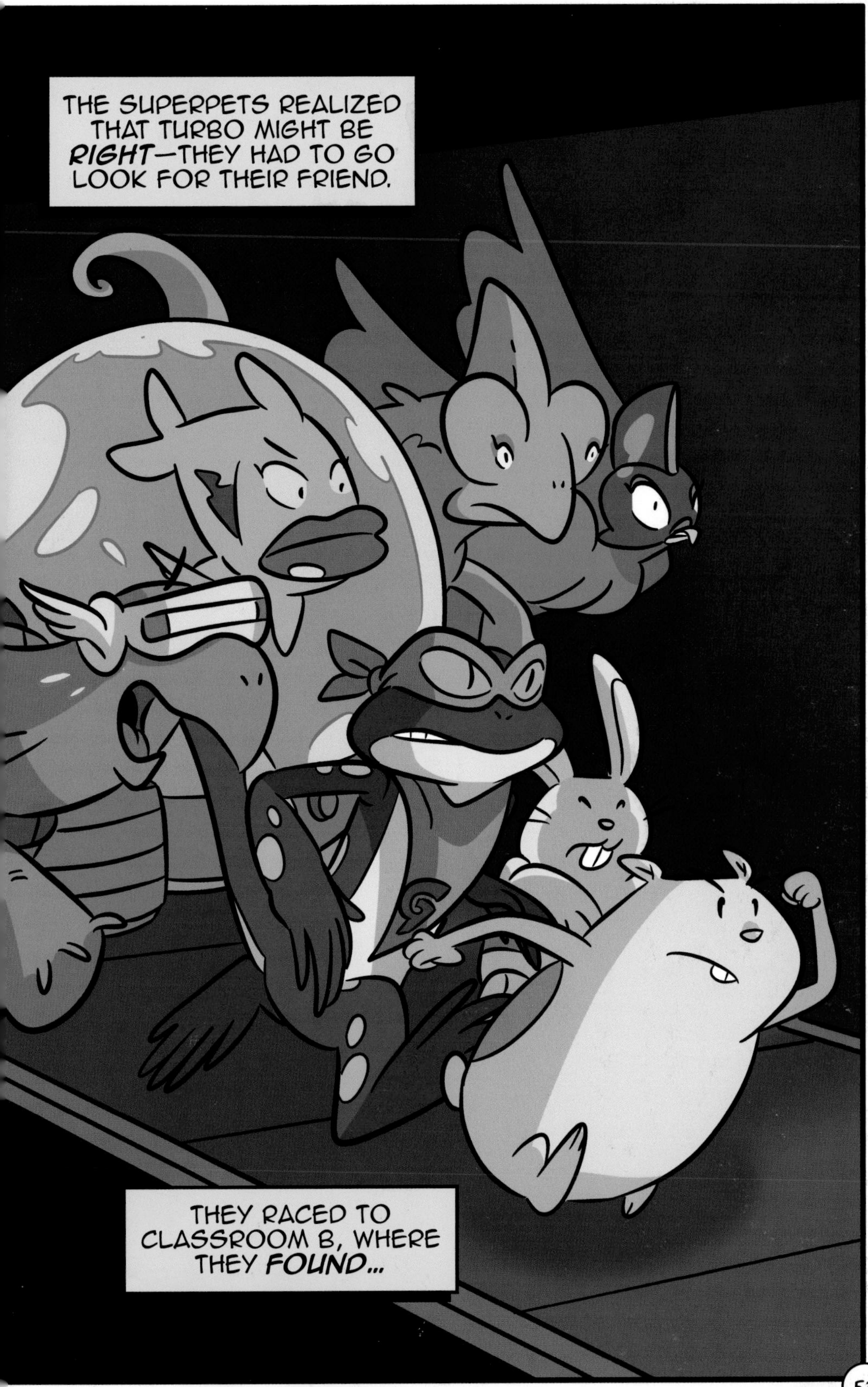
THE SUPERPETS REALIZED THAT TURBO MIGHT BE *RIGHT*—THEY HAD TO GO LOOK FOR THEIR FRIEND.
THEY RACED TO CLASSROOM B, WHERE THEY *FOUND*...

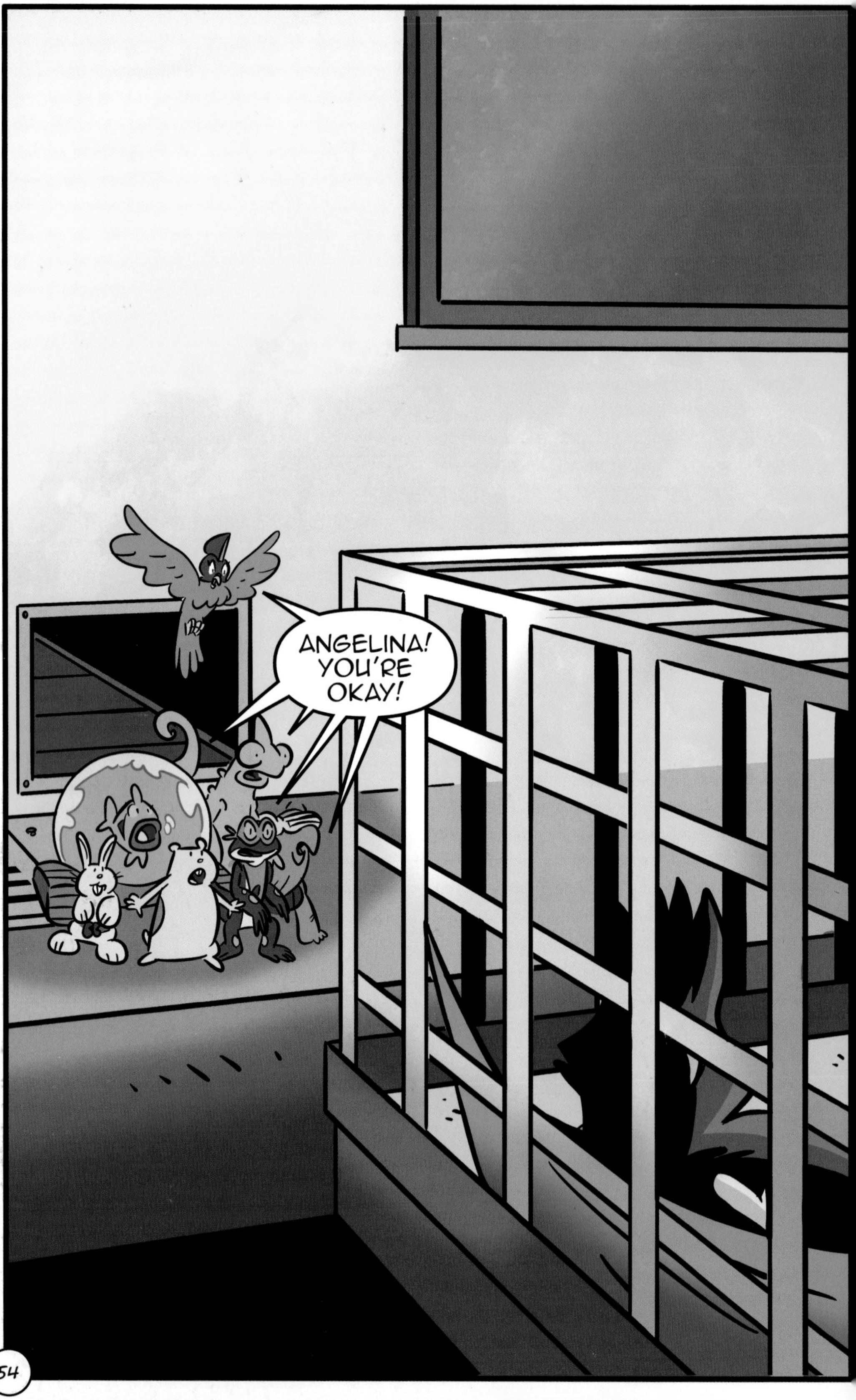
ANGELINA! YOU'RE OKAY!

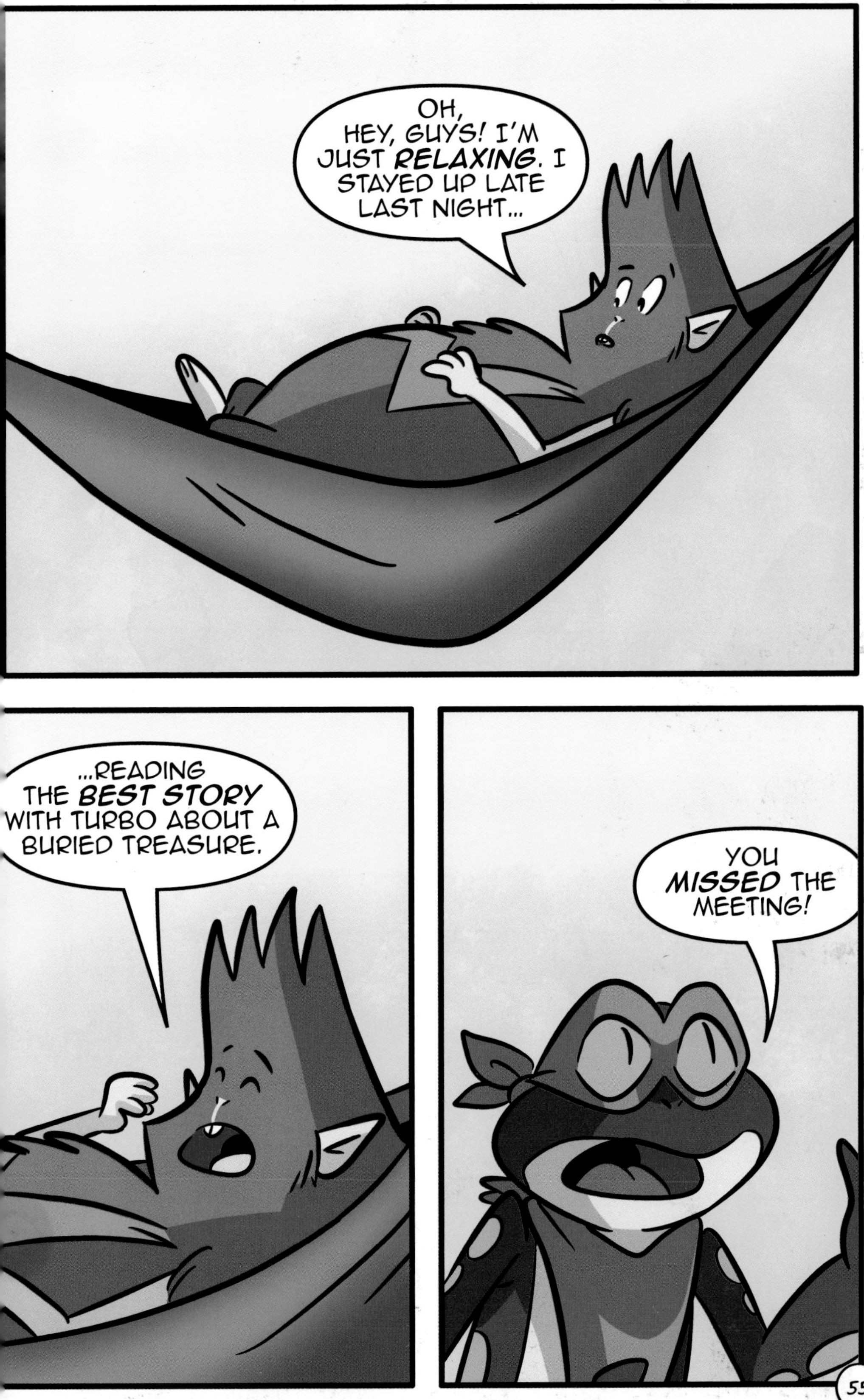
OH, HEY, GUYS! I'M JUST RELAXING. I STAYED UP LATE LAST NIGHT...
...READING THE BEST STORY WITH TURBO ABOUT A BURIED TREASURE.
YOU MISSED THE MEETING!

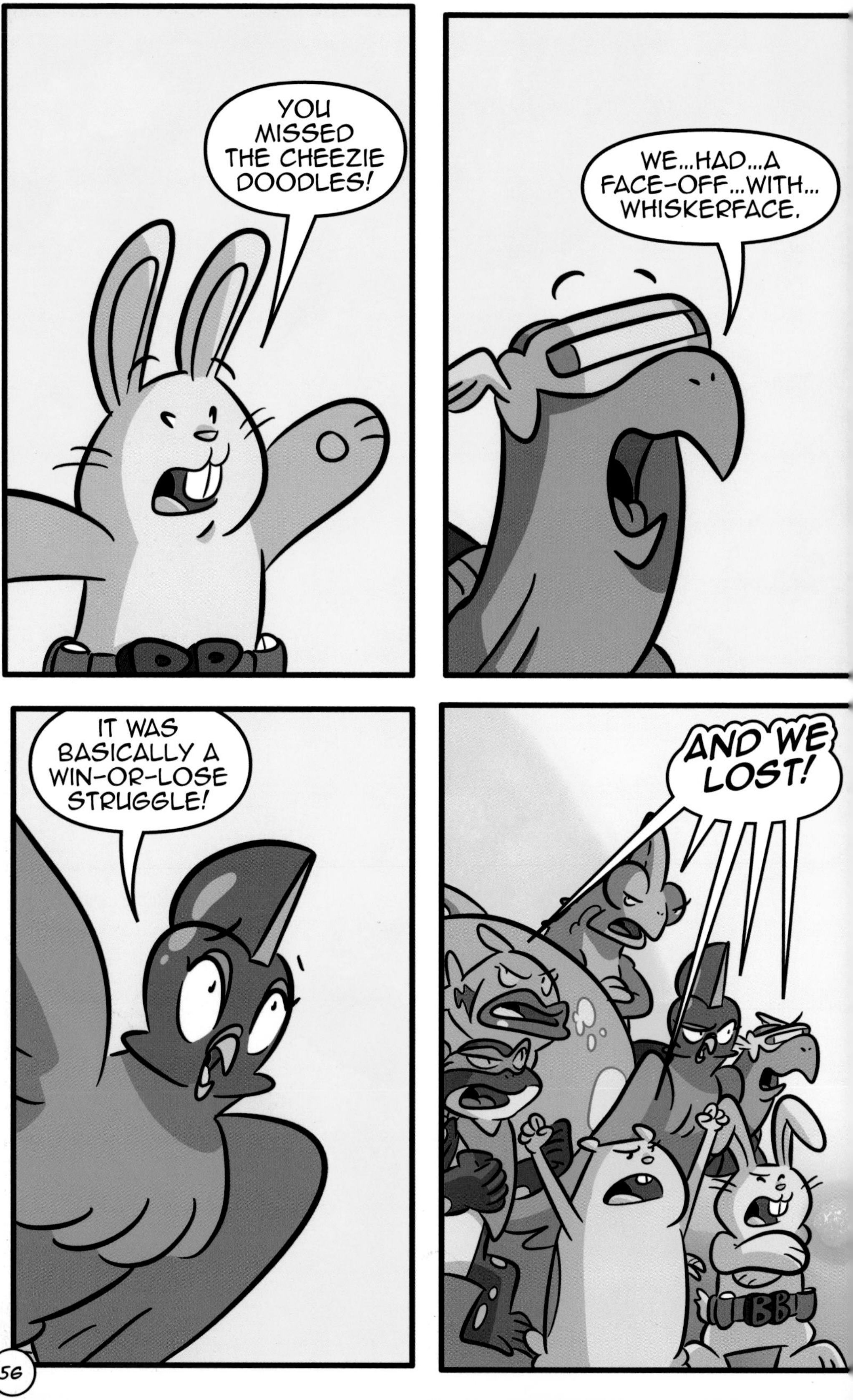
YOU MISSED THE CHEEZIE DOODLES!
WE...HAD...A FACE-OFF...WITH... WHISKERFACE.
IT WAS BASICALLY A WIN-OR-LOSE STRUGGLE!
AND WE LOST!

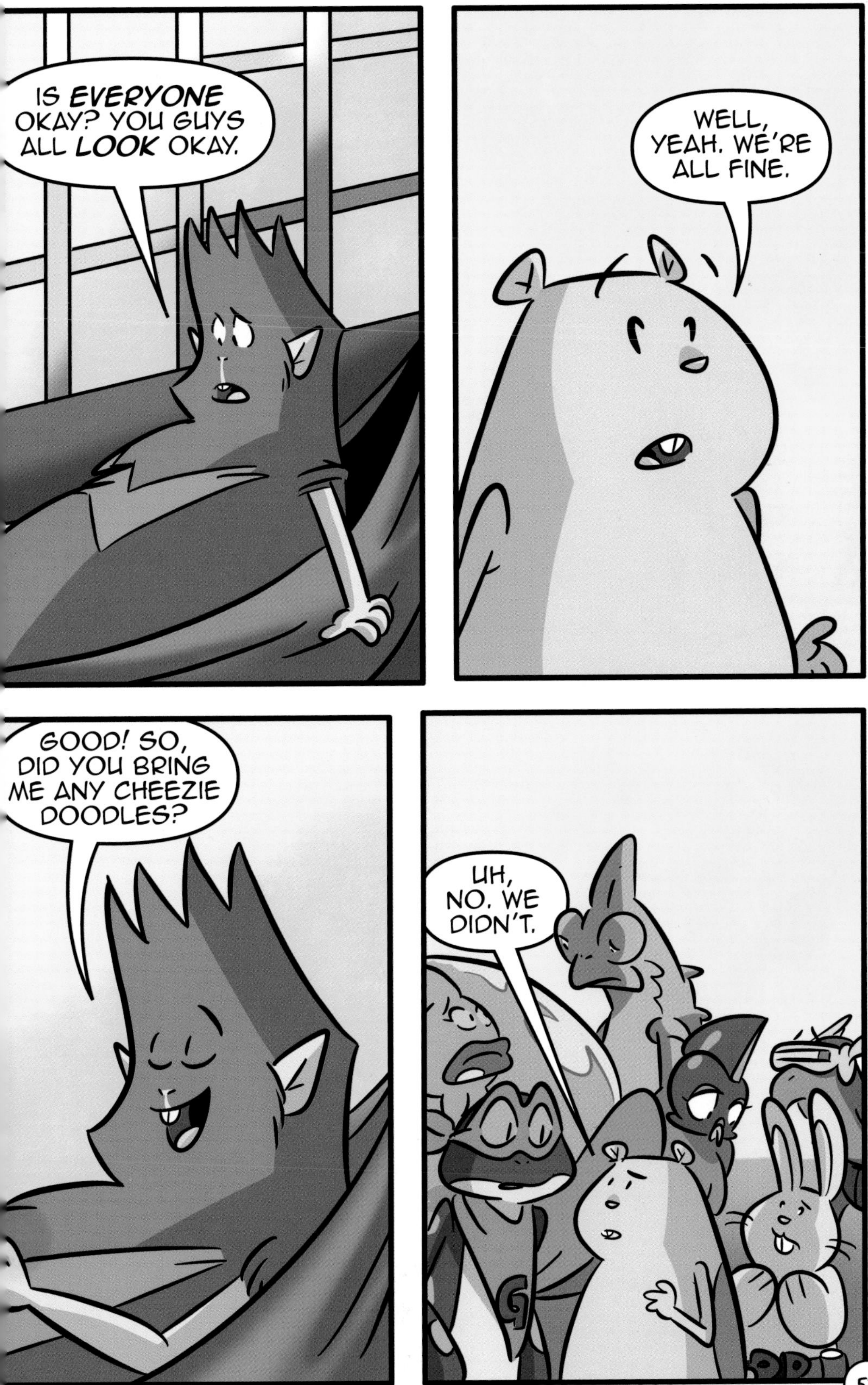
IS **EVERYONE** OKAY? YOU GUYS ALL **LOOK** OKAY.
WELL, YEAH. WE'RE ALL FINE.
GOOD! SO, DID YOU BRING ME ANY CHEEZIE DOODLES?
UH, NO. WE DIDN'T.

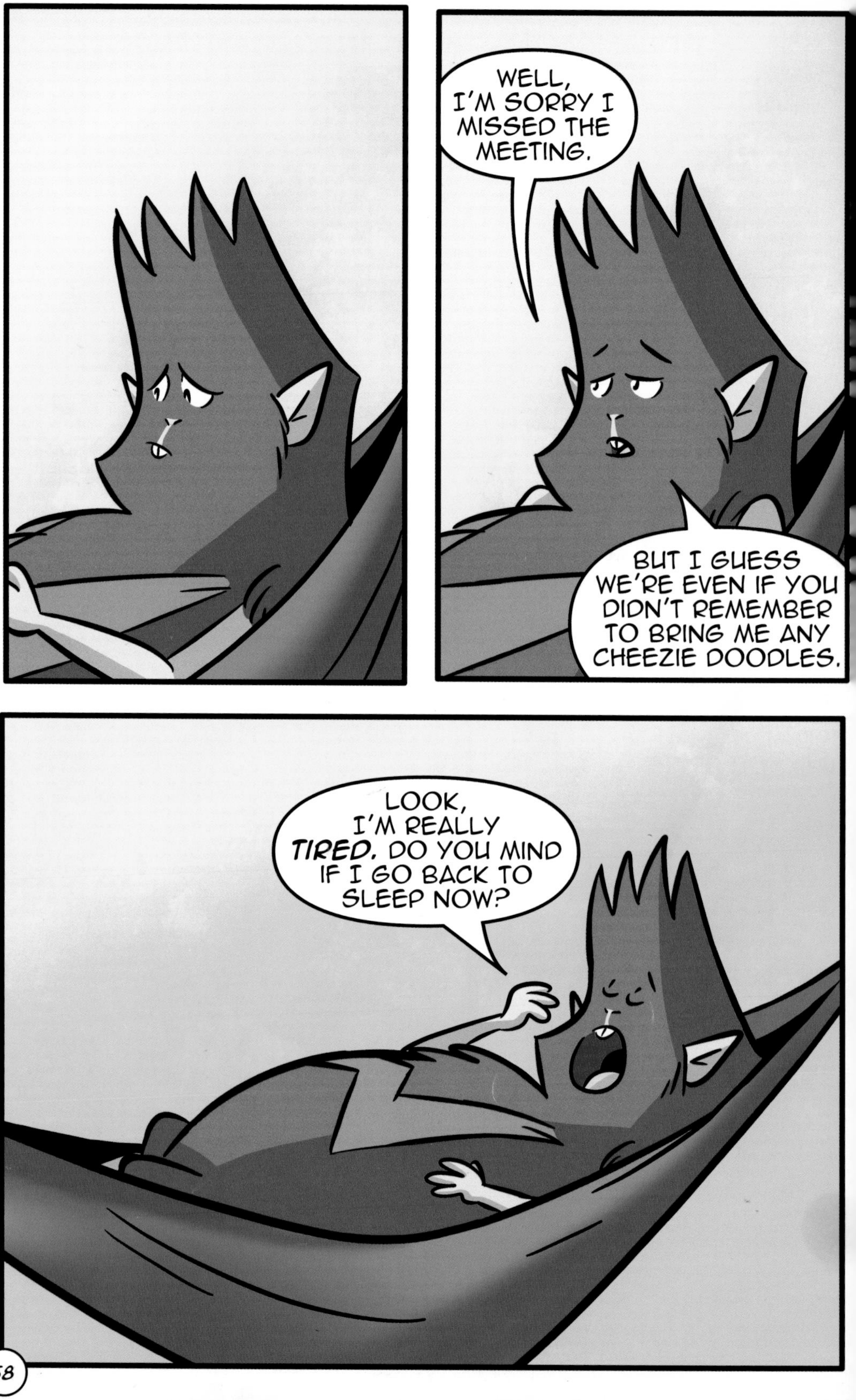
WELL, I'M SORRY I MISSED THE MEETING.
BUT I GUESS WE'RE EVEN IF YOU DIDN'T REMEMBER TO BRING ME ANY CHEEZIE DOODLES.
LOOK, I'M REALLY *TIRED.* DO YOU MIND IF I GO BACK TO SLEEP NOW?

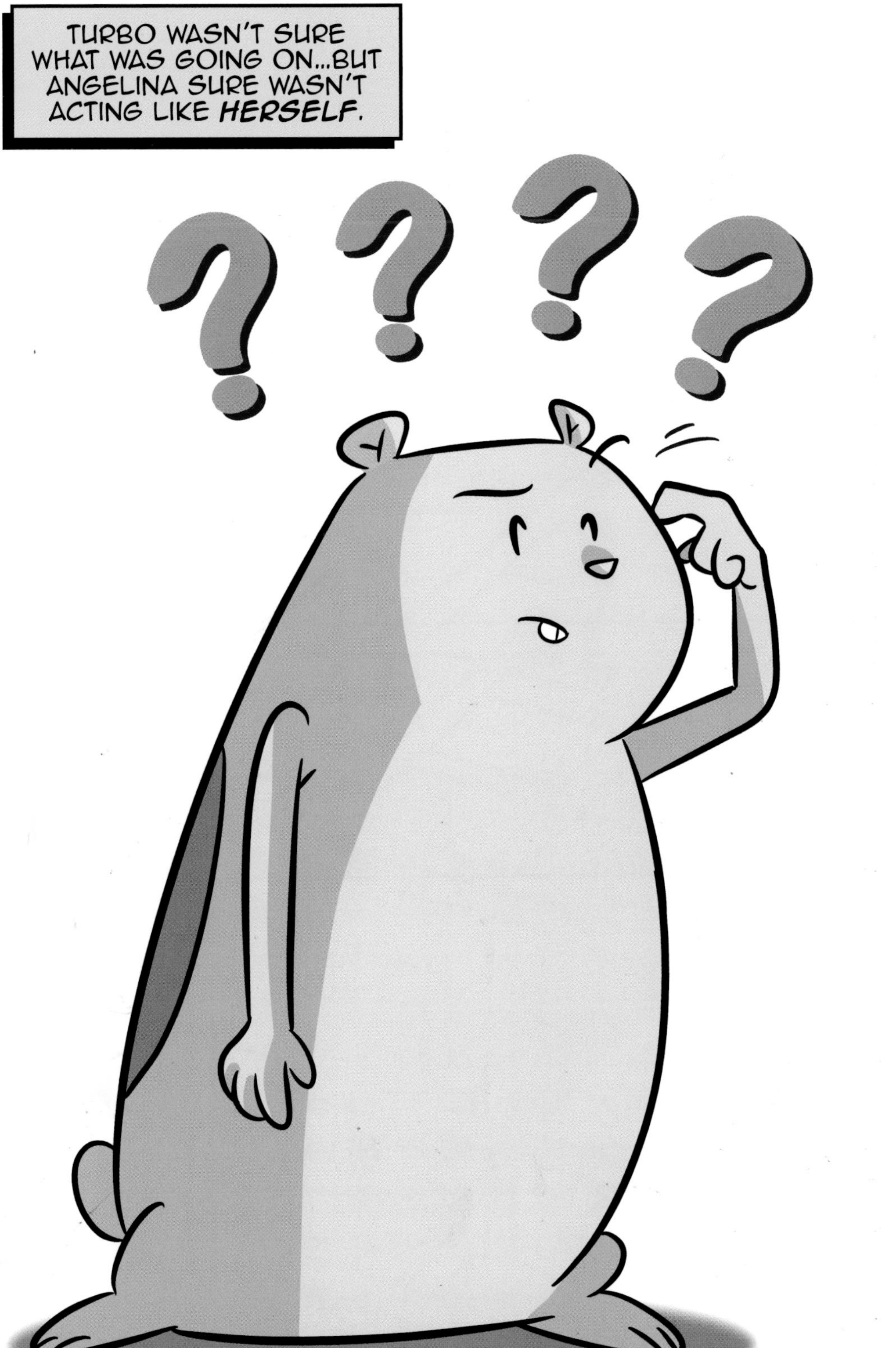
TURBO WASN'T SURE WHAT WAS GOING ON...BUT ANGELINA SURE WASN'T ACTING LIKE ***HERSELF***.

CHAPTER 5

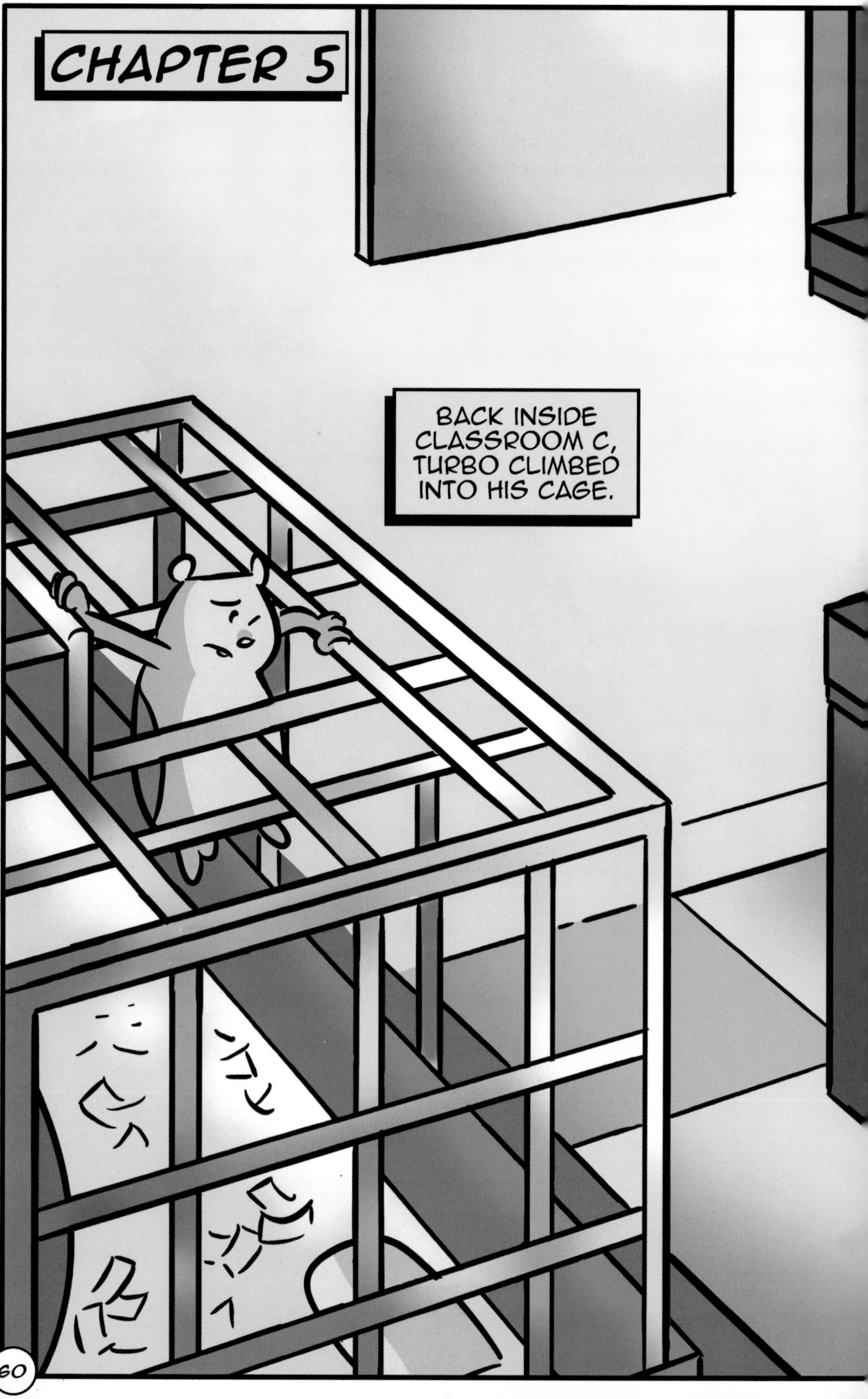
BACK INSIDE CLASSROOM C, TURBO CLIMBED INTO HIS CAGE.

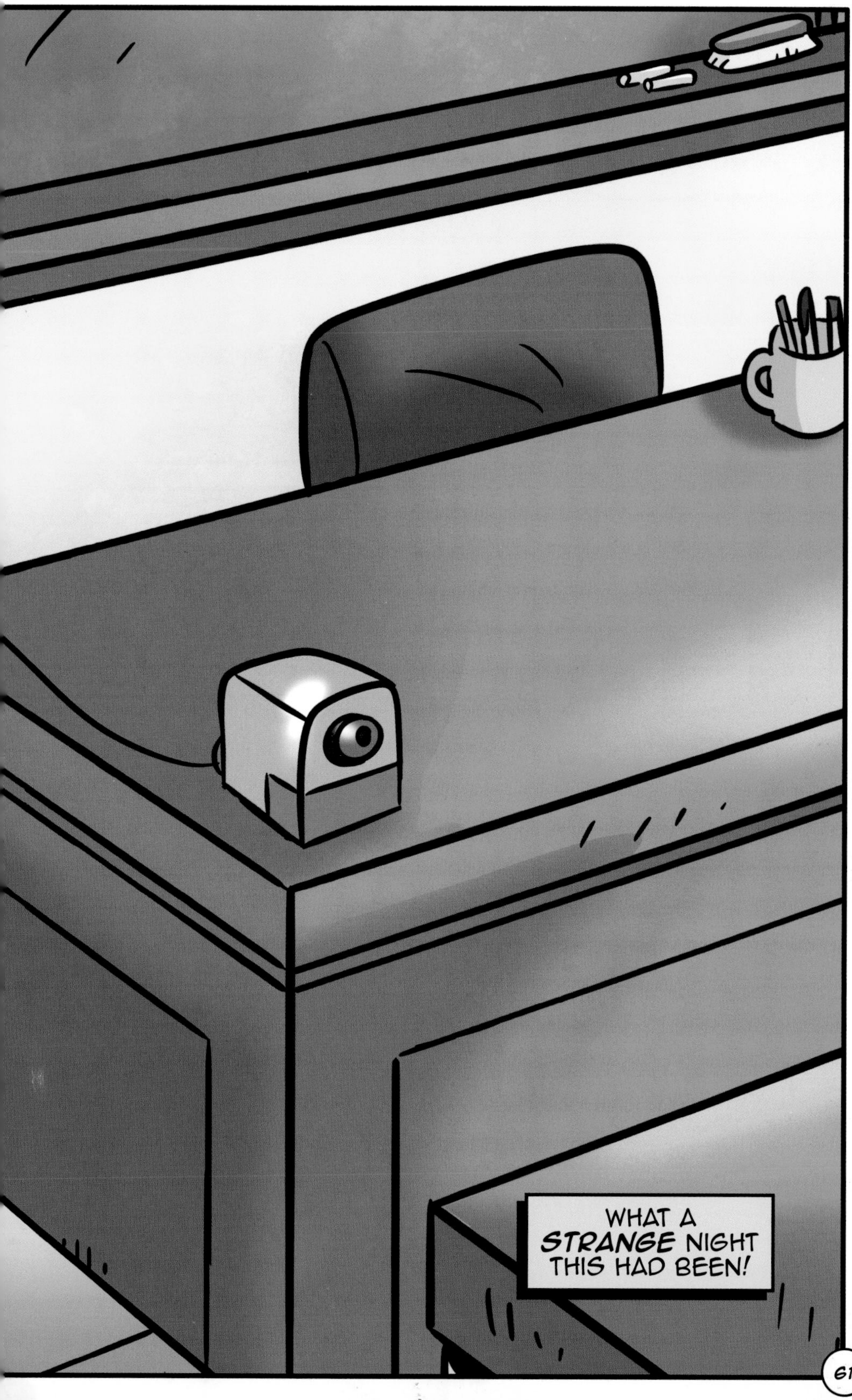
WHAT A STRANGE NIGHT THIS HAD BEEN!

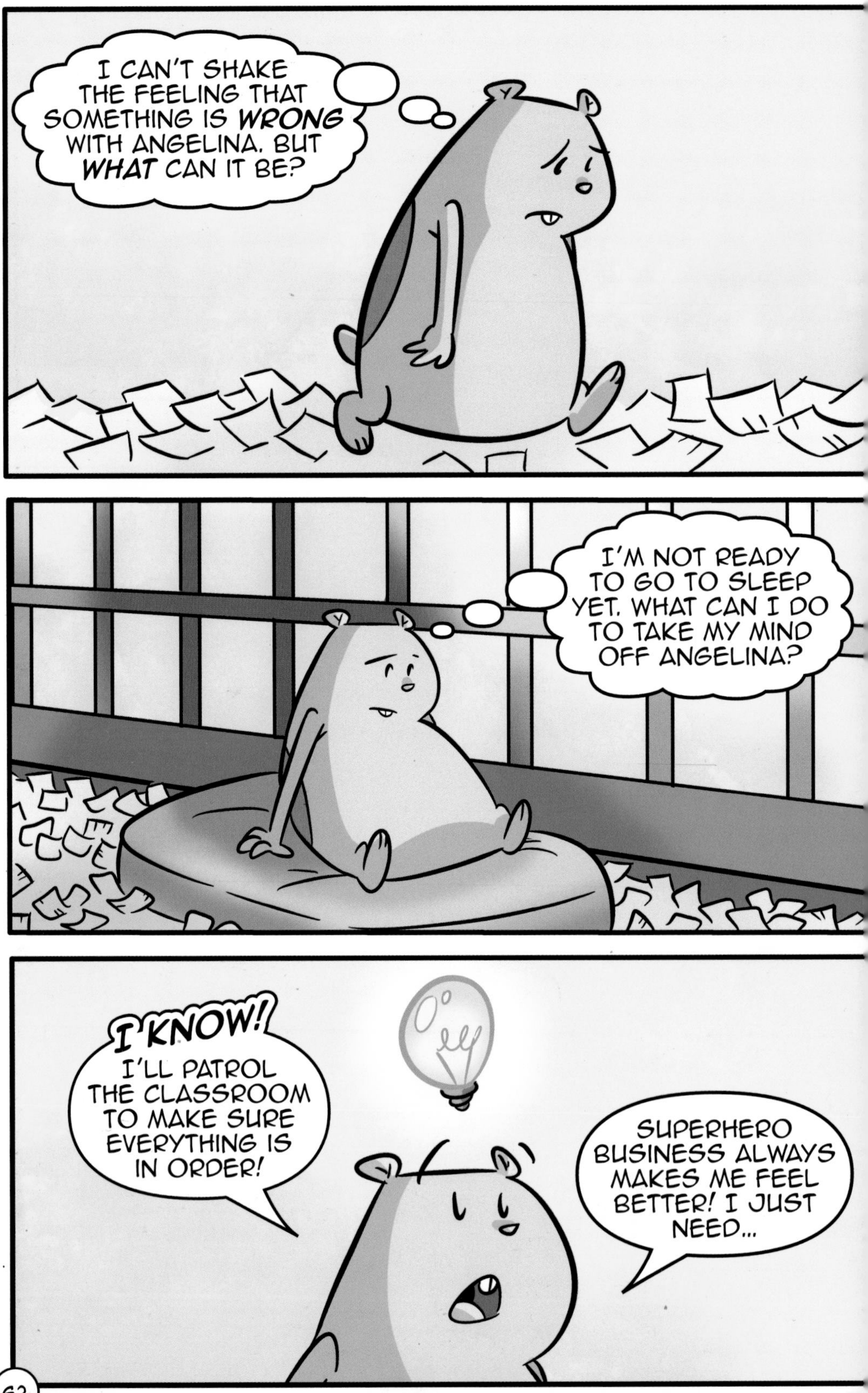

I CAN'T SHAKE THE FEELING THAT SOMETHING IS **WRONG** WITH ANGELINA. BUT **WHAT** CAN IT BE?
I'M NOT READY TO GO TO SLEEP YET. WHAT CAN I DO TO TAKE MY MIND OFF ANGELINA?
I KNOW! I'LL PATROL THE CLASSROOM TO MAKE SURE EVERYTHING IS IN ORDER!
SUPERHERO BUSINESS ALWAYS MAKES ME FEEL BETTER! I JUST NEED...

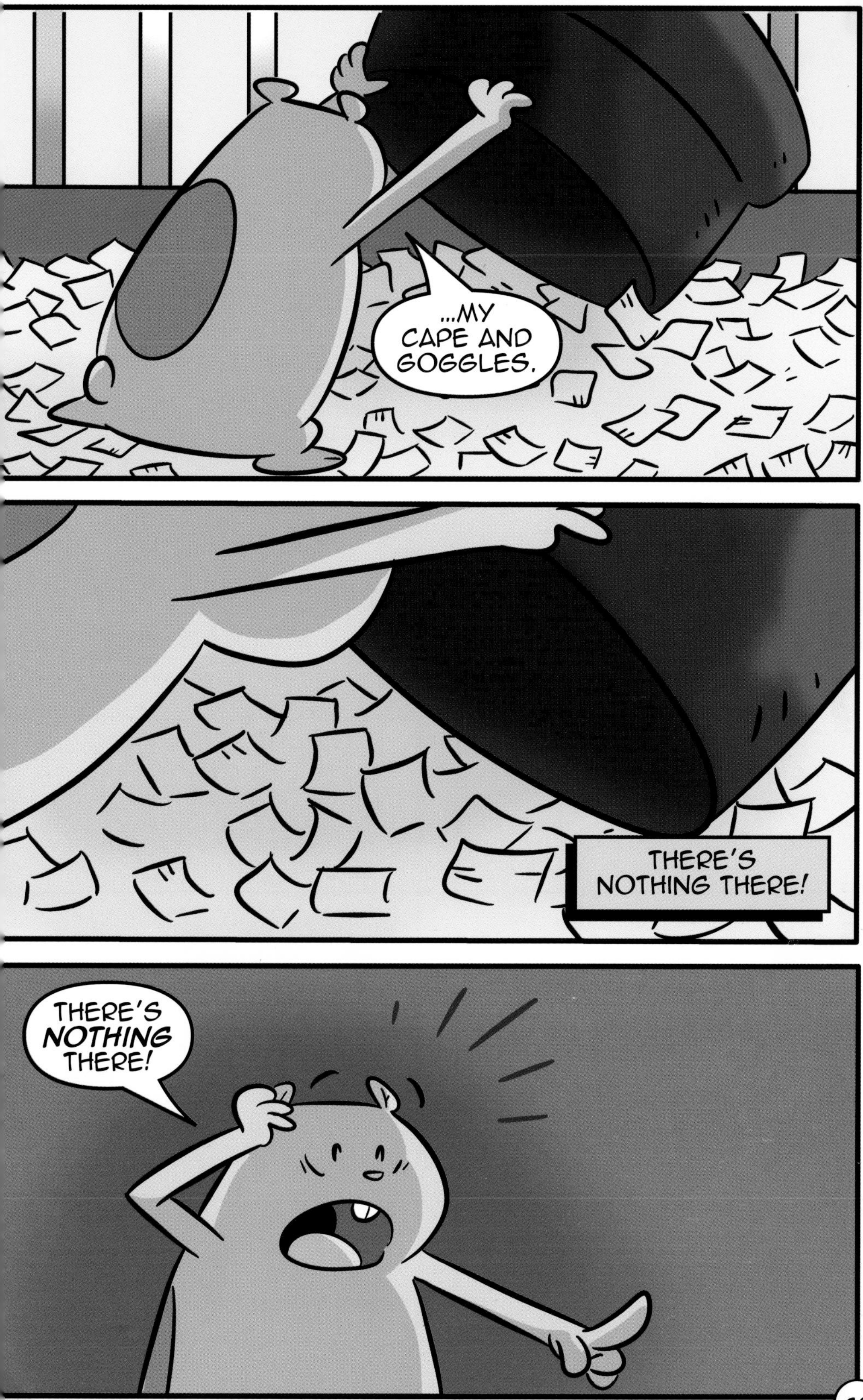
...MY CAPE AND GOGGLES.
THERE'S NOTHING THERE!
THERE'S *NOTHING* THERE!

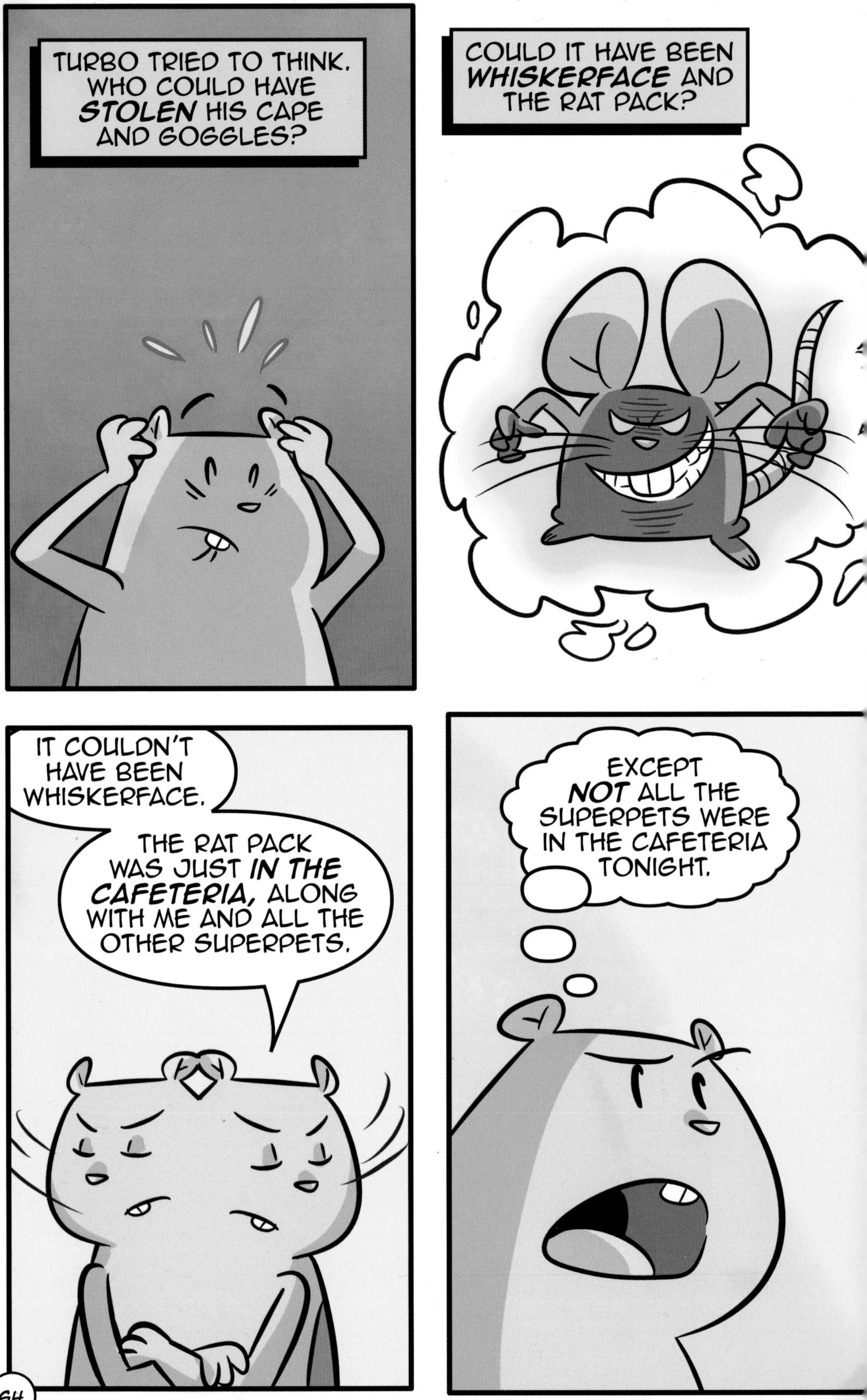
TURBO TRIED TO THINK. WHO COULD HAVE STOLEN HIS CAPE AND GOGGLES?
COULD IT HAVE BEEN WHISKERFACE AND THE RAT PACK?
IT COULDN'T HAVE BEEN WHISKERFACE.
THE RAT PACK WAS JUST IN THE CAFETERIA, ALONG WITH ME AND ALL THE OTHER SUPERPETS.
EXCEPT NOT ALL THE SUPERPETS WERE IN THE CAFETERIA TONIGHT.

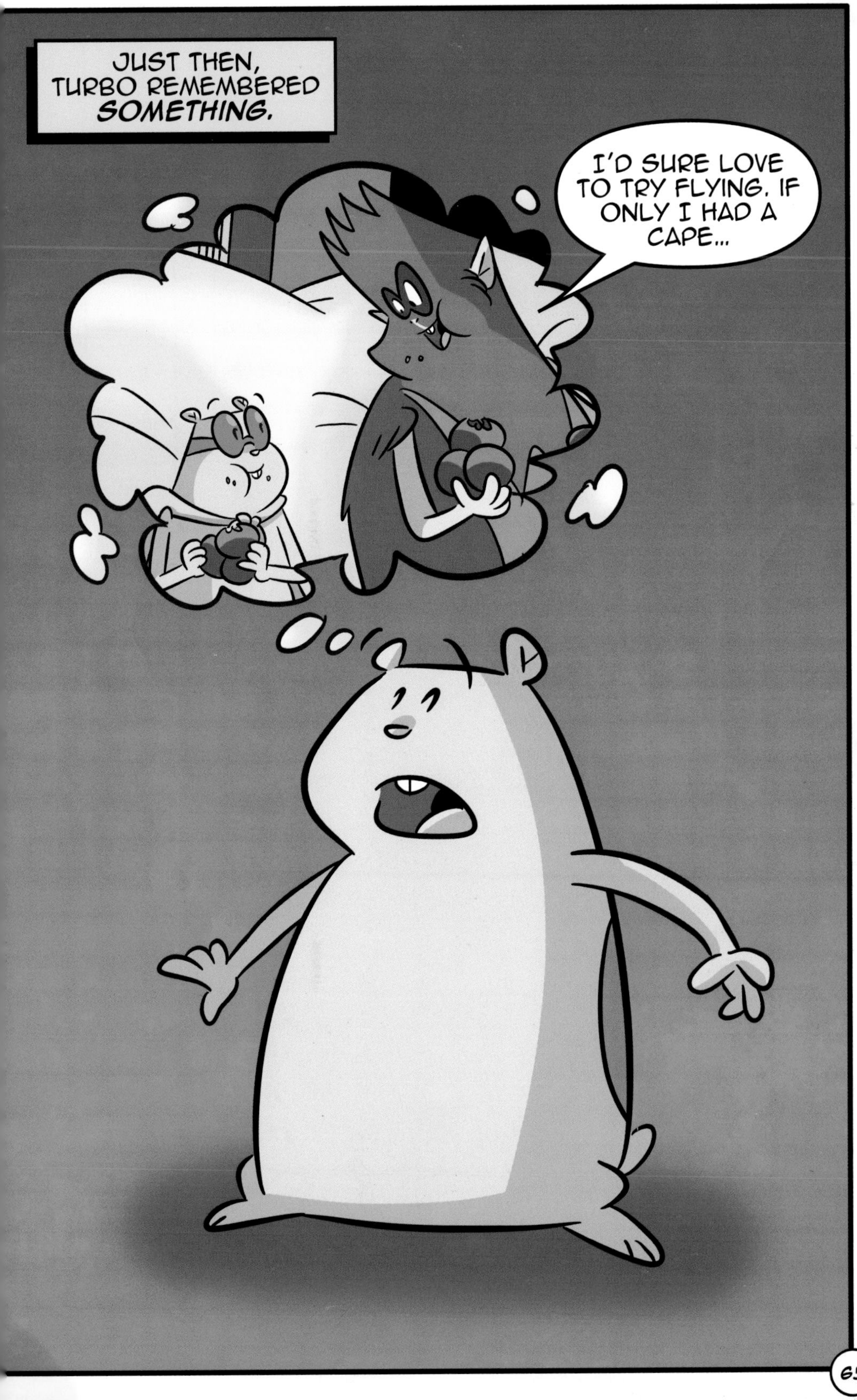
JUST THEN, TURBO REMEMBERED *SOMETHING.*
I'D SURE LOVE TO TRY FLYING. IF ONLY I HAD A CAPE...

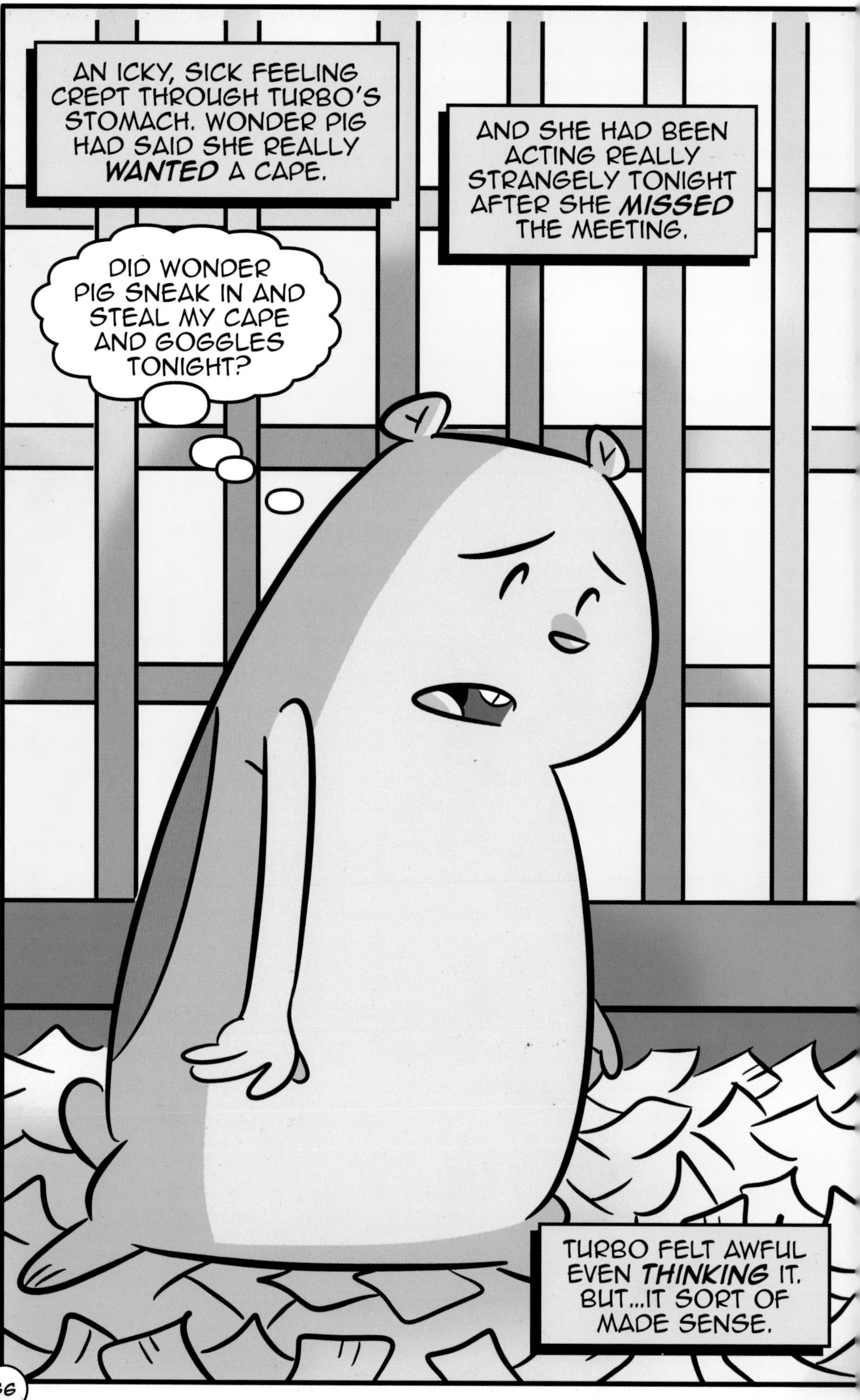
AN ICKY, SICK FEELING CREPT THROUGH TURBO'S STOMACH. WONDER PIG HAD SAID SHE REALLY *WANTED* A CAPE.
AND SHE HAD BEEN ACTING REALLY STRANGELY TONIGHT AFTER SHE *MISSED* THE MEETING.
DID WONDER PIG SNEAK IN AND STEAL MY CAPE AND GOGGLES TONIGHT?
TURBO FELT AWFUL EVEN *THINKING* IT. BUT...IT SORT OF MADE SENSE.

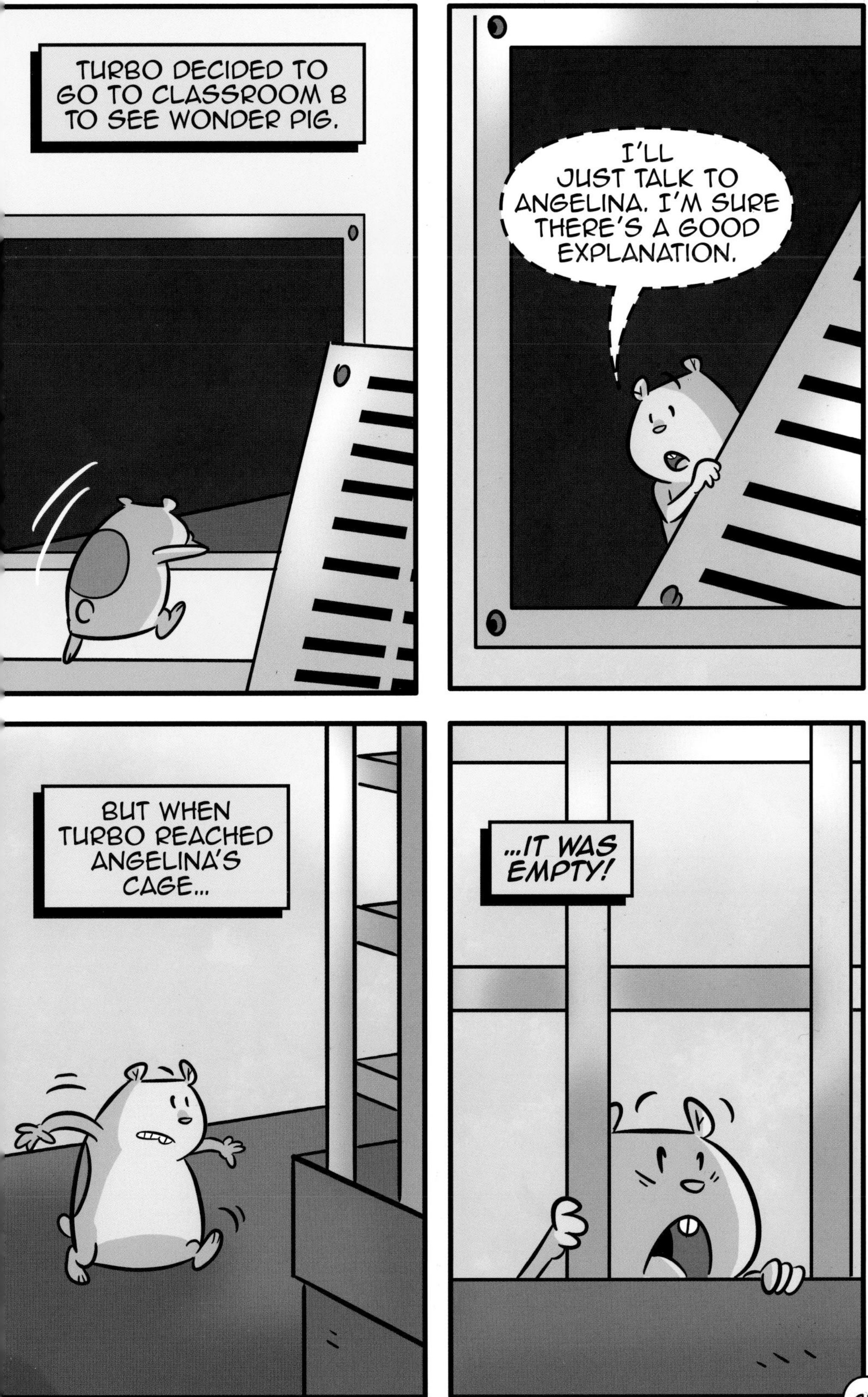
TURBO DECIDED TO GO TO CLASSROOM B TO SEE WONDER PIG.
I'LL JUST TALK TO ANGELINA. I'M SURE THERE'S A GOOD EXPLANATION.
BUT WHEN TURBO REACHED ANGELINA'S CAGE...
...IT WAS EMPTY!

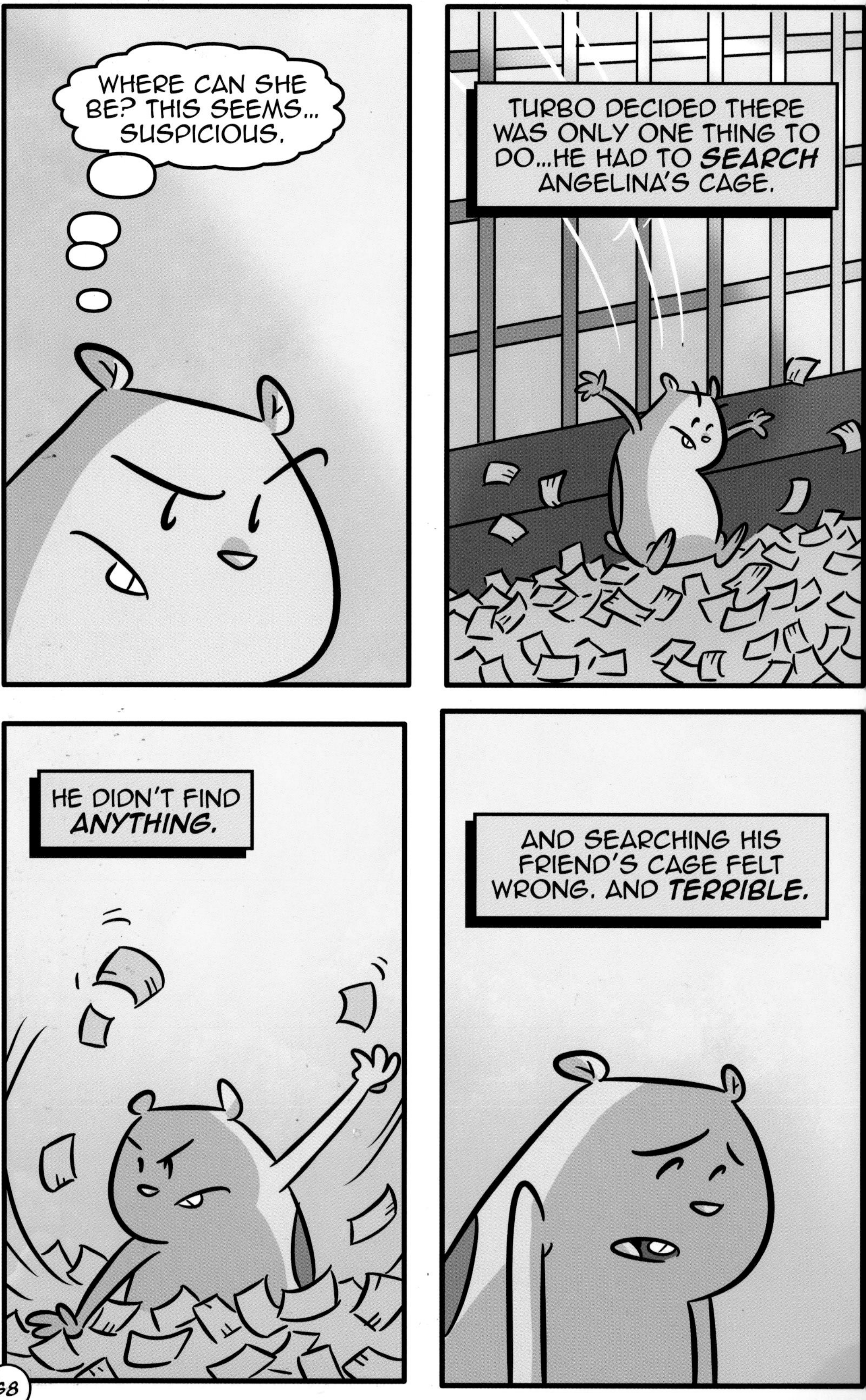
WHERE CAN SHE BE? THIS SEEMS... SUSPICIOUS.
TURBO DECIDED THERE WAS ONLY ONE THING TO DO...HE HAD TO SEARCH ANGELINA'S CAGE.
HE DIDN'T FIND ANYTHING.
AND SEARCHING HIS FRIEND'S CAGE FELT WRONG. AND TERRIBLE.

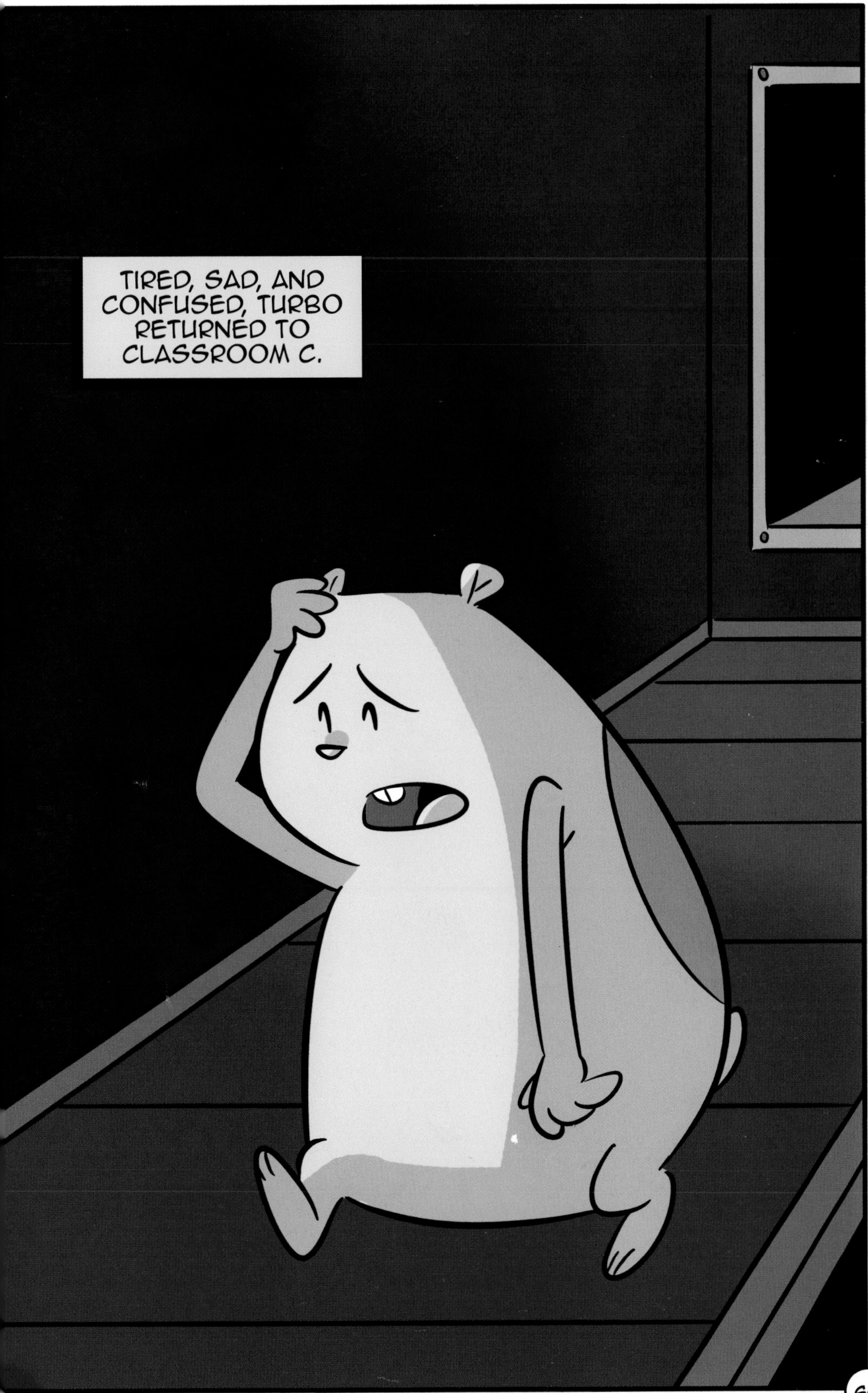
TIRED, SAD, AND CONFUSED, TURBO RETURNED TO CLASSROOM C.

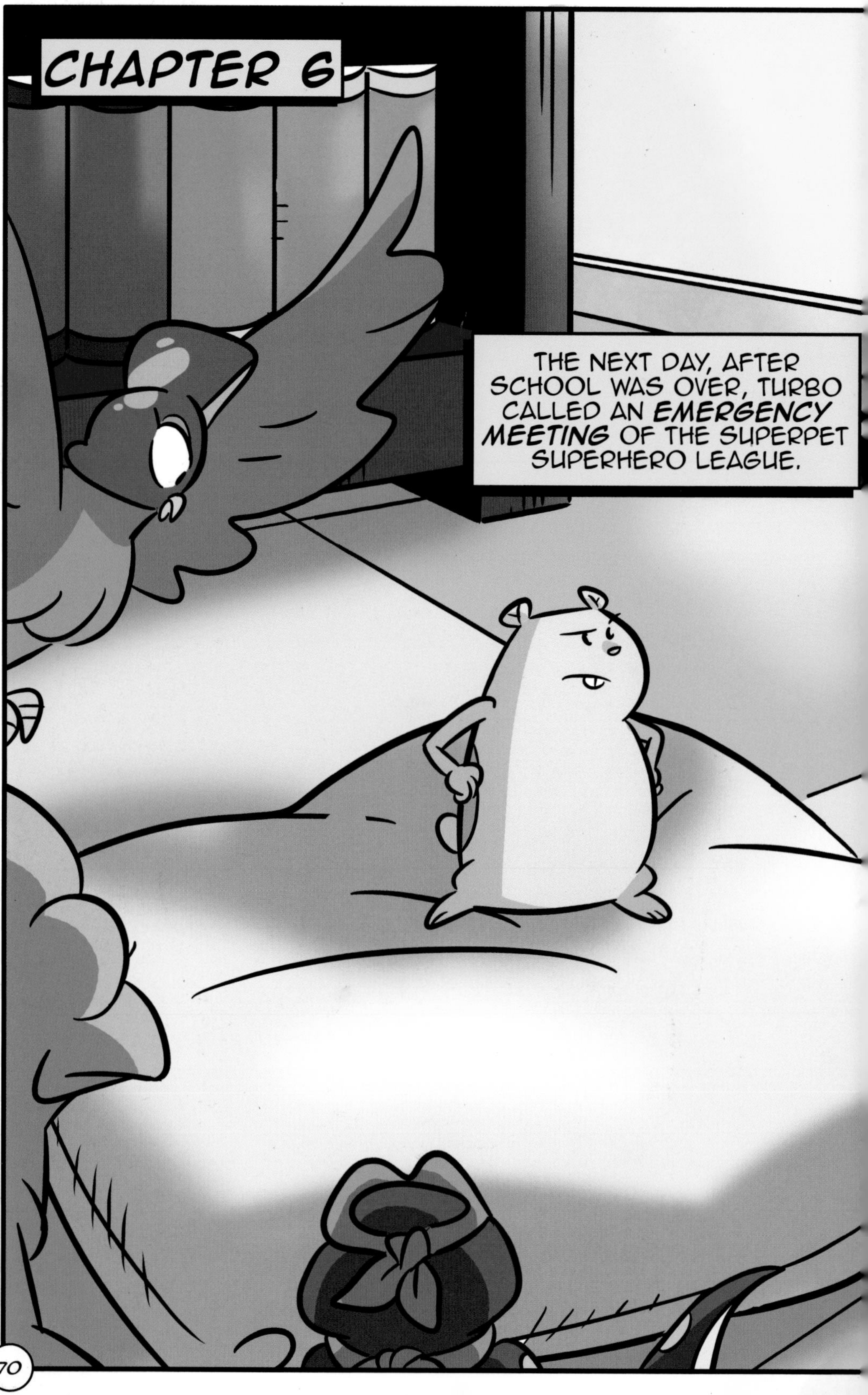
CHAPTER 6
THE NEXT DAY, AFTER SCHOOL WAS OVER, TURBO CALLED AN EMERGENCY MEETING OF THE SUPERPET SUPERHERO LEAGUE.

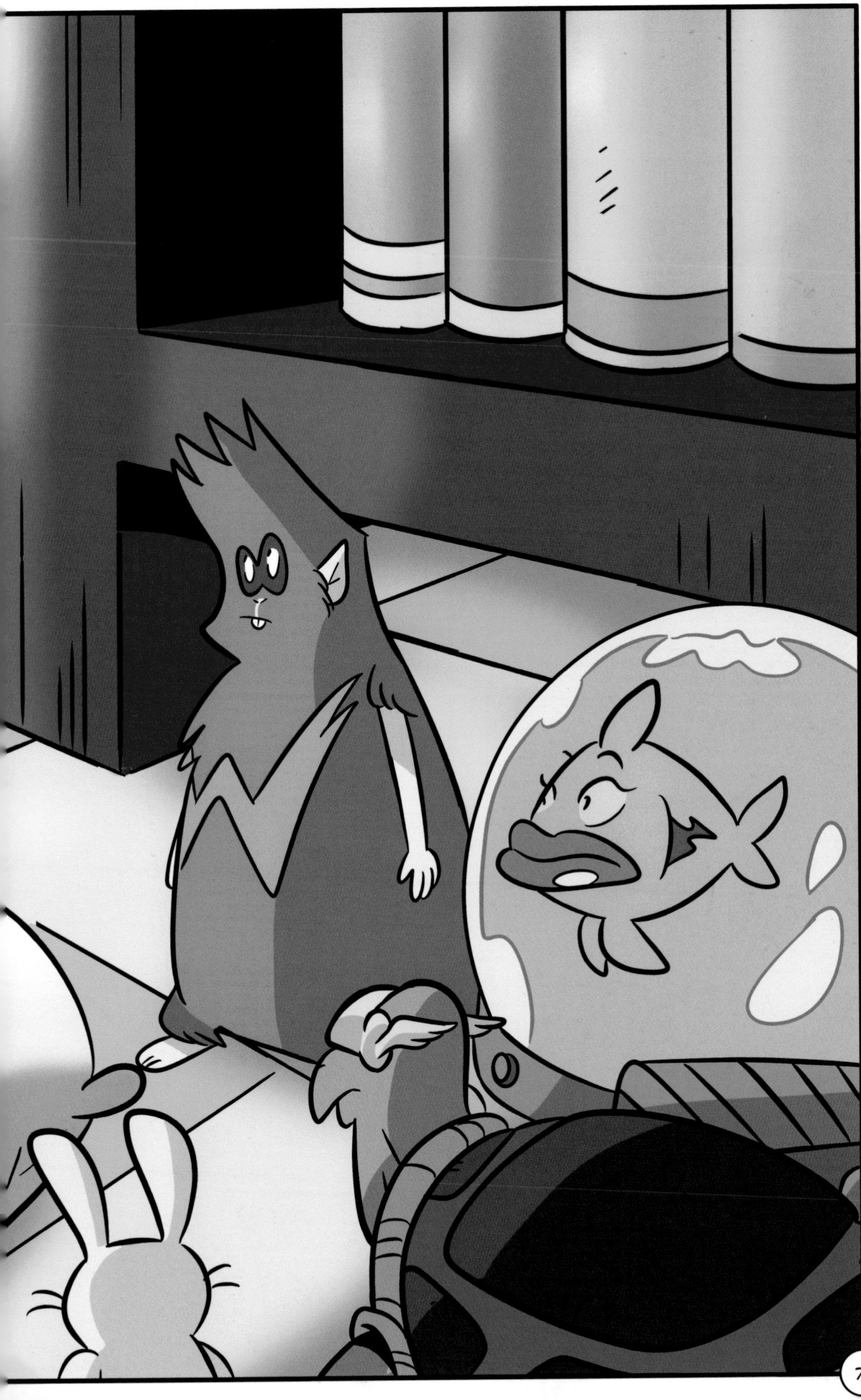

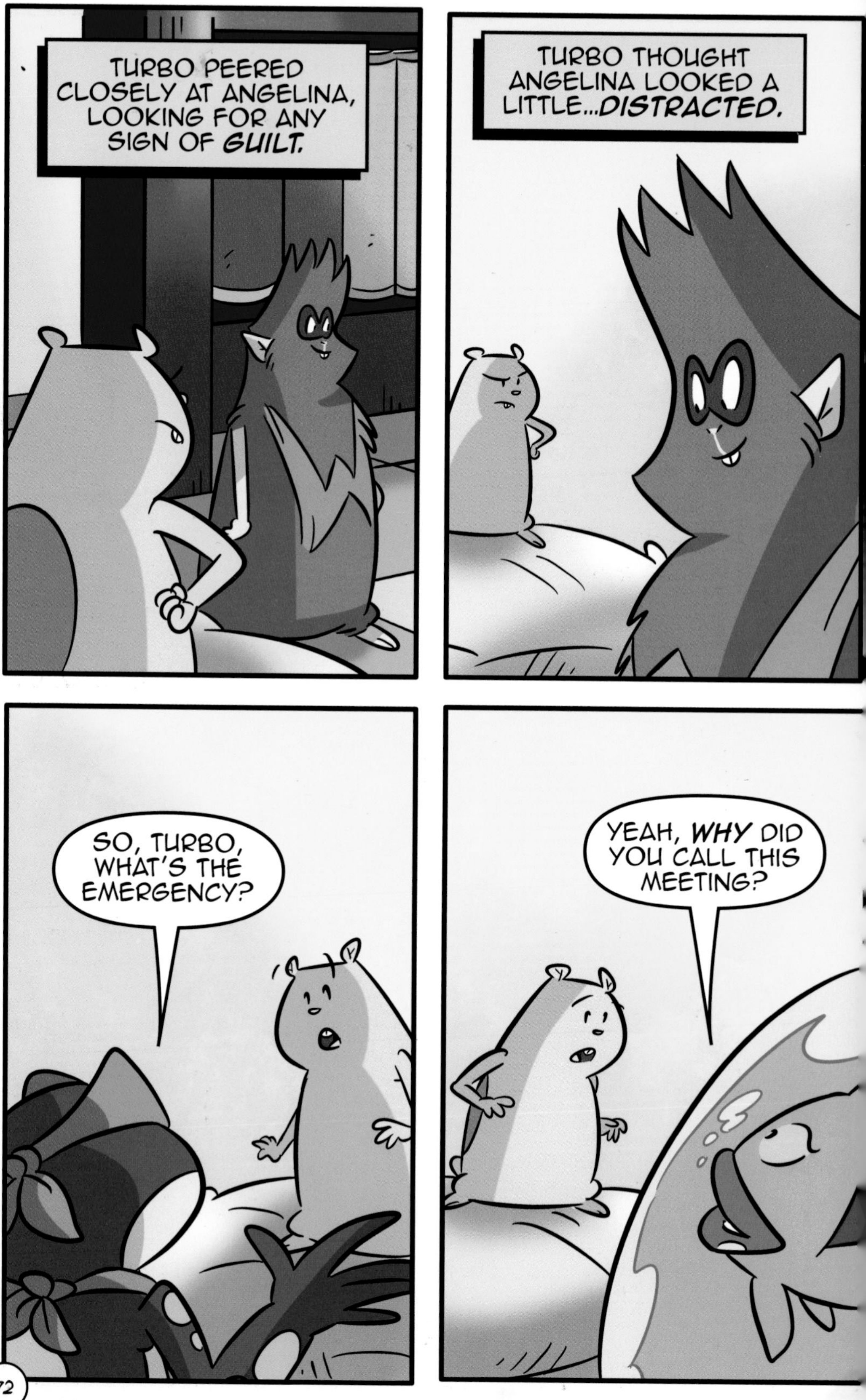
TURBO PEERED CLOSELY AT ANGELINA, LOOKING FOR ANY SIGN OF GUILT.
TURBO THOUGHT ANGELINA LOOKED A LITTLE...DISTRACTED.
SO, TURBO, WHAT'S THE EMERGENCY?
YEAH, WHY DID YOU CALL THIS MEETING?

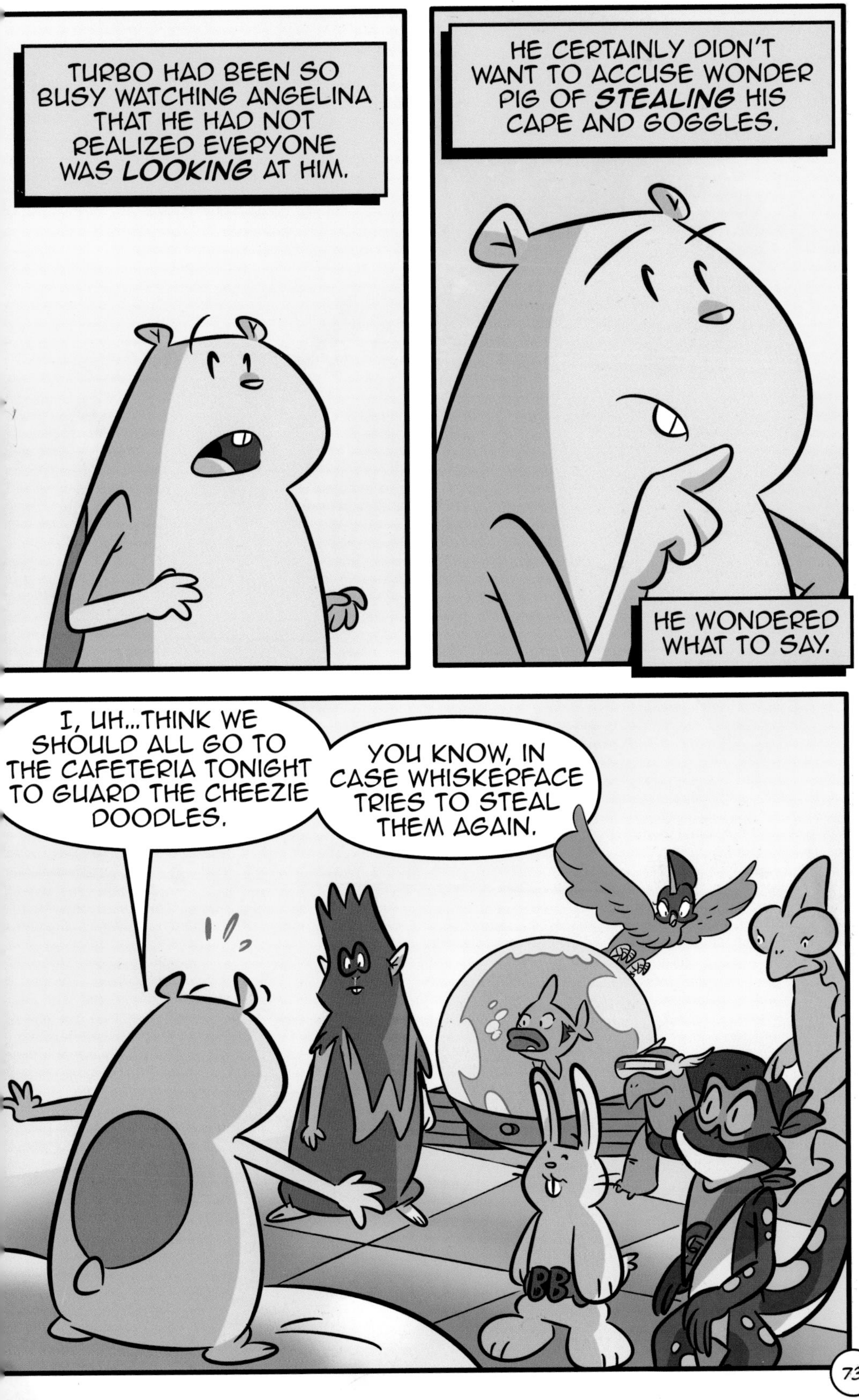
TURBO HAD BEEN SO BUSY WATCHING ANGELINA THAT HE HAD NOT REALIZED EVERYONE WAS LOOKING AT HIM.
HE CERTAINLY DIDN'T WANT TO ACCUSE WONDER PIG OF STEALING HIS CAPE AND GOGGLES.
HE WONDERED WHAT TO SAY.
I, UH...THINK WE SHOULD ALL GO TO THE CAFETERIA TONIGHT TO GUARD THE CHEEZIE DOODLES.
YOU KNOW, IN CASE WHISKERFACE TRIES TO STEAL THEM AGAIN.
BB

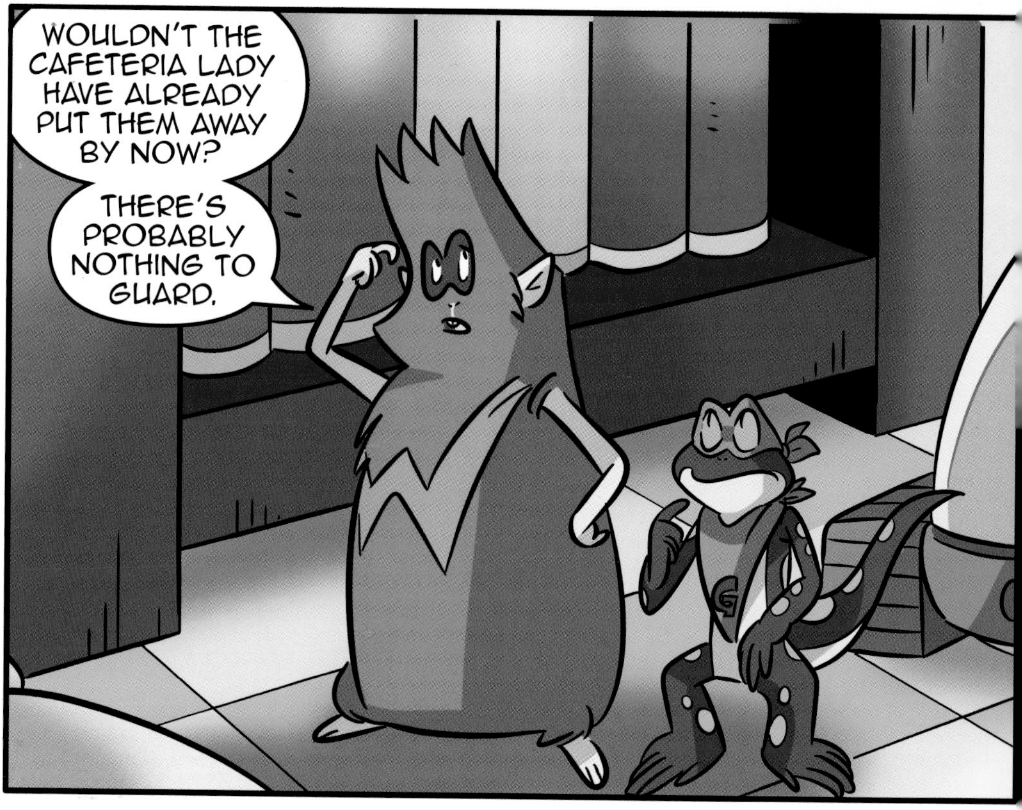
WOULDN'T THE CAFETERIA LADY HAVE ALREADY PUT THEM AWAY BY NOW?
THERE'S PROBABLY NOTHING TO GUARD.

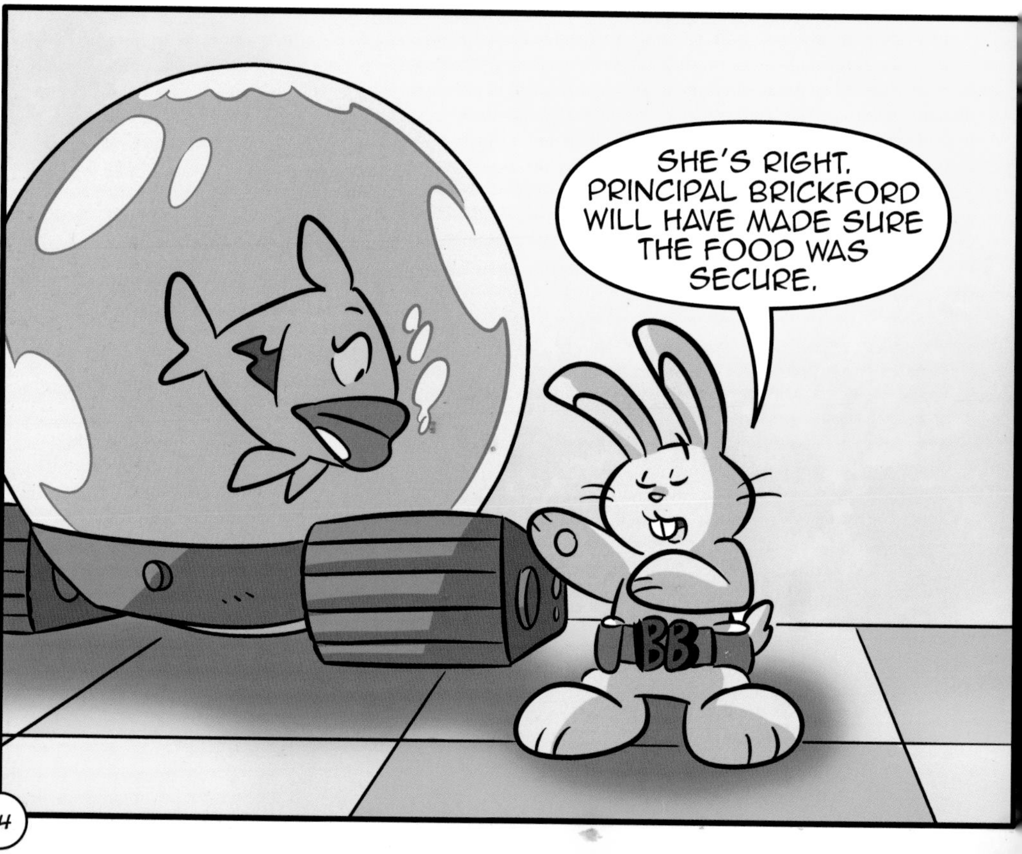
SHE'S RIGHT. PRINCIPAL BRICKFORD WILL HAVE MADE SURE THE FOOD WAS SECURE.
BB

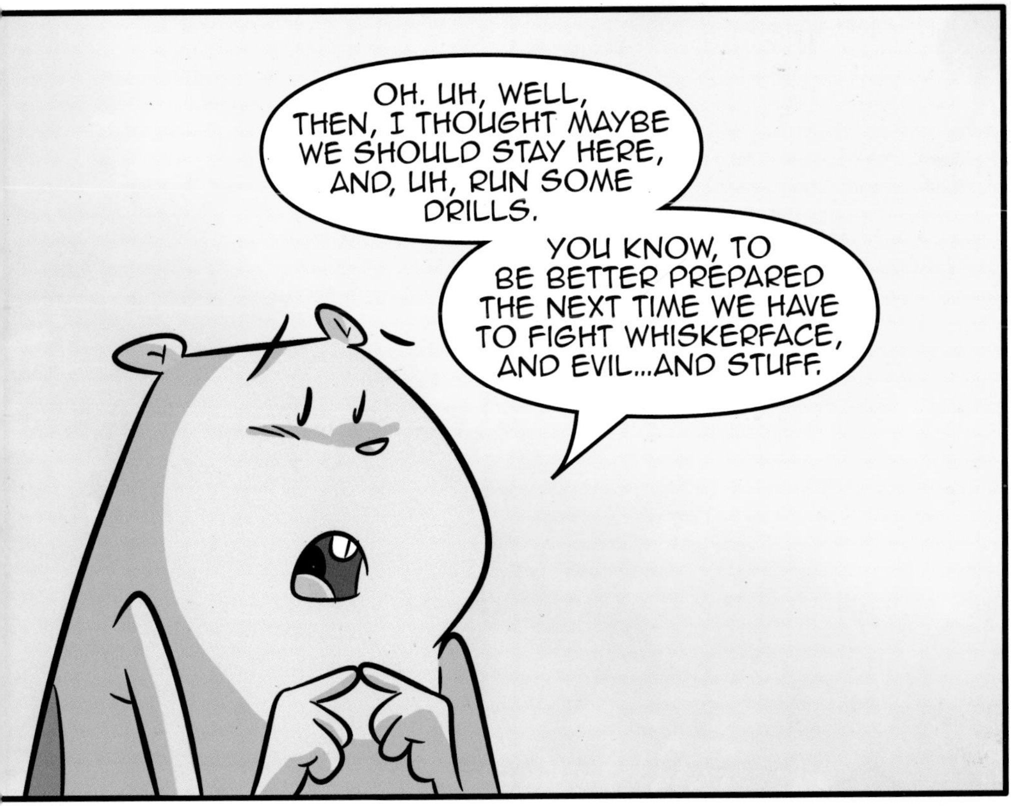
OH. UH, WELL, THEN, I THOUGHT MAYBE WE SHOULD STAY HERE, AND, UH, RUN SOME DRILLS.
YOU KNOW, TO BE BETTER PREPARED THE NEXT TIME WE HAVE TO FIGHT WHISKERFACE, AND EVIL...AND STUFF.

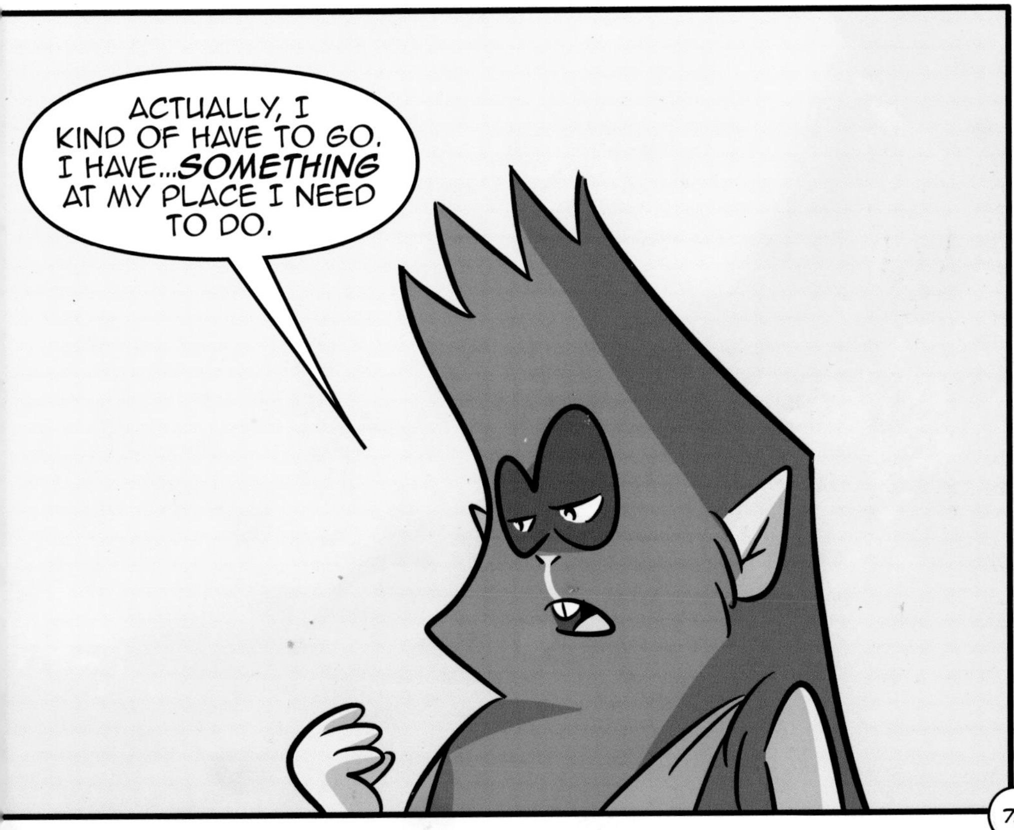
ACTUALLY, I KIND OF HAVE TO GO. I HAVE...*SOMETHING* AT MY PLACE I NEED TO DO.

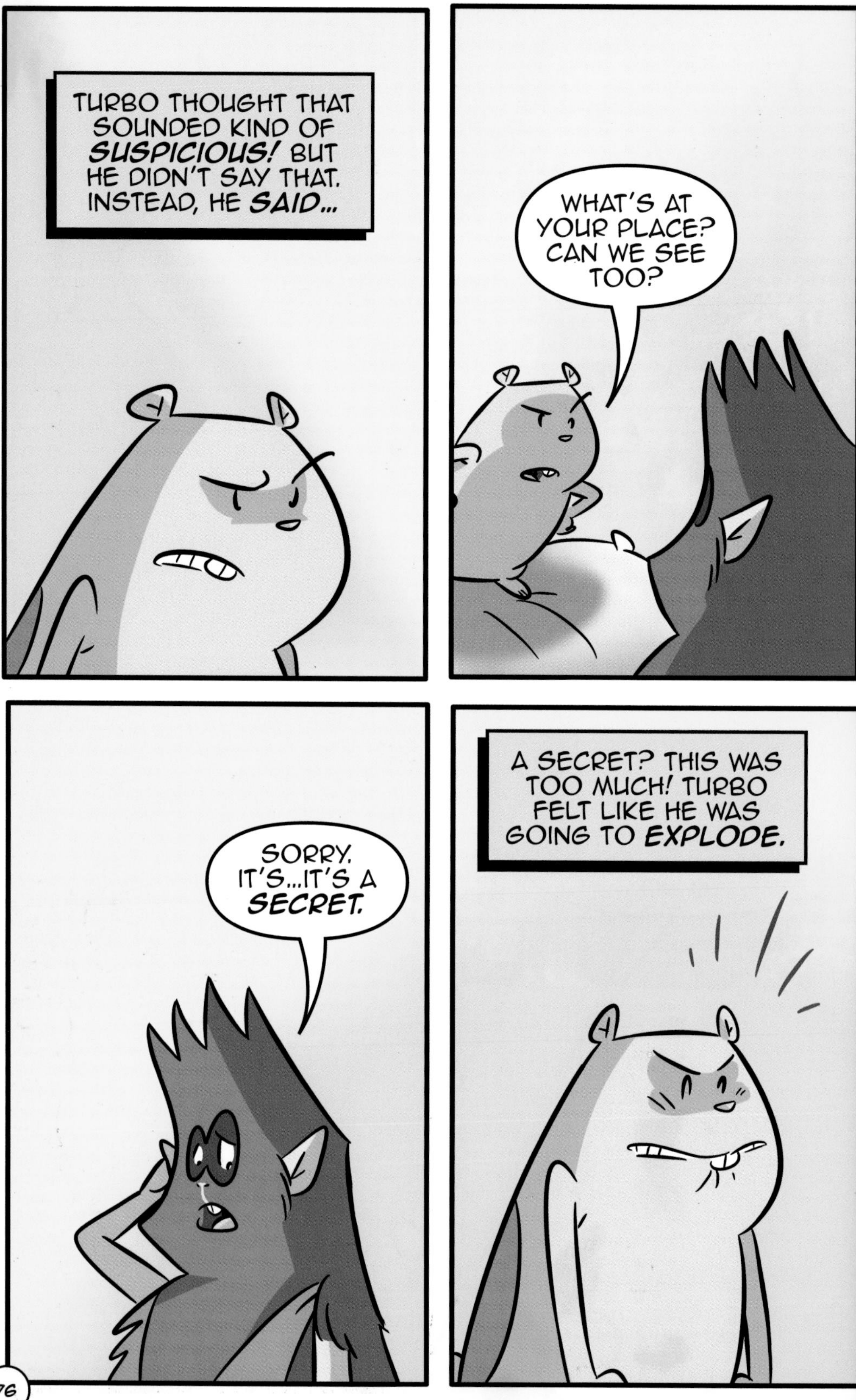
TURBO THOUGHT THAT SOUNDED KIND OF SUSPICIOUS! BUT HE DIDN'T SAY THAT. INSTEAD, HE SAID...
WHAT'S AT YOUR PLACE? CAN WE SEE TOO?
SORRY. IT'S...IT'S A SECRET.
A SECRET? THIS WAS TOO MUCH! TURBO FELT LIKE HE WAS GOING TO EXPLODE.

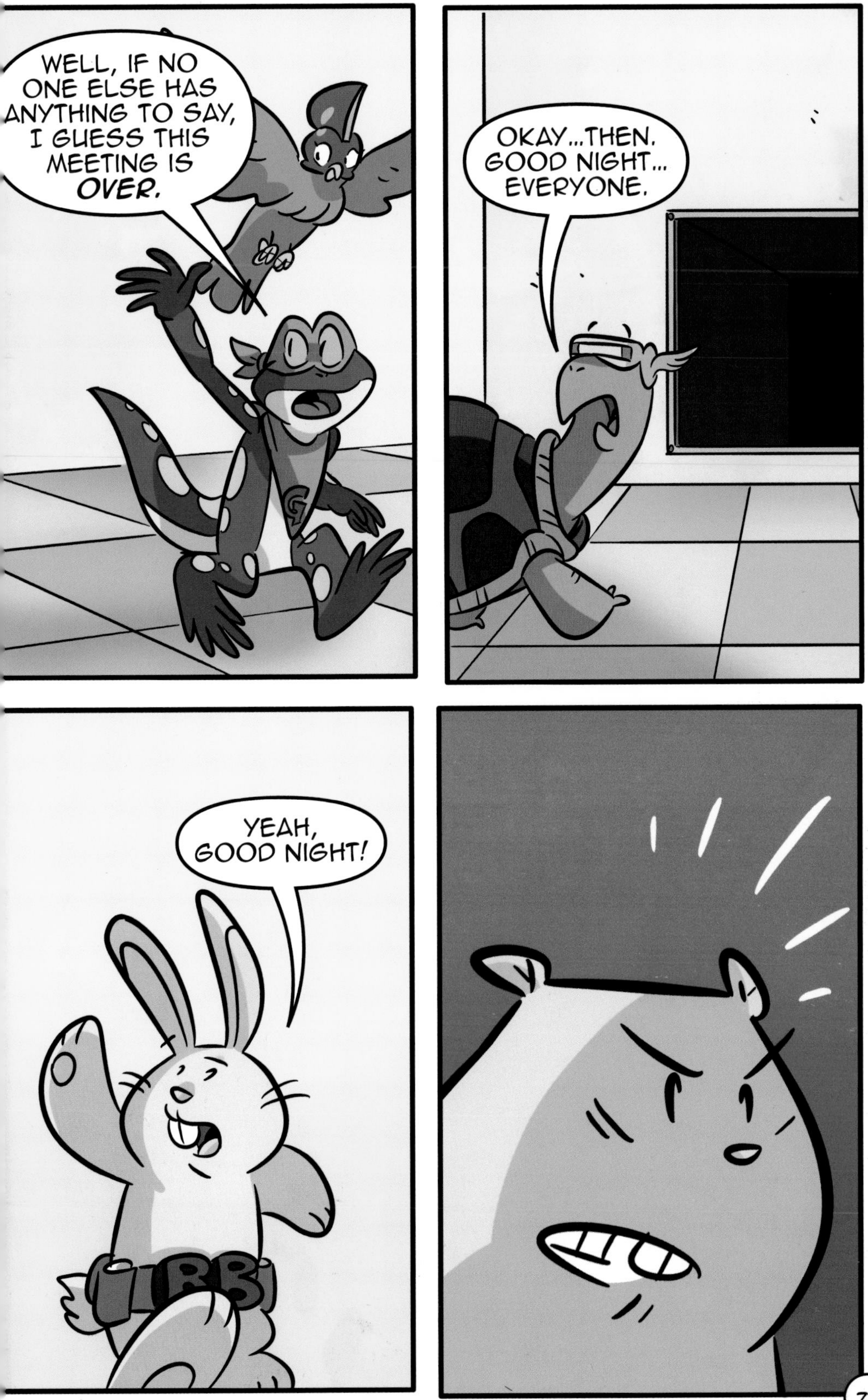
WELL, IF NO ONE ELSE HAS ANYTHING TO SAY, I GUESS THIS MEETING IS *OVER.*
OKAY...THEN. GOOD NIGHT... EVERYONE.
YEAH, GOOD NIGHT!

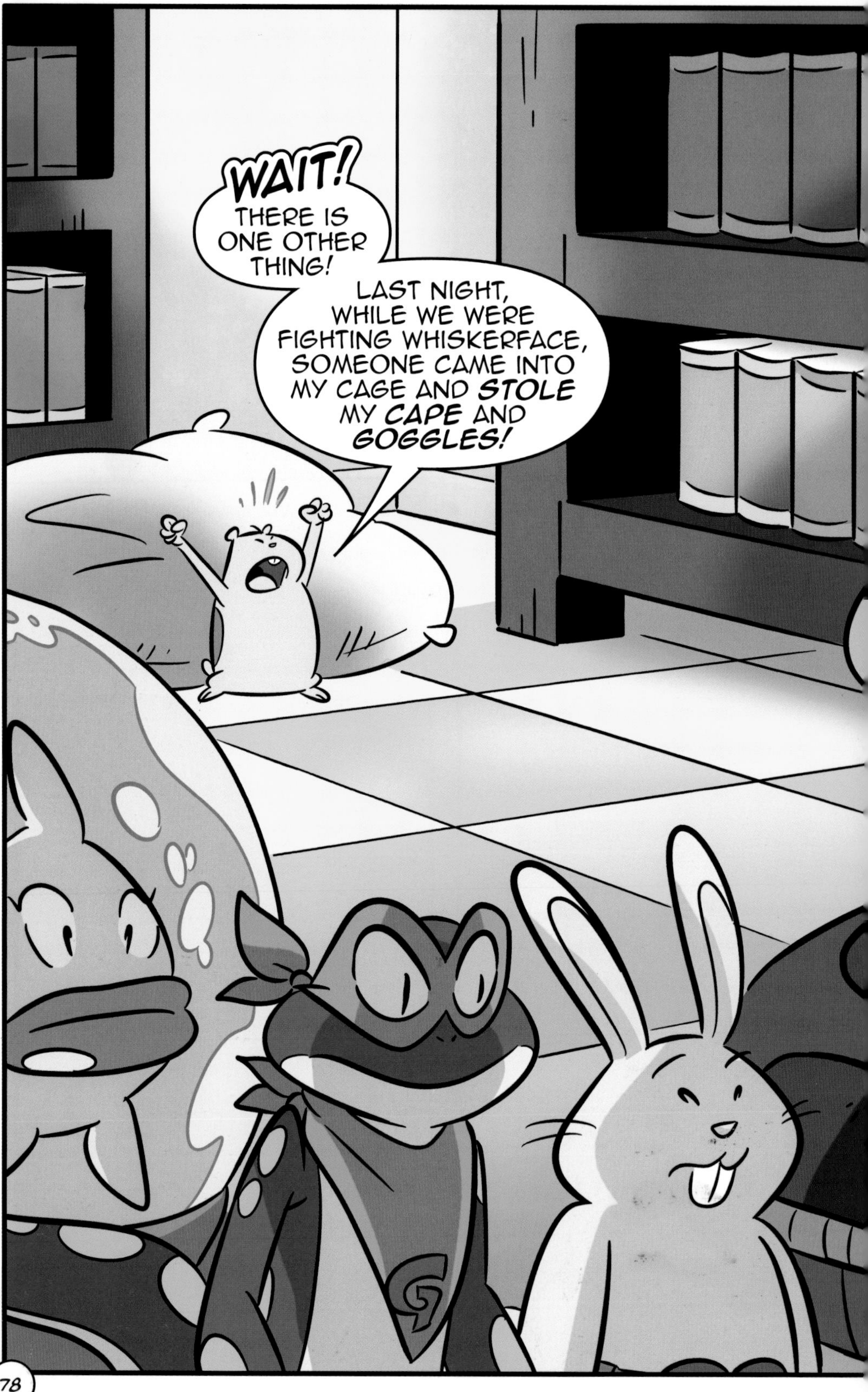
WAIT! THERE IS ONE OTHER THING!
LAST NIGHT, WHILE WE WERE FIGHTING WHISKERFACE, SOMEONE CAME INTO MY CAGE AND STOLE MY CAPE AND GOGGLES!

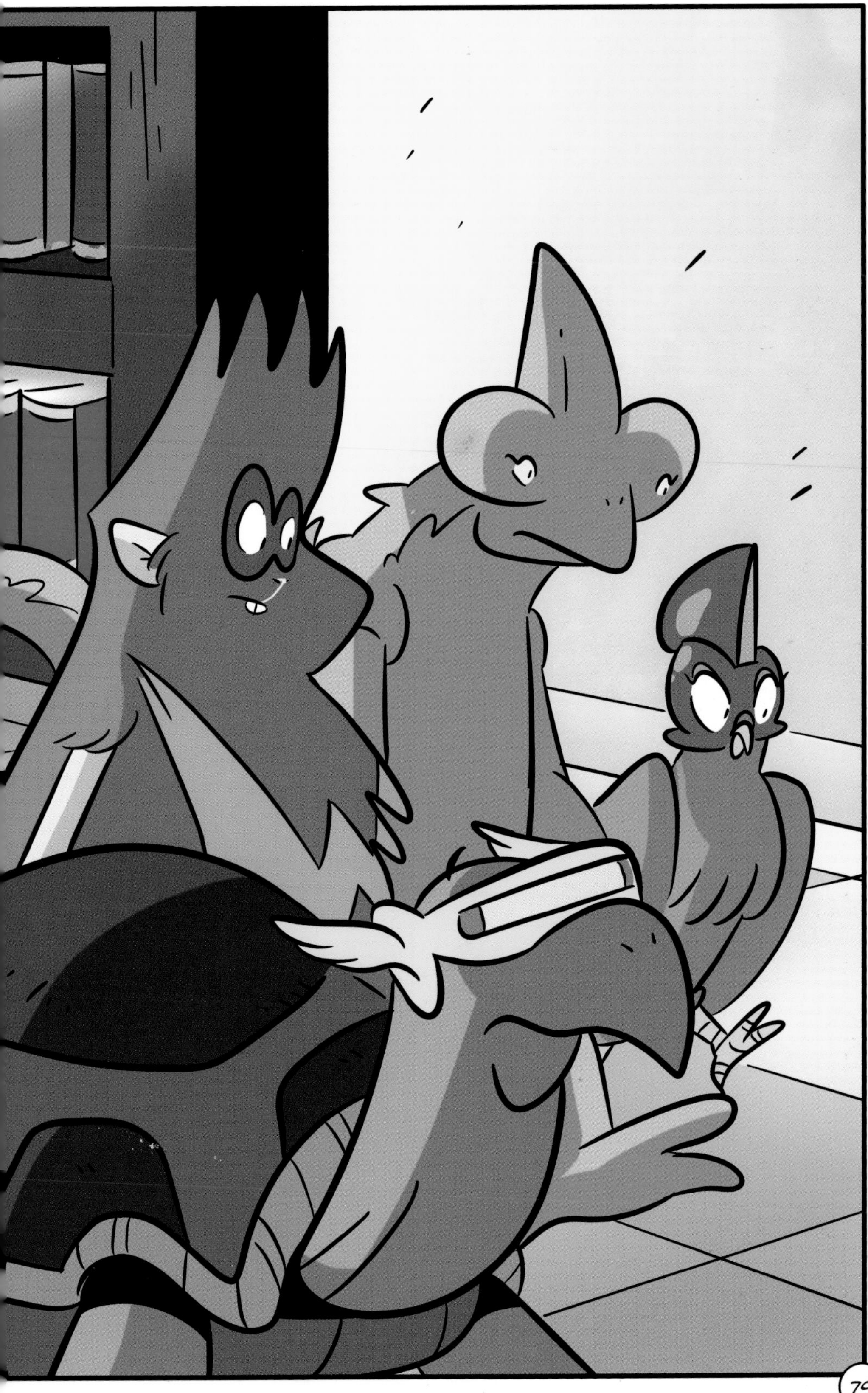

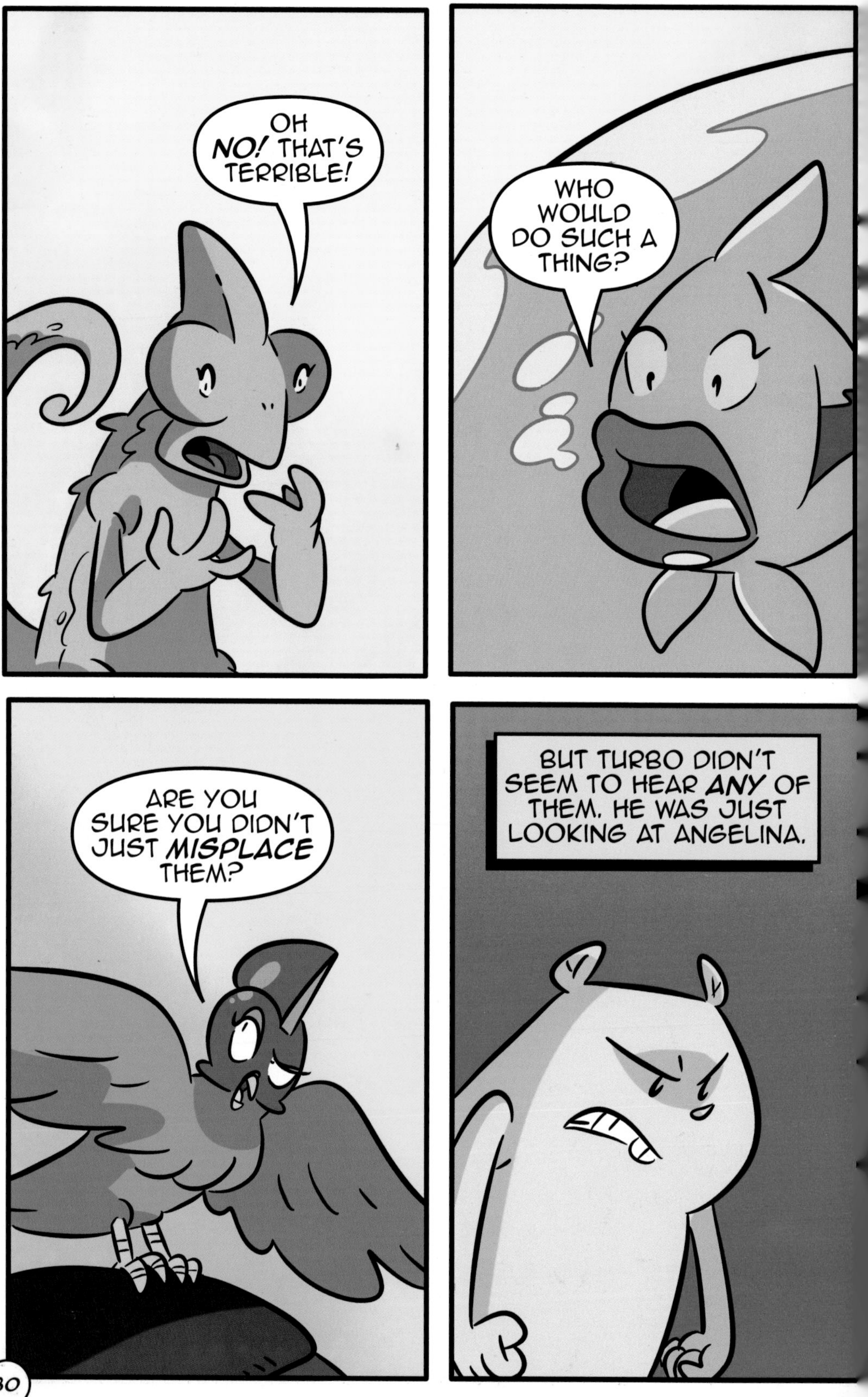
OH **NO!** THAT'S TERRIBLE!
WHO WOULD DO SUCH A THING?
ARE YOU SURE YOU DIDN'T JUST ***MISPLACE*** THEM?
BUT TURBO DIDN'T SEEM TO HEAR ***ANY*** OF THEM. HE WAS JUST LOOKING AT ANGELINA.

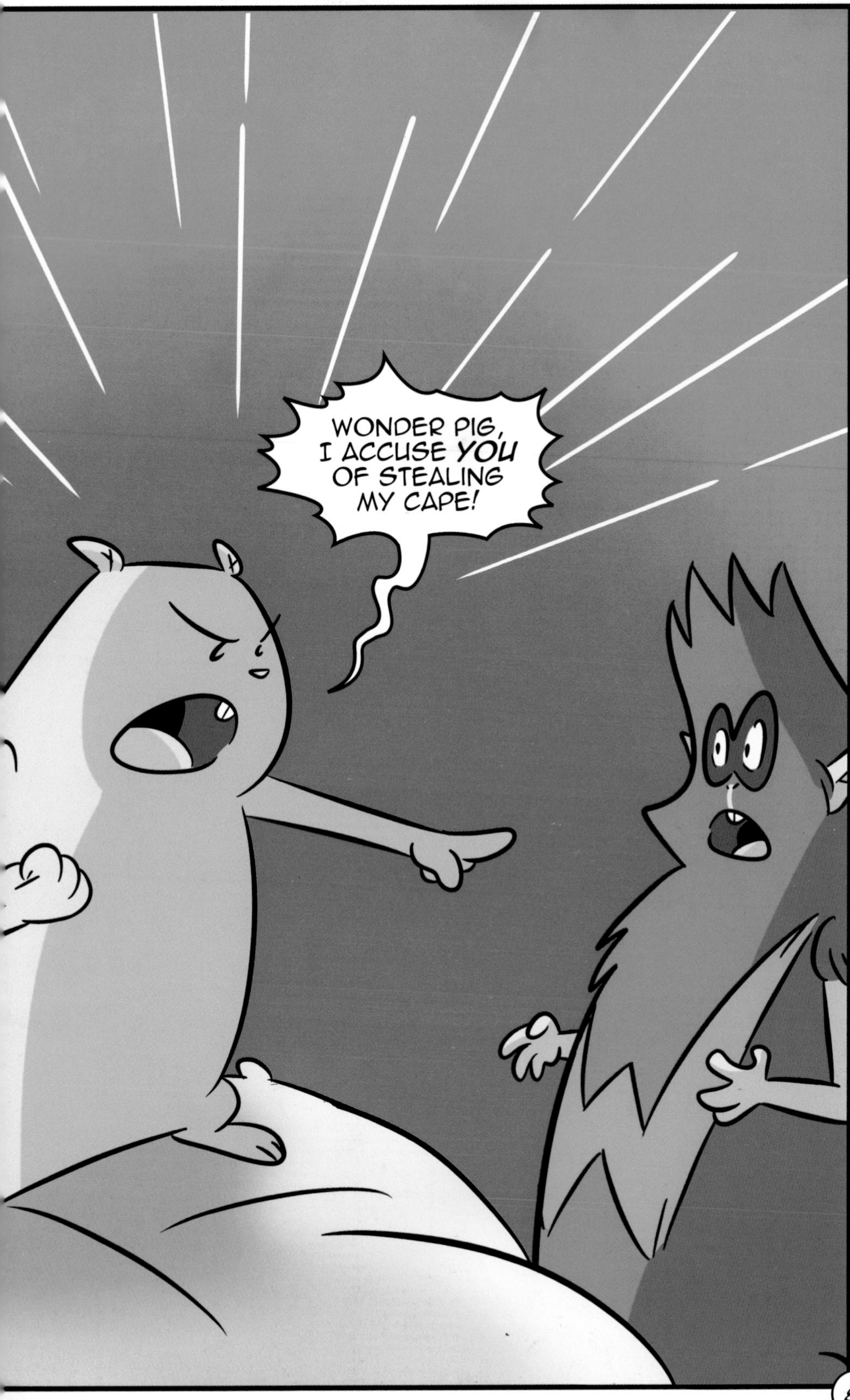
WONDER PIG, I ACCUSE YOU OF STEALING MY CAPE!

CHAPTER 7

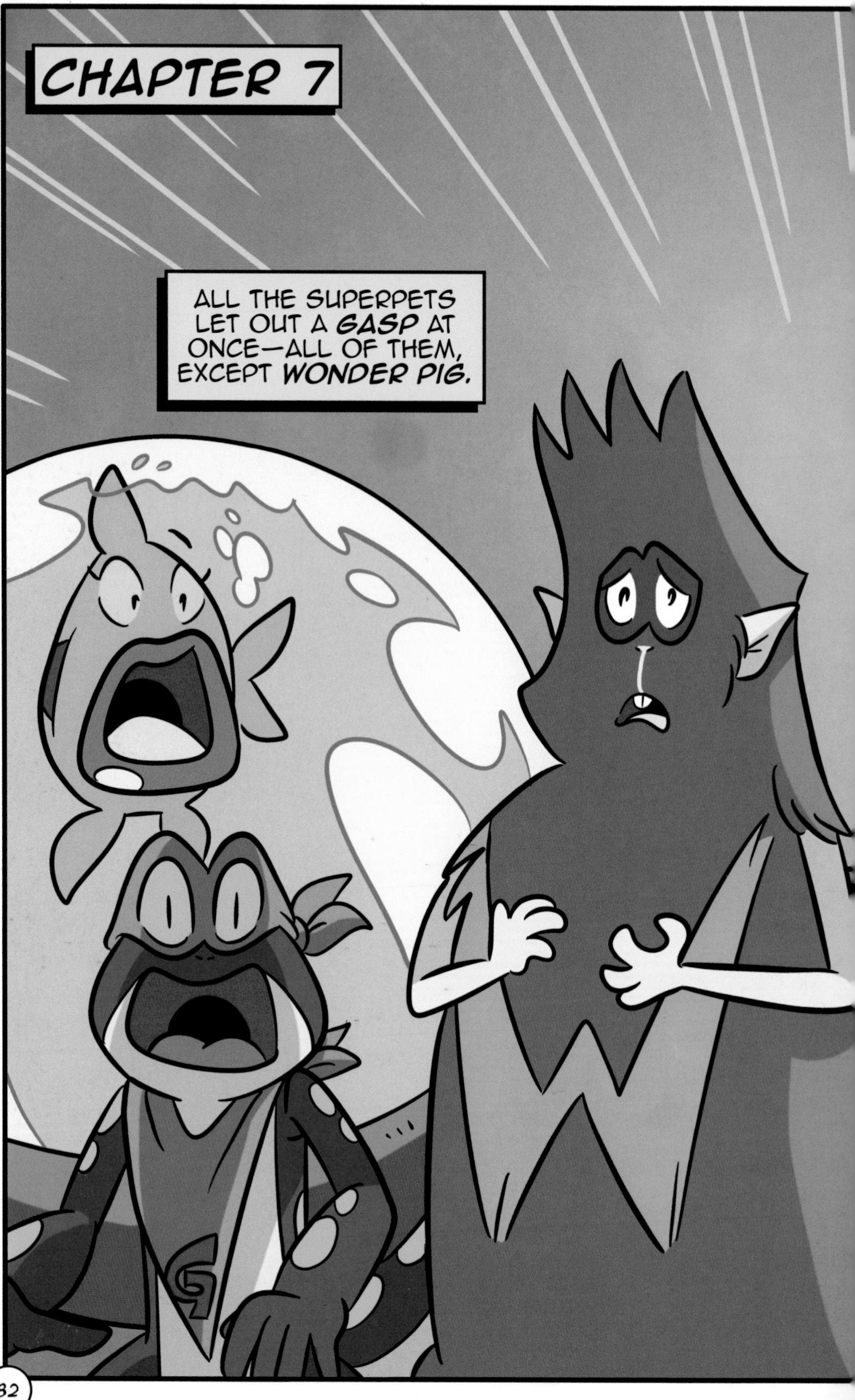
ALL THE SUPERPETS LET OUT A *GASP* AT ONCE—ALL OF THEM, EXCEPT **WONDER PIG.**

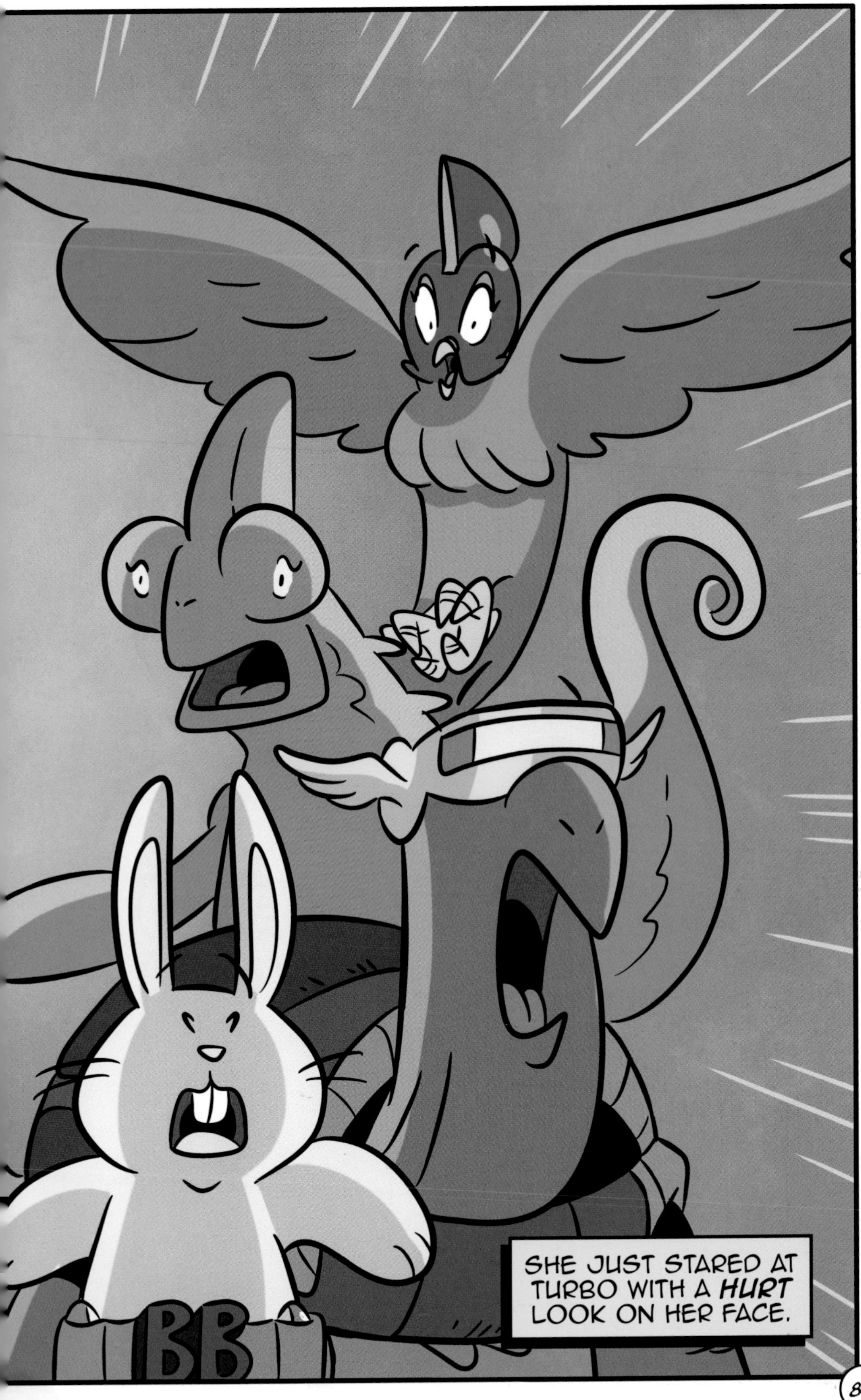
SHE JUST STARED AT TURBO WITH A *HURT* LOOK ON HER FACE.
BB

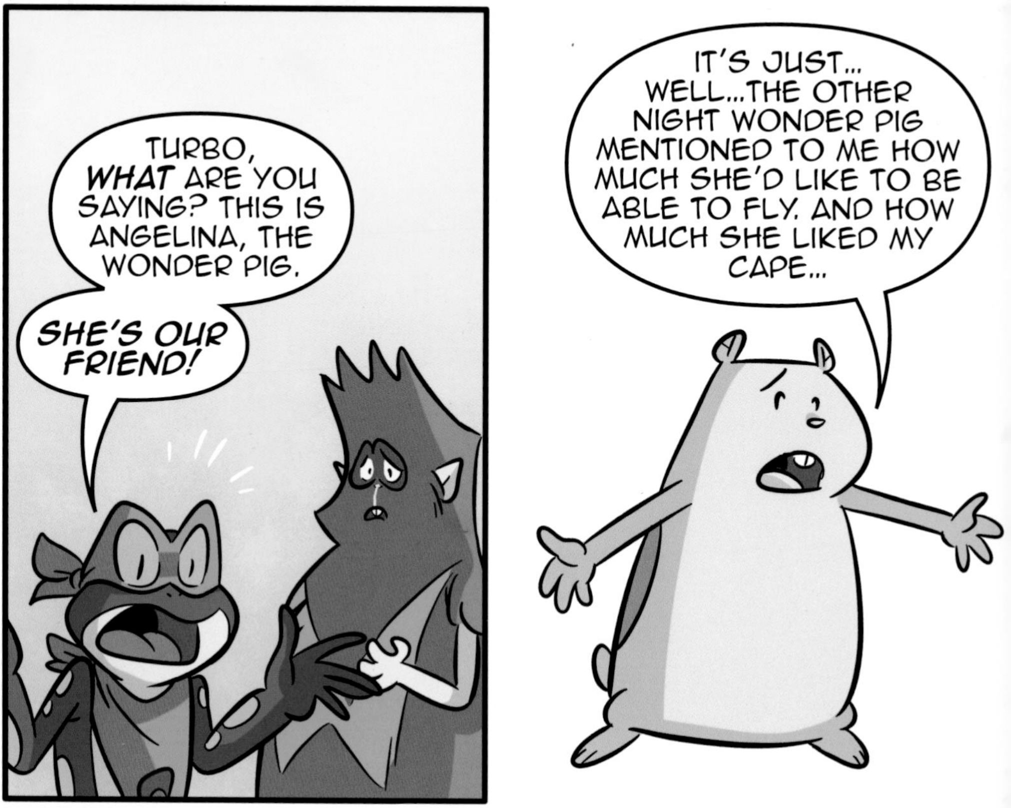
TURBO, **WHAT** ARE YOU SAYING? THIS IS ANGELINA, THE WONDER PIG.
SHE'S OUR FRIEND!
IT'S JUST... WELL...THE OTHER NIGHT WONDER PIG MENTIONED TO ME HOW MUCH SHE'D LIKE TO BE ABLE TO FLY. AND HOW MUCH SHE LIKED MY CAPE...

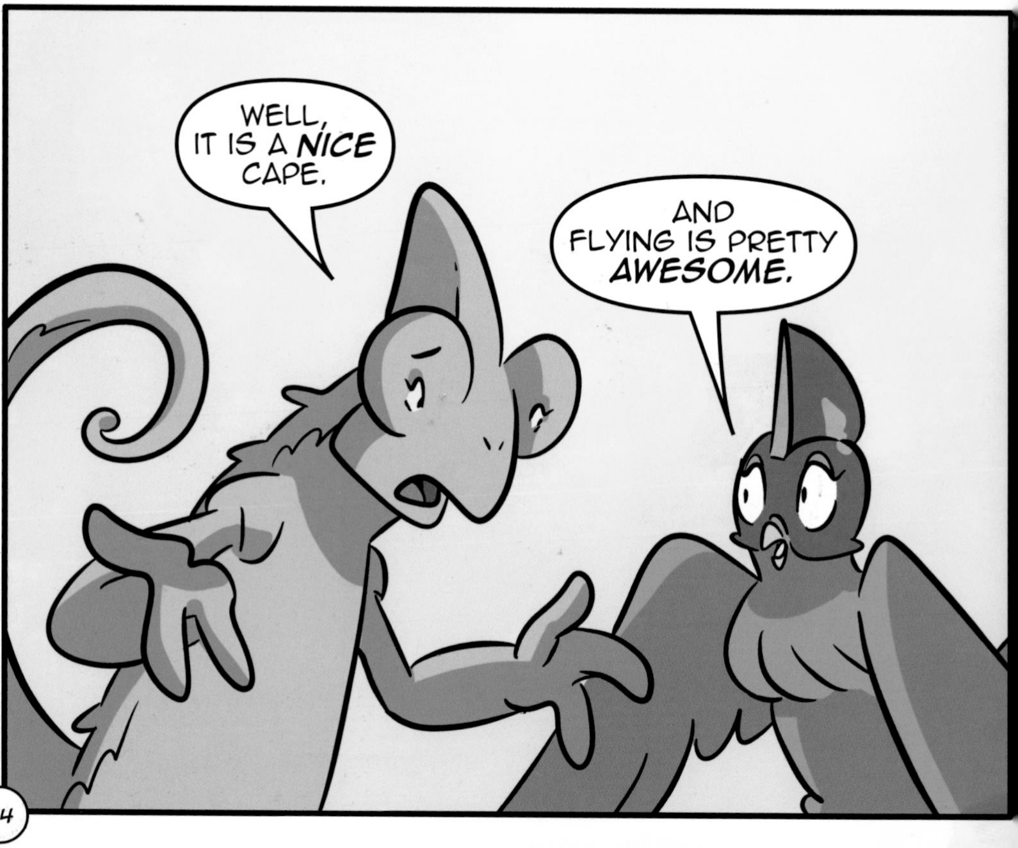
WELL, IT IS A **NICE** CAPE.
AND FLYING IS PRETTY **AWESOME.**

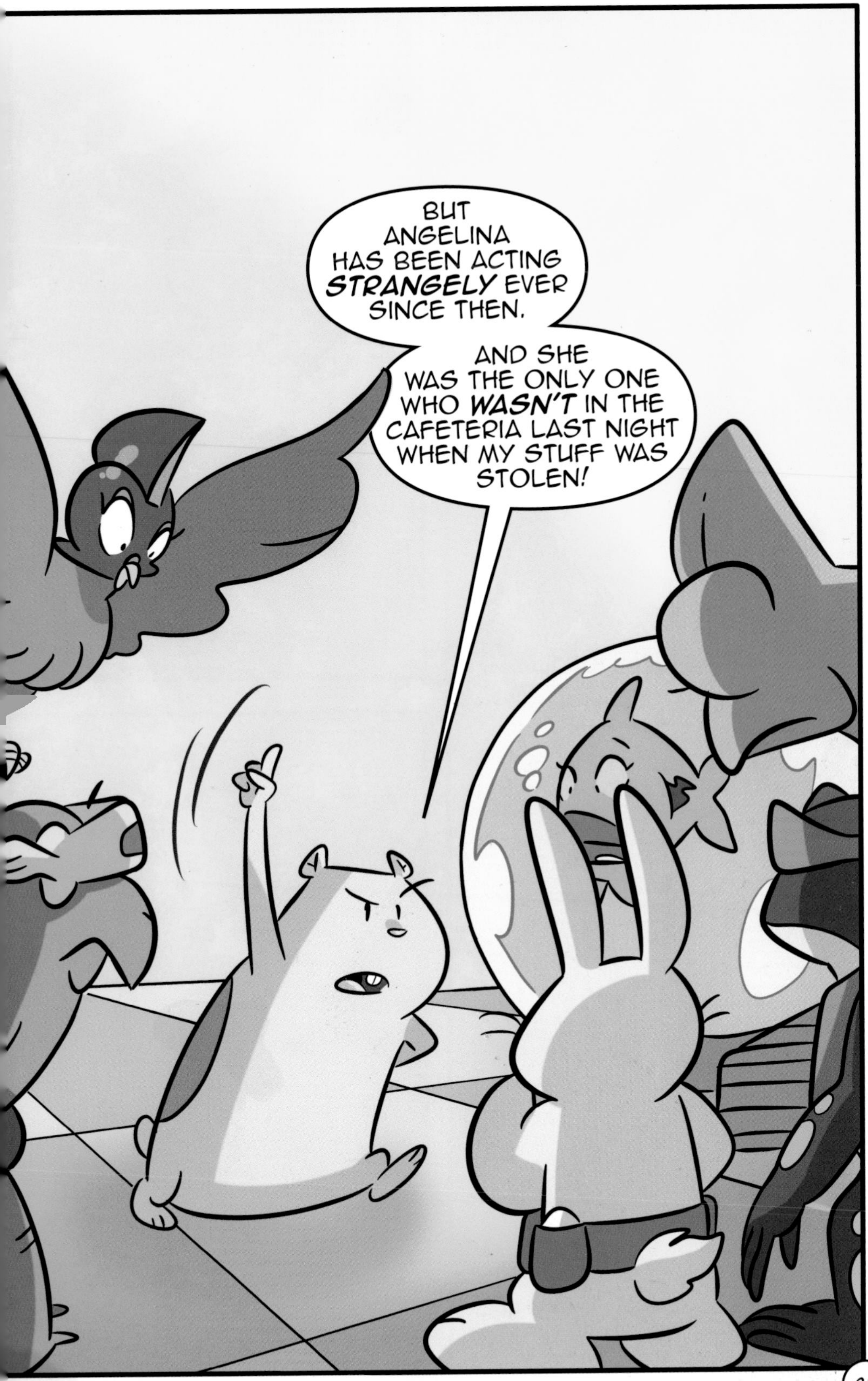
BUT ANGELINA HAS BEEN ACTING STRANGELY EVER SINCE THEN.
AND SHE WAS THE ONLY ONE WHO WASN'T IN THE CAFETERIA LAST NIGHT WHEN MY STUFF WAS STOLEN!

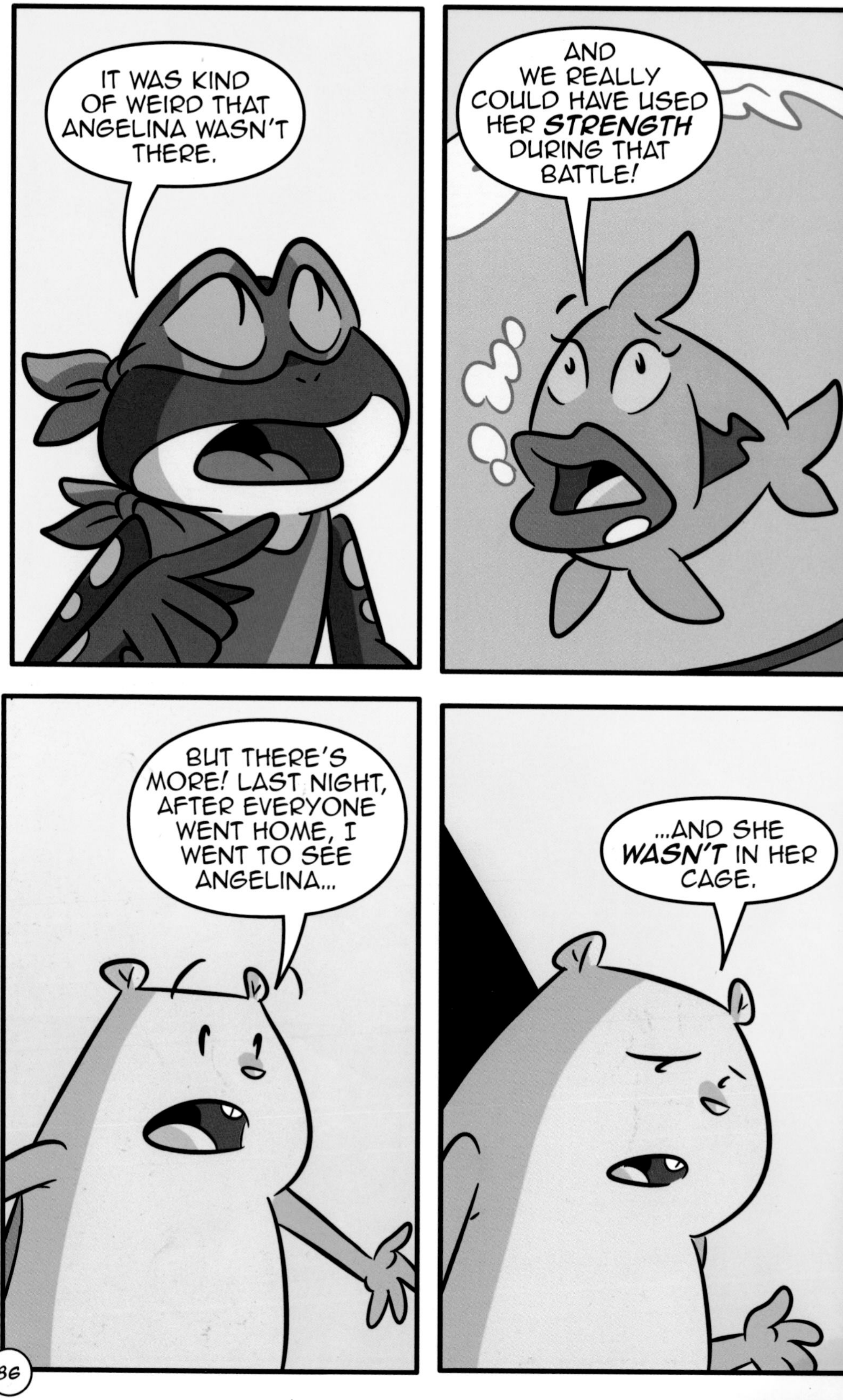
IT WAS KIND OF WEIRD THAT ANGELINA WASN'T THERE.
AND WE REALLY COULD HAVE USED HER **STRENGTH** DURING THAT BATTLE!
BUT THERE'S MORE! LAST NIGHT, AFTER EVERYONE WENT HOME, I WENT TO SEE ANGELINA...
...AND SHE **WASN'T** IN HER CAGE.

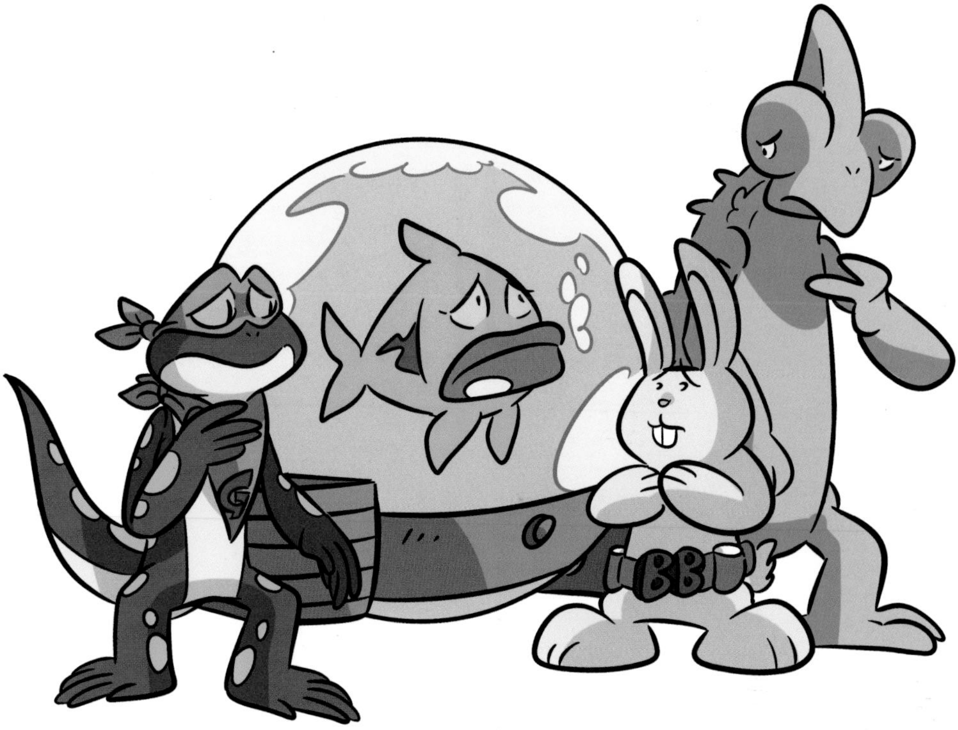

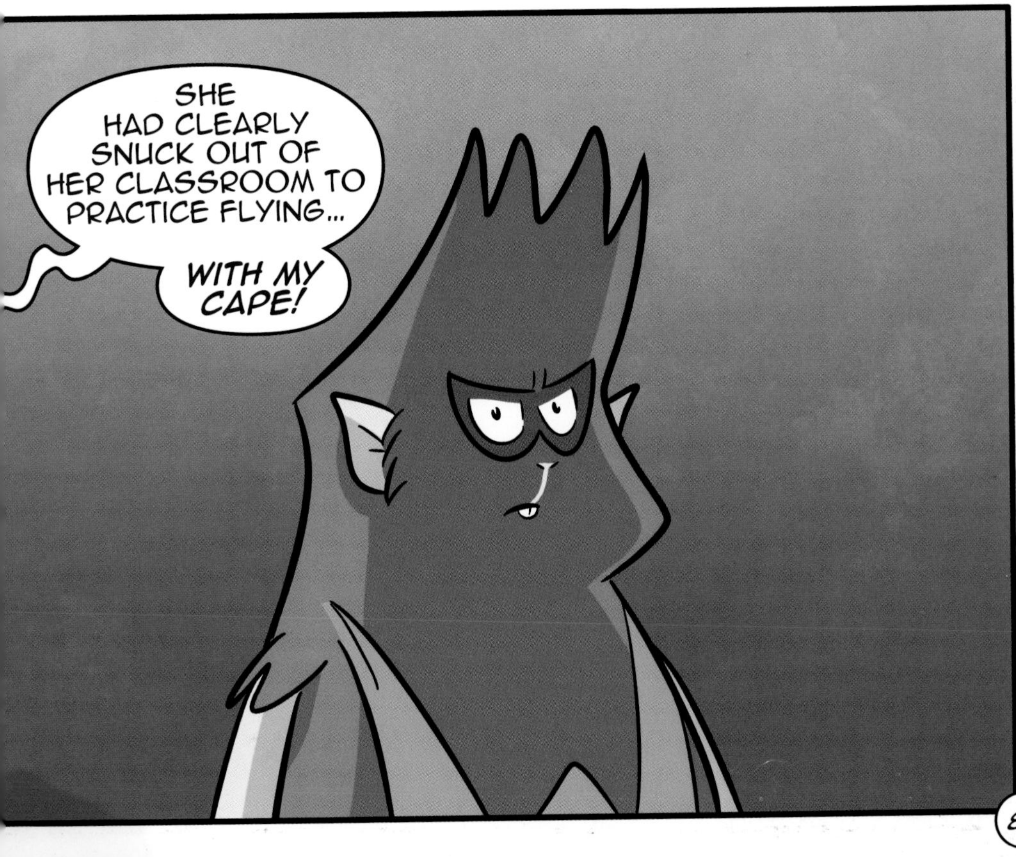
SHE HAD CLEARLY SNUCK OUT OF HER CLASSROOM TO PRACTICE FLYING...
WITH MY CAPE!

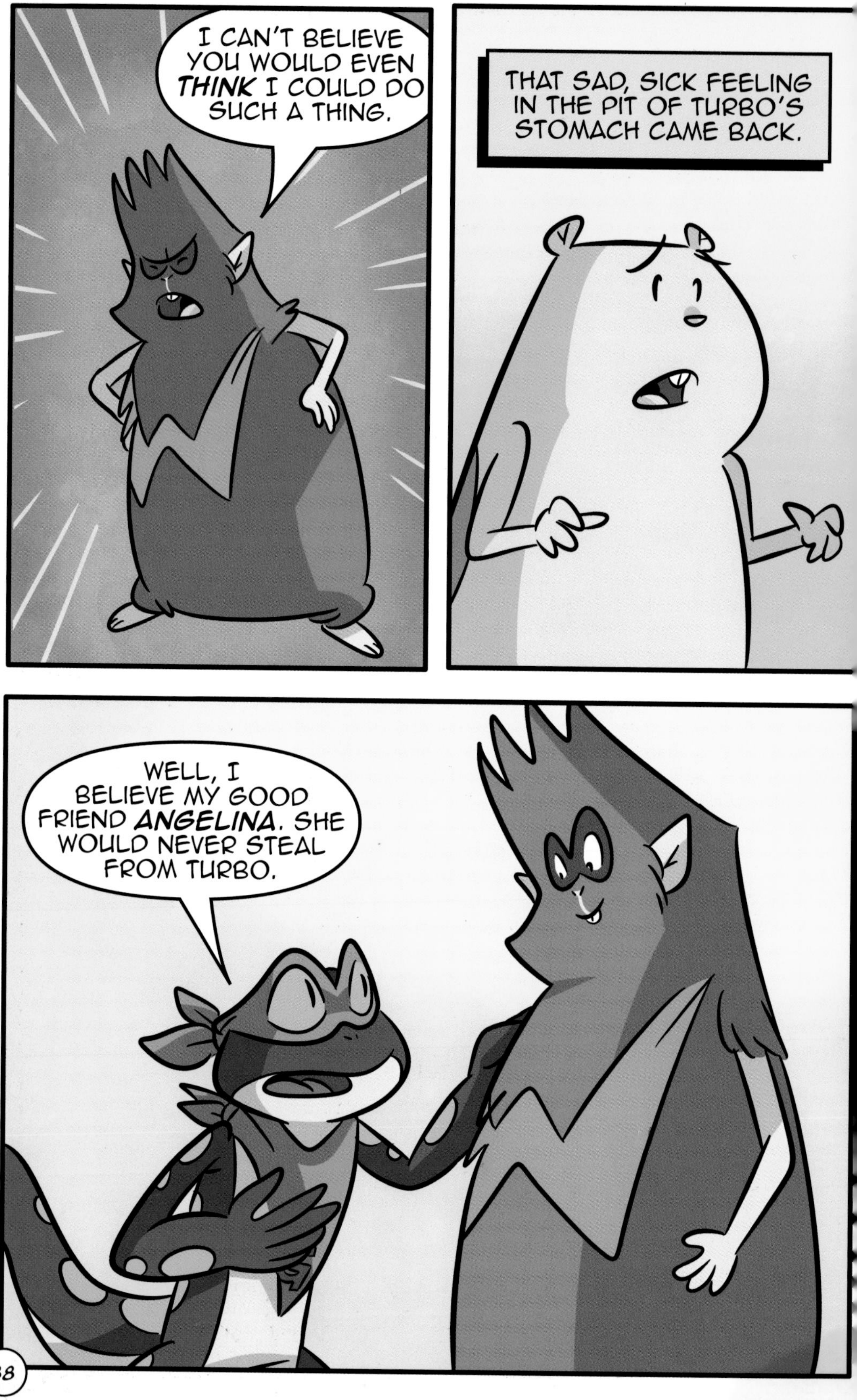
I CAN'T BELIEVE YOU WOULD EVEN *THINK* I COULD DO SUCH A THING.
THAT SAD, SICK FEELING IN THE PIT OF TURBO'S STOMACH CAME BACK.
WELL, I BELIEVE MY GOOD FRIEND *ANGELINA*. SHE WOULD NEVER STEAL FROM TURBO.

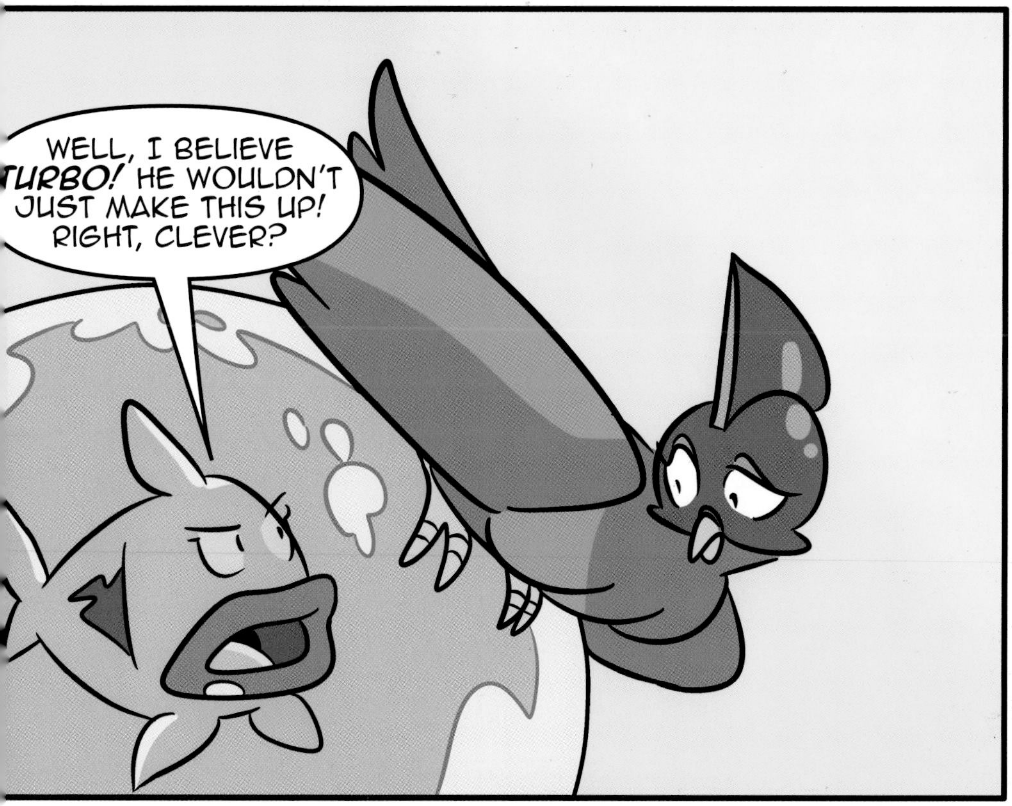
WELL, I BELIEVE TURBO! HE WOULDN'T JUST MAKE THIS UP! RIGHT, CLEVER?

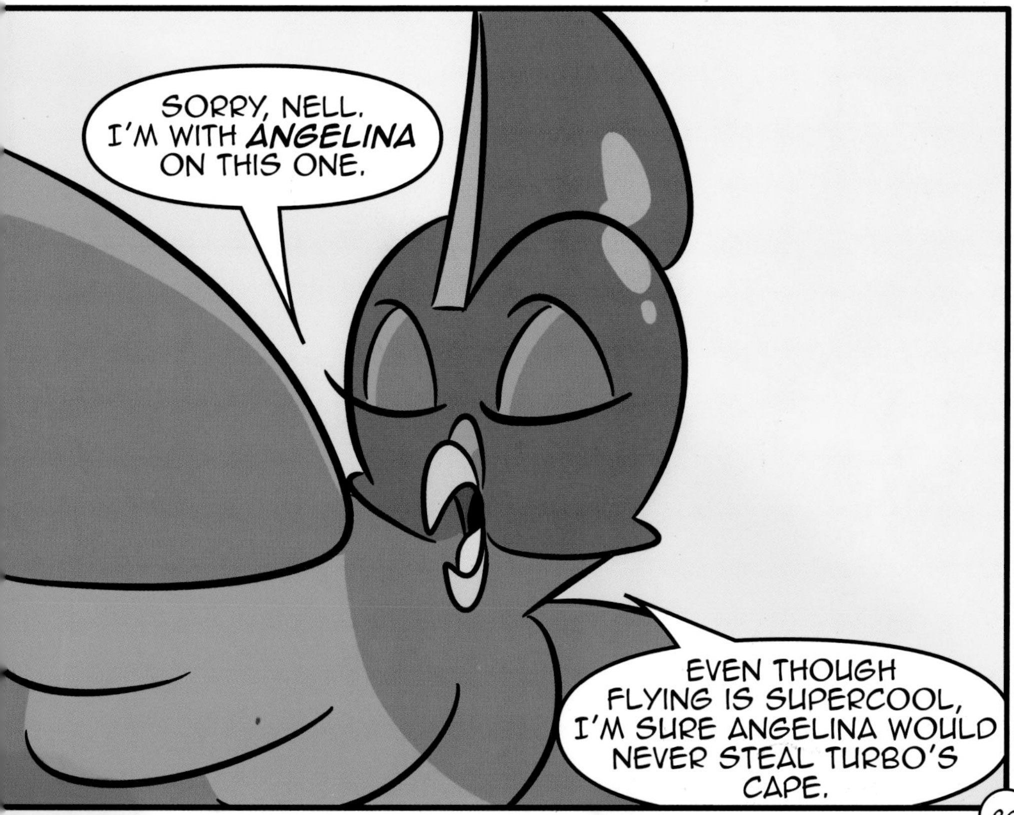
SORRY, NELL. I'M WITH ANGELINA ON THIS ONE.
EVEN THOUGH FLYING IS SUPERCOOL, I'M SURE ANGELINA WOULD NEVER STEAL TURBO'S CAPE.

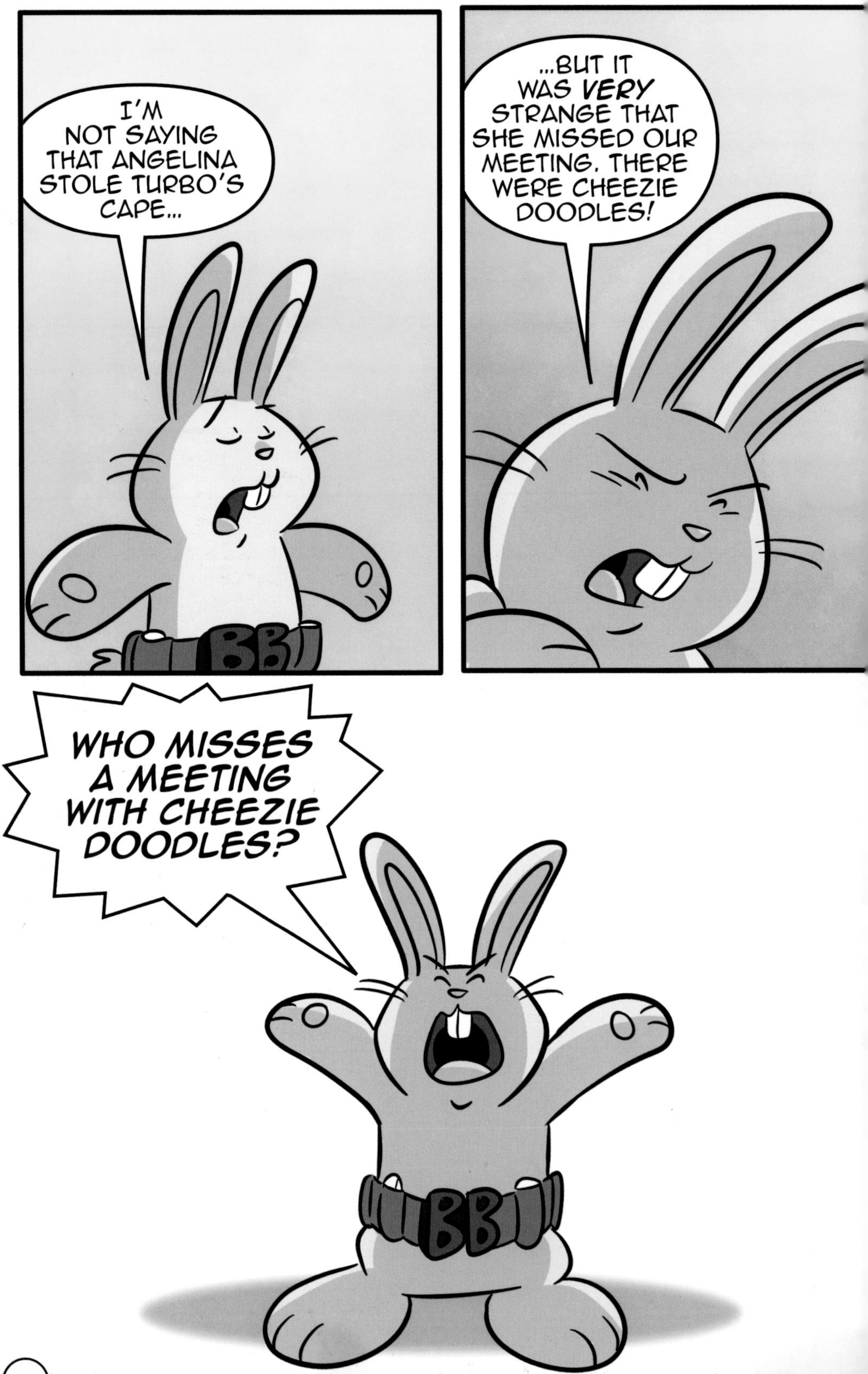
I'M NOT SAYING THAT ANGELINA STOLE TURBO'S CAPE...
...BUT IT WAS VERY STRANGE THAT SHE MISSED OUR MEETING. THERE WERE CHEEZIE DOODLES!
WHO MISSES A MEETING WITH CHEEZIE DOODLES?

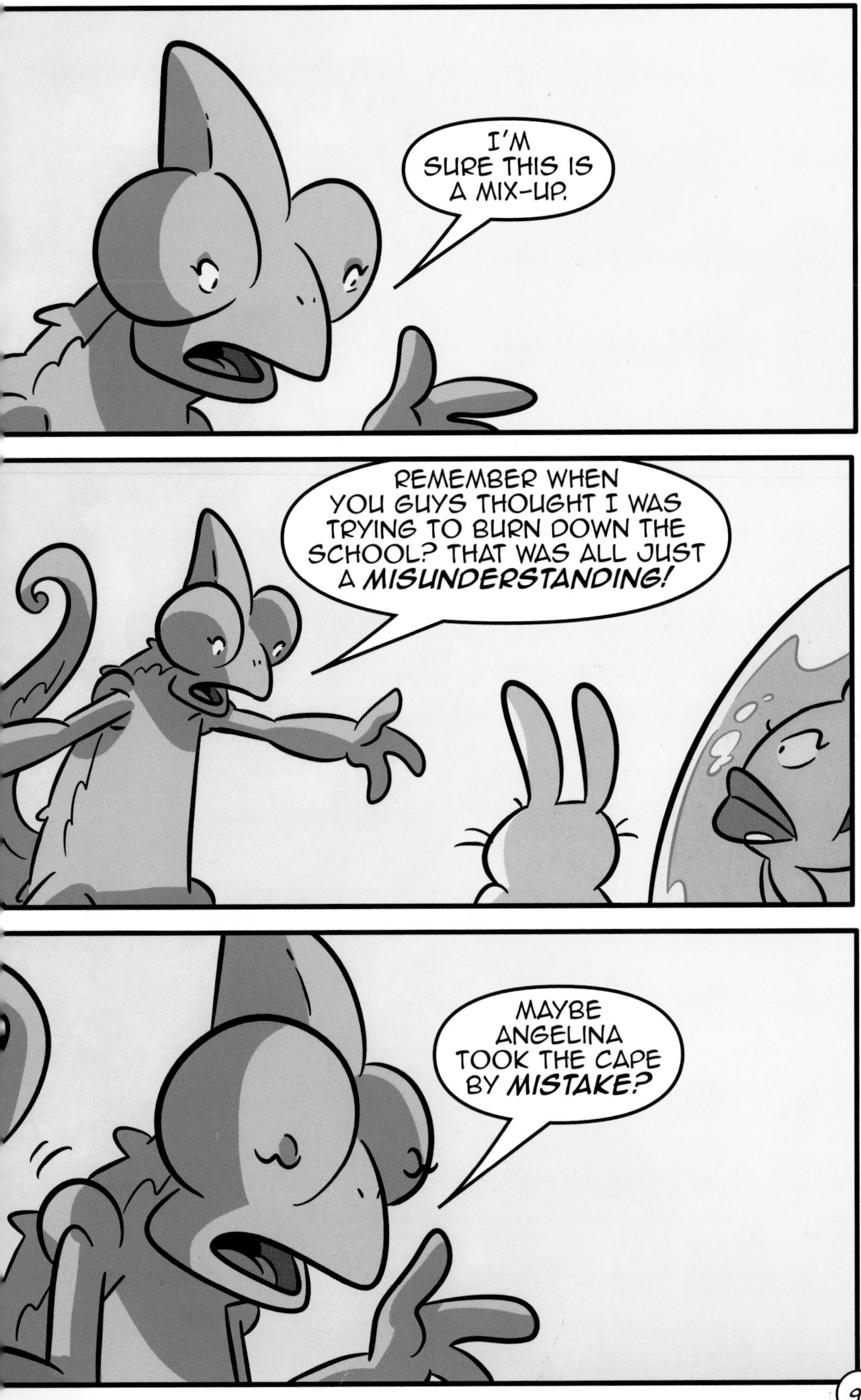
I'M SURE THIS IS A MIX-UP.
REMEMBER WHEN YOU GUYS THOUGHT I WAS TRYING TO BURN DOWN THE SCHOOL? THAT WAS ALL JUST A MISUNDERSTANDING!
MAYBE ANGELINA TOOK THE CAPE BY MISTAKE?

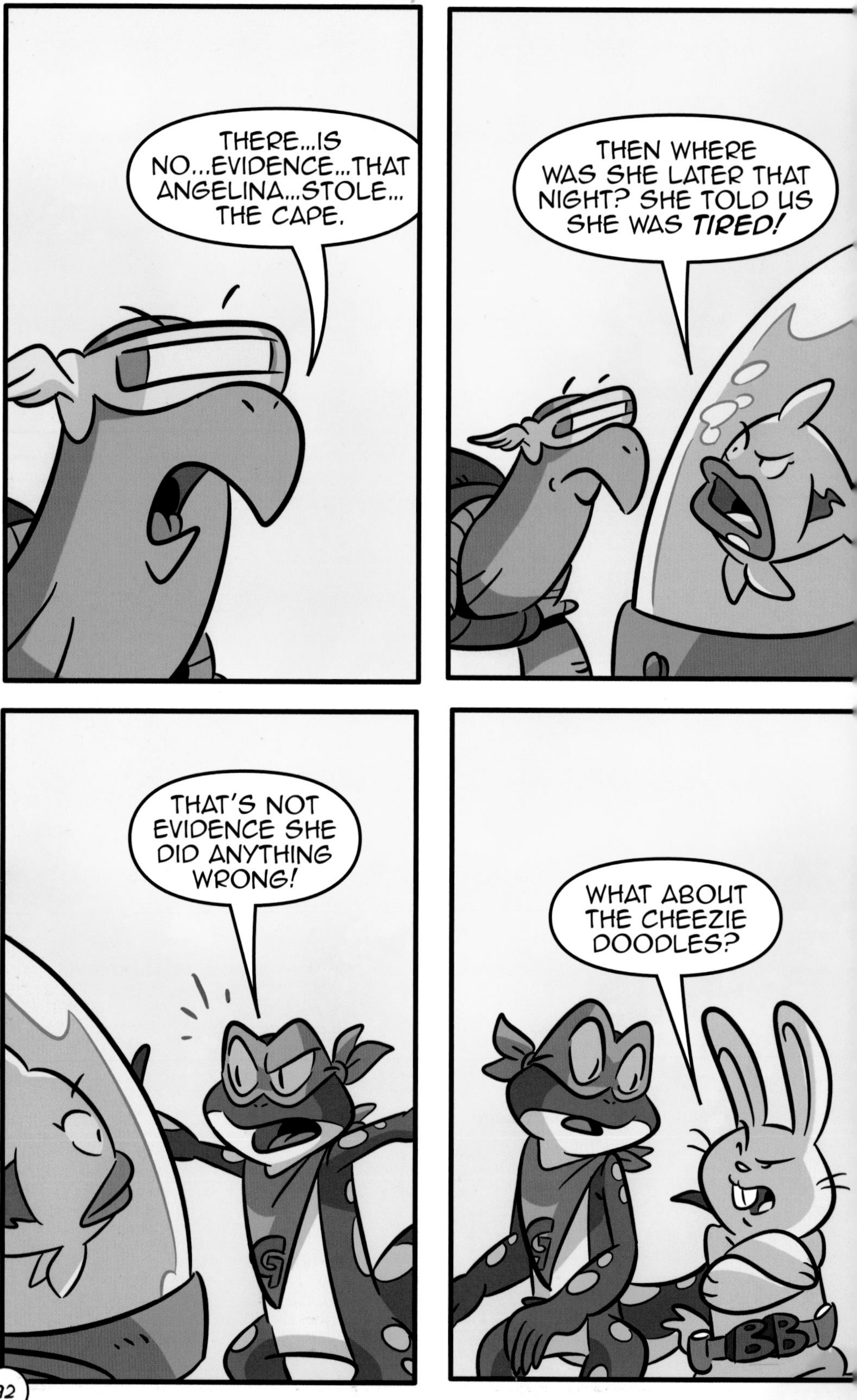
THERE...IS NO...EVIDENCE...THAT ANGELINA...STOLE... THE CAPE.
THEN WHERE WAS SHE LATER THAT NIGHT? SHE TOLD US SHE WAS *TIRED!*
THAT'S NOT EVIDENCE SHE DID ANYTHING WRONG!
WHAT ABOUT THE CHEEZIE DOODLES?
BB

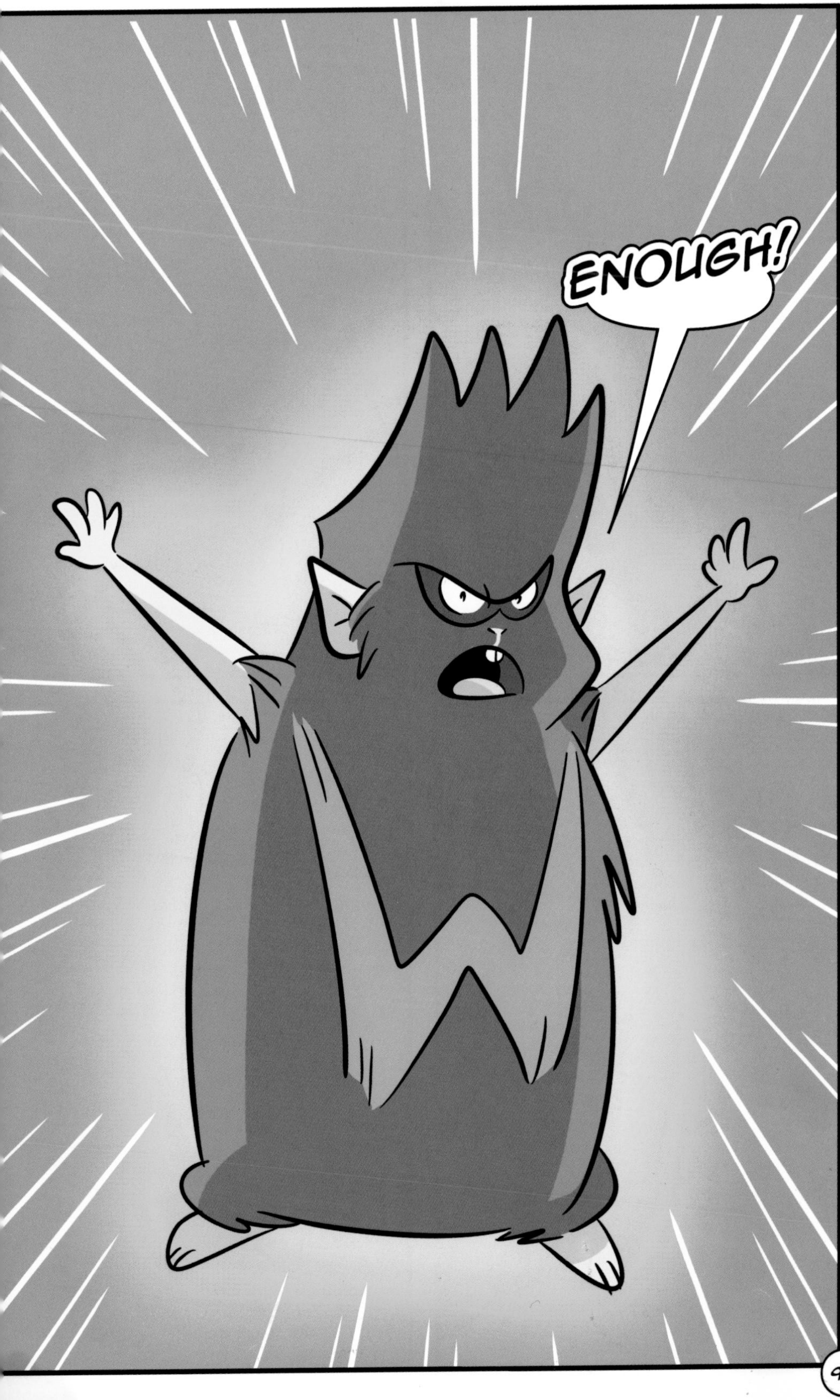
ENOUGH!

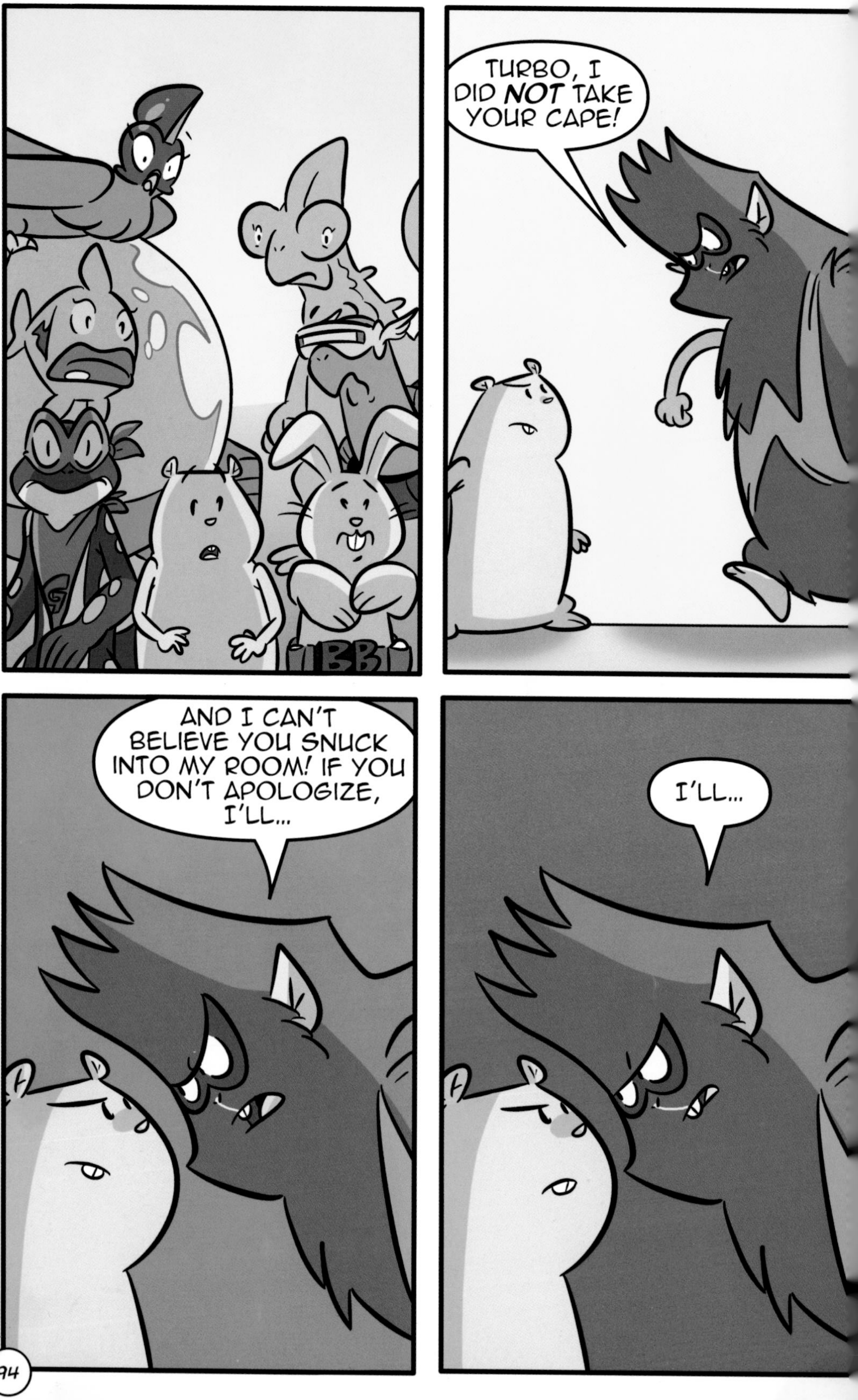
BB
TURBO, I DID NOT TAKE YOUR CAPE!
AND I CAN'T BELIEVE YOU SNUCK INTO MY ROOM! IF YOU DON'T APOLOGIZE, I'LL...
I'LL...

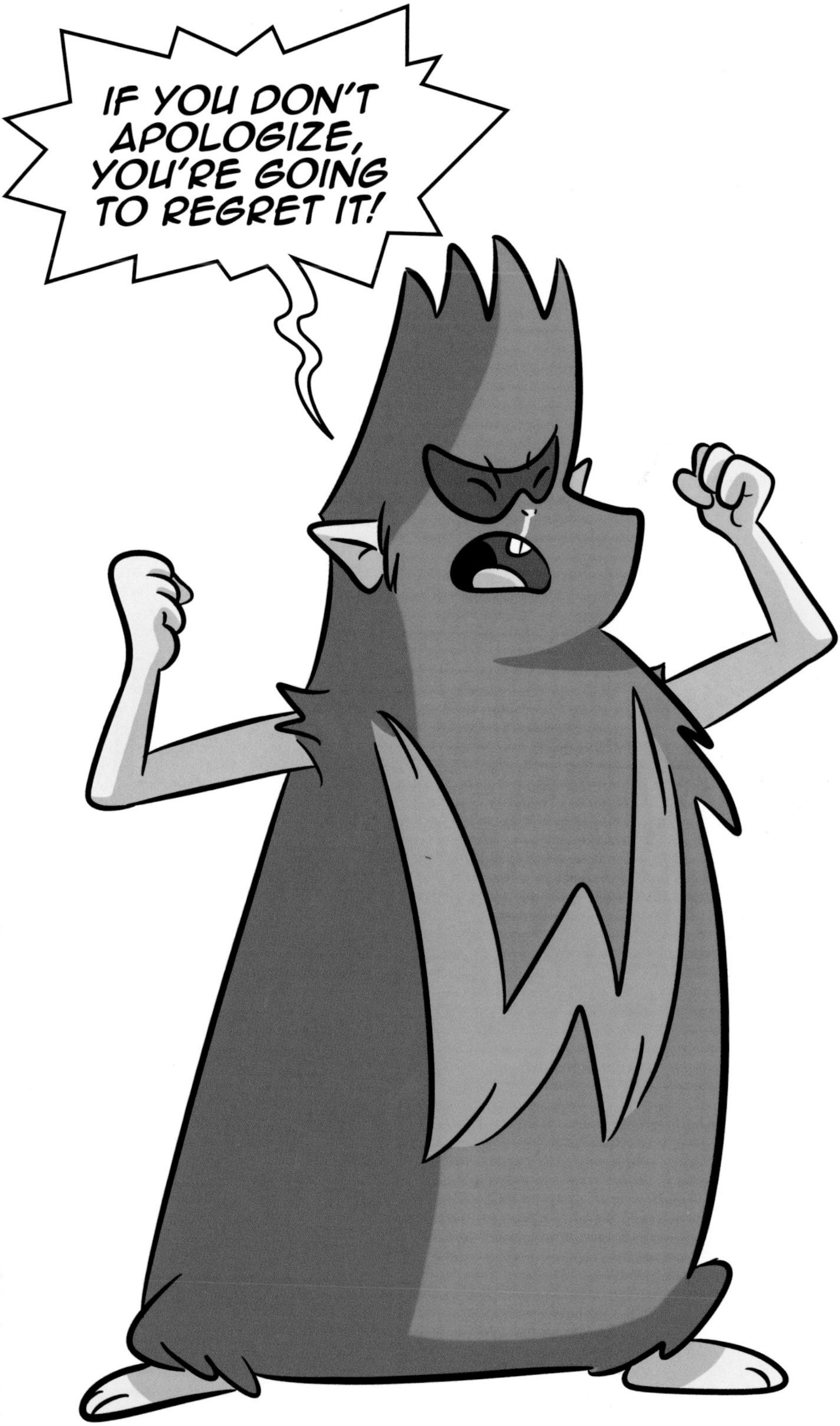
IF YOU DON'T APOLOGIZE, YOU'RE GOING TO REGRET IT!

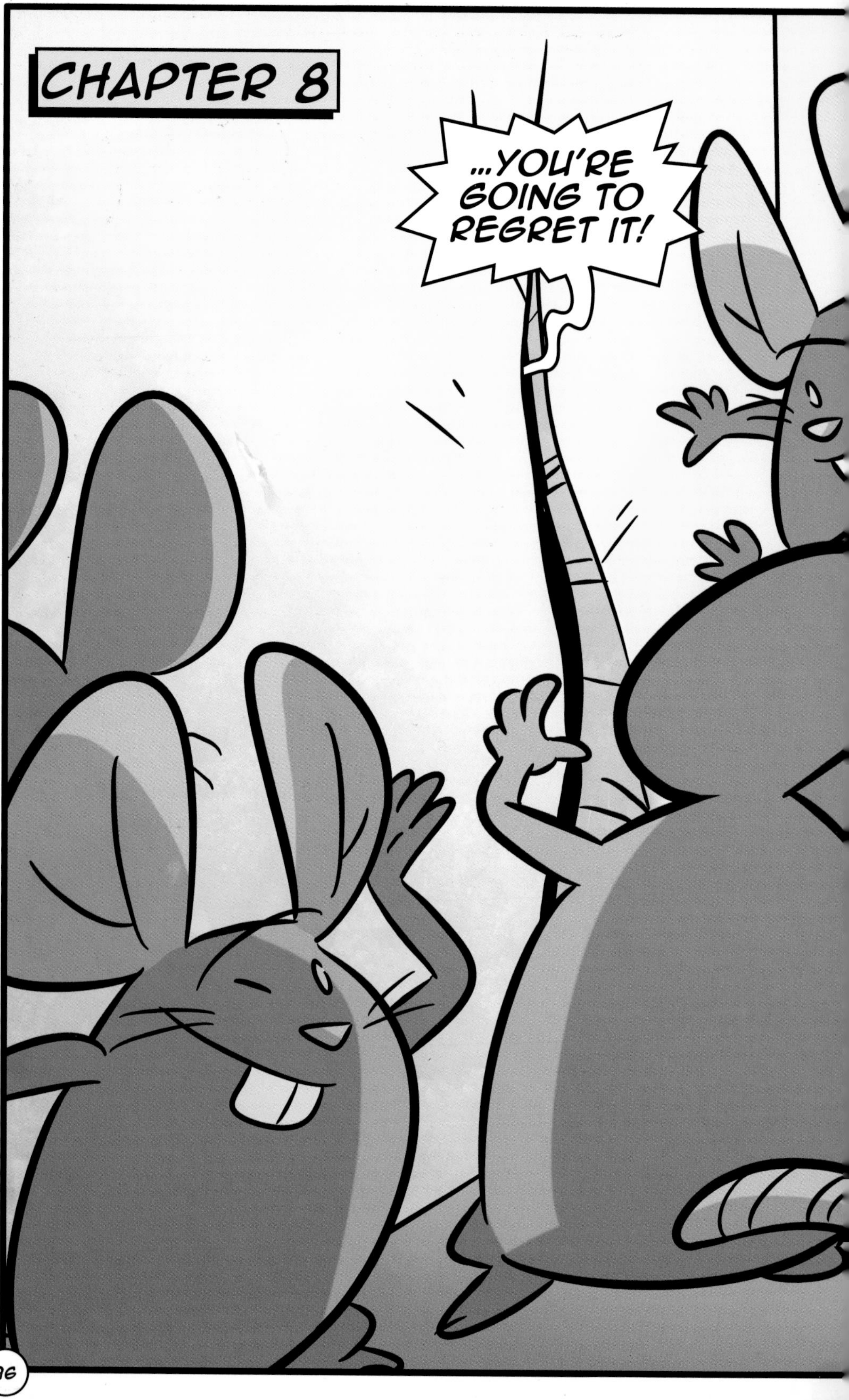
CHAPTER 8
...YOU'RE GOING TO REGRET IT!

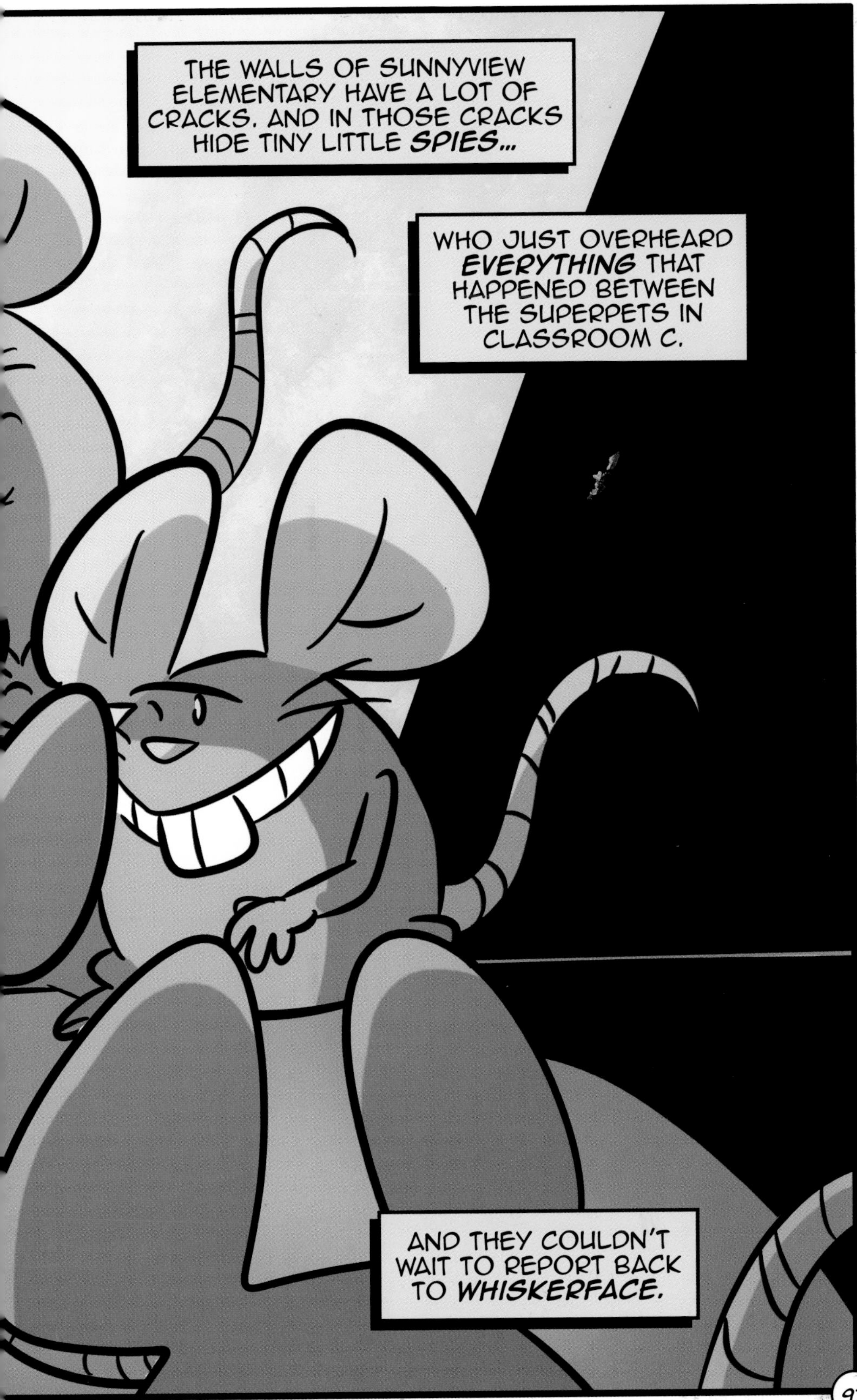
THE WALLS OF SUNNYVIEW ELEMENTARY HAVE A LOT OF CRACKS. AND IN THOSE CRACKS HIDE TINY LITTLE SPIES...
WHO JUST OVERHEARD EVERYTHING THAT HAPPENED BETWEEN THE SUPERPETS IN CLASSROOM C.
AND THEY COULDN'T WAIT TO REPORT BACK TO WHISKERFACE.

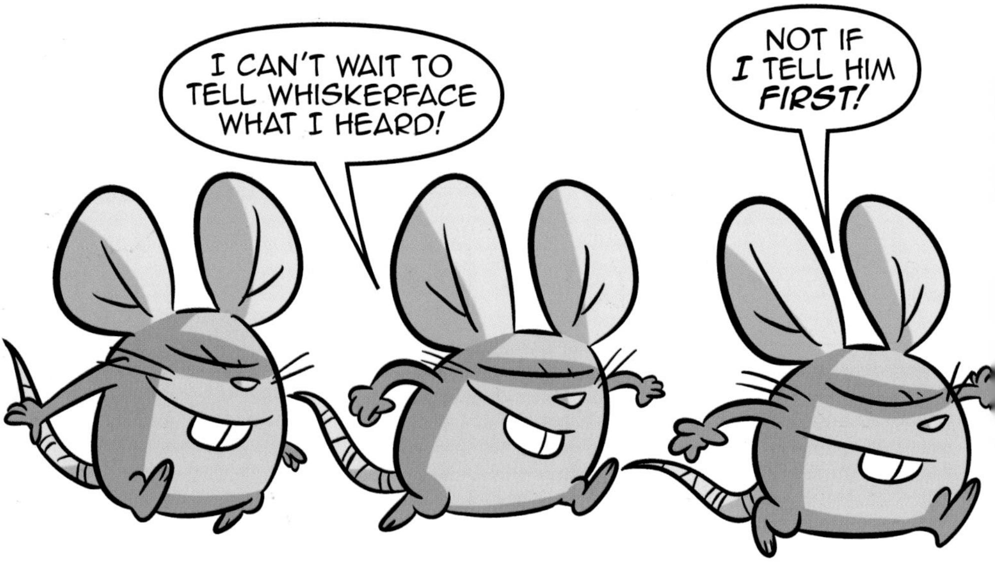
I CAN'T WAIT TO TELL WHISKERFACE WHAT I HEARD!
NOT IF I TELL HIM FIRST!

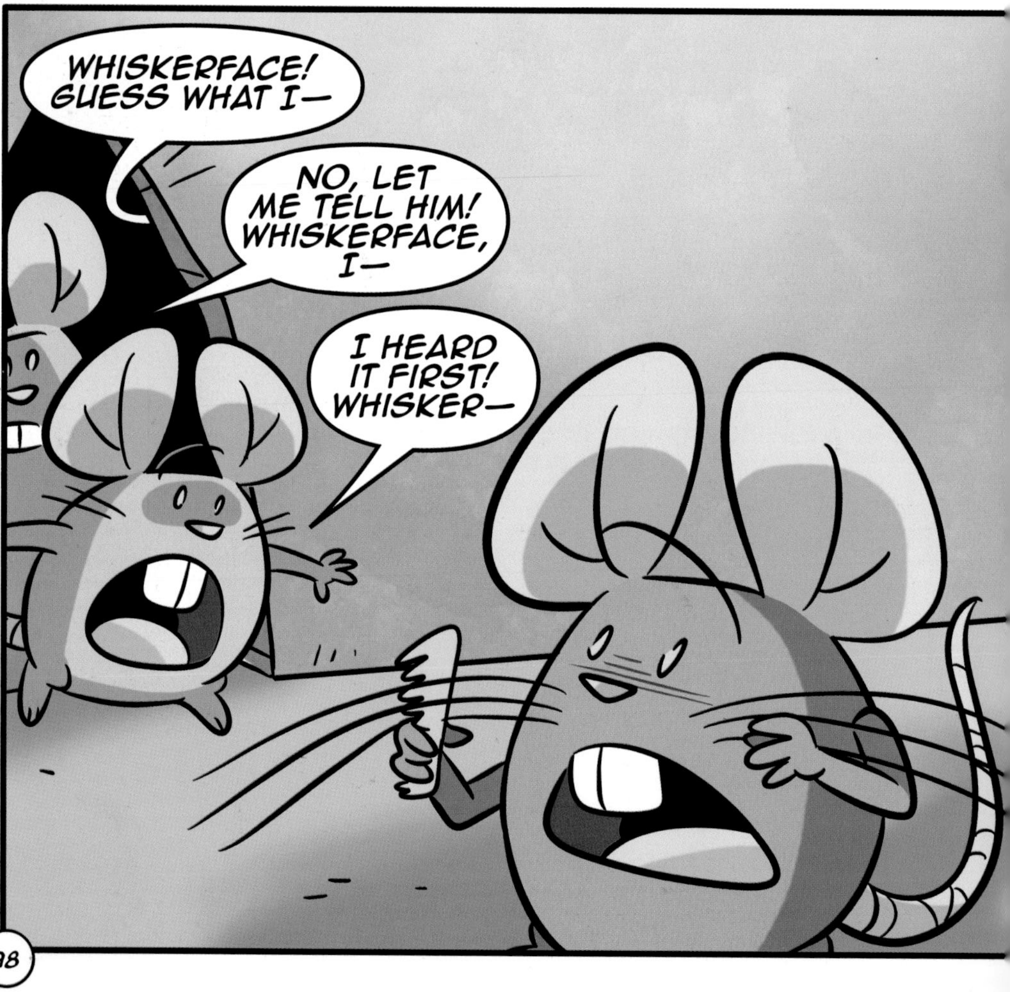
WHISKERFACE! GUESS WHAT I—
NO, LET ME TELL HIM! WHISKERFACE, I—
I HEARD IT FIRST! WHISKER—

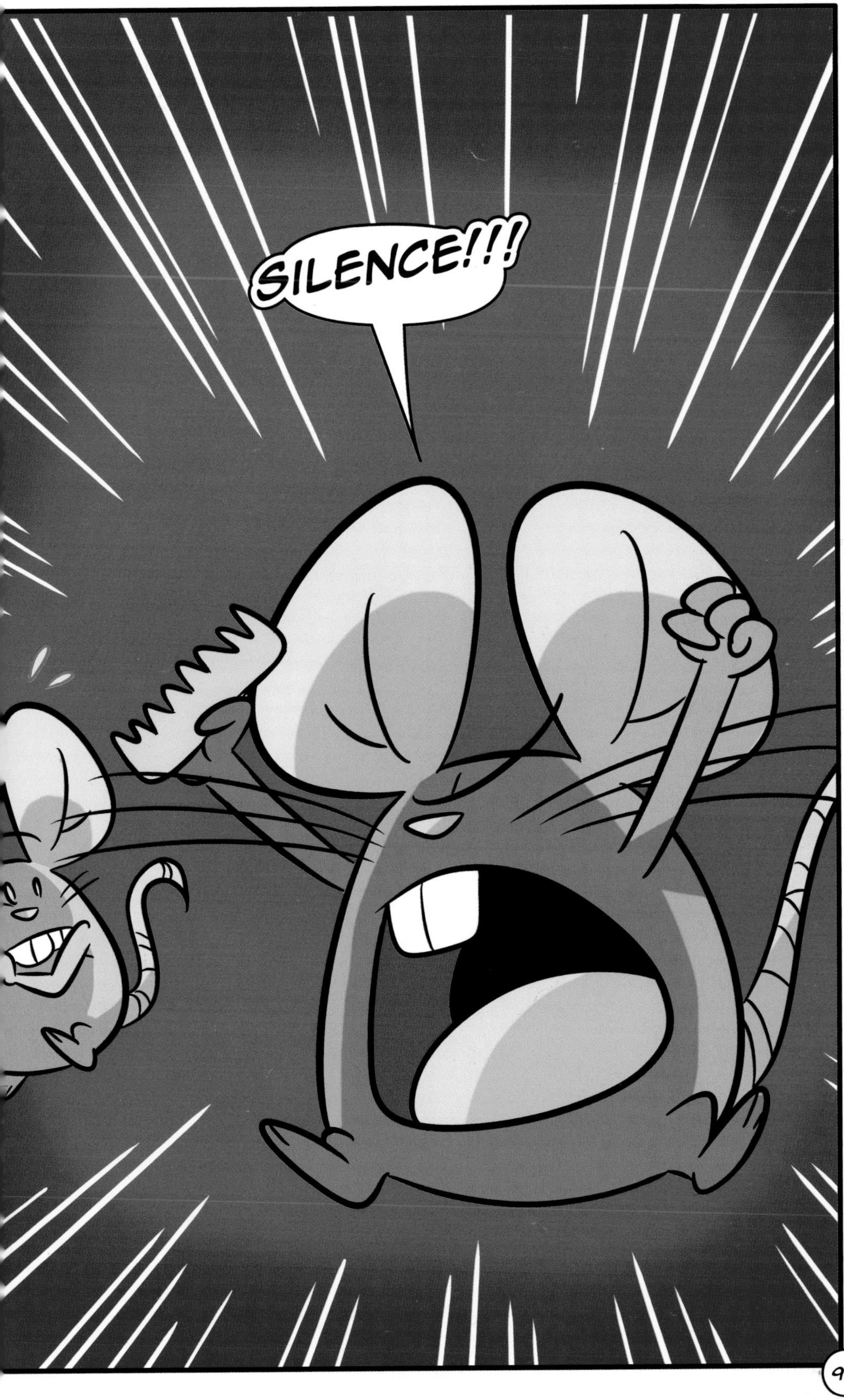
SILENCE!!!

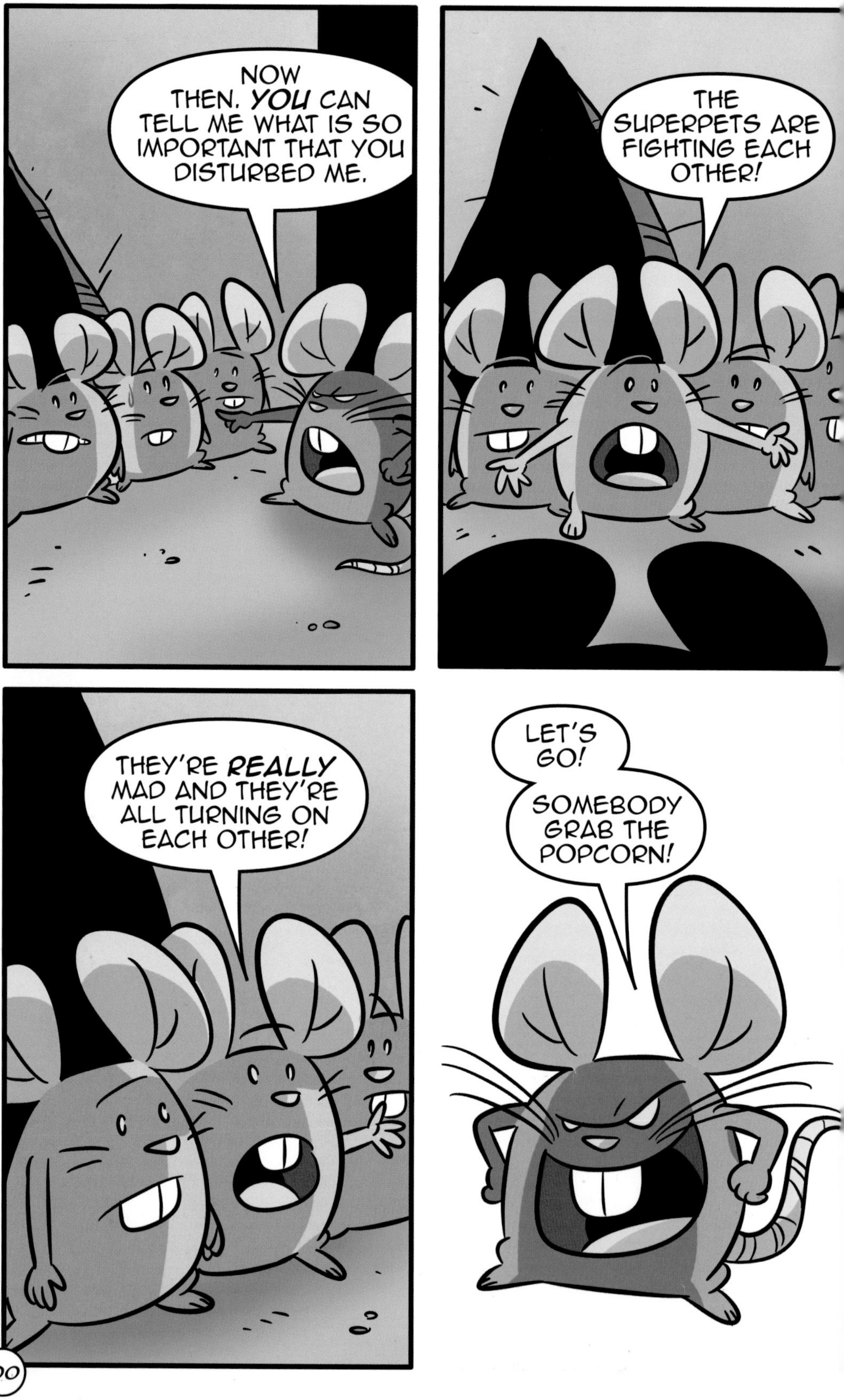
NOW THEN. YOU CAN TELL ME WHAT IS SO IMPORTANT THAT YOU DISTURBED ME.
THE SUPERPETS ARE FIGHTING EACH OTHER!
THEY'RE REALLY MAD AND THEY'RE ALL TURNING ON EACH OTHER!
LET'S GO!
SOMEBODY GRAB THE POPCORN!

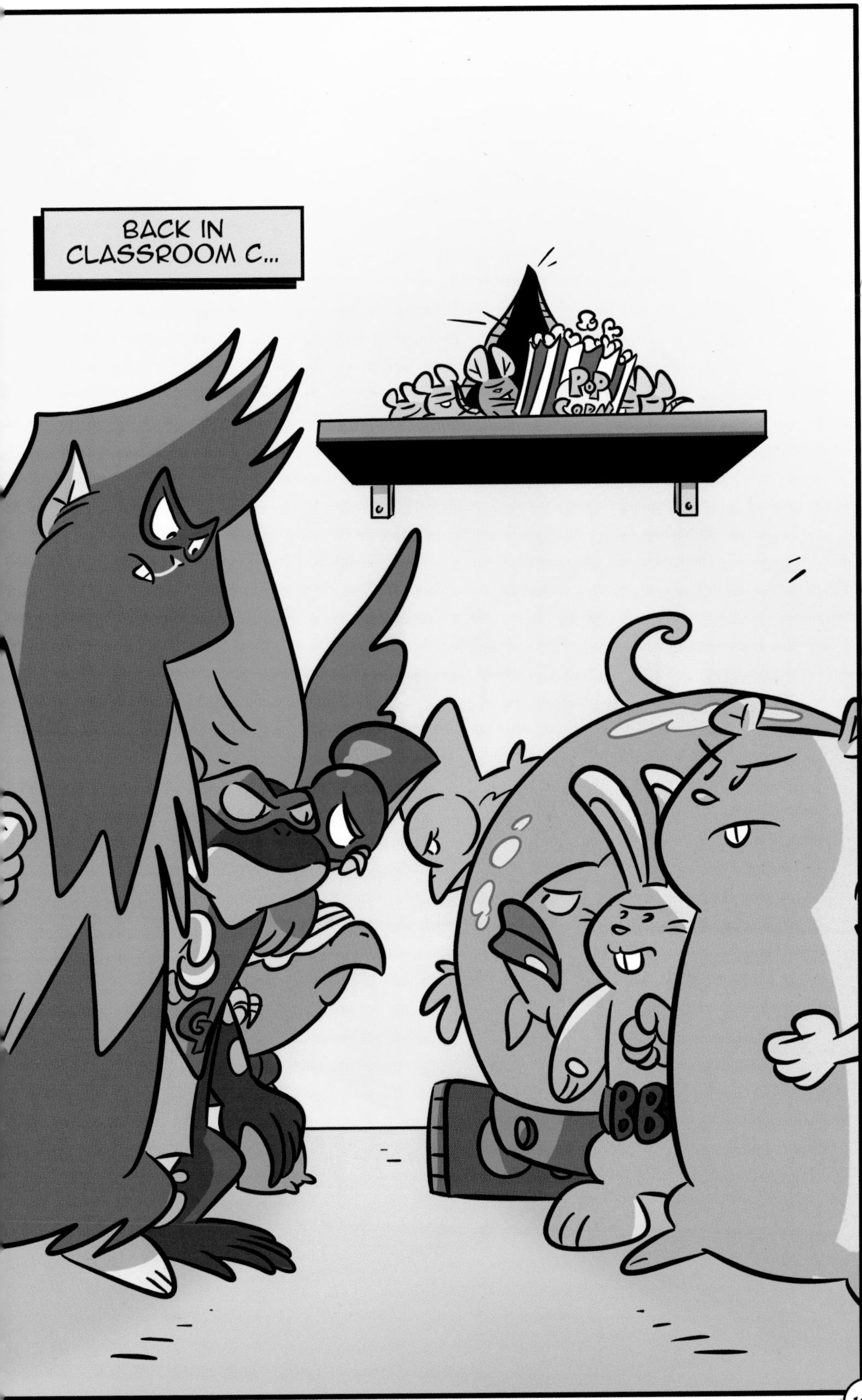
BACK IN CLASSROOM C...
POP CORN

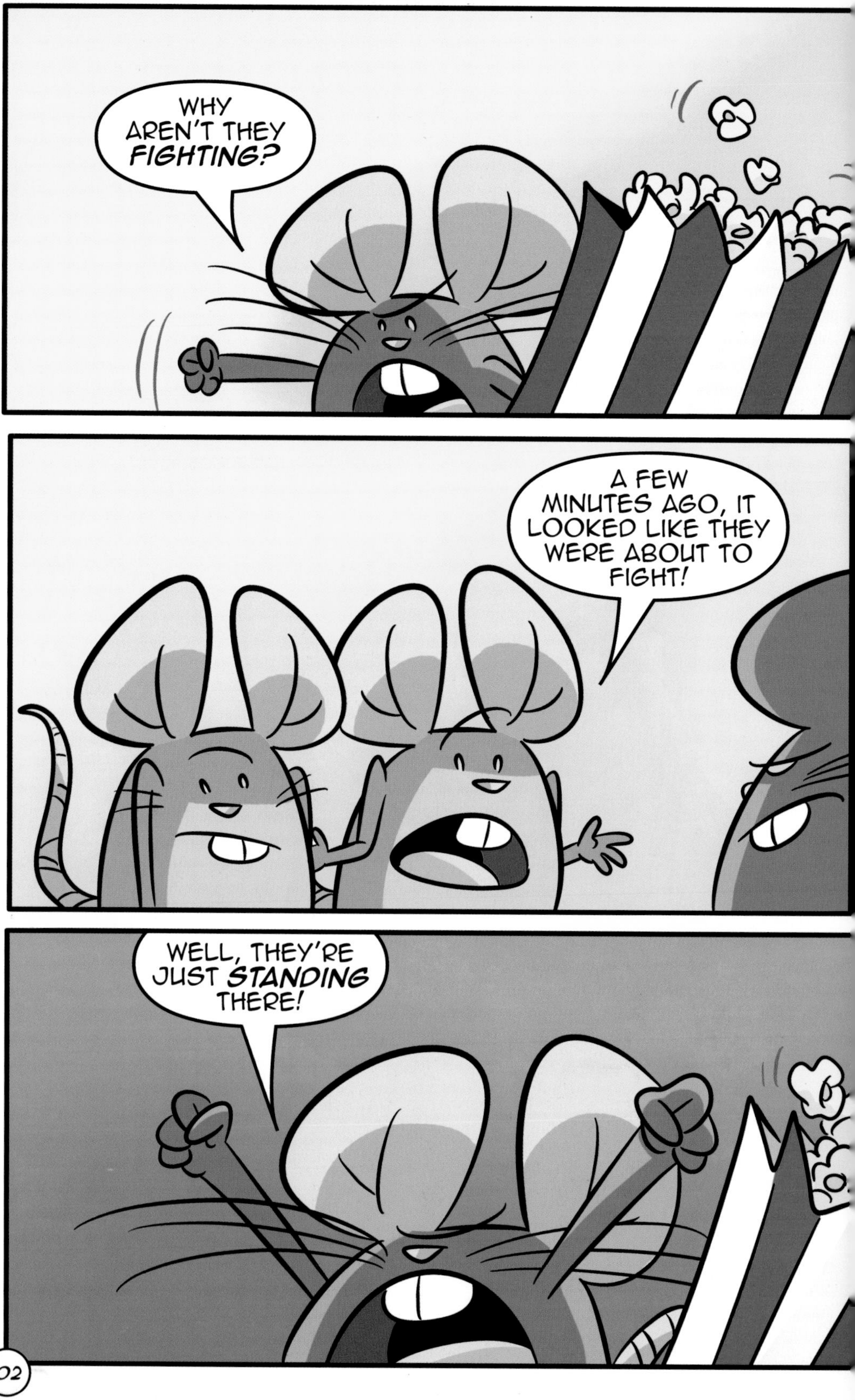
WHY AREN'T THEY *FIGHTING?*
A FEW MINUTES AGO, IT LOOKED LIKE THEY WERE ABOUT TO FIGHT!
WELL, THEY'RE JUST *STANDING* THERE!

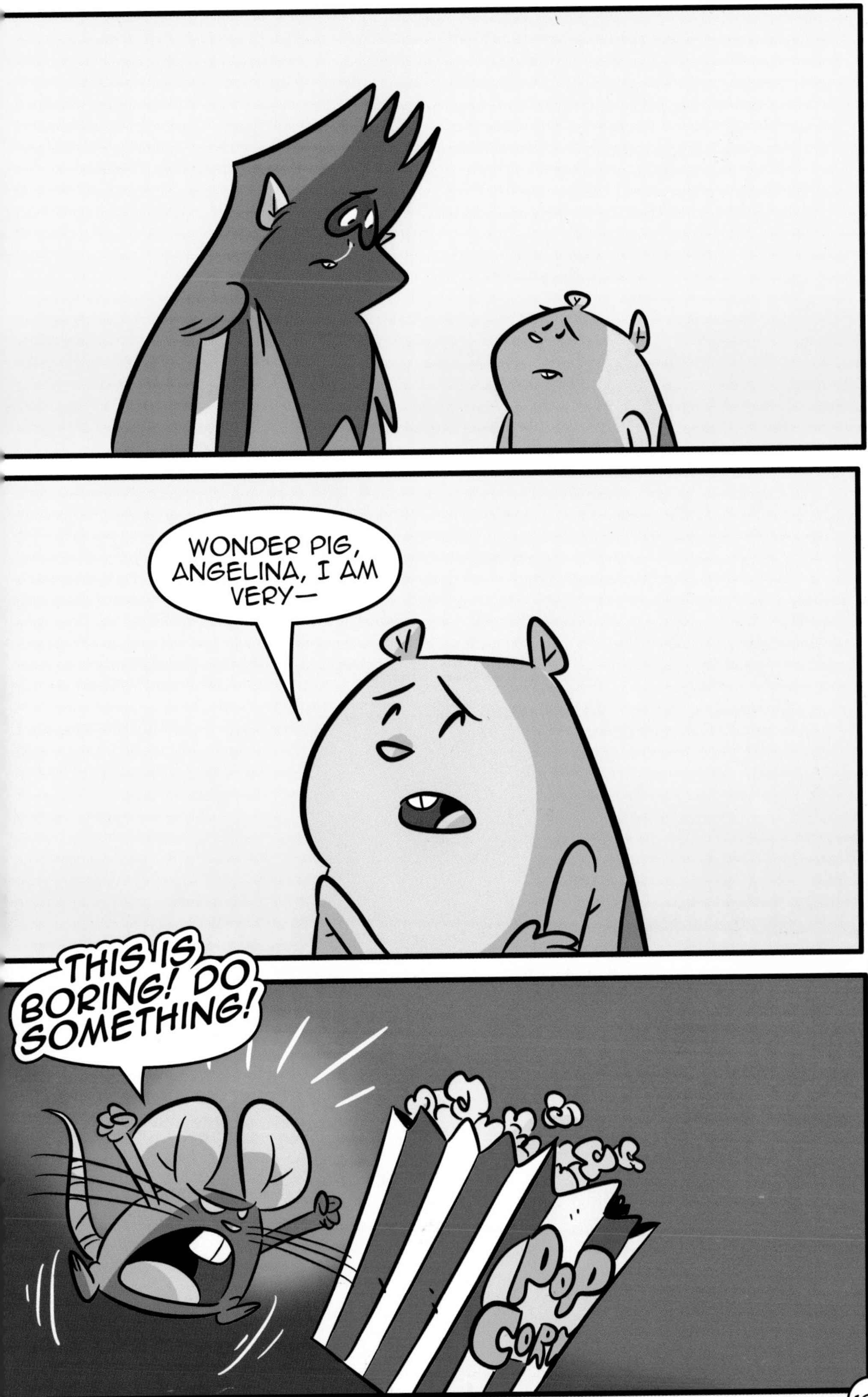
WONDER PIG, ANGELINA, I AM VERY—
THIS IS BORING! DO SOMETHING!
POP CORN

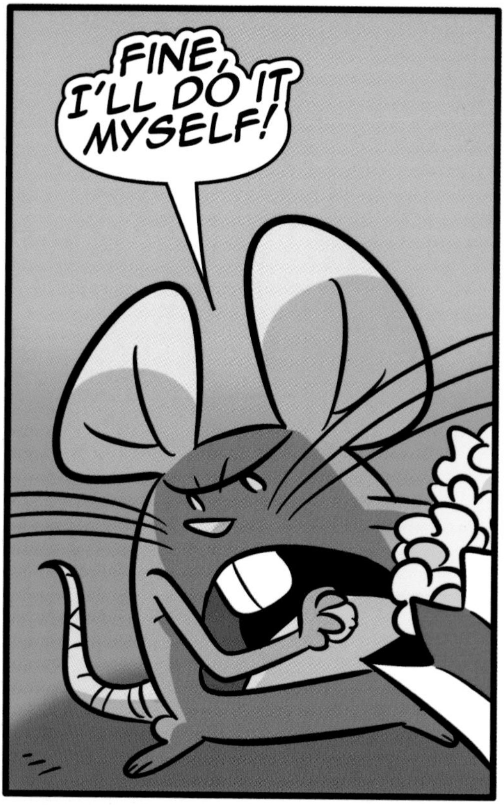
FINE, I'LL DO IT MYSELF!

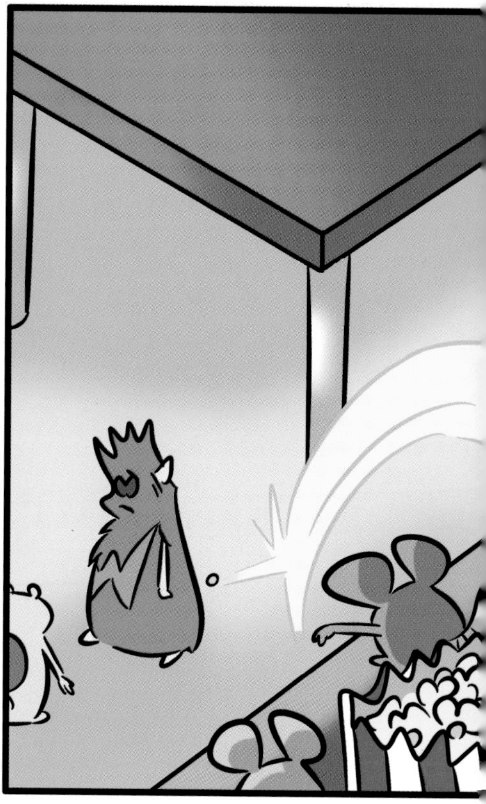

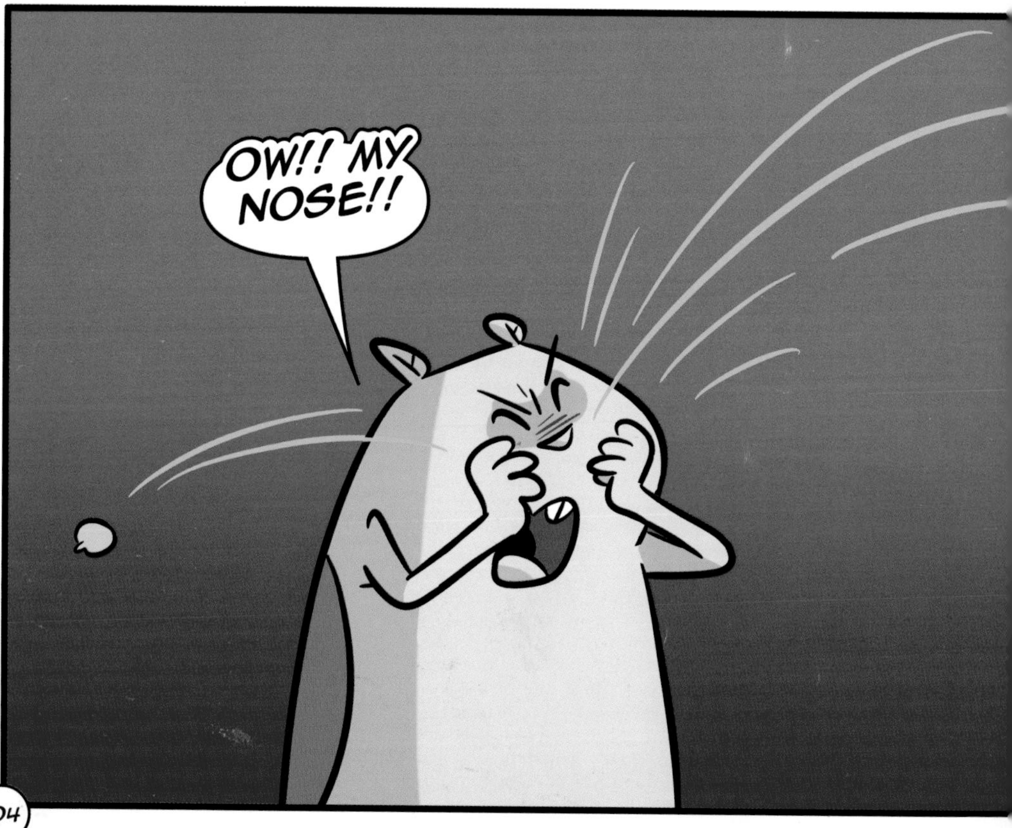
OW!! MY NOSE!!

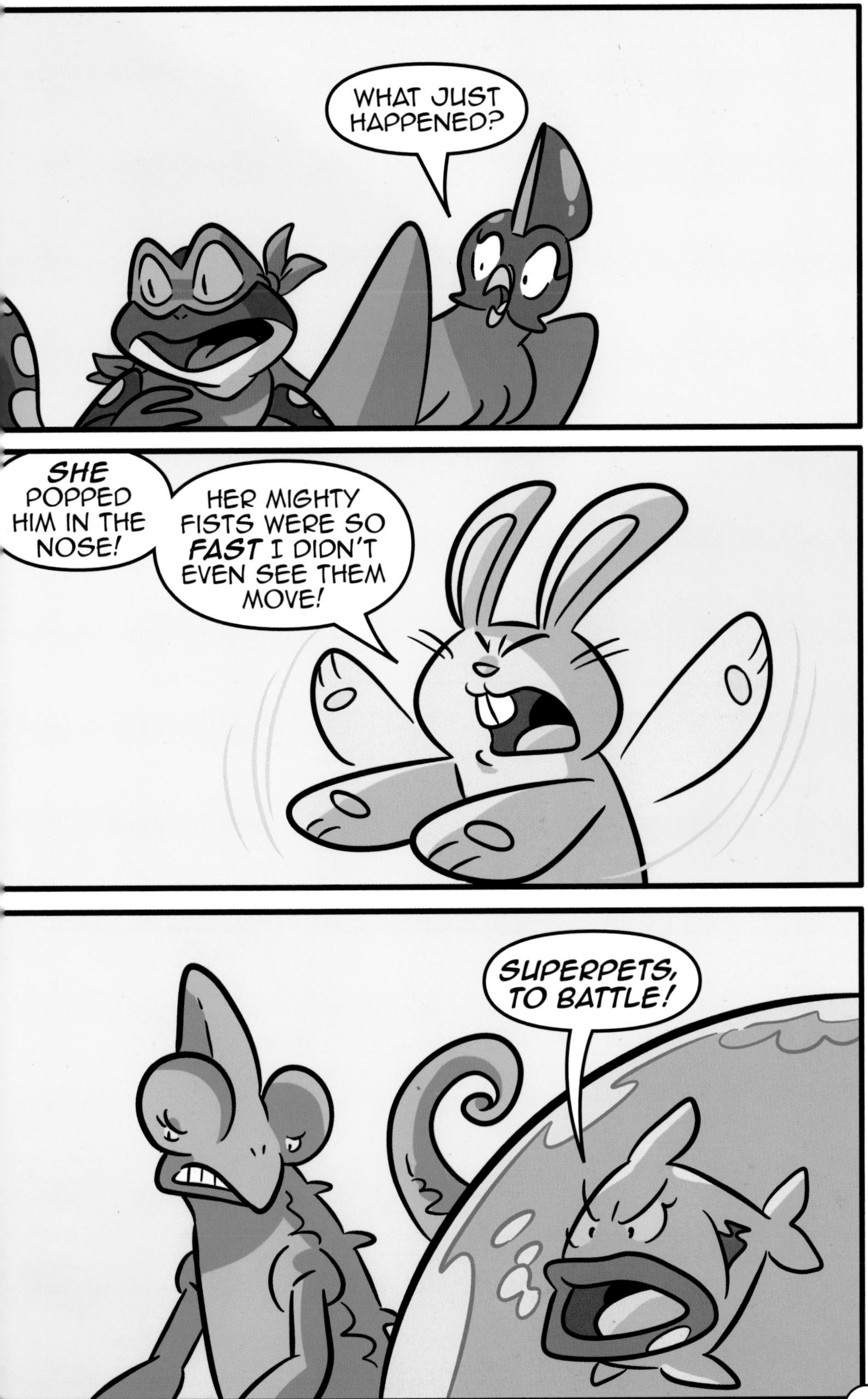
WHAT JUST HAPPENED?
SHE POPPED HIM IN THE NOSE!
HER MIGHTY FISTS WERE SO FAST I DIDN'T EVEN SEE THEM MOVE!
SUPERPETS, TO BATTLE!

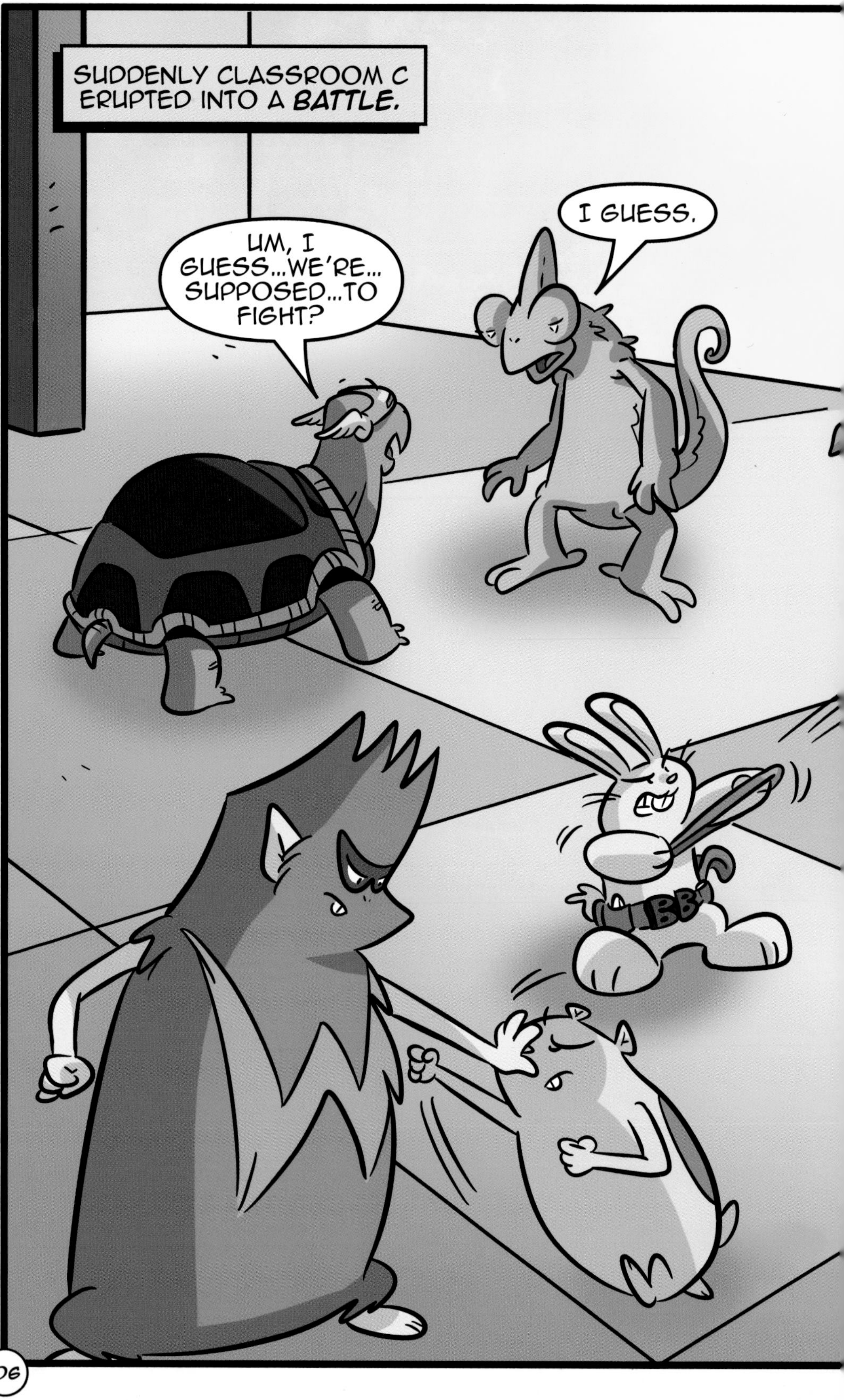
SUDDENLY CLASSROOM C ERUPTED INTO A *BATTLE.*
UM, I GUESS...WE'RE... SUPPOSED...TO FIGHT?
I GUESS.
BB

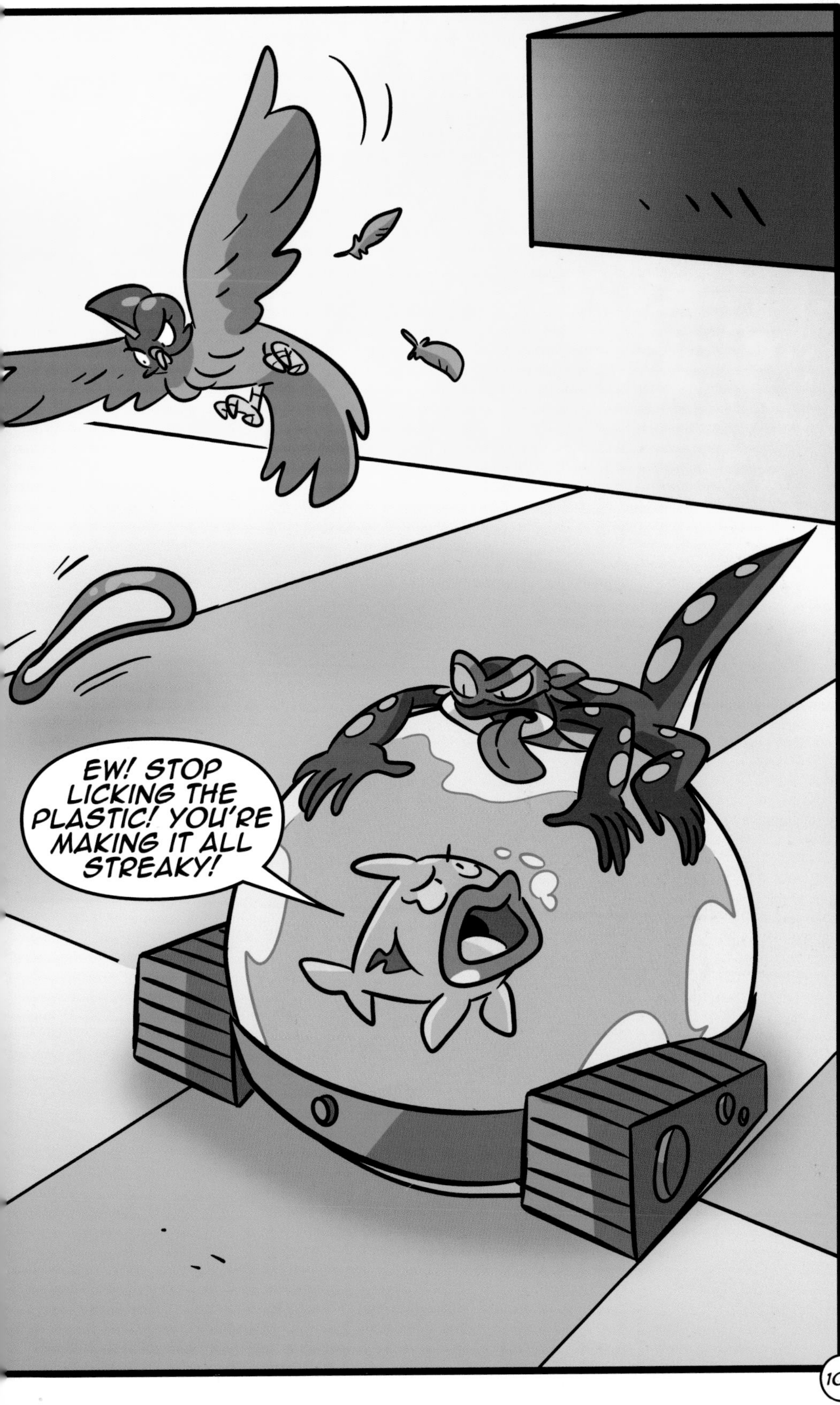
EW! STOP LICKING THE PLASTIC! YOU'RE MAKING IT ALL STREAKY!

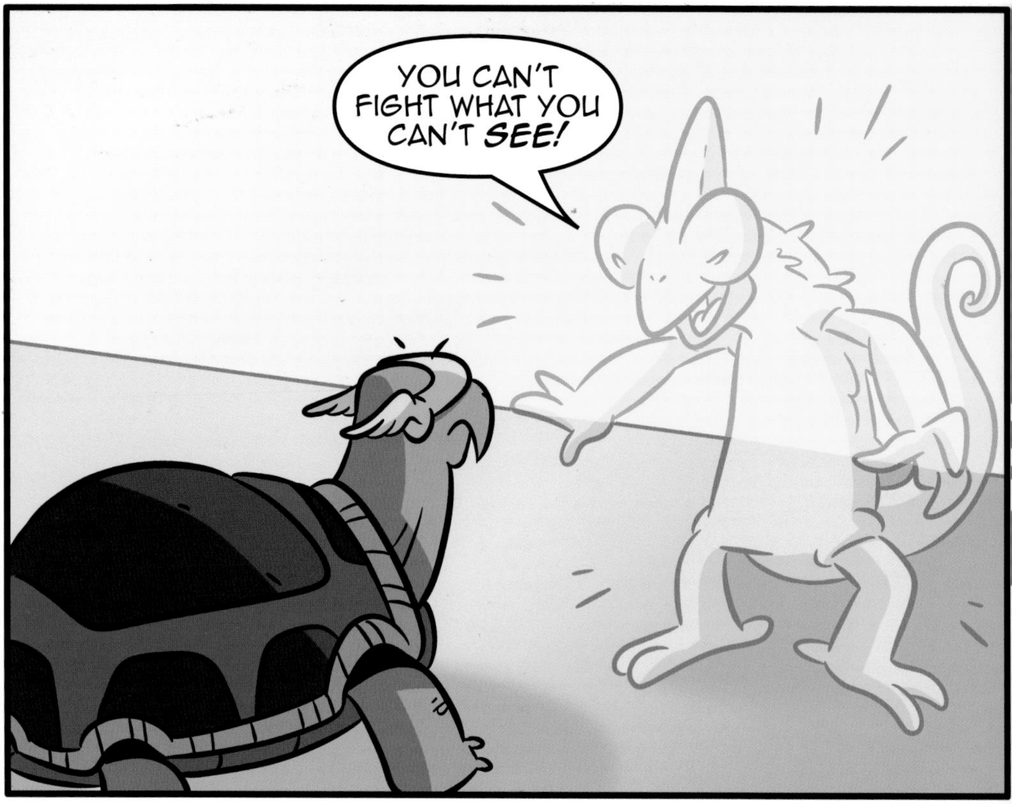
YOU CAN'T FIGHT WHAT YOU CAN'T SEE!

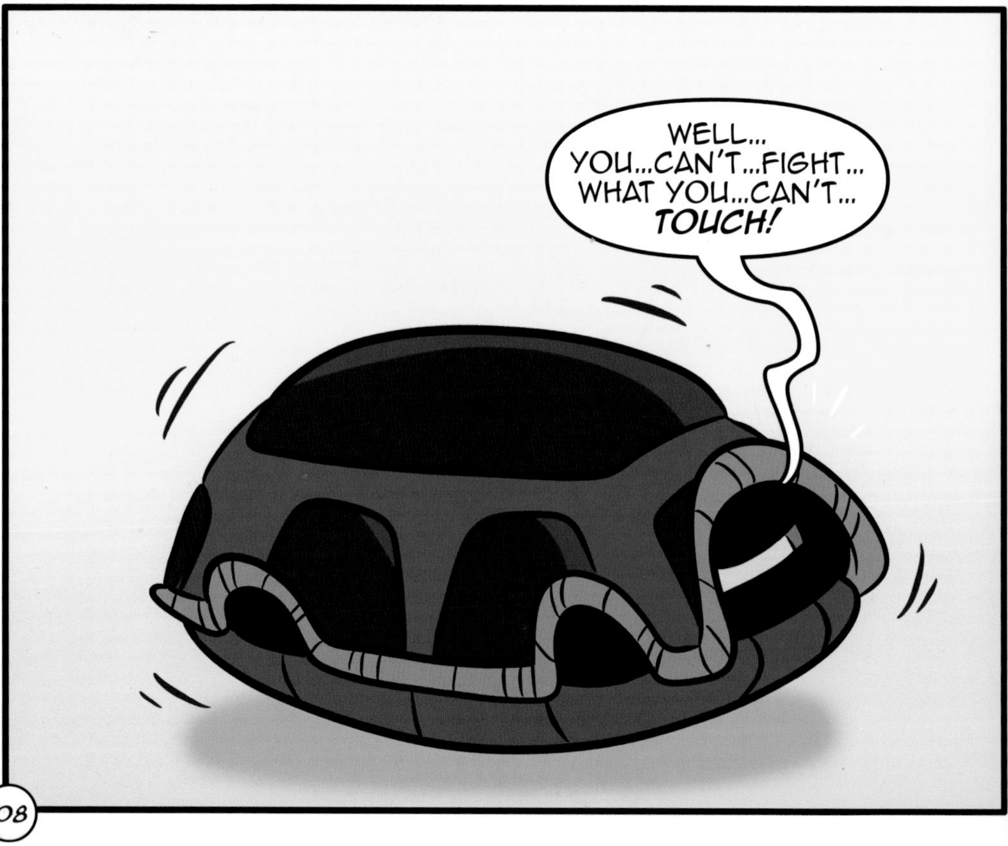
WELL... YOU...CAN'T...FIGHT... WHAT YOU...CAN'T... TOUCH!

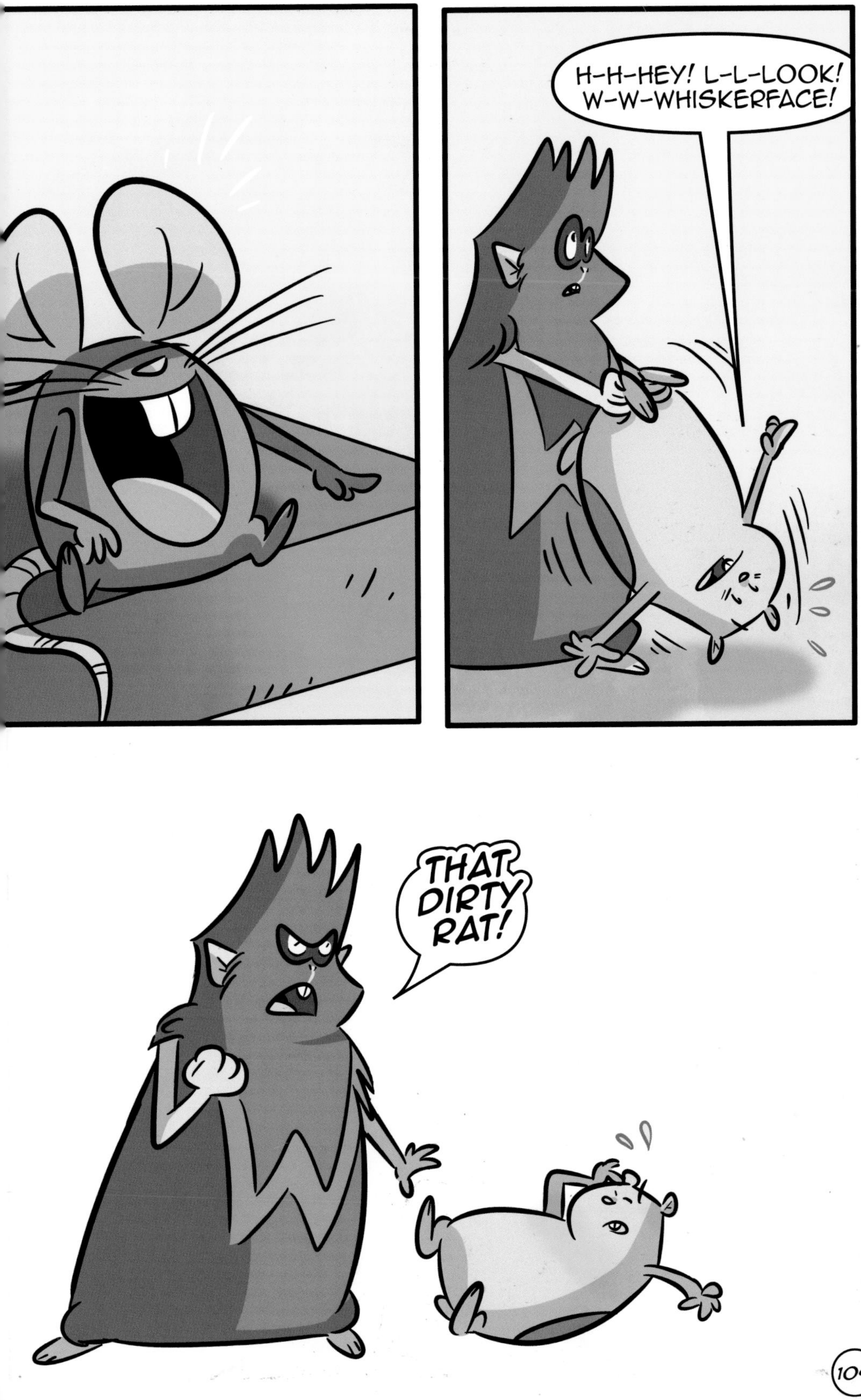
H-H-HEY! L-L-LOOK! W-W-WHISKERFACE!
THAT DIRTY RAT!

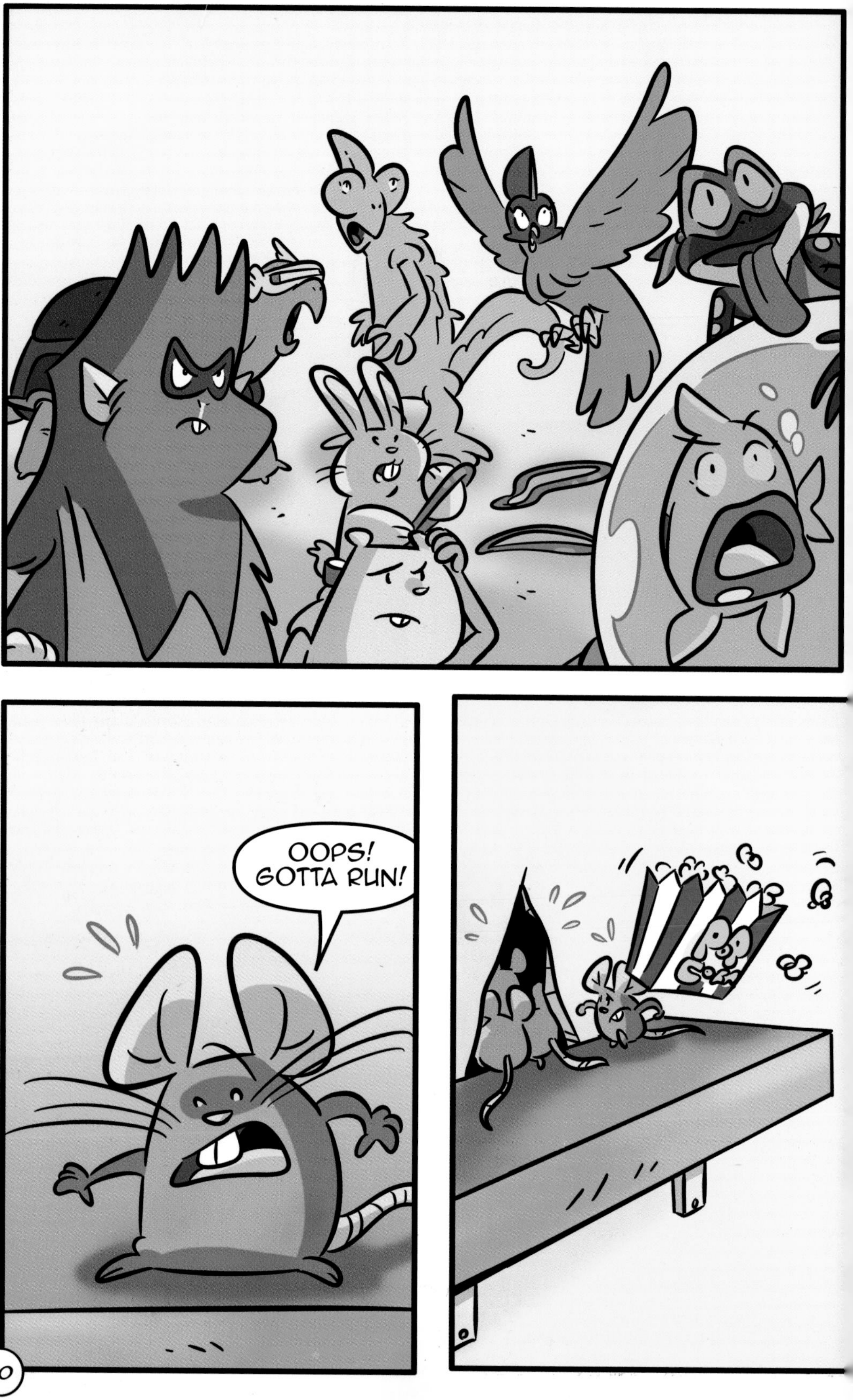
OOPS!
GOTTA RUN!

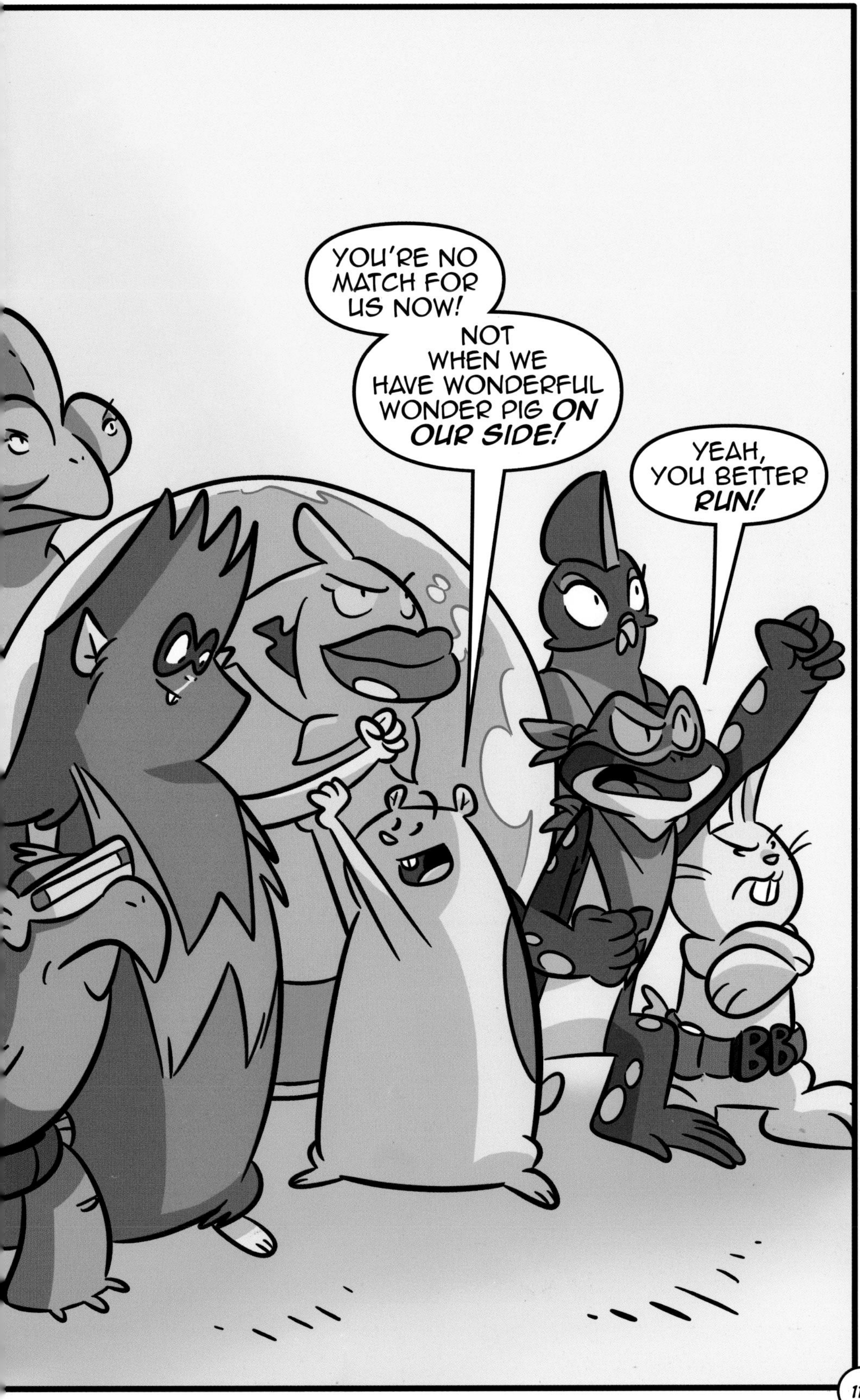
YOU'RE NO MATCH FOR US NOW!
NOT WHEN WE HAVE WONDERFUL WONDER PIG ON OUR SIDE!
YEAH, YOU BETTER RUN!
BB

CHAPTER 9

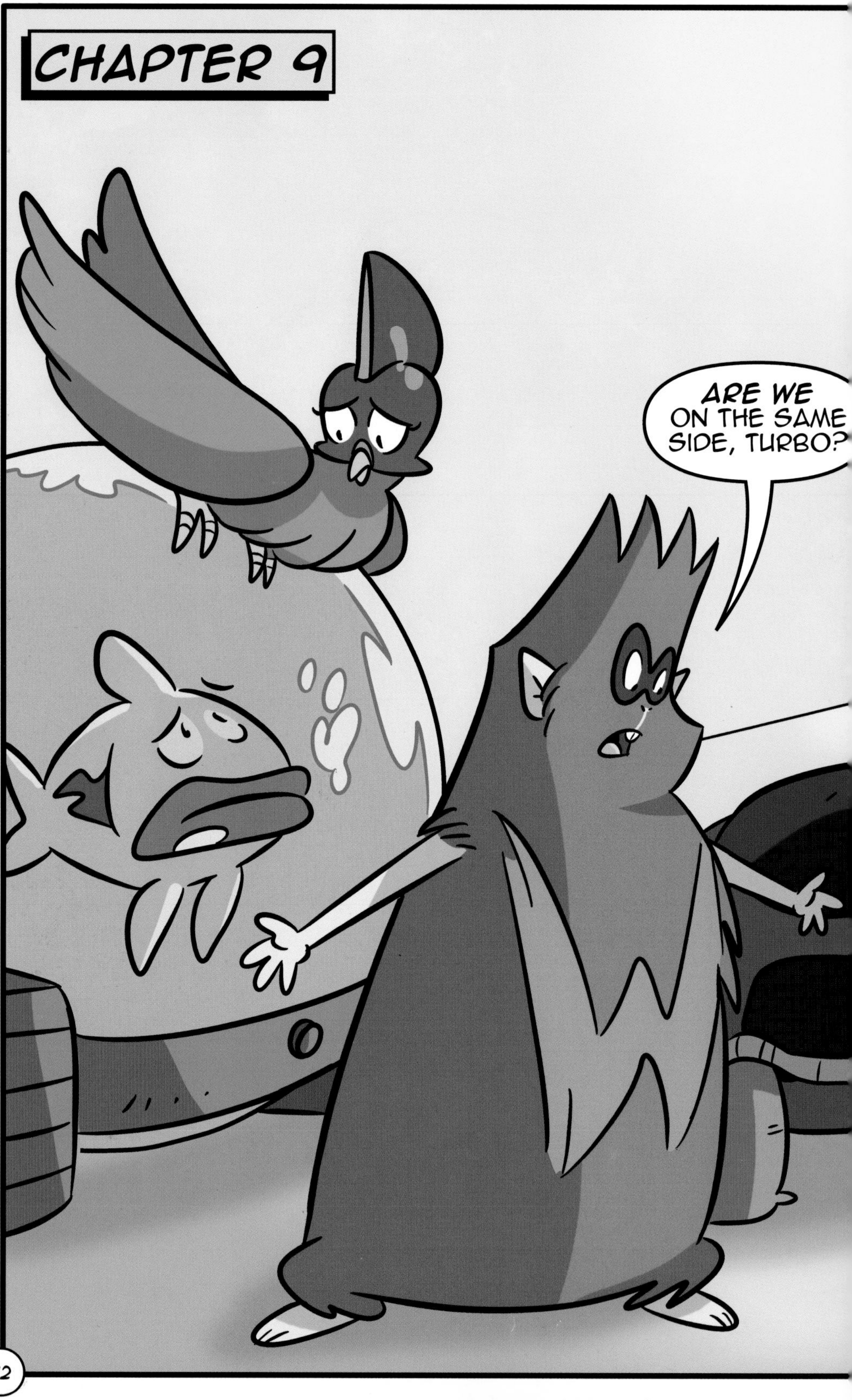
ARE WE ON THE SAME SIDE, TURBO?

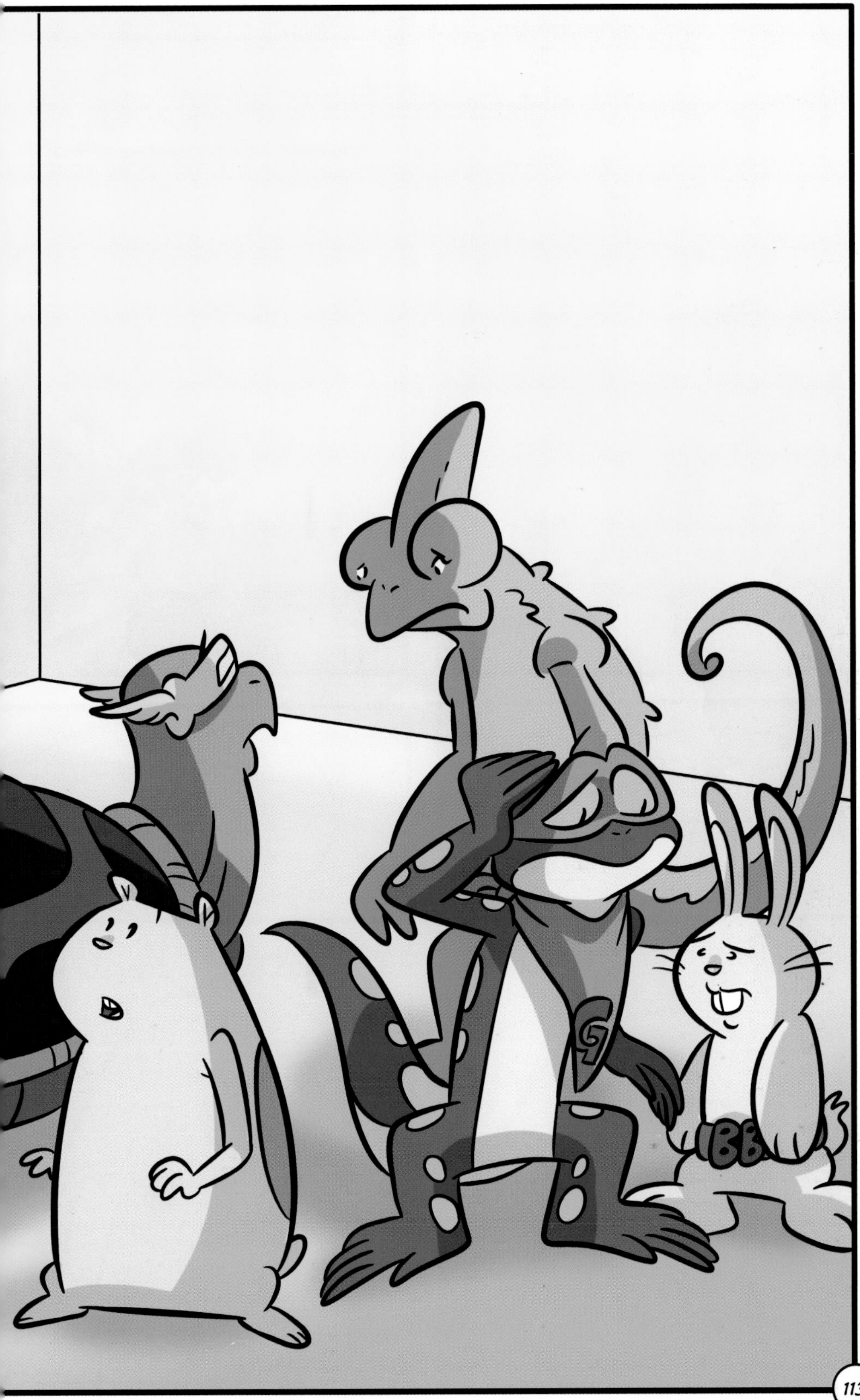

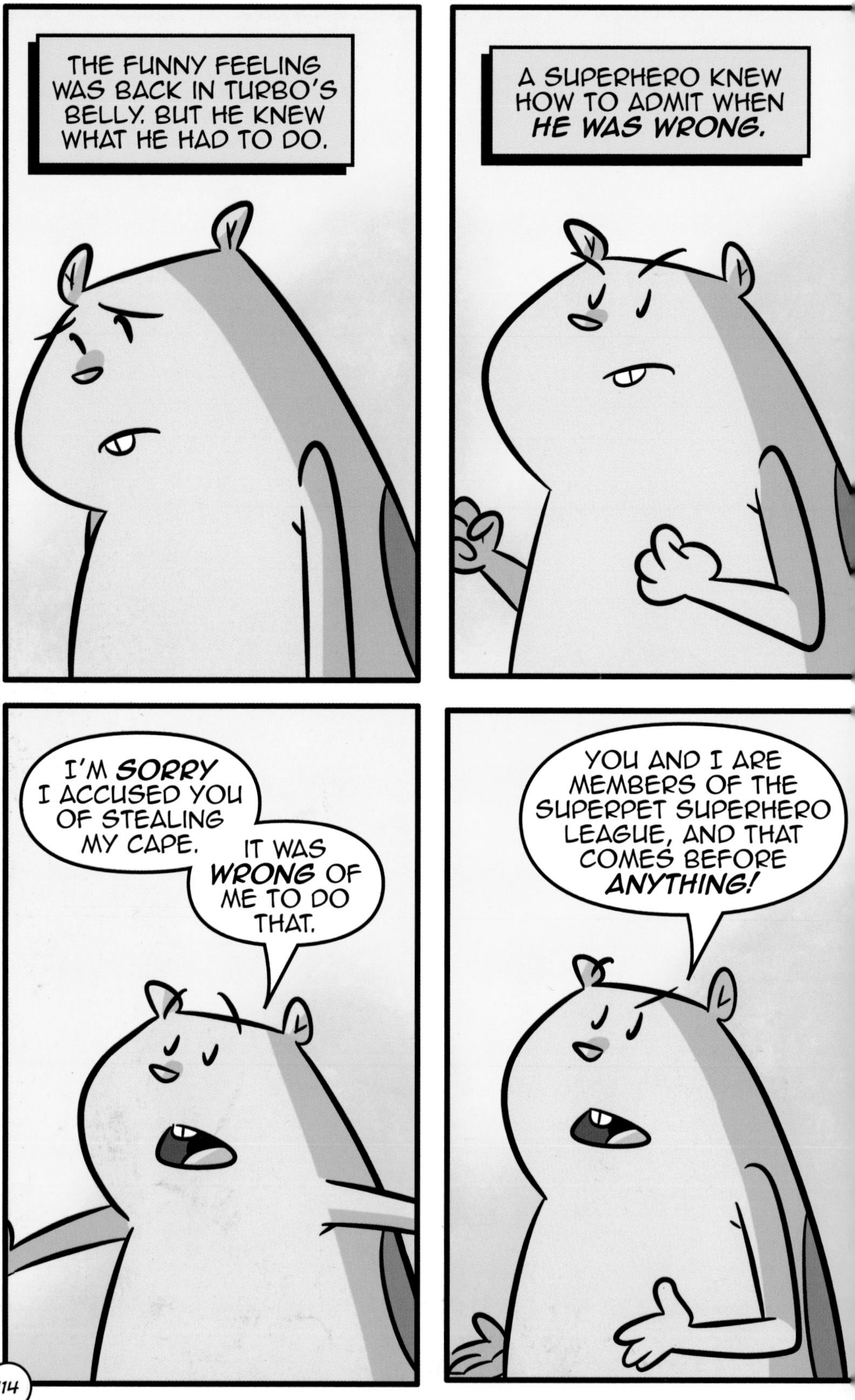
THE FUNNY FEELING WAS BACK IN TURBO'S BELLY. BUT HE KNEW WHAT HE HAD TO DO.
A SUPERHERO KNEW HOW TO ADMIT WHEN *HE WAS WRONG.*
I'M *SORRY* I ACCUSED YOU OF STEALING MY CAPE.
IT WAS *WRONG* OF ME TO DO THAT.
YOU AND I ARE MEMBERS OF THE SUPERPET SUPERHERO LEAGUE, AND THAT COMES BEFORE *ANYTHING!*

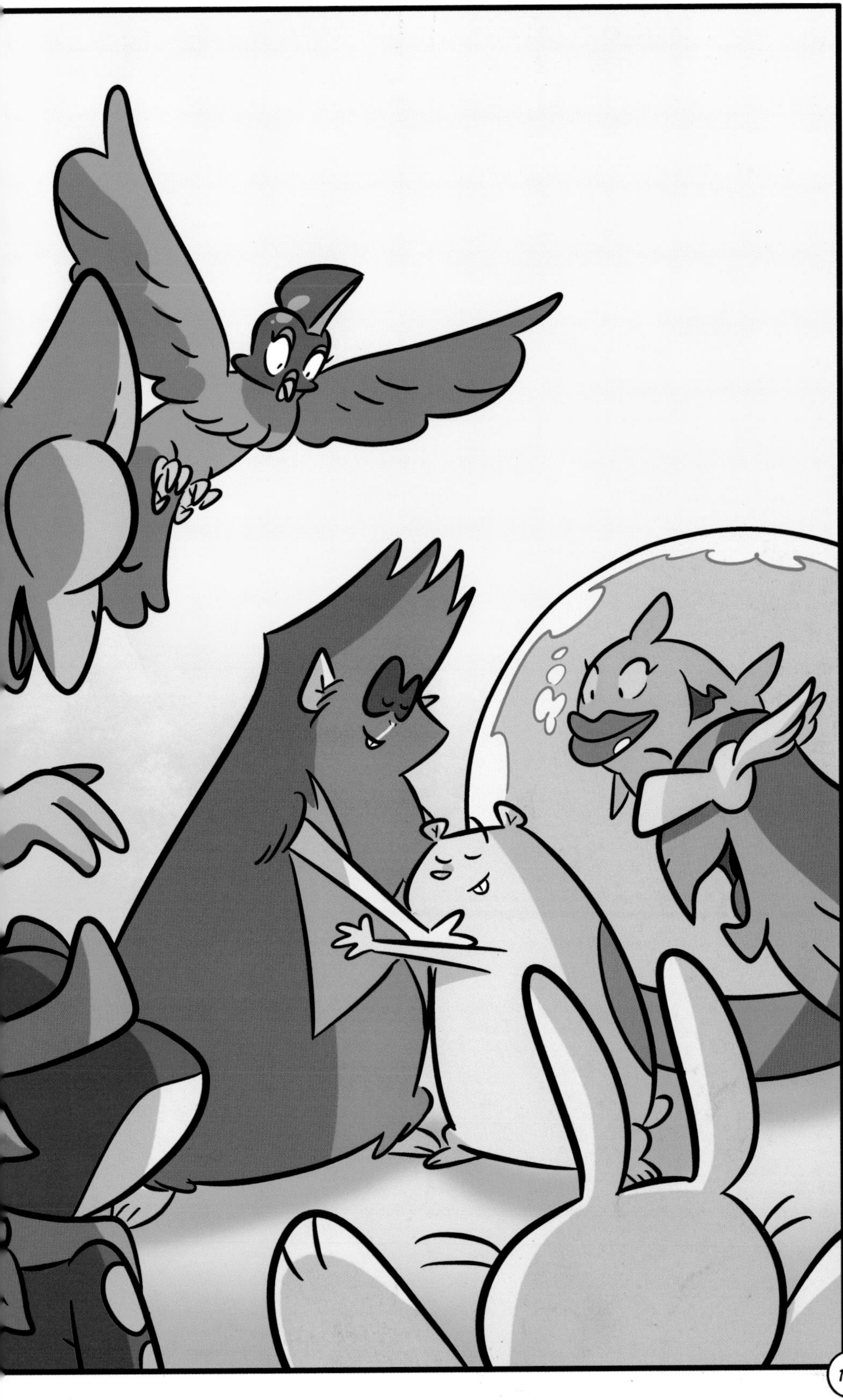

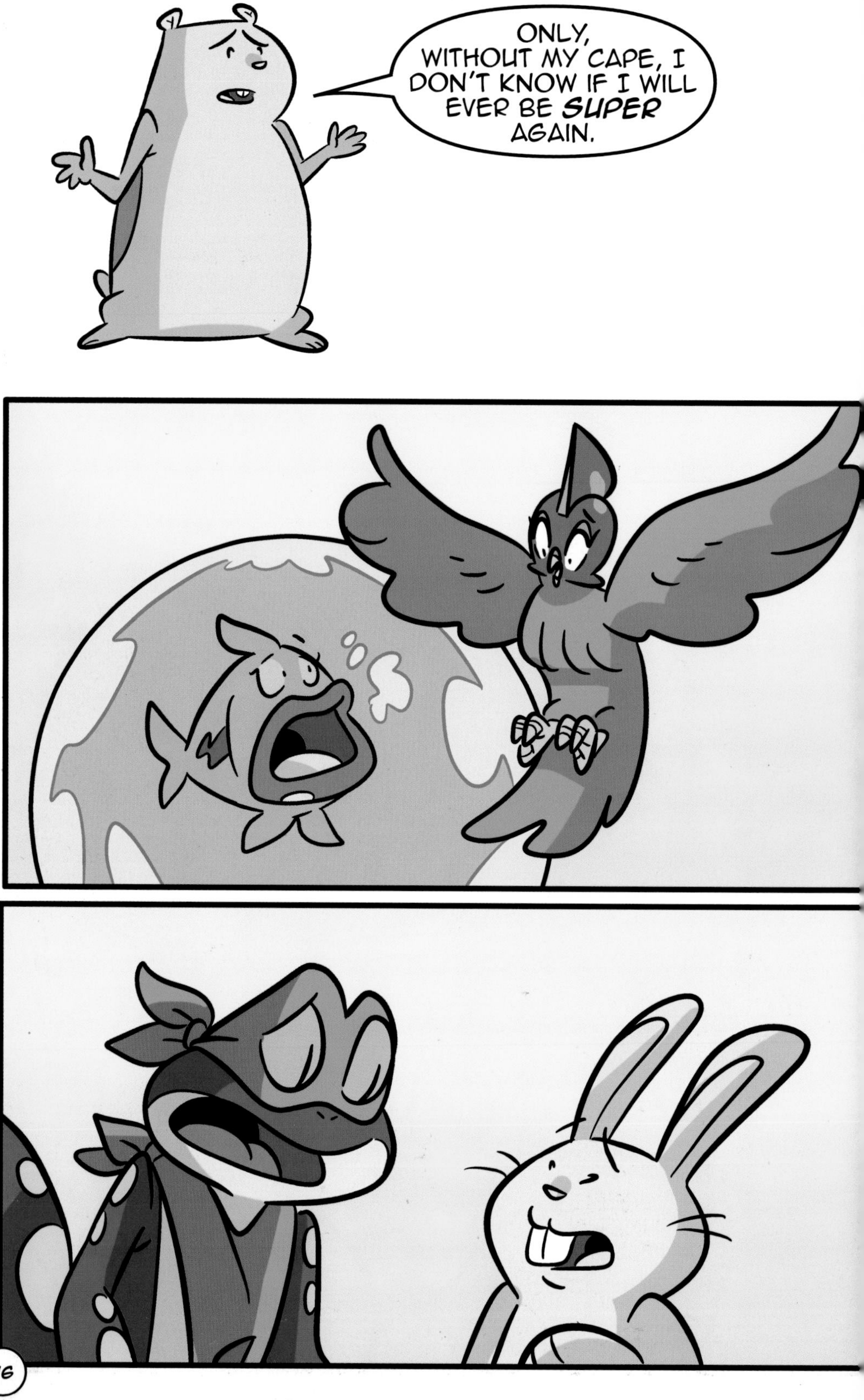
ONLY, WITHOUT MY CAPE, I DON'T KNOW IF I WILL EVER BE SUPER AGAIN.

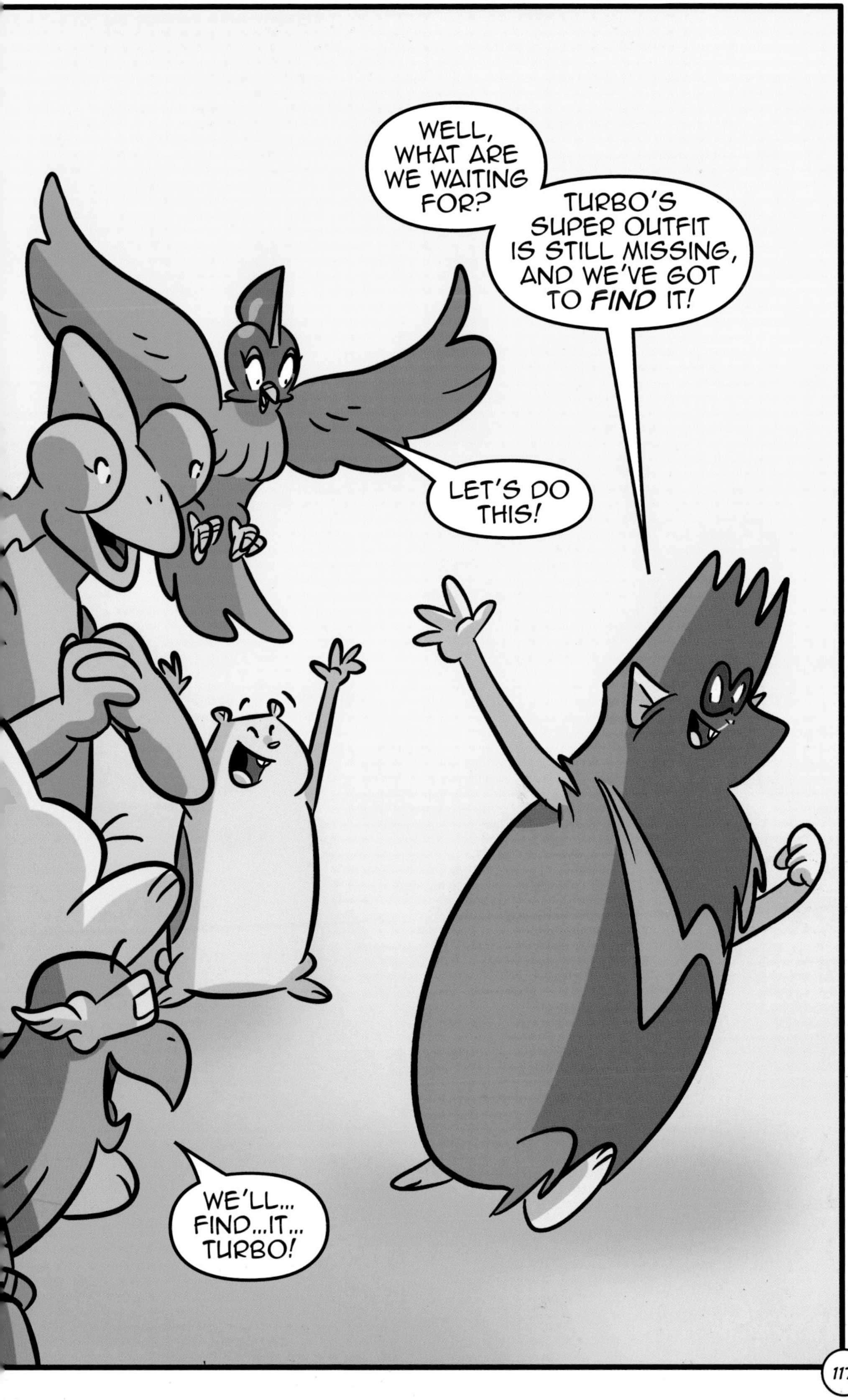
WELL, WHAT ARE WE WAITING FOR?
TURBO'S SUPER OUTFIT IS STILL MISSING, AND WE'VE GOT TO *FIND* IT!
LET'S DO THIS!
WE'LL... FIND...IT... TURBO!

THE SUPERPETS LOOKED *HERE.*

OVER *HERE.*

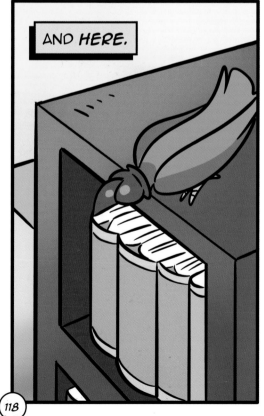

AND *HERE.*

IN *THERE.*

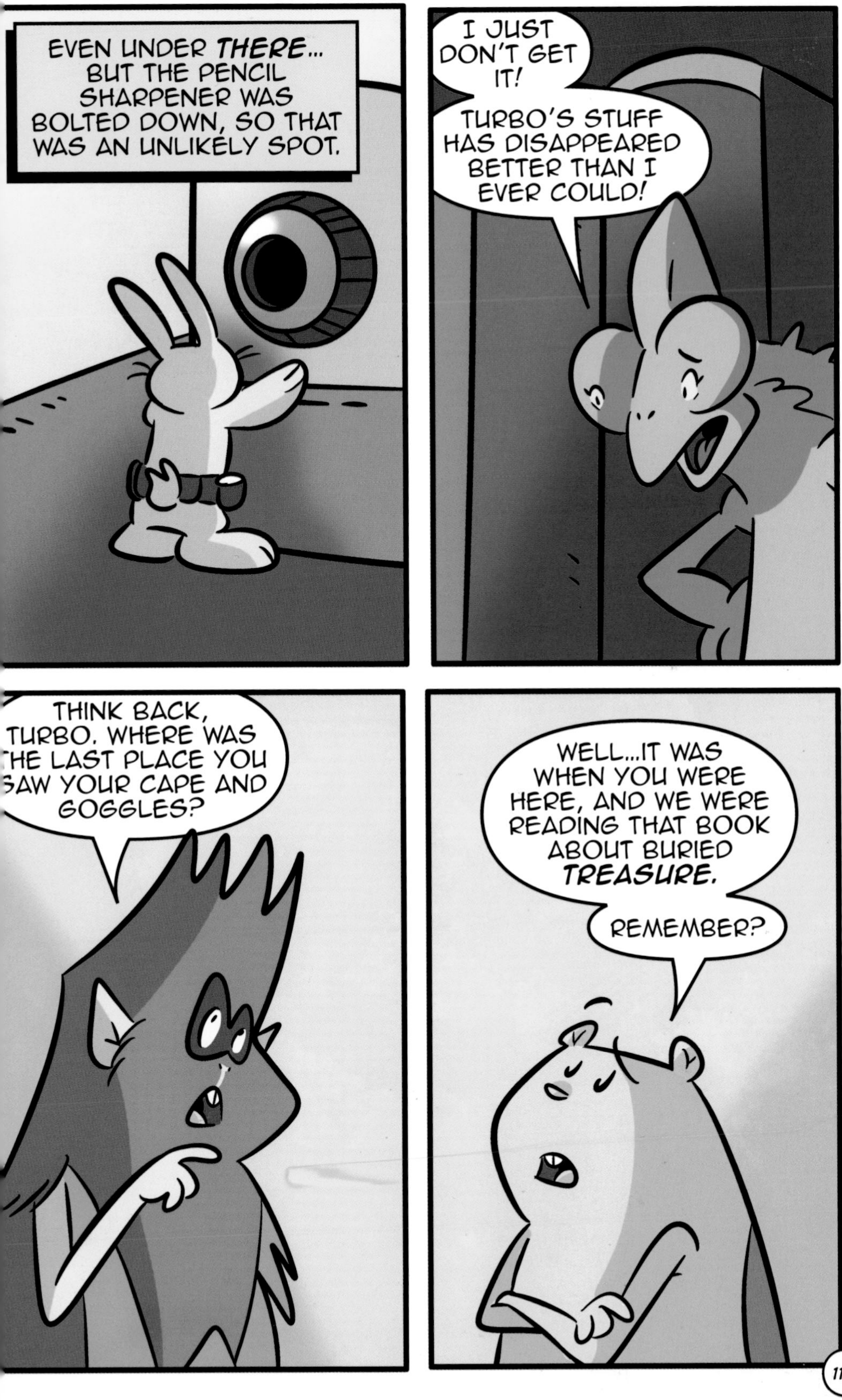
EVEN UNDER *THERE*... BUT THE PENCIL SHARPENER WAS BOLTED DOWN, SO THAT WAS AN UNLIKELY SPOT.
I JUST DON'T GET IT!
TURBO'S STUFF HAS DISAPPEARED BETTER THAN I EVER COULD!
THINK BACK, TURBO. WHERE WAS THE LAST PLACE YOU SAW YOUR CAPE AND GOGGLES?
WELL...IT WAS WHEN YOU WERE HERE, AND WE WERE READING THAT BOOK ABOUT BURIED *TREASURE.*
REMEMBER?

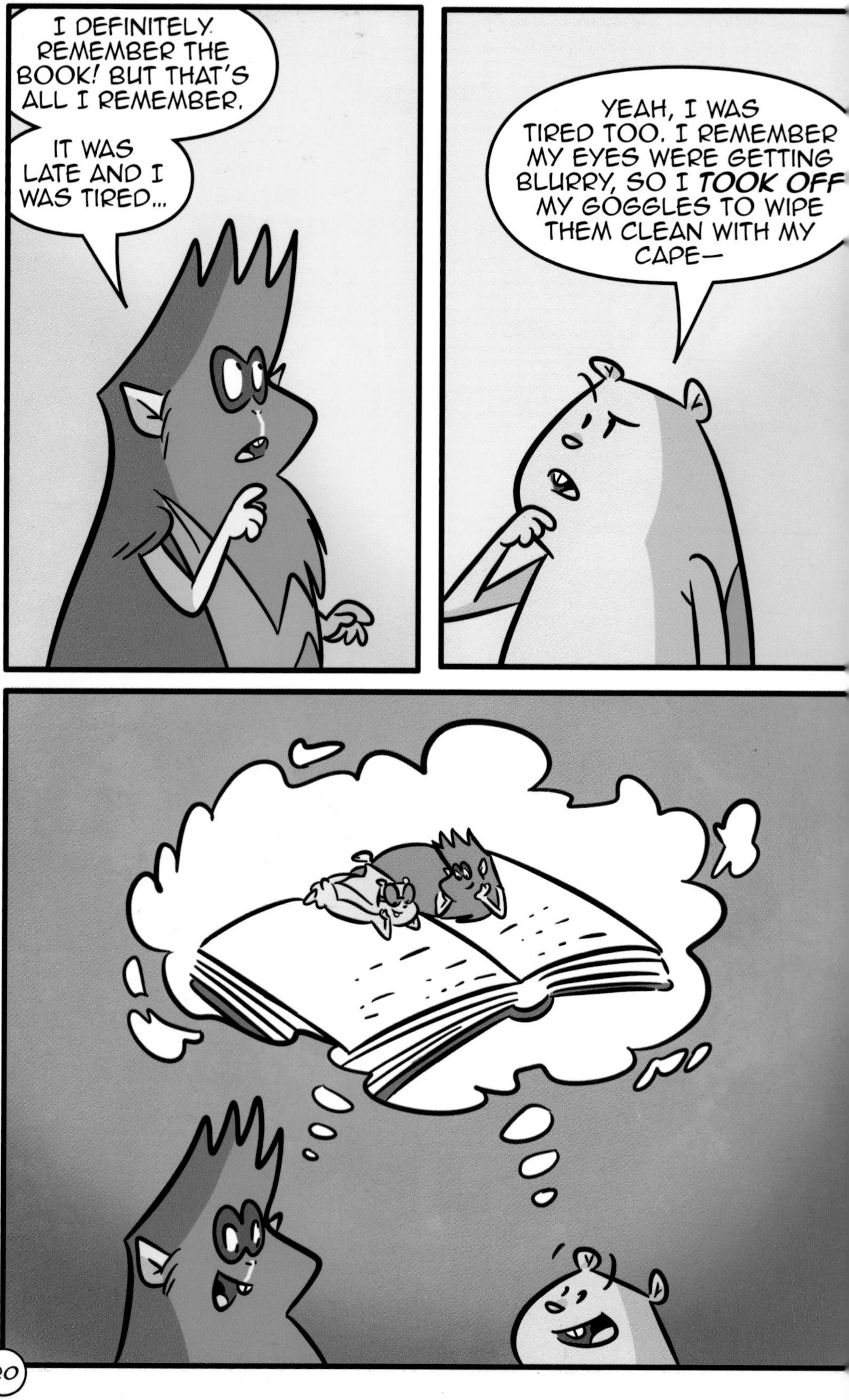
I DEFINITELY REMEMBER THE BOOK! BUT THAT'S ALL I REMEMBER.
IT WAS LATE AND I WAS TIRED...
YEAH, I WAS TIRED TOO. I REMEMBER MY EYES WERE GETTING BLURRY, SO I ***TOOK OFF*** MY GOGGLES TO WIPE THEM CLEAN WITH MY CAPE—

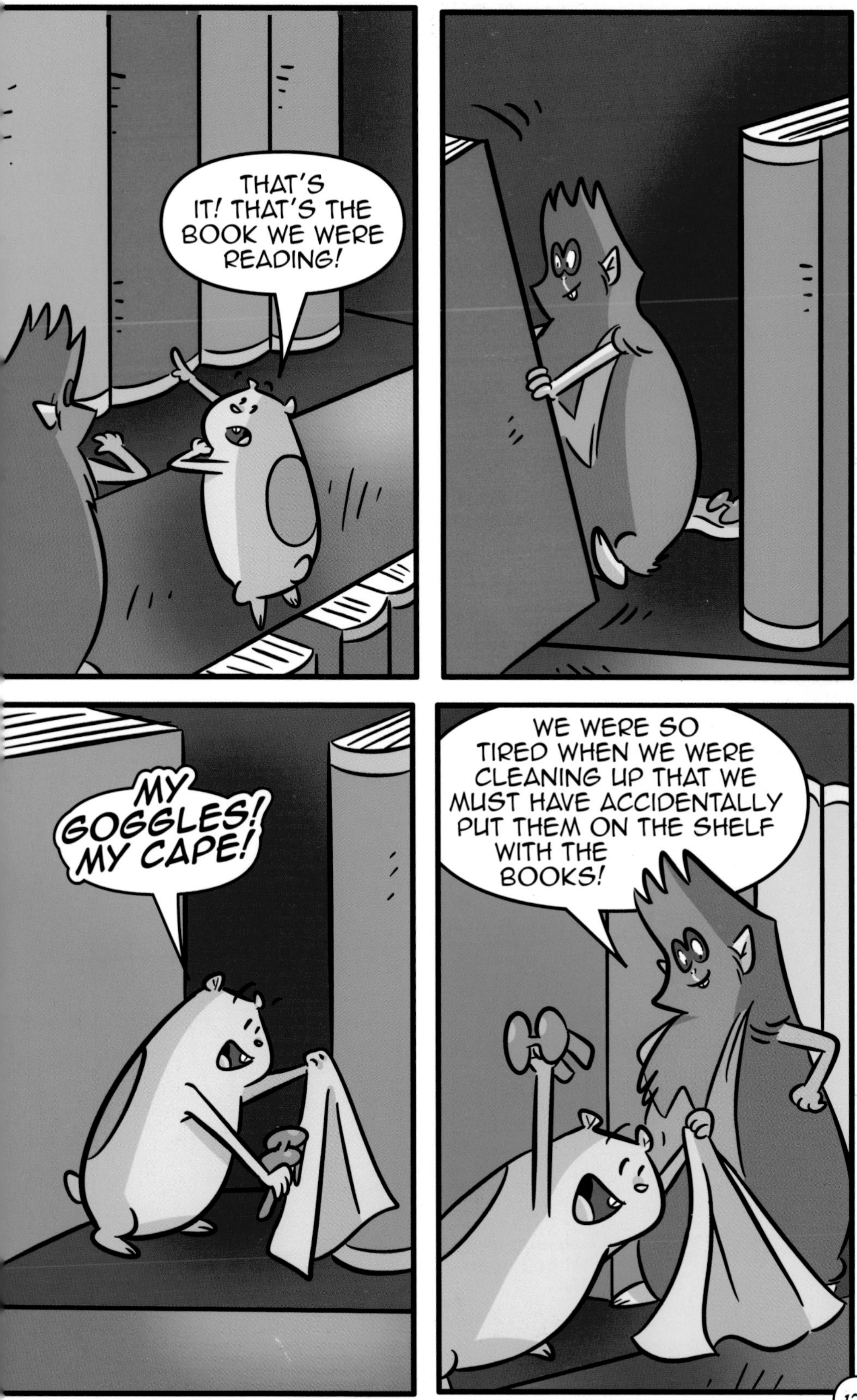
THAT'S IT! THAT'S THE BOOK WE WERE READING!
MY GOGGLES! MY CAPE!
WE WERE SO TIRED WHEN WE WERE CLEANING UP THAT WE MUST HAVE ACCIDENTALLY PUT THEM ON THE SHELF WITH THE BOOKS!

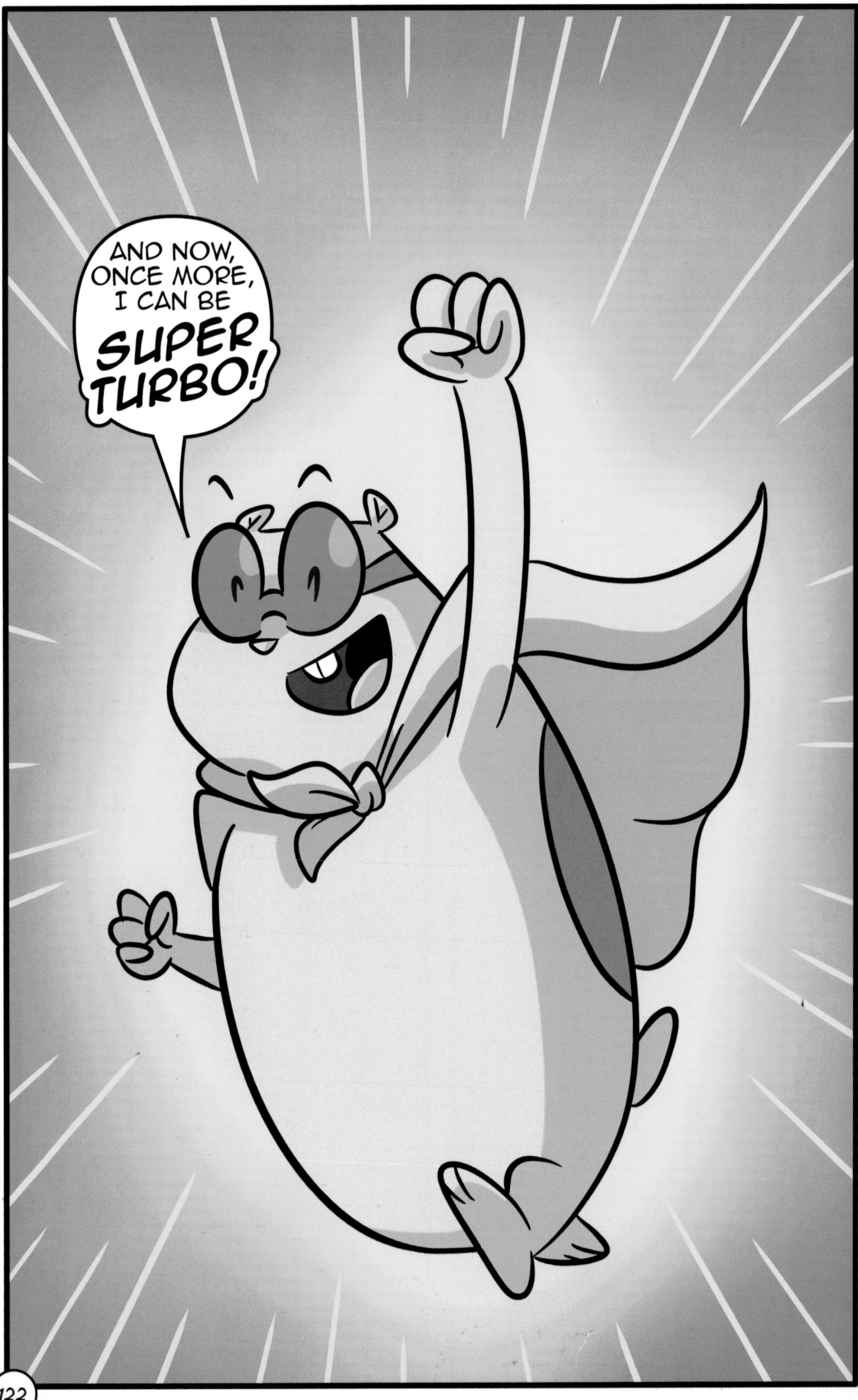
AND NOW, ONCE MORE, I CAN BE SUPER TURBO!

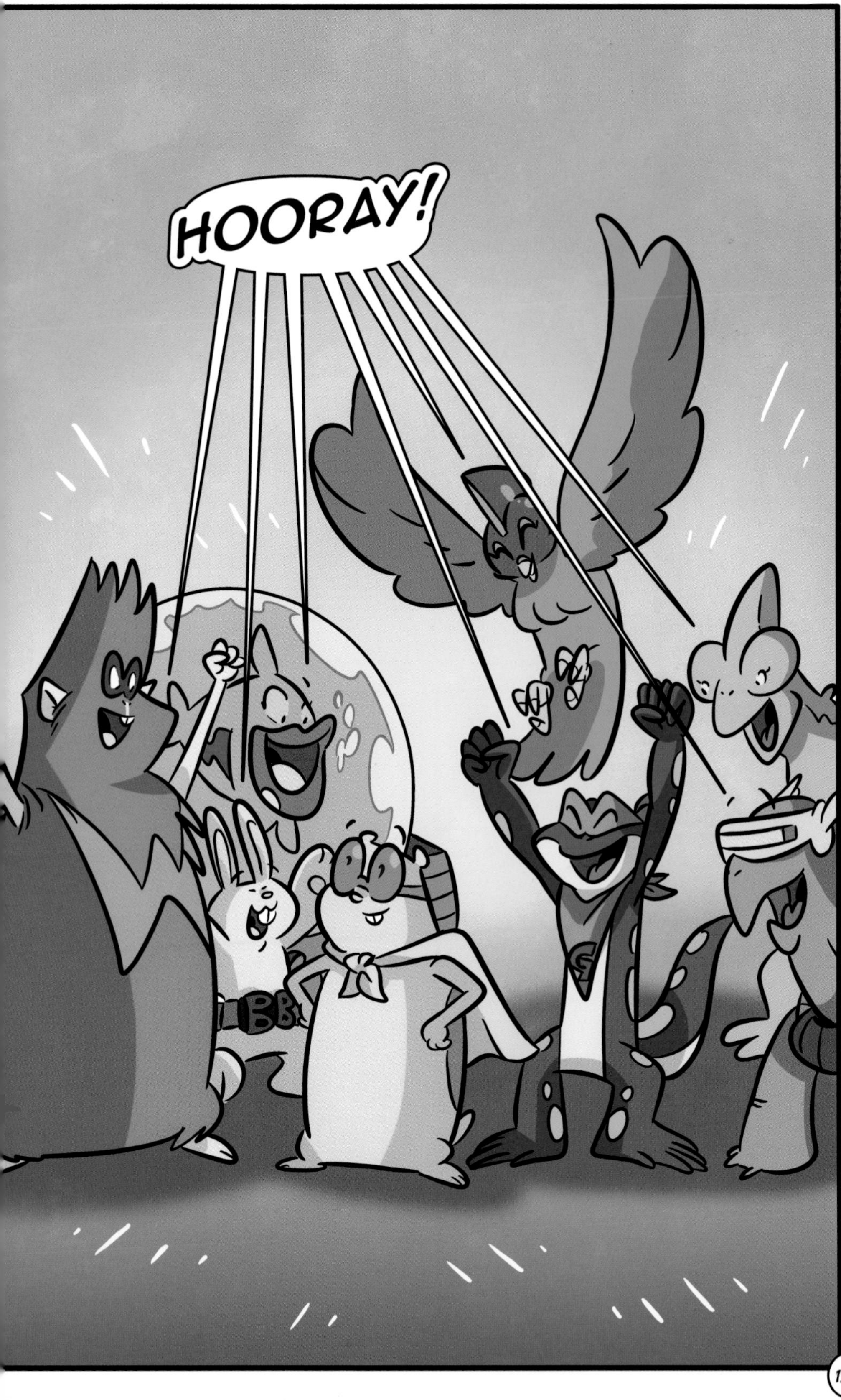
HOORAY!
BB

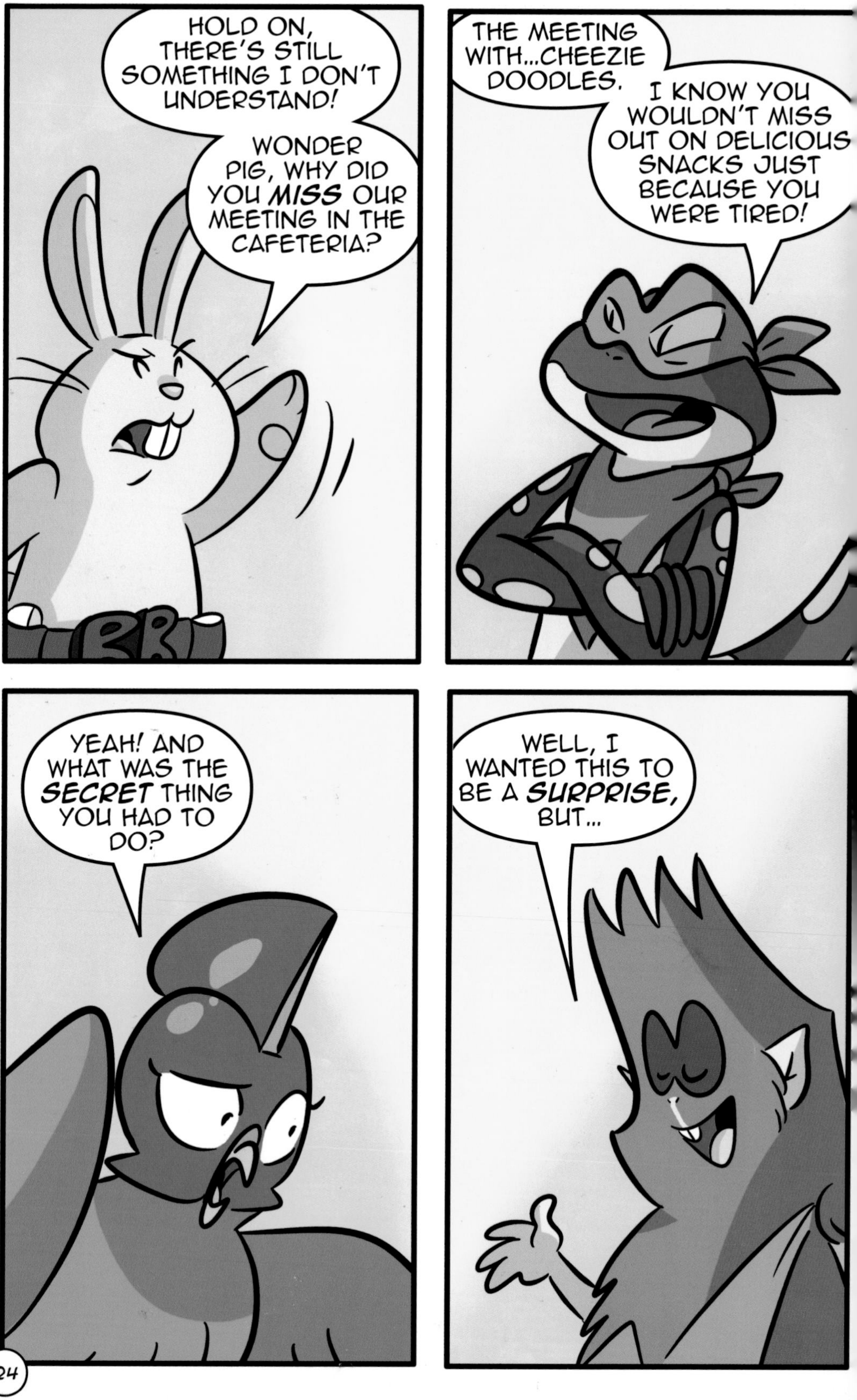
HOLD ON, THERE'S STILL SOMETHING I DON'T UNDERSTAND!
WONDER PIG, WHY DID YOU *MISS* OUR MEETING IN THE CAFETERIA?
THE MEETING WITH...CHEEZIE DOODLES.
I KNOW YOU WOULDN'T MISS OUT ON DELICIOUS SNACKS JUST BECAUSE YOU WERE TIRED!
YEAH! AND WHAT WAS THE *SECRET* THING YOU HAD TO DO?
WELL, I WANTED THIS TO BE A *SURPRISE,* BUT...

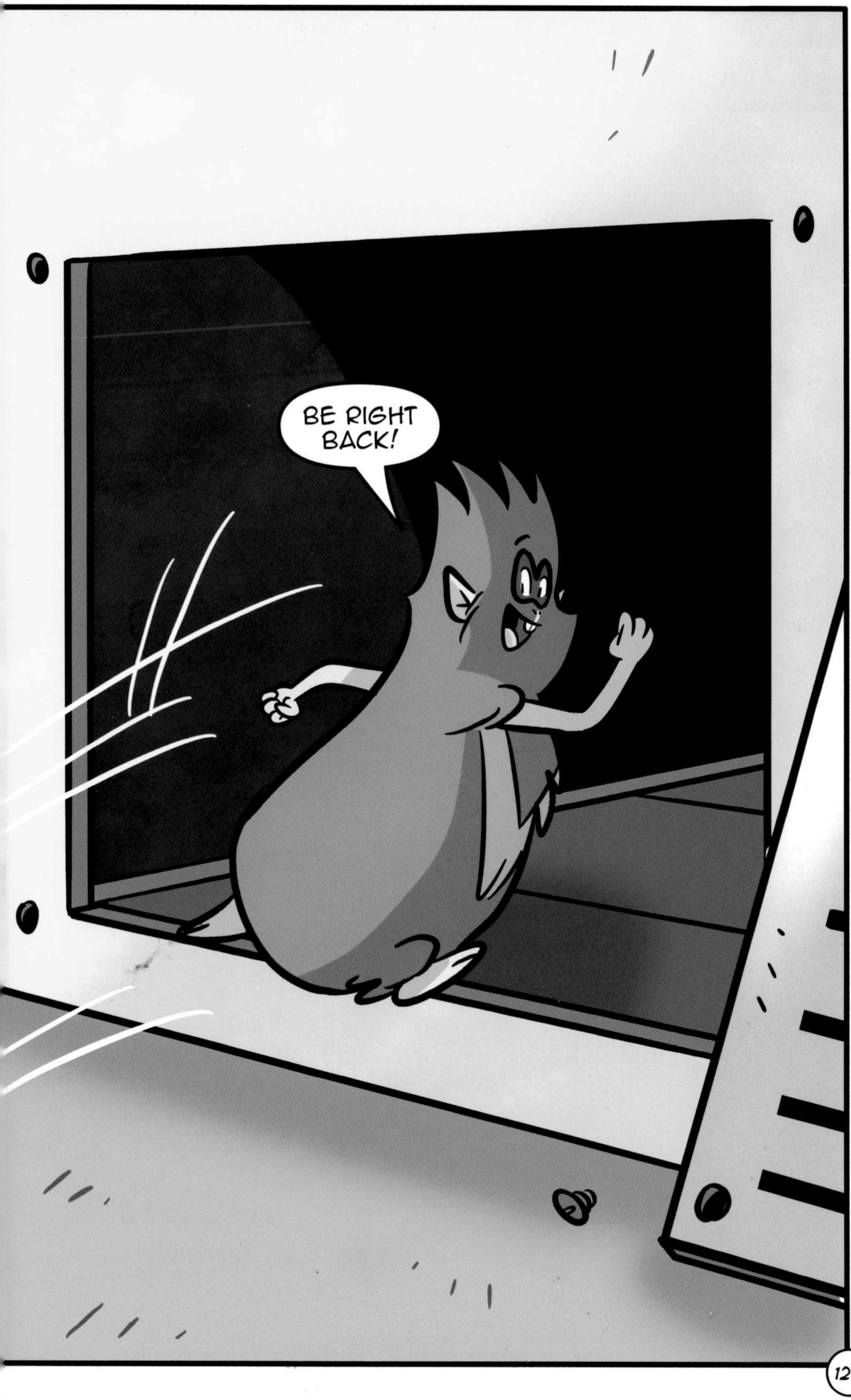
BE RIGHT BACK!

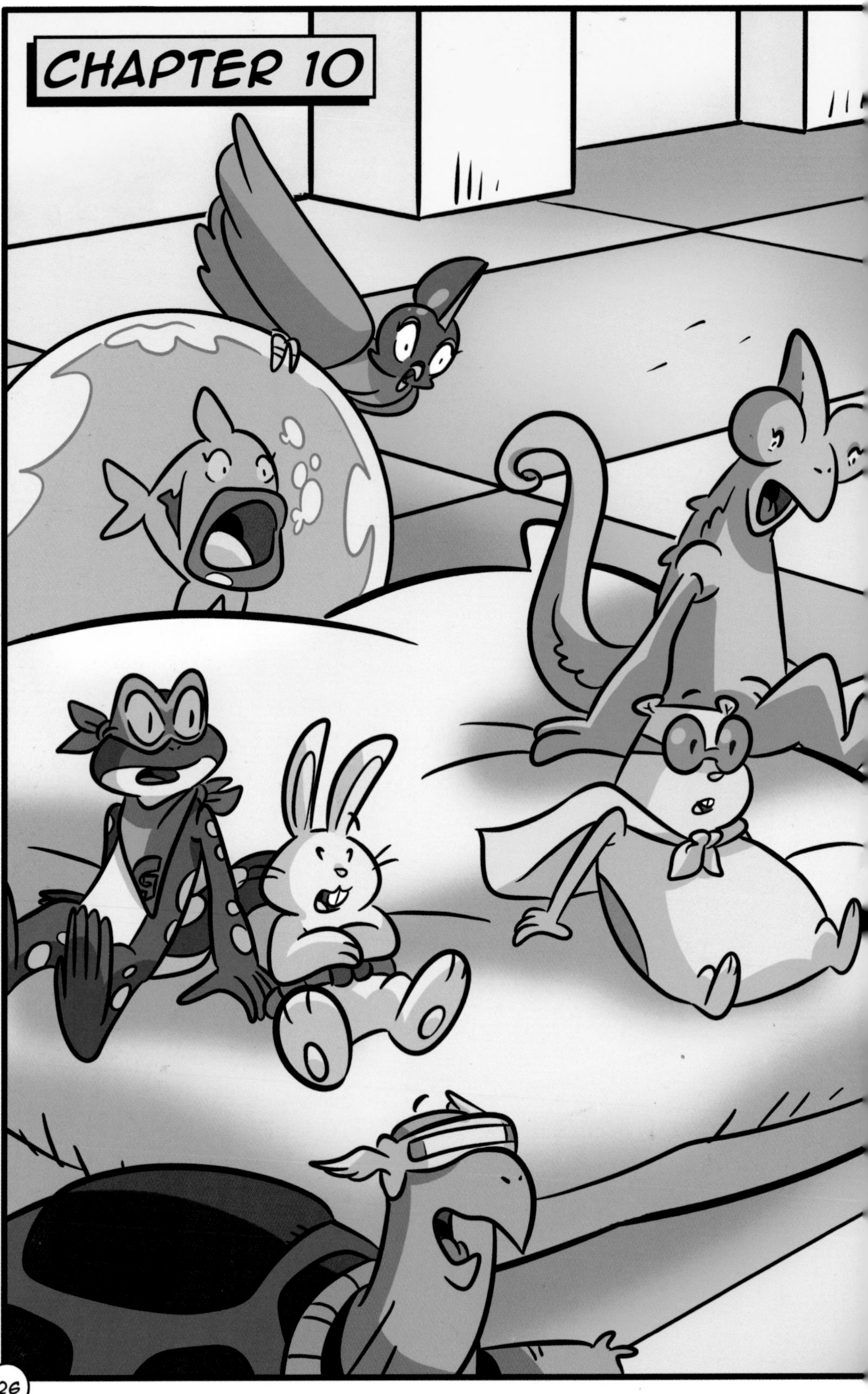
CHAPTER 10

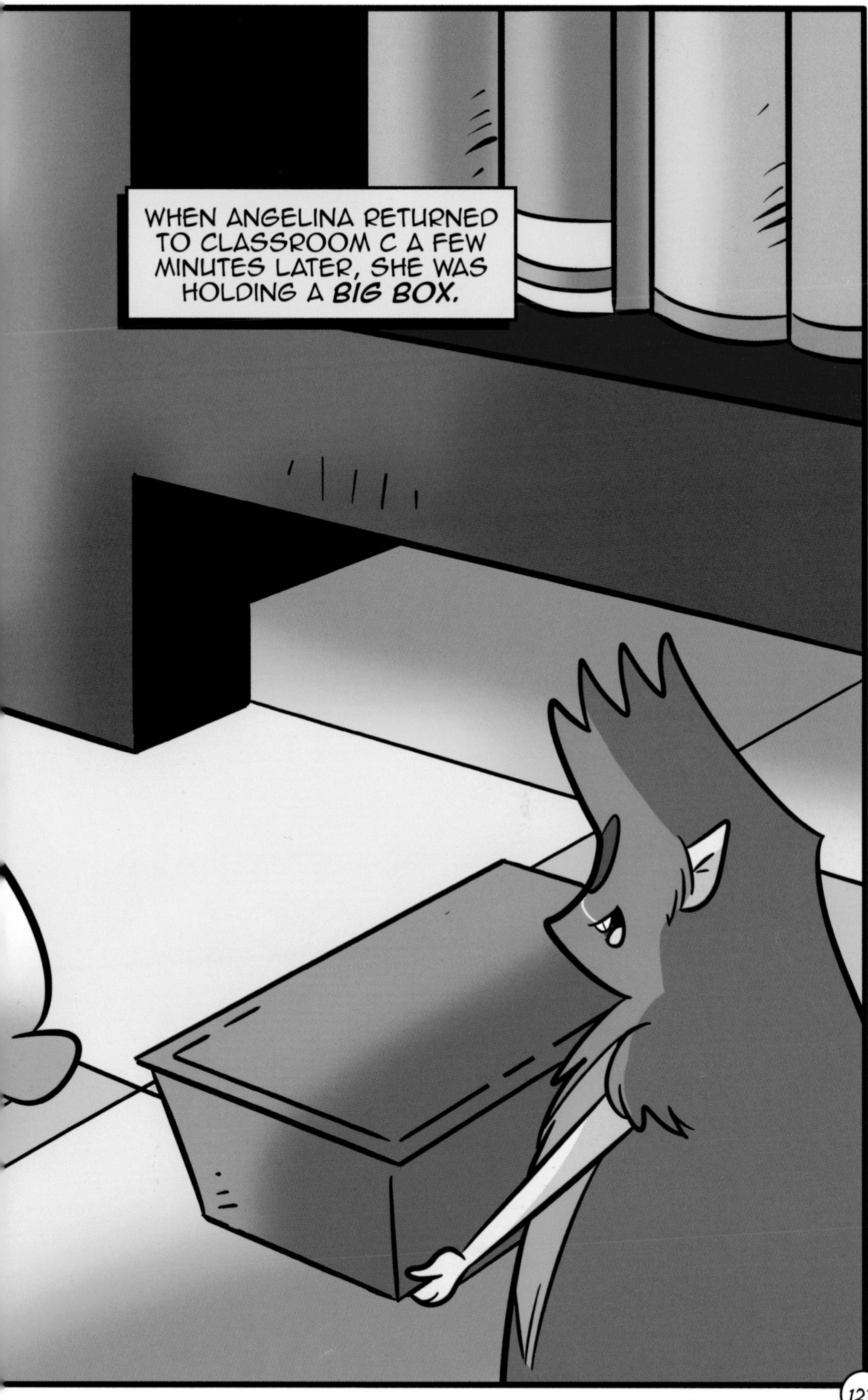
WHEN ANGELINA RETURNED TO CLASSROOM C A FEW MINUTES LATER, SHE WAS HOLDING A BIG BOX.

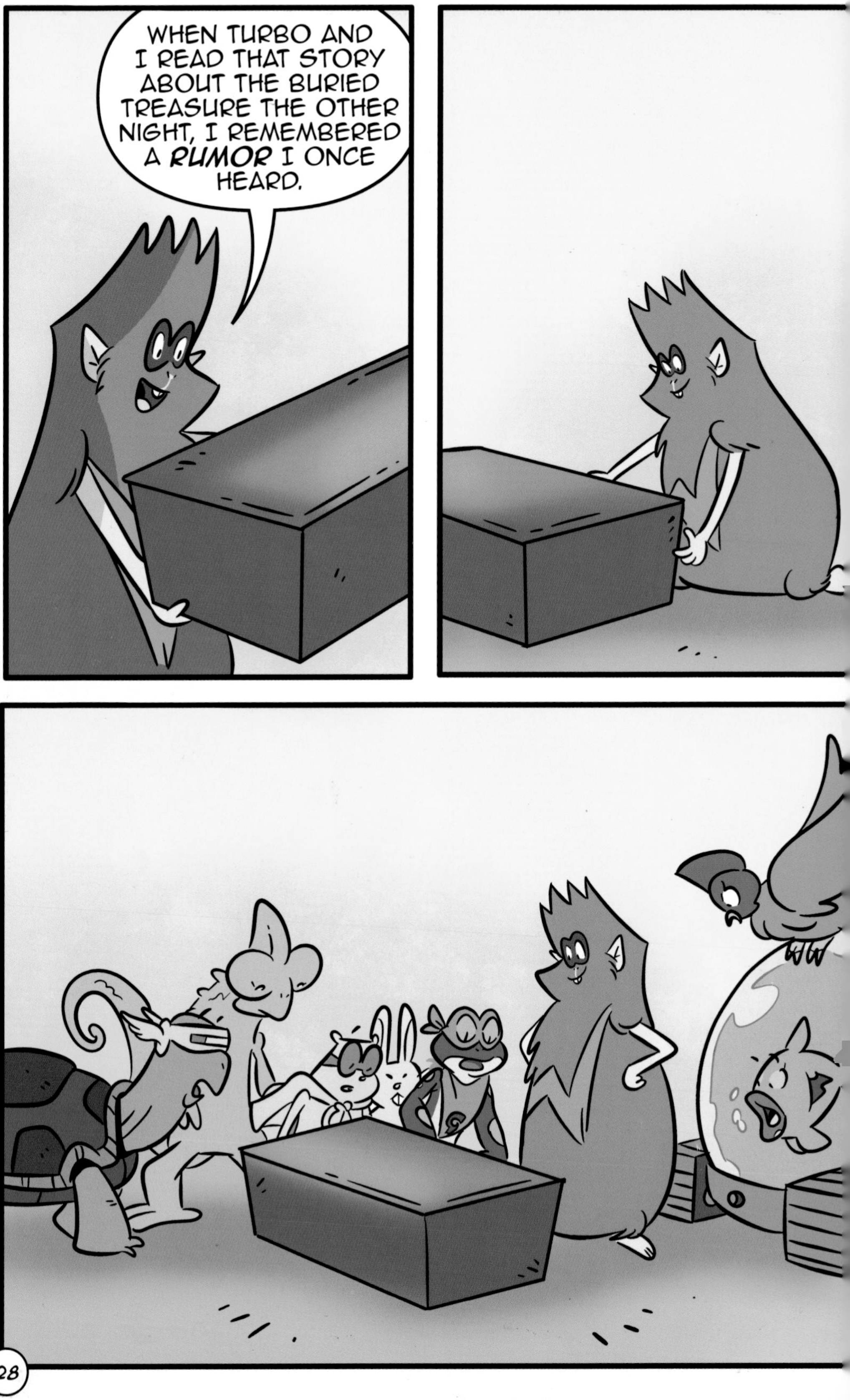
WHEN TURBO AND I READ THAT STORY ABOUT THE BURIED TREASURE THE OTHER NIGHT, I REMEMBERED A RUMOR I ONCE HEARD.

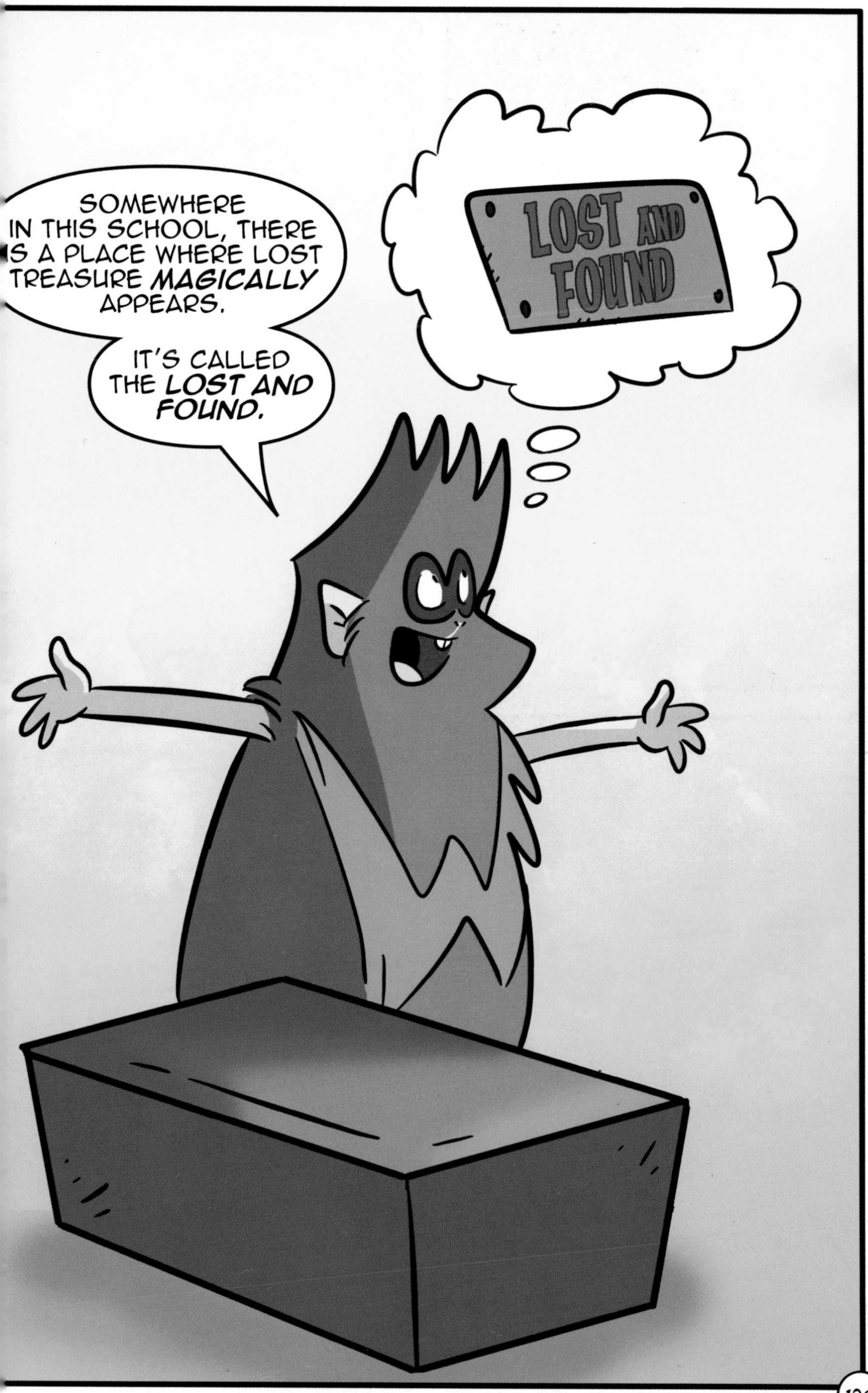
SOMEWHERE IN THIS SCHOOL, THERE IS A PLACE WHERE LOST TREASURE *MAGICALLY* APPEARS.
IT'S CALLED THE ***LOST AND FOUND.***
LOST AND FOUND

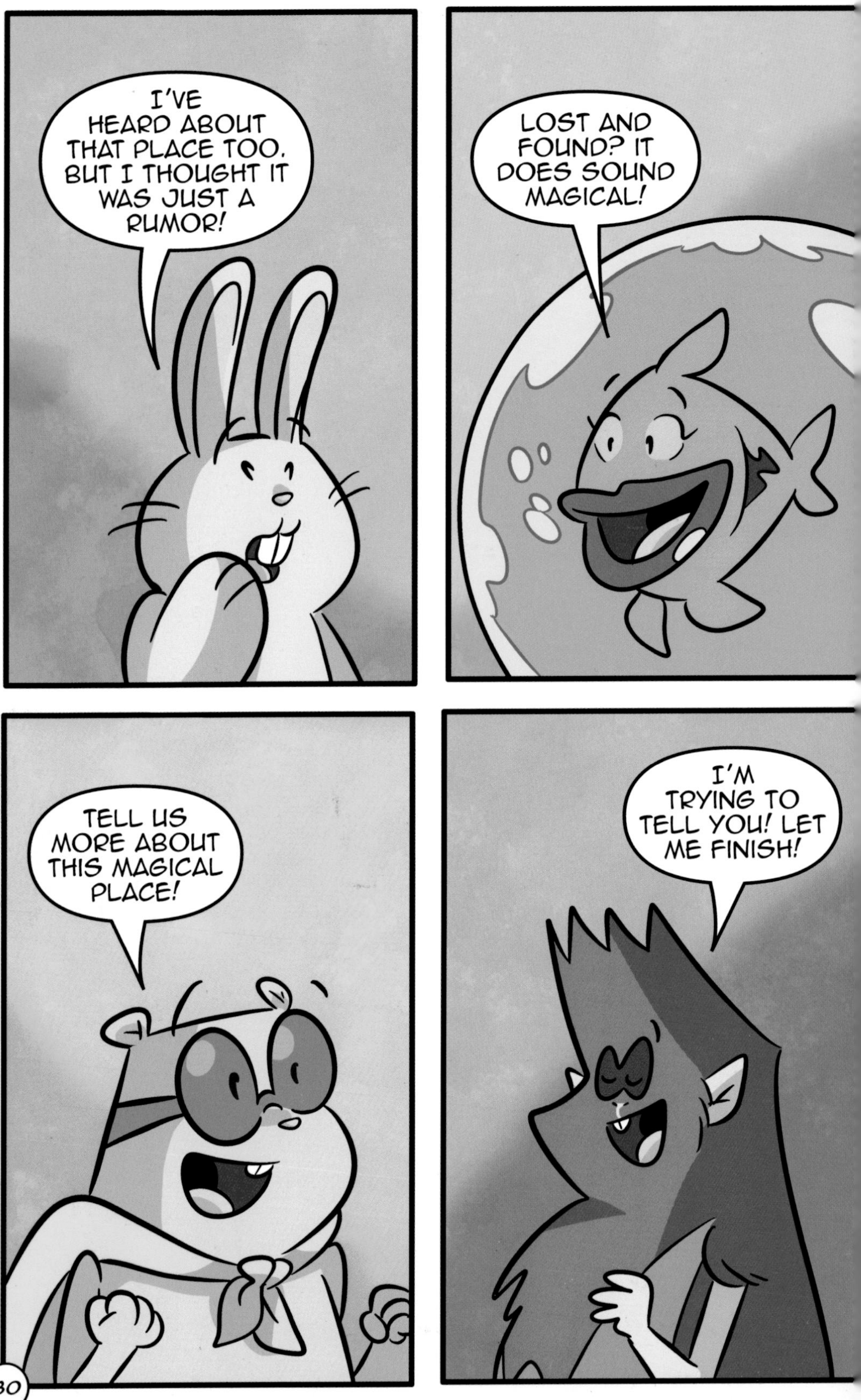
I'VE HEARD ABOUT THAT PLACE TOO. BUT I THOUGHT IT WAS JUST A RUMOR!
LOST AND FOUND? IT DOES SOUND MAGICAL!
TELL US MORE ABOUT THIS MAGICAL PLACE!
I'M TRYING TO TELL YOU! LET ME FINISH!

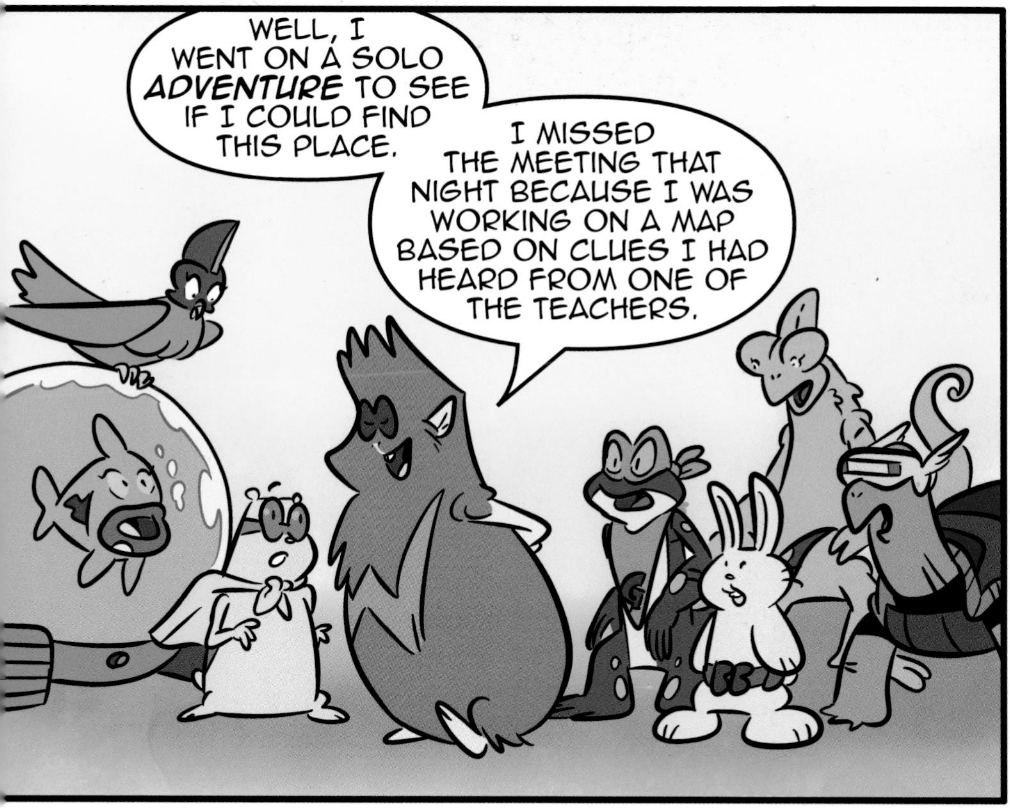
WELL, I WENT ON A SOLO *ADVENTURE* TO SEE IF I COULD FIND THIS PLACE.
I MISSED THE MEETING THAT NIGHT BECAUSE I WAS WORKING ON A MAP BASED ON CLUES I HAD HEARD FROM ONE OF THE TEACHERS.

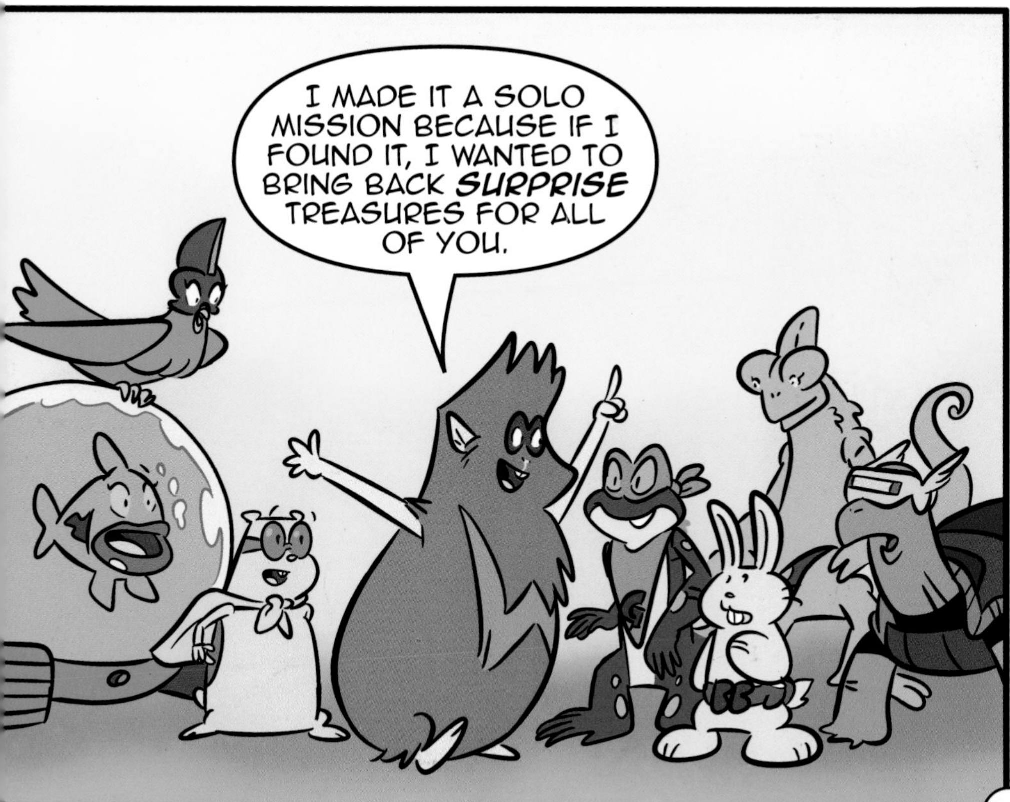
I MADE IT A SOLO MISSION BECAUSE IF I FOUND IT, I WANTED TO BRING BACK *SURPRISE* TREASURES FOR ALL OF YOU.

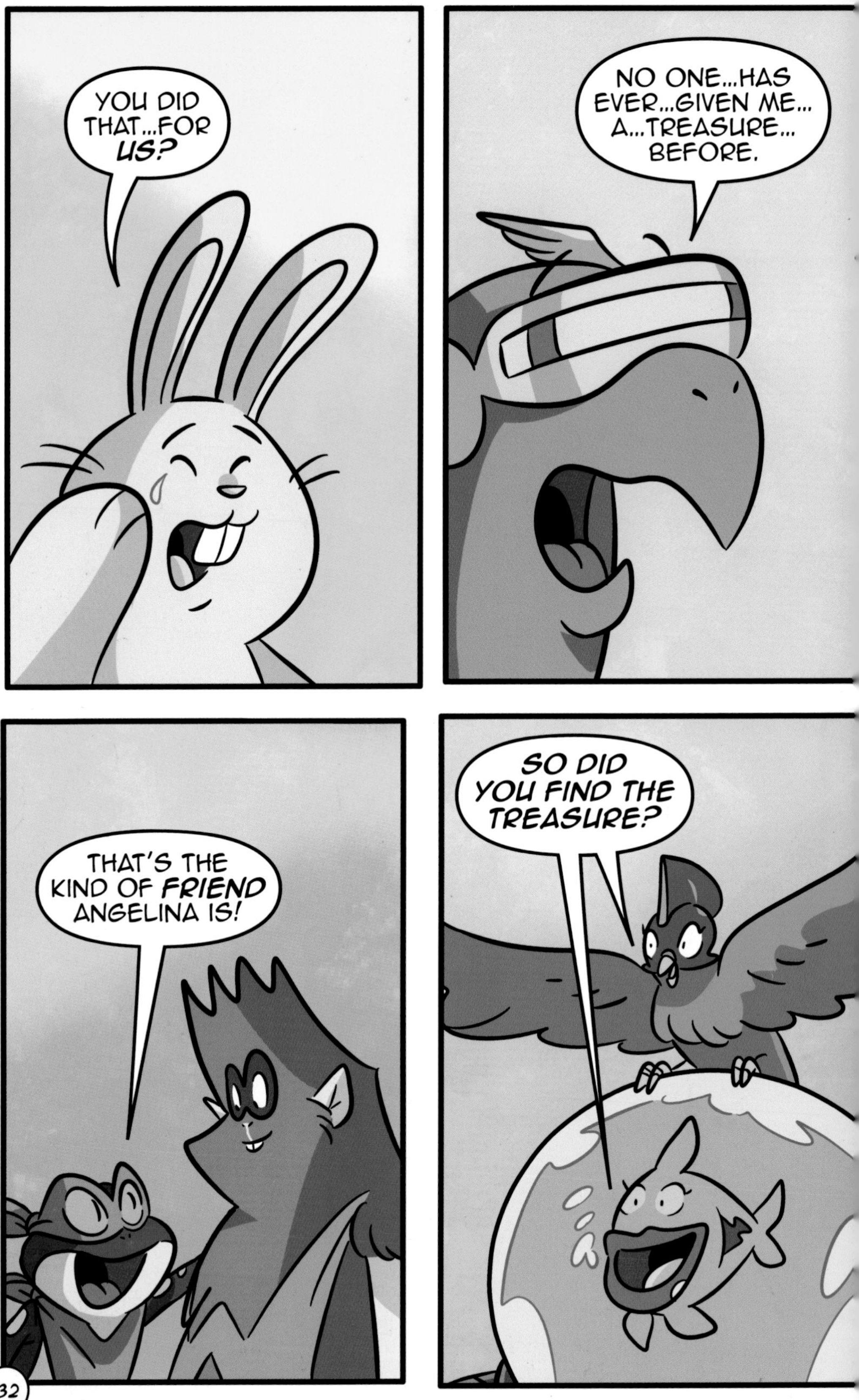
YOU DID THAT...FOR US?
NO ONE...HAS EVER...GIVEN ME... A...TREASURE... BEFORE.
THAT'S THE KIND OF FRIEND ANGELINA IS!
SO DID YOU FIND THE TREASURE?

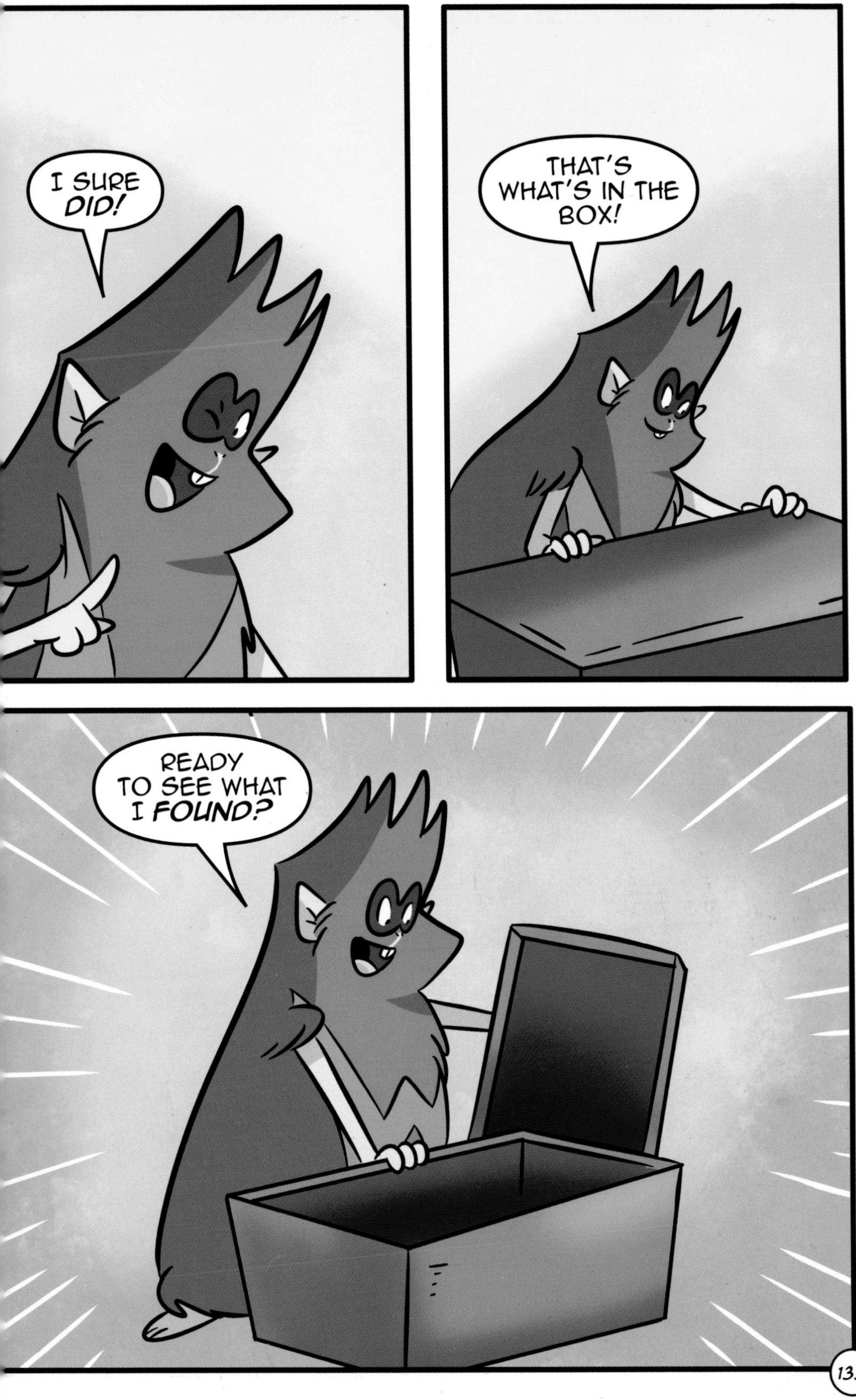
I SURE *DID!*
THAT'S WHAT'S IN THE BOX!
READY TO SEE WHAT I *FOUND?*

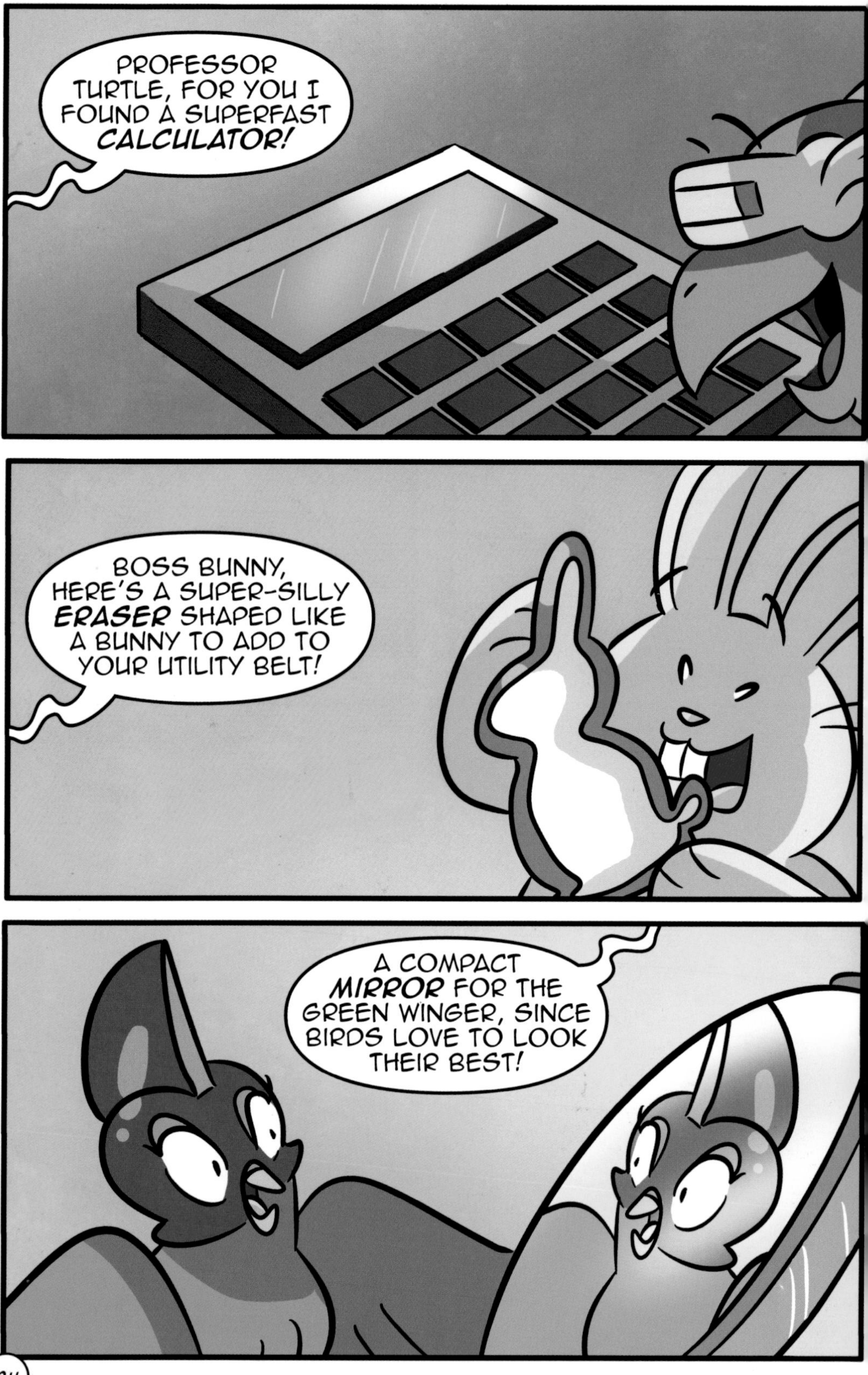
PROFESSOR TURTLE, FOR YOU I FOUND A SUPERFAST CALCULATOR!
BOSS BUNNY, HERE'S A SUPER-SILLY ERASER SHAPED LIKE A BUNNY TO ADD TO YOUR UTILITY BELT!
A COMPACT MIRROR FOR THE GREEN WINGER, SINCE BIRDS LOVE TO LOOK THEIR BEST!

A MINI **BULL'S-EYE**, PERFECT FOR THE GREAT GECKO'S TARGET PRACTICE!

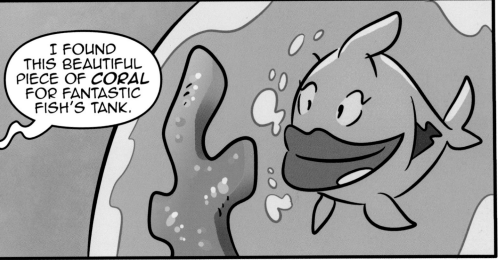

I FOUND THIS BEAUTIFUL PIECE OF **CORAL** FOR FANTASTIC FISH'S TANK.

PENELOPE, I PRESENT TO YOU A CAMOUFLAGE **BANDANNA** IN CASE YOU EVER GET TIRED OF CHANGING COLORS BUT STILL WANT TO HIDE.

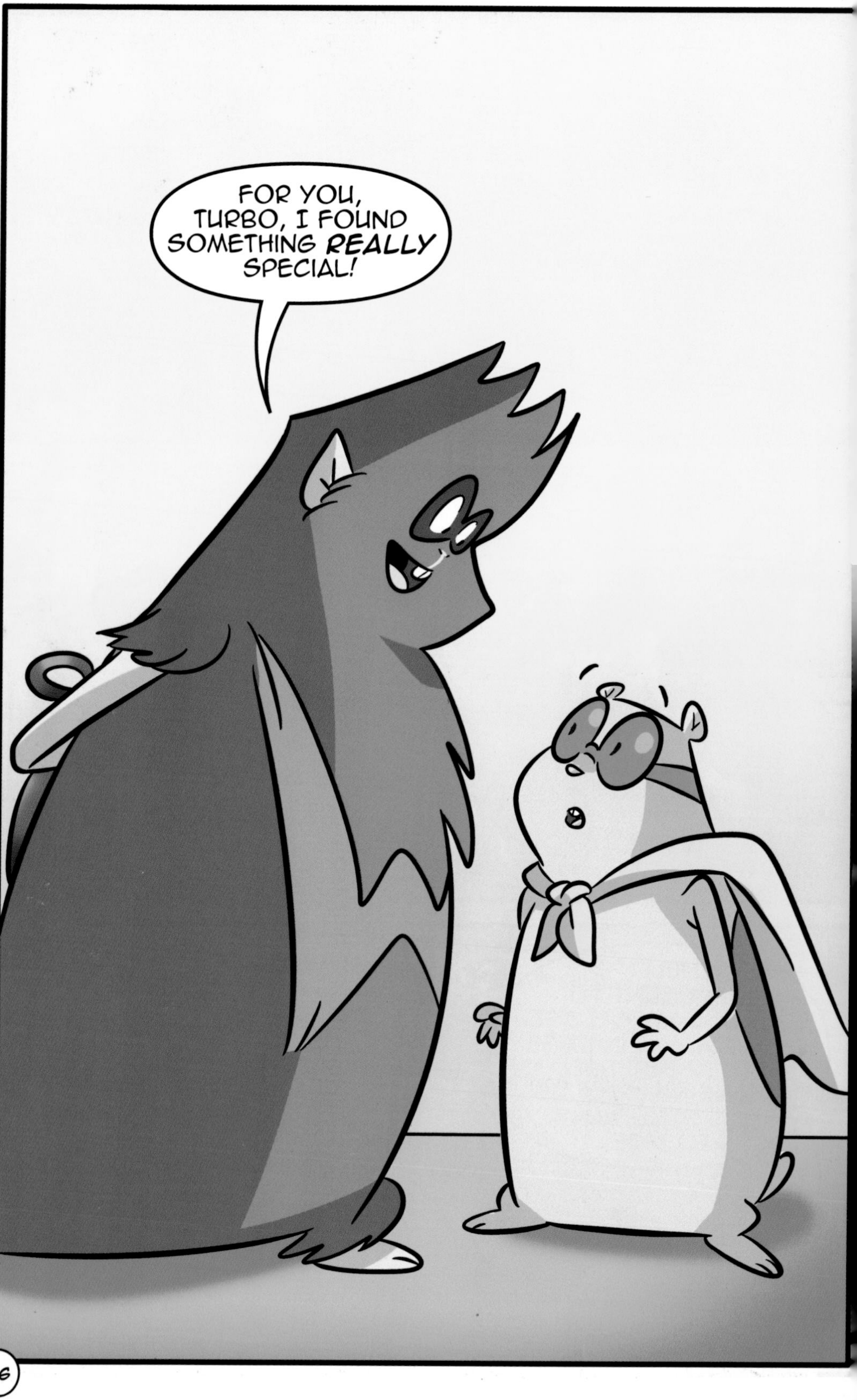
FOR YOU, TURBO, I FOUND SOMETHING REALLY SPECIAL!

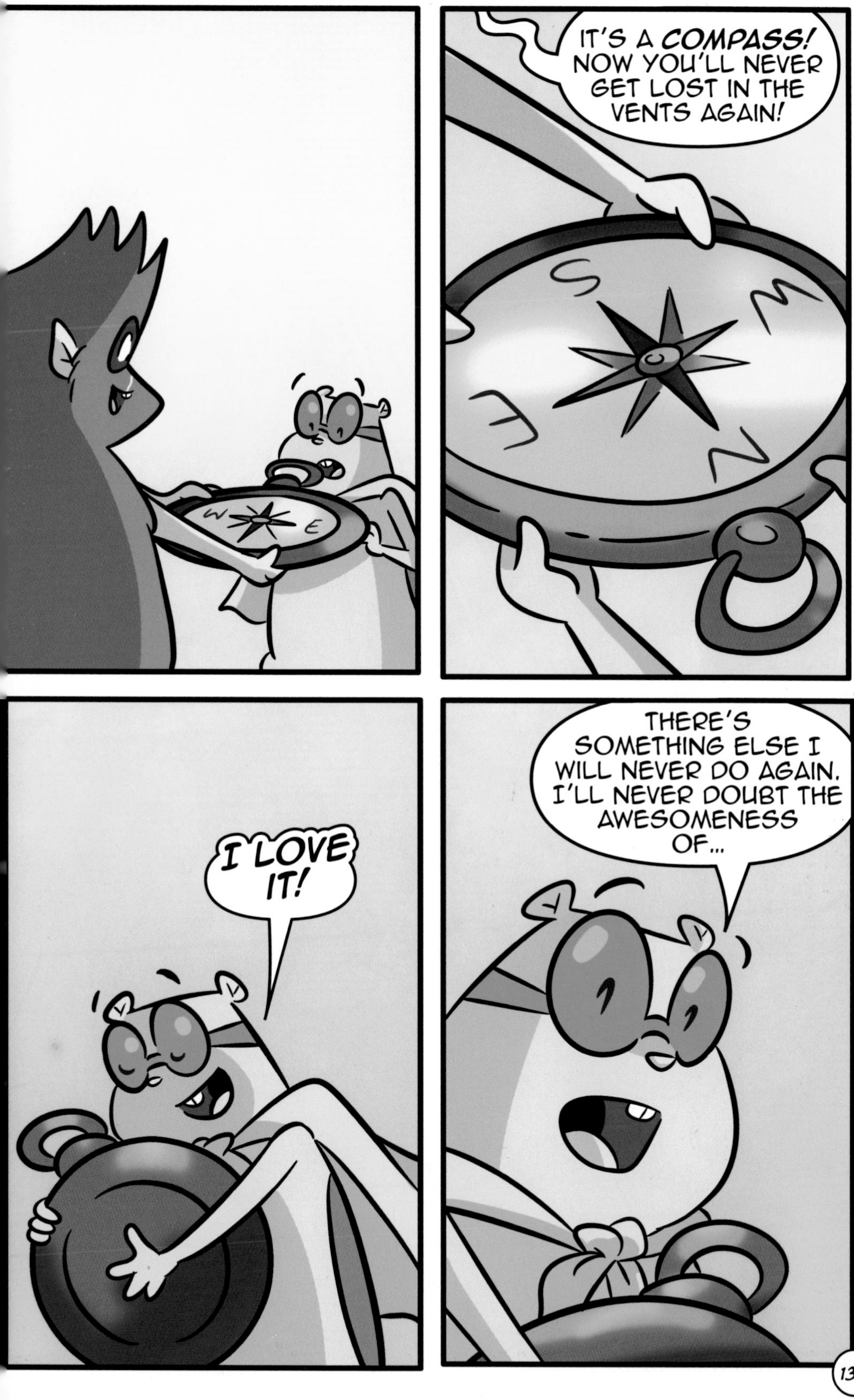
IT'S A COMPASS! NOW YOU'LL NEVER GET LOST IN THE VENTS AGAIN!
I LOVE IT!
THERE'S SOMETHING ELSE I WILL NEVER DO AGAIN. I'LL NEVER DOUBT THE AWESOMENESS OF...

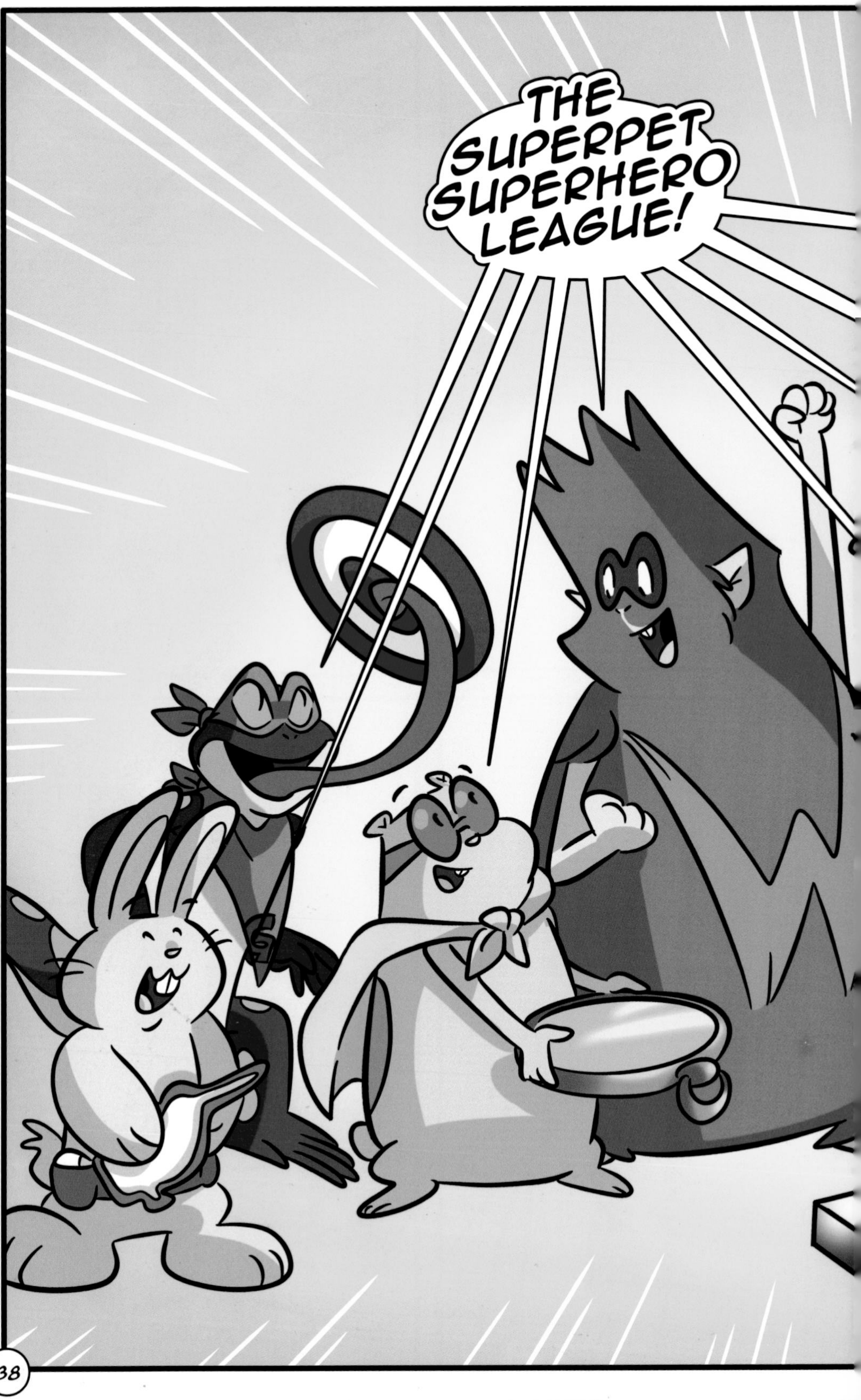
THE SUPERPET SUPERHERO LEAGUE!

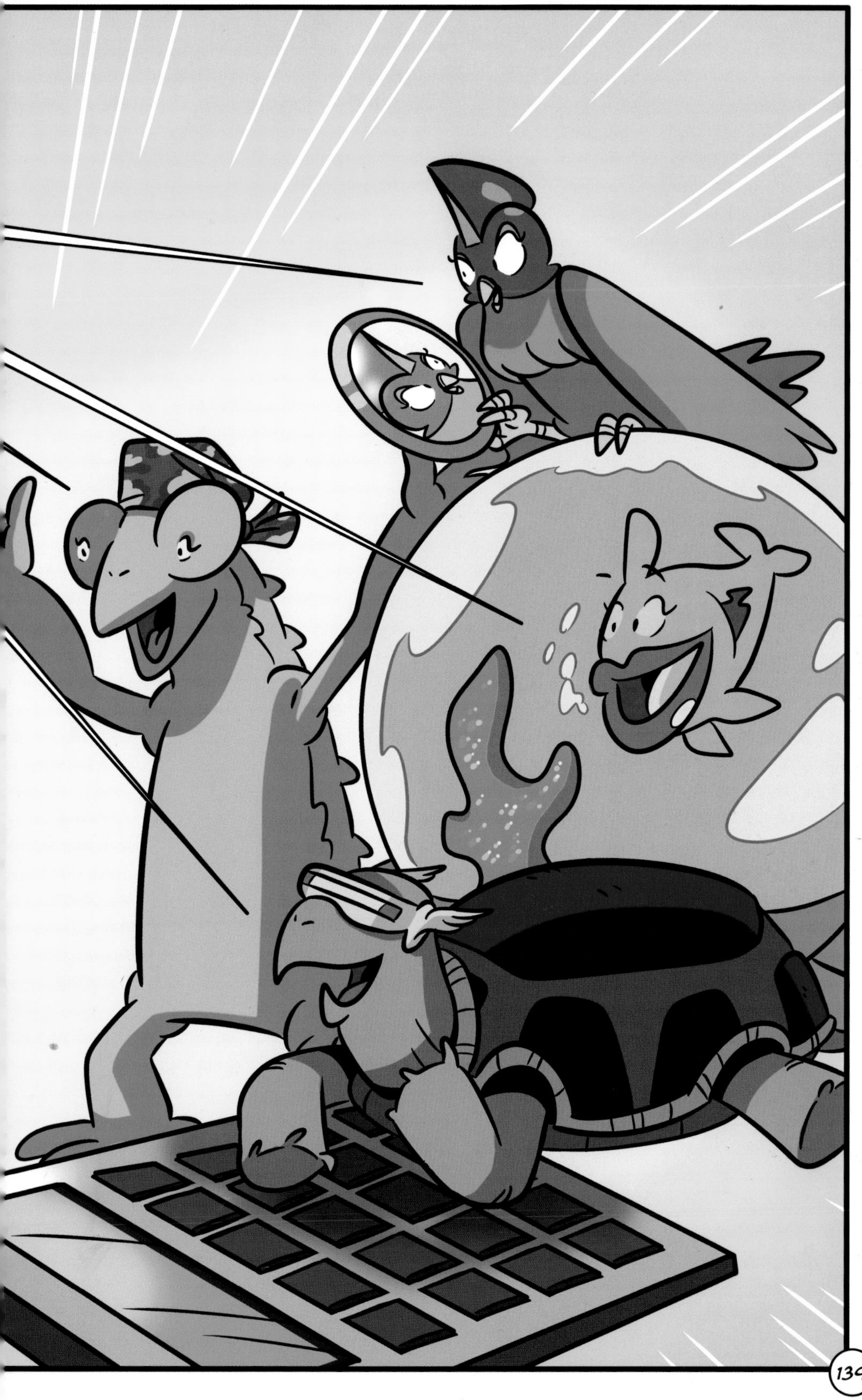

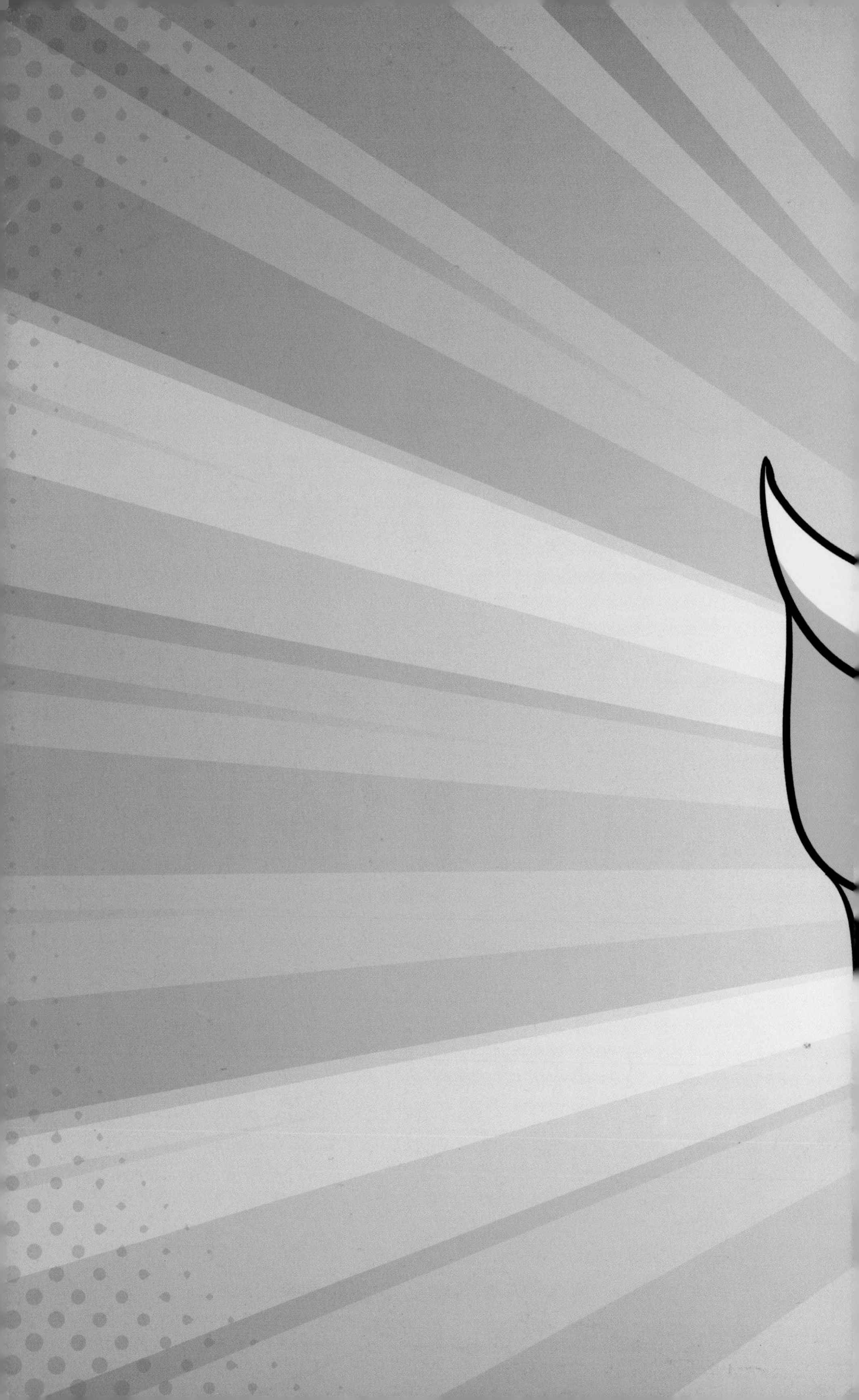

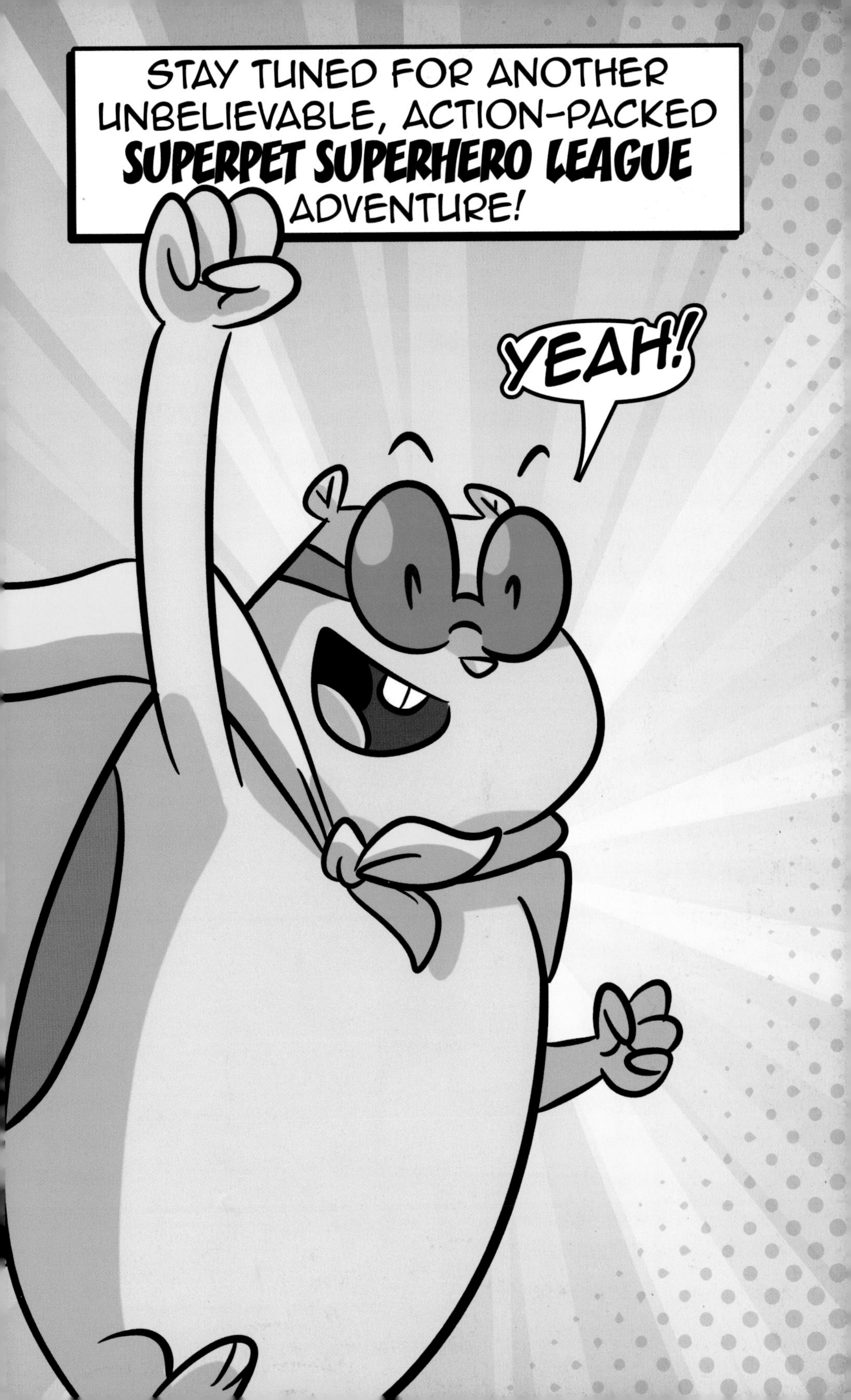
STAY TUNED FOR ANOTHER UNBELIEVABLE, ACTION-PACKED SUPERPET SUPERHERO LEAGUE ADVENTURE!
YEAH!

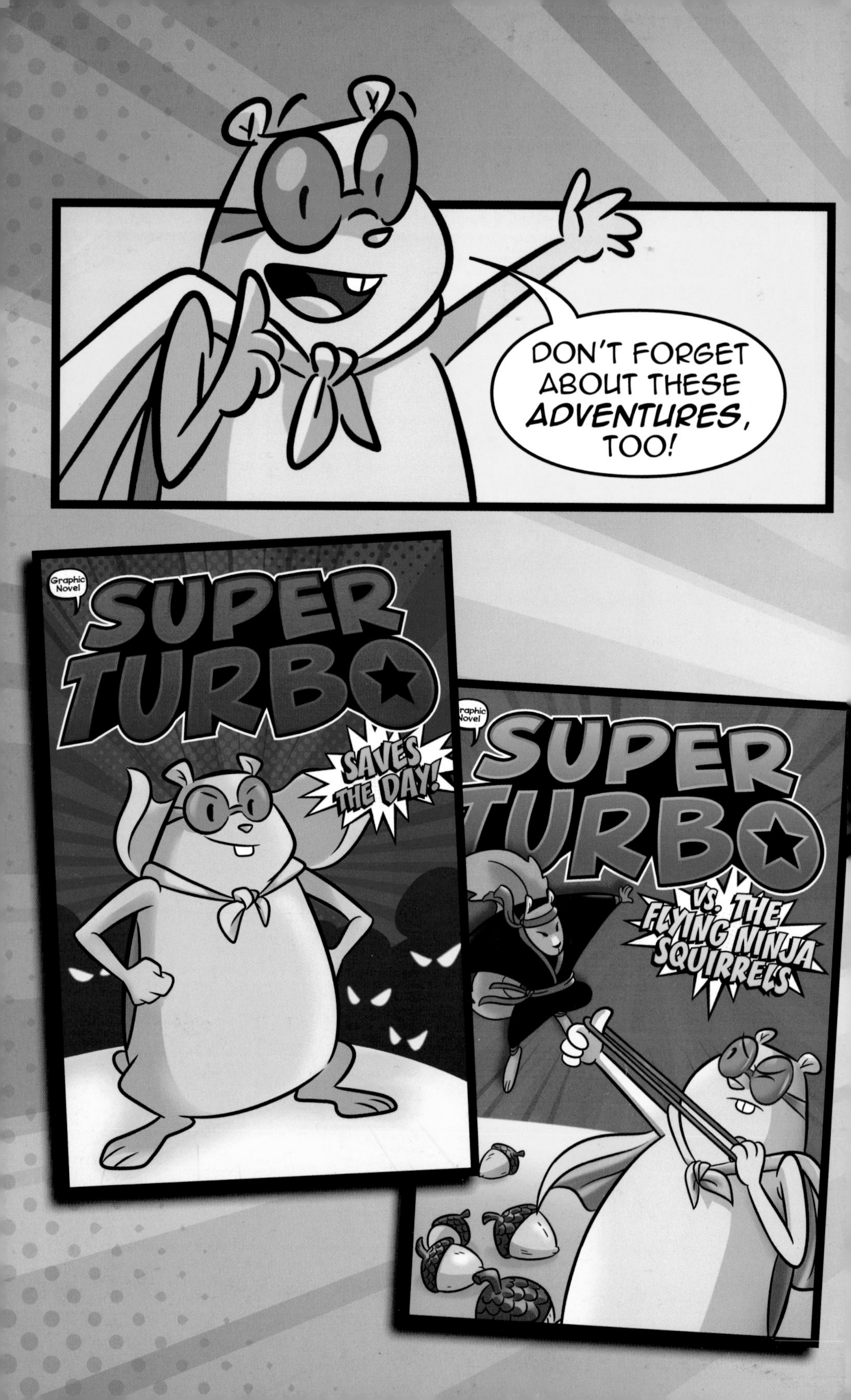
DON'T FORGET ABOUT THESE *ADVENTURES*, TOO!
Graphic Novel!
SUPER TURBO
SAVES THE DAY!
Graphic Novel!
SUPER TURBO
VS. THE FLYING NINJA SQUIRRELS

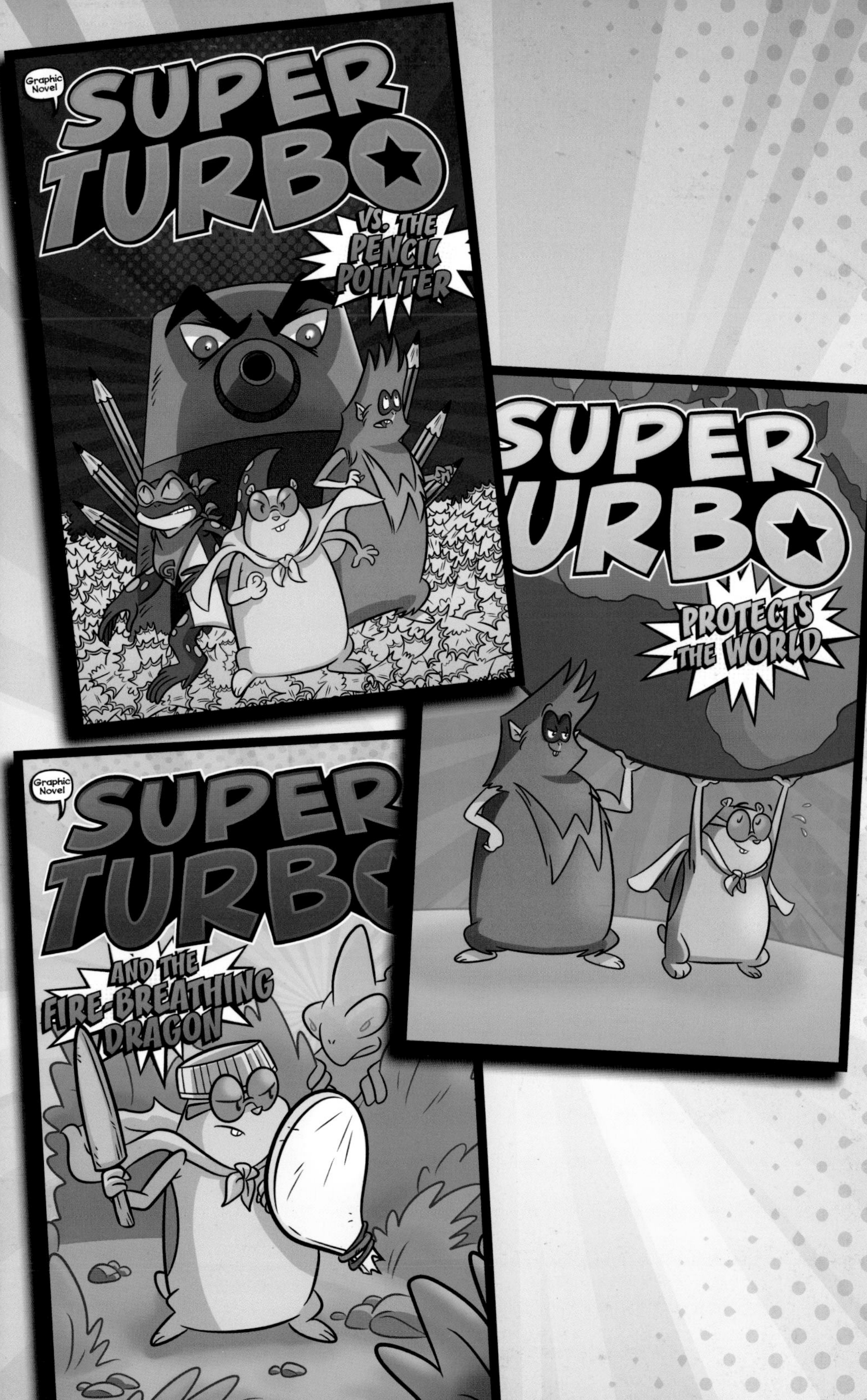
Graphic Novel
SUPER TURBO
VS. THE PENCIL POINTER
SUPER TURBO
PROTECTS THE WORLD
Graphic Novel
SUPER TURBO
AND THE FIRE-BREATHING DRAGON